Revealed Truth

A Journey from Fear to Faith

Eve M. Harrell

Original Copyright © 2023 Eve M. Harrell
Expanded Edition © Copyright 2024 Eve M. Harrell
Revealed Truth – A Journey from Fear to Faith
Revealed Book Series™ By Eve M. Harrell
ISBN: 979-8-9905489-1-6 (Volume 2 – Paperback)

Cover Artwork by:
Olha Volynska and Kara Starcher of Mountain Creek Books

Editing provided by:
Lauren Sanchez
Natalie Hendrix

A Daughter's Journey LLC - https://evemharrell.com

To Tony,

Thank you for encouraging me to face my fears.

Table of Contents

PROLOGUE 1

BEGINNINGS 3

FAMILY TIES...11

A PARTING FAVOR 19

GRAMMY KNOWS BEST 29

A PROMISING REVELATION..39

CONFIRMATIONS' SONG 48

ENDLESS POSSIBILITIES 56

THE DESTRUCTION OF PEACE 68

SEARCHING FOR HOPE IN A FALLEN WORLD.....79

AN UNCERTAIN FUTURE...90

BROKEN PIECES..99

A COCOON OF FEAR..109

CONNECTING THE DOTS 120

TRUTH REVEALED 131

LIGHT SHINES IN THE DARKNESS 143

A NEW NORMAL 153

RELEASING THE BURDEN 161

ALL IN A DAY'S WORK..171

HOMECOMING 183

LETTING GO 193

LOVE'S GIFT 201

TENDING TO THE ROOTS 209

WINTER RETREAT 217

CAPTIVE THOUGHTS 228

A MOUNTAIN OF DOUBT 241

PROTECTIVE COVERING 253

REVENGE OF A BIRD WATCHER 262

AN UNEXPECTED DROP 271

A SHIELD OF FAITH 278

A COUNTERFEIT PEACE 287

RESCUE! 297

EPILOGUE 303

APPALACHIAN DICTIONARY 312

ACKNOWLEDGMENTS 326

ABOUT THE AUTHOR 333

Prologue

June 22
Wild Rock, Tennessee

Thunder rolled in the distance. Maddie sighed as she listened to raindrops fall on the metal roof overhead. While she knew Mother Nature could create quite the show, the calm before the storm revealed her heart. Taps became plops as a crescendo of summer rain attempted to lull her to sleep moments before the storm brought chaos to the world around her.

Her Grammy referred to these preludes as peace.

> *Maddie Ruth, never ferget yer Creator, she would say. He provides peace in the storm. This rain right here, why it was sent from Heaven, and God's word says it'll not return without waterin' the earth, makin' it bud and flourish, providin' seed for the sower an' bread for the eater. Jes' so, his word won't return to him empty but'll accomplish all he desires. Nothin' to fear child, yer Father in Heaven'll provide everythin' you need. This rain here's a sign that he'll always provide. There's no storm he cain't control.*

She loved her Grammy. Grace Bennett, an outspoken woman, embodied a passionate heart and a gentle spirit. Born in the Blue Ridge Mountains, Grace was a naturalist who lived on the land. She loved her God, her family, her rocking chair, and her snap beans, in that order. Maddie could still remember the smell as she would sit for hours on Grammy's porch snapping beans while listening to the barn-thumpin' rain overhead, as Grammy called it.

Glancing at her scarred hands, she reminisced about the simpleness of the bean, the bumpy feel of the pod as she broke it into pieces, and the earthy taste of the bean as she snuck a bite. Another sigh escaped her lips as nostalgia turned to anxiety. She could almost feel her mom's disgust over the ragged appearance of her hands as she wondered, *when did life become so complicated?*

On cue, her grandmother's voice again broke into her anxious thoughts.

Maddie Ruth, yer the little-blessed one and'll be a companion to many. God in Heaven is yer strong tower. Run to him child, and you'll be safe. Always remember this Love. Nobody can ever take this away from you, nobody.

Once again, peace filled her anxious heart.

As the firelight cast shadows over the sleeping figures of her little brother Matthew and her friend Rachel, she found herself grateful, even a little jealous of their slumber. Rest seemed to be out of reach for Maddie with so many thoughts going through her head. *So much has happened; what will tomorrow bring?* She pondered. The encouragement of Grammy's soft voice interrupted her musings once more.

Sleep, Child. Tomorrow'll be here soon enough and with trouble of its own. But tonight, my sweet, ya need ta rest.

And with that, her heavy lids fell, and the dream would begin.

CHAPTER 1

Beginnings

July 14 – A Year Earlier . . .
Marietta, Georgia

It was a beautiful, sunny day in the suburbs of the ATL. Excitement bubbled up as Maddie looked at herself in the mirror. The pencil-straight white pants and the cute pink top seemed to provide the look she was going for. Thankfully, her mom's fashion sense benefited her for once.

Finally, I'm fifteen, she thought—*no longer little Maddie. I can finally get some respect!*

Her soprano voice, belting out "As It Was" by Harry Styles, drowned out the sound of a knock on the door.

The reflection of long brown hair and freckles glared back at her as she mumbled, "Will I ever have a 'just us'?"

"Maddie, didn't you hear me knock?" Her older brother Mike barreled into her room. "Would you hurry up already? A gaggle of little girls are downstairs calling your name."

Rolling her eyes, she said, "Really, Mike? We'll be driving next year; no little girls here."

"Ha, be sure to tell me when that miracle happens so I can stay off the road." Mike turned away, leaving his best "mic-drop" impression.

"Michael!!!" Following her big brother into the hallway, she threw her teddy bear at his back, wondering, *Why are big brothers so irritating?*

Maddie took the stairs two at a time, excitely thinking,

Today is an excellent day; I WILL NOT let him ruin it for me! It's my birthday, and today I am FIFTEEN! Jumping from the bottom stair to the landing, she lifted her chin as her thick brown hair swished around her head dramatically.

With her hand on her hip, she looked at the girls in her living room and said, "Hello, beautiful ladies. Who's ready to party?"

Screaming at the top of their lungs, her friends met her on the landing, sharing Happy Birthdays as they fell into a heap on the floor.

A stern voice interrupted the growing chorus of female giggles, "Madelyn Ruth Bennett, you get up this instant! That outfit was too expensive for you to be on the floor making a mess of it!"

The room was suddenly quiet. Maddie stood and straightened her hair as she brushed off her new pants. "Yes, ma'am," Maddie melted under her mother's gaze.

Suddenly, a flash of red hair under a Yankee ball cap occupied by none other than her little brother yelled, "Maddie, Maddie, we won!" Unaware of the tension in the room, Matthew grabbed his sister in a big bear hug and said again, "We won!"

Oh, the joy one little brother brought to the Bennett household. Smitten from the first moment she looked into Matthew's eyes, she couldn't remember a time when she didn't love having her ten-year-old brother around. Smart, witty, and funny in the presence of his big sister, he was strangely quiet with others. But no matter, he was hers, and she loved him dearly. Matthew always lifted her spirits when others threatened to tear them down.

As her mom left the room, Maddie sighed with relief. Walking into the kitchen with little Matthew, she asked, "Hi, Mom, can I help?"

"Yes, dear. Can you and your brother please grab the groceries from the back of the truck? Where is Mike? Mike, Mike, please come down! We need help with the groceries for this party to happen."

"Mrs. Bennett, can we help too?" Maddie smiled with relief at her best friend, Rachel. With Matthew and her friends in tow, each grabbed a bag from the back of the black Tahoe.

Birthdays were her favorite time of year. Mom would allow her to invite four girls for a sleepover full of movies and junk food. This special occasion would be an exception to Mom's "no junk food" rule. Only on special occasions was she allowed to corrupt her body with all that sugar. But oh, what a special day this was to be. She was fifteen!

After helping her mom, Maddie, Rachel, Emma, Kaitlyn, and Jade huddled around the television with a bowl full of popcorn and a monstrous box of Junior Mints.

"What'll it be tonight, Maddie?" Emma asked.

"Road to Possession Hill is really scary," Kaitlyn suggested. "Wanna watch?"

Maddie saw Rachel fidgeting in her seat from the corner of her eye. Knowing her friend wasn't a fan of horror movies, she asked, "How about something funny?"

Quietly, Rachel piped in, "My mom and I are streaming this fantastic series called The Chosen. Maddie, I think you would love it."

"What's it about?" Maddie asked.

"Oh, It's great!" Rachel answered excitedly. "It's all about Jesus and His disciples . . ."

"Jesus," Jade piped in. "Aren't we a little old for fairy tales?"

"It's all about the disciples being called by Jesus and learning to follow him. It's wild how similar they are to you and me. I promise you'll love it, but Maddie, it's your birthday; you choose the movie."

Listening to the exchange, Maddie couldn't help being curious about Jesus. Grammy told her many stories of God and Jesus over the years. She was interested to catch a glimpse of him.

"The Chosen it is," she decided as she turned on the TV.

"Mary of Magdala," Jesus said.
"Who are you? How do you know my name?" She asked.

"Thus says the Lord who created you, and He who formed you, fear not for I have redeemed you. I have called you by name. You are mine."

Maddie's heart pounded as she watched Jesus hug Mary. The comforting music encouraged thoughts of the hugs she received from her dad.

Looking at Rachel, Emma asked, "Do you really believe God is with you?"

Blonde curls popped up from the other side of the bean bag chair as Rachel answered excitedly, "Absolutely!"

Emma looked away for a moment. Wiping her eyes, she quietly asked Rachel, "But, like, how do you know?"

Maddie hit pause.

As Rachel stood to turn on the light, the room became uncomfortably quiet. Maddie saw something different in her friend. It was obvious that she had a secret to tell and couldn't wait to share.

Rachel faced the group and said, "Everyone, circle up. Now close your eyes.

"It's summertime. You are in a meadow. Butterflies are hopping from flower to flower. In the distance, a bunny sits very still. His little mouth nibbling—hoping to go unnoticed. You give the bunny his space as your gaze lowers, your fingers softly pulling a flower from the ground. Dirt falls to the earth as you press the velvet petals into your palm. After breathing in a scent that reminds you of your Gram's sweet perfume, you open your eyes to a grand canopy above you—a blanket of leaves protecting you from the sun. As your gaze lowers, the leaves reflect on the water's surface of a slow-flowing brook. The reflection sparkles like little green diamonds shining below the gentle waves. Then, you see it." Rachel pauses for dramatic effect.

"See what?" Kaitlyn raised her head.

"Shhhh." Rachel laughed. "Close your eyes."

"But what does she see?" Whispered an exasperated Emma.

What is it that we see? Maddie thought to herself.

Closing her eyes, Rachel patiently mustered up the courage she needed to leave these girls with a most important truth. "As your eyes adjust to the dancing reflection, you see the most beautiful face staring back at you."

Rachel's poignant pause ended as a loud voice broke into the moment.

"Oh, my stars, what is this? The beautiful face staring back at you, oh Johnny, your beautiful face!"

"Muah, Muah, Muah, I love you Mikey-Poo!" Five sets of eyes glared at Mike Bennett and his friend Johnny's handsome good looks as they playfully embraced.

Maddie yelled, "Mike, HOW COULD YOU!" His face became target practice as he and his friend ran from the barrage of pillows.

Fuming with anger over her brother's antics, she looked down at her friend Rachel, the excitement on her face gone as she looked as if she wanted to cry. "What's the matter?" Maddie asked as she and the other girls surrounded her friend.

"Nothing," Rachel said, "it's nothing."

Maddie was immediately sad for her friend. Rachel was such a good storyteller, always had been. She had a way of painting a picture without even wielding a brush. And she wanted so very much for her friends to know Jesus. But the disappointment on her friend's face was apparent. Dropping to her knees, she placed her hands on Rachel's shoulders as she attempted to reset the mood. "Please tell us. What do we see?"

With tears in her eyes, Rachel stood and looked intently into each face. To each one, she said, "Don't you know?"

Maddie looked around at three questioning gazes as Kaitlyn piped in, "Know what, Rach?"

A deep sigh fell from her lips as she quietly answered, "When you focus on the reflection in the water, you see yourself through the eyes of your Heavenly Father."

Dazed stares fell on Rachel as they contemplated her explanation.

"God is all around us," she continued. "He is our Creator and has created everything: the flowers, the butterfly, the water, the trees, the bunny, you, me. Everything around us carries the touch of his hand." She was standing now, gesturing wildly as she explained God's presence. "So, in that very moment when you look into the water and see your reflection, you can see what he sees—you, fearfully and wonderfully made in his image, Imago Dei."

Rachel's magical picture reminded Maddie of summer days spent chasing butterflies in Grammy's front yard. Grammy always said the same thing: "God is everywhere."

Jade's impatient tone interrupted her thoughts. "Well, I don't know how you can conclude that God is everywhere when you can't even see him!"

Maddie looked up, ready to change the subject. Before she could say a word, Rachel's quiet voice broke the uncomfortable silence, "Jade, what do you breathe?"

"I breathe air, obviously," Jade exclaimed.

Four pairs of eyes returned to a salty Rachel, who replied, "Can you see it?"

Suddenly, pillows were everywhere as Maddie's brothers barreled into the living room with Mike's friend Johnny in tow. Pandemonium set in as the pillow fight ensued. Giggles and screams carried up the stairwell as the tension in the room disappeared.

Later that night, Maddie found herself wide awake amid the soft sleeping sounds of her friends. Her mind raced as she pondered Rachel's words. Grammy had much to say about God's Presence in her life. Truthfully, she wanted to invite Grammy's Jesus into her life, but she was never sure. Jade made a good point tonight about being unable to see God, but as Rachel said, we can't see air. Maddie found herself confused about the whole God subject.

Taking a chance, she whispered Rachel's name.

Sleepily, she answered, "Yeah?"

"Do you think I can see God?"

"Oh yes," Rachel replied, "everywhere."

"I want to. Grammy always talks about him, but I can never seem to make him appear."

Rachel sat up and said, "He's not a genie, Maddie. You can't make him appear."

"Then why can't I see him?" she asked.

"Maybe you're looking in the wrong places," she replied.

Maddie struggled with this response. She saw Rachel moving her lips quietly with her eyes closed.

Rachel opened her eyes and asked, "Doesn't Grammy have a dog?"

"Yes, Max is so sweet."

Yawning, Rachel continued, "You always tell me how loving he is."

"Yeah, every time I visit, he jumps off the porch to greet me." Chuckling, she added, "Oh, Rach, he's so funny when he runs. His stubby little legs and big paws are the cutest."

"And what does he do when he gets to you?"

She thought for a moment, "He slobbers all over me. Oh, and he loves to snuggle."

"Yeah, he loves you, doesn't he?" Rachel's eagerness to help her friend see through her eyes was palpable.

"Yes," Maddie smiled.

Rachel, getting a bit bolder, asked, "How about babies? Didn't your Aunt Lisa just have a baby?"

"Oh yes, a beautiful baby girl, she named her Eva Mae."

"Didn't you tell me that looking into her eyes was like looking at perfection?"

A bit perplexed, she asked, "Why yes, but what do Max and Eva have to do with God?"

"Remember, Maddie, God created everything. He created you, me, Max, and Eva, right?"

Confused, she answered, "Sure, if you say so."

"I believe that as we can see God in nature, we can also see him through the eyes of those we love. Max loves you, and Eva loves you. When you look into their eyes, you see his love looking back."

Maddie glanced up, puzzled. "I don't know, Rachel; it all sounds so weird."

"It's okay. You don't have to understand right away. Keep seeking, and you will.

"Rachel?"

Yawning a second time, Rachel responded sleepily, "Yeah?"

Trying to hide the tears that threatened her, Maddie said, "I want to feel Jesus with me, like Mary in the show."

"Yeah, I know." Rachel encouraged her friend by grabbing her hand.

"No, listen, Rachel, I want to feel him with me . . . so I'm not anxious all the time."

CHAPTER 2

Family Ties

Maddie began to stir as slivers of sun filtered into the room. A familiar male voice from downstairs caught her attention. Jumping up, she changed into a T-shirt and a pair of shorts and ran out of her room.

"Daddy!"

As she entered the kitchen, she found her favorite person in the whole world drinking coffee. She ran into his arms and exclaimed, "Daddy, you made it!"

Quickly setting his coffee cup down, her dad gave her a big hug and looked at his daughter with joy. At six feet two inches, David Bennett towered over his only daughter, but she didn't care. In his arms, she was safe.

"Well, here's my birthday girl! Or shall I call you a young woman now?"

David was born in the hills of Tennessee. After high school, he attended the University of Georgia on a football scholarship.

After meeting Maddie's mom, Jacque, at a sorority function in his junior year, they fell head over heels in love. Directly after graduating from college, he asked her to marry him, after which he entered the military and retired after twenty years of service.

Hopping onto the kitchen stool, Maddie asked, "I thought you were on a business trip?" With elbows on the counter and chin propped on her folded hands, she expectantly awaited to hear all about his trip.

Lifting his brow in disbelief, her daddy asked, "Now, Ruthie, do you really think I was going to miss the party of the century? I worked it out to come home just for you. I understand you have some of your friends over?"

Maddie was always sad when her dad went out of town. His job provided her family with a good life, but if truth be told, she just wanted him. Shaking the sad thoughts away, she realized that when he called her by her favorite nickname, "Ruthie," she forgot all about his absence. He always said that her name held a promise that one day he would reveal—something Grammy had a part in. But then her mom would always burst the bubble: *David, must we hear about this promise again? You're going to fill her head with unrealistic dreams.*

As she chatted with her dad, Matthew ran into the kitchen.

"Daddy!" Matthew jumped into his dad's arms to hug his neck. Maddie's bubble was once again secure as the love of family surrounded her.

"Good morning, Mr. Bennett," Rachel greeted as she and Maddie's friends entered the kitchen. "How was your trip?"

A bit offhandedly, David replied, "Oh, you know, a hacker's dream."

"What's a hacker, Daddy?" Matthew interrupted.

"Good question, Champ. Consider if somebody broke into one of the video games you enjoy playing and mixed up all the characters," Dad replied.

"Why would they do that?" Matthew asked, perplexed.

Maddie interjected, "Because they want to make you crazy, Matthew!"

"Be nice to your brother now. Matthew, there are bad guys in this world who enjoy creating chaos in big corporations. Your daddy gets to beat them at their own game."

Rachel laughed at the exchange, "Yeah, my dad says you are a pretty good gamer."

"He would know," David amusingly agreed.

As her dad talked to Matthew and Rachel, Maddie wondered what her daddy did when he went out of town. A glance at her mom revealed that perhaps she wondered the same.

Mom was so excited when he came home. Often, in her excitement, she would take her daughter on a day-long shopping spree. She and her mom weren't very close, but when they went shopping, her mom would shower her with attention as she bought new outfits for them both. They would then spend an hour enjoying a special brunch where they would talk about her younger years of debutante balls and beauty queen parades.

Jacquelyn Montgomery Bennett was a beautiful woman with long red hair and green eyes, which her dad said were piercing, whatever that meant. She was the only daughter of a prominent southern family who graduated from the Lamar Dodd School of Fine Arts at the University of Georgia with a degree in Interior Design. Her dad, Maddie's granddad, Grandpa Jack, was a famous businessman who bought land and sold it to wealthy companies. Grandma Pauline died when Maddie was a young baby, but family pictures revealed a woman as beautiful as her daughter.

A bit embarrassed as her mom caught her staring, she asked, "Mom, can I help you?"

"Yes, Maddie, thank you. Can you please grab the eggs out of the fridge? We need to get a move on with this breakfast. Grandpa Jack will be here soon for your party."

"Grandpa Jack is coming?" She gave the eggs to her mom. Maddie seldom saw her grandpa but was excited he was coming. As big as a lumberjack, Grandpa Jack always had warm hugs. "Who else is coming?"

"Well, we do have a surprise for you," her dad interjected.

"A surprise? What is it?" Rachel, Kaitlyn, Jade, and Emma surrounded her and began guessing what the surprise might be.

David let the girls continue their guesses for about five minutes before he called Maddie to him, "Close your eyes."

Both excited and nervous simultaneously, she obeyed as her dad covered her eyes and turned her around.

Hearing gasps all around her, she repeated, "What is it?"

Her dad lifted his hands, and with eyes big as saucers,

Maddie focused on her Grammy, Aunt Lisa, and baby Eva Mae. Through tear-filled eyes and a full heart, she threw herself into her Grammy's arms, reveling in the familiar deep Tennessee drawl.

"Come 'ere and gimme some sugar, Dahlin'!"

Since Grandpa George had died three years before, Grammy secluded herself in the Blue Ridge Mountains of Tennessee. George and Grace had been the epitome of the grand love affair. Their love for one another grew quickly after their first meeting and as teenage sweethearts, they married within a year. At the young age of nineteen, Grace found herself enamored as her David entered the world.

When Grandpa George passed away, Maddie was so sad, but Grammy would always encourage her that he was home with Jesus. Resting in the comfort of her Gram's extravagant hug, she thought, *I wish Jesus would share Grandpa with us today* as she breathed in the smells of cinnamon and sugar. Casting the sad thought away, she clasped Grammy even tighter. She was so loved by her family.

"Maddie Ruth, my beautiful Granddaughter, yer fifteen today." Grammy placed her warm hands on her face and looked at her intently.

"Yes, ma'am, I am."

With a serious look, Grammy continued, "Ya know somethin' special's 'bout to happen, right?"

"What's that?"

"My Dear, yer 'bout to begin an amazin' journey; yer whole life's gonna change."

"Now, Grace, please don't speak nonsense to her," Mom interrupted.

Grammy, never one to back down, looked earnestly into her granddaughter's eyes. "Child, the next year is critical. Ya need to know Jesus is with you. Ya need to learn to trust him."

Anxious when her grandmother's eyes filled with tears, she asked, "Grammy, what is it? What's wrong?"

Wrapping her granddaughter in a big hug, she replied, "Oh, nothin' Beautiful Girl. I'm jes' so happy yer becomin' a young woman!"

Grammy had been quite emotional over the last three years. While Maddie knew she was loved, she felt nervous when Grammy began talking to her about Jesus. *Why did Grammy say that the next year is critical? Was she going to die like Grandpa George? Is that why Grammy cried?*

With a warm smile, Grammy kissed her granddaughter and looked toward her daddy as she exclaimed, "David Bennett, come 'ere boy and give yer momma a hug!"

As Maddie's thoughts continued their downward spiral, fear grabbed hold. Her heart was pounding, her breathing labored. The room started to spin as she was suddenly overwhelmed and didn't know what to do.

Walking discreetly over to her friend, Rachel touched her shoulder and said, "Breathe, Maddie."

After a few moments, she began to feel better and smiled at her friend.

As she regained control of her breathing, she joined the others who were loving on little Eva Mae.

Emma asked Aunt Lisa what being a new mom was like.

"With this bundle of joy, it's the greatest gift ever!" Eva Mae opened her eyes and looked at her momma. "See what I mean? How could you not love this beauty?"

"Breakfast is ready," Mom called out.

As everyone entered the dining room, David placed his arms around his little girl and asked, "Is everything all right, Ruthie?"

Looking at a spot on the floor, she answered quietly, "Yes, Sir, I'm fine. Why?"

"You looked a little pale a moment ago."

"It's okay, just a little anxiety." The spot seemed to grow as she stared.

Gently lifting Maddie's chin, Dad asked, "You know you can talk to me, right?"

"She's fine, David," Mom interjected, "it's just hormones."

"Hmm," he replied.

As everyone settled around the table, Rachel whispered in

her ear, "Can I pray over the meal?"

She smiled at her and asked, "Daddy, do you mind if Rachel says the blessing?"

"Why sure, that would be great."

Maddie was thankful to have everyone she loved at the same table.

As everyone bowed their heads, Rachel began, "Father, we thank You for the opportunity to share in Maddie's fifteenth birthday. Lord, please bless this year. Give her the courage and strength to do all You have called her to. We thank You for everyone at this table and for the love You have poured into her through each person. We pray You will bless this food to our bodies and our bodies to Your service. In Jesus' Name, amen."

"Amen," everyone replied in harmony. The feast of French toast, eggs, bacon, oranges, orange juice, and coffee soon became the talk of the table as everyone dug in.

After feeding Eva Mae, Aunt Lisa asked, "So Maddie, what are yer plans for the rest of the summer?"

"Well, we plan to go swimming and swimming, and oh, did I say we were going swimming, right girls?

Nodding, with a piece of French toast dangling off her fork, Kaitlyn added, "And don't forget the movies."

"Oh yeah, and we're going to the movies."

"Ahem," Maddie's mom cleared her throat, "And you will finish your summer reading."

"Yes, ma'am," she said, looking at Aunt Lisa. "And my summer reading."

"Whatcha readin'?" Aunt Lisa asked.

Popping the last bite of egg in her mouth, she answered, "I'm reading Moby Dick for Language Arts."

"Manners, Maddie," Mom reminded her.

Aunt Lisa cut through the awkward silence, "I love Moby Dick. I never did understand why Captain Ahab believed he'd fight evil alone. Although my heart was happy when Ishmael survived the Pequod's sinkin'."

"But why do they have to go after the whale? What did he

ever do?" Jade interjected.

"Well, Ahab saw the whale as all that was evil." Aunt Lisa replied.

"Doesn't that sound familiar?" Mike mumbled.

"What do you mean?" David asked.

"With all the evil in the world, our President might as well be Ahab, thinking he can fight everyone."

"Now, Mike, don't speak of what you don't know. You need to gather your facts before spouting lies about our President."

"Whatever, Dad. That man thinks he can go after whoever is in his way, at whatever cost, while innocent people are losing their rights."

Maddie's brother was often outspoken toward his dad, especially when politics were involved. She was conflicted about whether she should interrupt.

"Mike, the current climate in our country requires an active President at the helm. One day, if you become President, you might understand the difficulties the job entails."

"Hmph, I guess," Mike mumbled.

"My dad says we may be in the last days," Rachel said as she stared at her food. The conversation died as the adults glanced at one another and then at Rachel.

David said, "Rachel, some dangerous things are happening now, but nothing history hasn't seen before. You have nothing to worry about."

Grammy perked up as she looked him in the eye. "David, ya might wanna read that book again."

"What book?" Matthew asked.

Grammy chuckled, "Well, that'd be Revelation, Matthew. We should all be readin' it these days."

"Mom, aren't they a little young to read that particular book of the Bible?" David argued.

"Never too young, Son. If ya don't prepare 'em now, how'll they ever be ready to fight when the spiritual battle comes?"

Maddie gulped her milk, swallowing down the old, familiar burning sensation as she struggled with her feelings. Fear, an ugly emotion, would paralyze her in a dark place. She was once told that fear was a good thing as it warned of impending danger; however, she just couldn't shake her body's response to it. Her palms were sweaty, her breathing shallow, and her heartbeat thumping like crazy; she wanted to run.

Rachel touched her arm, "Breathe," she whispered under her breath. "Maddie, look at me," Rachel continued.

All at once, everyone turned to look.

Maddie's face turned ten shades of red.

Her dad walked over and crouched down to her level. "Maddie, what's wrong?"

"I - don't – know."

Emma broke the silence in the room as she asked, "Maddie, do you have panic attacks?"

"What - do - you - mean?" She rasped.

Not wanting to upset her friend, Emma said, "Mr. Bennett, a panic attack is an overwhelming feeling of anxiety. Your heart rate goes up and you may find it hard to breathe. My mom gets them a lot, so we've had to learn coping skills to help her find calm when she has an attack. Maddie shows all the symptoms."

Looking at his daughter, David grabbed her hands and asked, "Are you afraid?" The oranges on her plate became the most exciting thing in the room as tears fell down her cheeks.

"Yes," she replied, still trying to catch her breath.

"What are you afraid of?" her dad asked.

"Mr. Bennett, no disrespect, but Maddie needs a minute to catch her breath," Rachel encouraged as she looked at her friend. "She'll be okay. Won't you?"

The tears were coming full tilt now as she realized she couldn't hold them in. David put his arms around his daughter as he comforted her, "It's okay, Ruthie. I've got you."

"Well, I'll be the air here is thicker than butter. Did somebody mention Moby Dick? Do I need to call my old pal Ishmael?" Everyone moved their attention from Maddie to the booming voice at the end of the room.

"Grandpa Jack!" Wiping her cheeks, Maddie ran into the giant arms of her beloved Grandpa.

CHAPTER 3

A Parting Favor

After the awkward silence was broken, everyone carried their empty plates to the kitchen.

Maddie dodged another bullet. Sweeping her fears under the rug was much easier than facing them. However, she couldn't help but wonder if another wasn't far behind. Well, no matter, she decided that bullet could wait another day. For now, everyone she loved was under one roof, including her Grandpa Jack.

At over six feet tall, Grandpa Jack was a big man with silver-black hair, a ruddy face, and a beard. Jack Ruby was a high-powered developer who sold real estate. His keen eye and quick wit served him well in the boardroom. Not a man in the city of Atlanta dared to cross Jack without bearing the brunt of his fury. But to his grandchildren, he was a big papa bear who gave the best hugs.

Jade hooked arms with Maddie as she said, "Come on, there's a room upstairs with the perfect fit for the perfect party." Arm in arm, they made their way toward the back stairs.

Maddie blew a kiss and a wave behind her, "Bye, Grandpa Jack!"

"Bye, sweet Girl, see you in a few." He waved back.

"Maddie Ruth, there are dishes to be done, young lady!"

Disappointed, she responded, "Yes, ma'am."

"Go ahead, I'll be up in a few minutes," she called up to her friends.

Rachel grabbed her hand and said, "Come on Girls. Five

are better than one." The girls all bounded down the stairs to help her in the kitchen.

As the adults found their way to the back patio to set up for the party, ten hands quickly cleaned up after breakfast. Suddenly, Emma and Rachel broke into song.

As they harmonized to "Good, Good Father," Maddie's heart found a normal rhythm. Kaitlyn was quiet, looking at her friend's faces as they sang their duet. Kaitlyn and Jade didn't believe in Rachel and Emma's God, but Maddie wondered about this love her friends had found. Her thoughts moved to God more and more of late. *Who is God truly? Why do some people need him so much while others can live fine without him?* Her parents, for example, Dad didn't go to church due to his work schedule, while Mom seemed to have something against God. *But they were just fine, weren't they? I mean, we have everything we need. Everyone is happy, right? Why do we need God?* Reminded of her conversation with Rachel about wanting to feel God in her life, Maddie stood confused as she dried the dish in her hand.

Several important people in her life believed in God. Emma went to Church and loved to sing about her Father. Rachel talked about God as if he were her best friend. Then there was Grammy. Maddie smiled as she thought about the stories Grammy loved to share about God.

Elbowing her friend in the ribs, Rachel asked, "That plate is dry about now, don't you think? What are you thinking about?"

"I was thinking about God," Maddie replied.

Rachel's eyes lit up like Christmas morning as she said, "Oh, do tell!"

Maddie placed the plate she was drying in the cabinet and asked, "Rachel, how do you know that God loves you?"

Hopping onto the island, she leaned forward and looked intently at her friends.

"Here we go," Kaitlyn smirked.

Maddie glared at Kaitlyn as she turned her attention back to Rachel.

"Remember when my mom had to stay in the hospital after

delivering my sister?"

"Yeah," Maddie responded.

"Did you know the doctor told my mom she was going to die?" Everyone stared at Rachel with big eyes.

Shivering, Rachel began to remember her feelings of fear as she said, "I screamed at God, 'Please don't take my momma away, please heal her!' I remember being so afraid and crying so hard that I thought I would cry myself into a puddle. But then, I was alright. I can't explain it except to say that I knew everything was going to be okay. I guess God encouraged me to BELIEVE he would heal her. And then HE DID!"

"How do you explain that to those who aren't healed?" Kaitlyn asked honestly.

"After my mom came home, I shared my prayer with her, and she told me this, 'Rachel, God loves you so much, and he heard your prayer, but my healing was only temporary. My healing will be complete when I come face to face with my Savior. Until that day, I trust that God will be with me no matter what I face, even death.' She said it's okay to ask for healing but always to ask for God's will to be done because he has a plan for each of us. Momma said that one day he would take her to be with him, but until that day, he had a plan for her here. Since then, I have tried to learn everything I can about him."

Maddie had a hundred questions for her friend. As she considered the first one, Matthew ran into the kitchen, "Maddie, Maddie, you will never guess what?!?"

"What, Matthew?" She asked.

"It's a surprise!" Matthew called over his shoulder as he ran back outside.

Deciding to wait until later to ask her questions, she finished the dishes, and she and her friends ran upstairs. She was so excited about her party and couldn't wait for her surprise!!!

After Maddie and her friends left the kitchen, the adults gathered around the kitchen island for a pow-wow.

Grandpa Jack turned to look at his son-in-law as he asked, "David, what's going on with Maddie? She was shaking like a leaf."

David looked at Jacque, "I'm not sure. I never noticed it before."

Annoyed, Jacque interjected, "It's nothing. She's fifteen. She'll be fine."

He looked at his wife patiently, "When she begins to exhibit physical signs, it becomes much more than nothing."

"I know my daughter, David, she is fine."

"Jacque, do ya mind if I talk to 'er?" Grammy asked.

"Well, Grace, I don't mind, but please don't fill her head with that God nonsense. That's the last thing she needs right now."

"That's cute," Emma said.

Looking at herself in the mirror, Maddie tucked the front of her T-shirt into her new pink shorts and tied the pink sash. "Aw, thanks, Girl. Don't we all look cute? Let's take a selfie!"

All five girls crowded in as Maddie lifted her phone in the air for a group selfie. Click - Click - Click.

"Text it to the group chat," exclaimed Rachel.

"Don't forget to tag me," Jade added.

A quiet knock sounded on the door. "Maddie, can you come downstairs, please? We have a birthday girl to celebrate."

She opened her door to find her dad on the landing with a rose in his hand.

David looked down and kissed her cheek, "This is for you, Daughter."

Four "awes" echoed from behind her as she took the rose from her dad.

"Thank you, Daddy," Maddie flushed.

Looking at her intently, her dad asked, "May I have your arm?" At the top of the stairs, he stopped his daughter, "Ruthie, are you okay?"

Shrugging her shoulder, she replied, "Yes, sir, it's fine."

"How often do you have these anxiety attacks?"

"Well, I don't know that they're attacks, but I guess every once in a while, why?"

"We need to talk about your anxiety. I want to know when and what triggers these attacks, okay?"

"Yes, Sir."

"Enough of that for now. Let's celebrate my beautiful daughter's fifteenth birthday!"

"YAY!" Maddie and her dad entered the living room arm-in-arm. She couldn't ever remember a time when she felt so loved. Even her mom displayed a slight sign of emotion as her daughter entered the room with her husband.

As Maddie looked at her family and friends, she felt sure there would never be another day like this one.

Rachel walked over to her friend with a handkerchief in hand. "Turn around and close your eyes. We can't have you peek at your surprise!" Rachel covered her eyes and guided her through the house. Maddie was so excited. *What could it be?*

Her friend removed the handkerchief as they crossed the threshold into the backyard. Maddie had to shield her eyes from the bright sun. As her eyes regained their focus, she caught the most incredible sight of her fifteen years while her friends and family broke into a chorus of happy birthdays.

Daisies, her favorite flower, were everywhere. A big sign was attached to her two favorite shade trees: "HAPPY BIRTHDAY MADDIE." A handful of beautifully wrapped presents surrounded a big cake designed like a keyboard. Maddie's heart soared over the new keyboard with a MacBook and microphone set up in front of the table.

"Oh, my goodness, oh my goodness, finally, I can record music!" Running to her parents, standing side by side, she hugged them both and exclaimed, "Thank you, thank you, thank you!"

Maddie walked over and touched the keys. Gliding her fingers along the smooth surface, a song popped into her mind. This was a regular occurrence for her. Out of the blue, she would hear a melody in her mind and start humming. Strangely enough, she couldn't recall the song, and most often, she would have an overflow of words that followed. Not knowing what to do with the anomaly, she added them to her notes app for later. She was so excited as she realized, *TODAY WAS LATER! I only need the courage to share them with the world.*

"A YouTube influencer you will become!" Emma interrupted her thoughts with ideas for Maddie's new toy. "Hey, now we can write a worship song together!"

"Really?" Maddie asked, "We can do that?"

"Well, of course!" Emma clapped. "I've always wanted to write one, but I can only sing the tune; I have no idea how to write the words."

"I don't know." Doubt began to creep in. "I don't think I'm good enough to write a worship song."

"Why not? You're only writing a letter to God."

"Well, if it's that easy, why can't you do it?"

"Good question," Emma laughed, "but, hey, you have the hardware now, so let's do it together!"

Rachel, Kaitlyn, Emma, and Jade surrounded Maddie as they congratulated her on her new toy. Emma burst into song, encouraging her to step out of her comfort zone.

Five voices suddenly began harmonizing to "Who Says" by Selena Gomez. *Yeah, who says I'm not good enough?* Maddie played the chords on her new keyboard as she agreed, "Yeah! Yeah! Yeah!"

Grammy, Mom, Dad, and Matthew found Maddie for one last gift as the party wrapped up. Looking at Maddie with a gleam in his eye, Dad announced, "Maddie, we have one more surprise."

"Really? Another one?" She asked.

"You and Matthew will be going to Grammy's house for two weeks."

"WHAT? REALLY? NO WAY!!!" She excitedly tripped over her words.

Looking up at his sister, Matthew grabbed her hands, "Isn't that awesome, Maddie? Aren't you excited?"

"Oh yes, but Dad, what about baseball?"

"Well, the season is over, so Matt can go to Grammy's, can't you, Sport?" Dad tipped Matthew's hat lovingly.

Out of the corner of her eye, Maddie saw her mom give Dad "the look." *Hmmm, what was that about?*

After everyone left the party, Maddie took all her new things to her room. As she walked past her dad's study, she heard her parents arguing.

"Why, David? Must you go now? You've only just arrived!" Leaning in to listen, she could hear fear in her mom's voice.

"You know how this works, Jacque. When they call, I come. Dangerous things are going on in Washington now, and I am needed."

"But what about your job?" Jacque asked.

"The Pennington case is complete, so my docket is clean. Besides, they understand."

"Please, please don't go. I spent twenty years waiting for you to come home. I thought this ended when you retired from the Navy," Jacque pleaded.

Maddie's dad wrapped his arms around her mom as she wept. "My Love, if I could stay home, I would. My priority is my family, and then my country. If either one is in danger, I must do my duty."

Her dad lifted her mom's chin and gave her a soft kiss. As he looked into her eyes, he said, "Jacque, I need you to do something for me." She looked at her husband as he wiped a tear from her cheek. "I need you to talk to Maddie about this anxiety."

Suddenly, Maddie's mom stiffened and looked away. "She does not have anxiety. I told you, she's fifteen."

David let go of his wife, "Jacque, please sit down and talk to her; find out why she's so afraid."

Opening her mouth to argue, she began, "But I don't believe . . ."

Gently caressing her lips, he asked, "If you won't talk to her, at least be open to Mom talking to her, okay? She has been through a lot. I believe her strong faith can help Maddie."

"David, have you ever been a fifteen-year-old girl with hormones? Trust me. She is fine."

Deep in thought, Maddie walked away from the door and up the stairs. *Was it hormones, or was she suffering from panic attacks, as Emma suggested? I don't want to be afraid,* she thought to herself.

After placing her new keyboard in the corner of her room, her thoughts moved to her parent's conversation as she picked up a T-shirt and folded it in her suitcase.

As if he heard her thoughts, her dad walked into the room.

"You're leaving again, aren't you?" Maddie asked.

Sitting on the edge of her bed, her dad answered, "Yes, but only for a little while."

With one lonely tear escaping, she asked, "The Navy?"

"Were you listening downstairs?"

"Well . . ." She looked down, pretending to tighten the sash on her shorts.

"Ruthie, you know that I love you very much, right?"

Looking up, she softened in the care found in her dad's eyes. "Yes, sir."

"Everything I do is for you and this family. I will always answer my country's call to keep you, your mom, and your brothers safe. Do you understand?"

"Can't somebody else do it?" She asked timidly.

David cupped Maddie's chin, "Sweetheart, I promise I will return soon. In the meantime, I want you to enjoy visiting Grammy's house. I have a big favor to ask; I would like you to sit down and talk with her about your anxiety, okay?"

She returned to tightening the sash on her shorts, "Okay."

"Promise?" He asked.

Knowing what would come next, she smiled and said, "Promise."

With a serious look, her daddy asked, "Pinky promise?"

Grabbing his pinky in her own, she looked up into her daddy's big brown eyes as he made her give her solemn vow. "Pinky promise."

DOBBINS AIR FORCE BASE

"Thanks, Bill." David grabbed his luggage from the uniformed driver and hefted it from the black unmarked car.

"Yes, sir, Commander. Be safe now, ya here?"

Forcing a smile, he picked up his luggage and went to the waiting Learjet on the runway.

After he retired from the Navy, David worked for Magnum Lock Security as a professional hacker. The cryptology skills he'd obtained in the military prepared him to help others find their IT vulnerabilities. Unfortunately, the Navy would not let him go. Two years after retirement, the Navy recalled him into the reserves as an Information Warfare Dominance Officer under the direct command of the National Security Administration.

"Commander Bennett." An E5 Petty Officer saluted as he mounted the steps of the plane. "May I take your luggage?"

"Yes, thank you, Petty Officer Davis."

Lowering his head to enter, David stepped onto the plane and turned toward the cabin. *Hmm, it looks like I'll be flying solo this round.*

"Can I get you anything, Sir?" The steward asked.

He removed his jacket and answered, "Ice water, thank you."

After settling in his seat, he pulled out his laptop. Waiting for the logon screen, he gazed at the jets outside his window. Mesmerized by the engine's rotation, he recalled the argument with his wife over his leaving. *She just doesn't understand that my country needs me. The future of my family depends upon my service.*

David ran his hand through his wavy chestnut brown hair for the fiftieth time that day. While he was loyal to his country, he couldn't ignore how the stressful effects of the job took their toll. Listening to the ring of the secure uplink, he mentally prepared for the pending conversation.

"Good afternoon, Commander; thank you for being available on such short notice."

"Admiral Osborne, it's good to hear your voice. Thank you for waiting to call until after my daughter's birthday party." He answered, hoping to hide his frustration.

"Please forgive us, Dave, but we have a situation."

David softened at his mentor's tone. "I figured as much. How can I serve you, Rick?"

Admiral Richard Osborne worked closely with David's team before his retirement. In the wake of DataGate, he was promoted to Admiral—a promotion well deserved after the sabotage their team had thwarted in London. After his promotion, he called David into his office and asked if he would return. The years had brought the two together on many occasions, and Rick Osborne knew his protégé could be counted on for difficult missions.

Peering intently through the screen, Admiral Osborne replied, "Well, Son, you're going to Israel."

CHAPTER 4

Grammy Knows Best

Maddie loved the Tennessee mountains. As Aunt Lisa slowed around the curves in the road, Maddie began to recognize familiar rock formations. Everything was lush and green in the summertime and much cooler here than in the Atlanta sun.

Deep in thought over her last conversation with her dad, she wondered: *What was Dad called away for? He said he must keep us safe.* While she mulled these thoughts in her head, Matthew chatted eagerly with Grammy.

Being the shy one in the family, Matthew was typically quiet with everyone. But in the presence of Maddie and Grammy, he became a chatty Cathy. Her friends would ask if she was ever annoyed with her little brother, but she loved him so much that she'd listen to him talk all day. Looking at his coppery red hair, she thought about when he got sick. She couldn't imagine losing her little brother.

Maddie remembered Rachel's prayer when her mom was sick and wished she had faith like her friend. Her Grammy talked about faith, too. "Ya only need faith as big as a mustard seed," she would say. "Don't be 'fraid, have a lil' faith!"

A passionate woman, Grammy was never afraid to share her faith and her God with everyone she met. Even the servers at restaurants would experience her love for God. Maddie remembered the first time Grammy asked a waitress if she could pray for her over the meal. The waitress teared up a little as she answered, "Yes, please pray for my son who is in prison." Grammy proceeded to share Jesus with the waitress after the meal, even to pray for her to accept him into her heart!

Maddie wished she believed as Grammy did, but so many questions were on her mind. *Oh, I forgot to ask Rachel about God,* she thought disappointedly. *I can call her later.*

Or you can ask Grammy, a voice popped into her head.

As Aunt Lisa rounded the last bend at the top of Wild Rock Mountain, Maddie's heart leaped as the familiar white house and red roof came into view. A familiar flurry of long brown ears and white paws bound across the front yard as they drove up to the house. Jumping out of the car, she knelt to pet Grammy's beloved Basset Hound. Twelve-year-old Max was beginning to show his age a little, but he was loving and loyal as always.

Max and Maddie always had a beautiful reunion. She knelt as Max slowly walked before her and sat down in front of her. Wrapping her arms around Max as he laid his floppy-eared head on her chest, she rested her chin on his head. *Basset hugs are the best!*

"Max!" Fifty pounds of Basset peered around Maddie and promptly left her to retrieve his beloved duck as a gift for her brother. Max loved Matthew. From the first moment that Mom brought newborn Matthew to visit Grammy, two-year-old Max was enamored. Maddie laughed as she remembered the toddler's attempt to follow short Max around. Convinced that Max was an old man in a dog suit, she always wondered who was teaching whom!

"That dawg ain't no spring chicken, but he's still fast as greased lightnin'," Grammy laughed.

"Momma, I'll be back to pick ya up for church on Sunday. I gotta get Eva Mae home for bed." Aunt Lisa waved goodbye as she left.

"Come on young'uns, in the house with ya, let's warsh up for supper."

"Yes, ma'am," Maddie replied. It was going to be a great two weeks!

"Wow, something smells so good, Grammy. What is it?" She knew the answer; Grammy cooked much of the same every time she visited, but she loved to hear her dissertation.

"Well, Maddie girl, I picked up a roast at the Piggly Wiggly; and see here, we've got green beans, 'taters, and okra from my garden. Oh, and lookie here at these 'maters." Grammy proudly lifted the lid off each pot, revealing the yummy aromas inside. "We'll take a walk in the garden tomorrow. God's bounty is a'growin'!"

As they sat down to supper, Grammy asked Matthew to say grace. "Oh, I don't know, Grammy."

"Come now, Son, we've got Holy Spirit power in this room; let it out," she encouraged him.

"God, thank you for this bounty," he said nervously.

Maddie opened one eye and looked at her brother as he considered what came next.

"Bless us, amen."

"Now see, that wasn't so hard. R'member, when we pray, we're talkin' to God, that's it. Ain't no need to be a fancy pray'r, jes' share your heart. Now dig in!"

As they finished eating, Grammy looked at her Granddaughter intently. "Girl, tell me 'bout these Jim jams you been feelin'."

"What do you mean?" Maddie asked nervously.

"Well, lemme' see, as I r'call we were sittin' at the breakfast table when you couldn't breathe. I ain't been born yesterday, Girl. Spill the beans."

"It's nothing, Grammy, just a little anxiety."

"Anxi'ty? Did a doctor tell you that?"

"She's afraid," Matthew interrupted with his mouth full.

Irritated by her brother's interruption, Maddie yelled at her brother. "Matthew!"

"Get to the point, Girl; who told you this?"

"It's just the way I feel, Grammy. Lots of girls feel this way.

Like, ya know, your heart beats out of your chest, and it gets hard to breathe." Recognizing the vulnerable moment, she tried to squelch the fluttering of her stomach.

Looking at her granddaughter lovingly, Grammy asked, "So, what're you 'fraid of?"

"Nothing, I don't know, everything?" Maddie wanted to run but instead traced the pattern on the tablecloth.

Grammy placed her napkin on the table as she breathed in deeply. "Maddie Girl, come sit with yer ole' Grammy fer a spell." Chairs squeaked on the old oak floor as Maddie and Matthew followed their Grammy to the front porch with Max in tow.

As the screen door slammed behind them, Grammy found her favorite rocking chair and patted the one to her right. "Come sit."

Max must have sensed the strained conversation as he trotted over and laid down at Grammy's feet.

Minutes seemed like hours as Grammy rocked and rocked. Finally, her quiet voice broke the silence. "Tell me what you see out thar'."

Uncertain what Grammy was getting at, Maddie asked, "Trees?"

"What else?" Grammy asked patiently.

Studying the front yard, she said, "Flowers."

"C'mon Girl, what else do ya see?" Grammy prodded.

Maddie took a moment to consider what Grammy was searching for. *What am I supposed to say?*

Reminiscing past conversations with Grammy on this very porch, she answered sheepishly, "Peace?"

"Fireflies!" Matthew exclaimed as he jumped off the porch with Max following close behind.

Shaking her head with a laugh, Grammy looked at her granddaughter. Madelyn Ruth Bennett, God's Holy Word says that 'The Name of the Lord is a Strong Tower; the righteous run to it and are safe.' Now, do ya know the meanin' of this Word?

"That God's Name is strong, and we are safe with him?"

Maddie answered, a little proud of herself that it came out so quickly.

Looking intently into her granddaughter's eyes, Grammy continued, "That's right, sweet One, and do ya know what yer name means?"

She shook her head.

"Madelyn means strong tower. From the very beginnin' when you were growin' in your momma's tummy, I wanted ya t'know that you were safe with him. But Girl, it's up to you to believe."

The slight wobble of the rocking chair was soothing as Maddie looked at the trees and wondered if they were strong towers. "I don't know what I believe, Grammy. Rachel always talks about God, but I never see him."

Grammy began to wave her hands, "So whaddya see here? Peace was what ya said, so tell me what peace looks like."

Folding her hands in her lap, she replied softly, "I dunno."

"C'mon, think Girl," Grammy encouraged her.

Remembering Rachel's story, a light bulb came on in her head. "Well, God created the trees, the flowers, the fireflies, and he created you and me so . . . I guess that means I can trust him to care for me?"

"Whoo-wee, I think we've got a winner!" Grammy exclaimed as she hit her knee. "My Granddaughter through and through! Maddie Ruth, everythin' you see around ya is in the hand of Almighty God. He created every inch of whatcha see and feel. Now, whatcha gotta know is we're gonna suffer and we're gonna face trials, as James in the Good Book tells us. But we're never alone. God is always with us. Jes' as ya see in the beauty right here."

With imploring eyes, Grammy squeezed her Granddaughter's hand as she said, "Dear One, thar' ain't nothin' to be 'fraid of. Yer Strong Tower's got ya in his hand. Thar' ain't nothin' else I know to be truer than this."

Matthew ran up the stairs, "Look at what I caught, Grammy!"

"Well, if that don't just beat all! God placed light in the palm of this young'uns hand!" Maddie and Grammy oohed and awed over the black and red beetle cupped in Matthew's hand.

Matthew looked at his grandmother intently. "Grammy, did you know the firefly lights up when it mates?"

"Hmm, that might jes' be the most interestin' news I did hear all day. Do ya see over yonder?" Grammy pointed toward the clearing past the trees.

Matthew looked at the end of Grammy's hand intently.

"Ever' summer, jes' as these fine fireflies make thar reveal, the folks in Jake's Holler hold a festival called 'The Night of Lights.' Ya never would guess what we're celebratin'."

"Fireflies?" Matthew answered enthusiastically.

"Whoo, doggie, get him a cookie. Got that straight, boy. Now, I'll tell ya a little fact a' my own." Maddie and Matthew patiently waited as Grammy looked off into the distance. "At one of those thar' festivals, yer Grandpa George asked me to marry 'im."

"Wow, really?"

"Yup, as the fireflies were lightin' up like a choir, he got on one knee and said, 'Gracie, God placed a light in you brighter than all these fireflies. It'd be a might fittin' if you'd light up my life forever."

Maddie smiled at the thought of her Grandpa George asking Grammy to marry him.

After a few moments, Grammy straightened, "C'mon y'all, I reckon I'm worn slap out. Let's warsh the dishes and call it a night."

Under the dim light of the bedroom lamp, Maddie brushed her hair with the required one hundred strokes. The mundane task made it easy for her to mull over her worries. Grammy walked in as she was thinking about her dad. "Ready fer bed?" Grammy asked.

Lying down and tucking her covers under her feet, she

replied, "Yes, ma'am."

After laying something on the bedside table, Grammy sat down next to her granddaughter. She caught the glimmer of a tear escaping her granddaughter's eyes. "What's wrong, Love?"

Embarrassed, Maddie wiped her eyes quickly, seeking a distraction in the bed covers. A fray in the quilt satisfied her gaze for the moment. "I dunno, I miss Daddy, I guess." Grammy's brown eyes tenderly pierced Maddie's heart, *just like Daddy*. She thought.

"Worried?" Grammy asked.

She shrugged her shoulders in response as her gaze followed the trail of her fingers in the fray.

"I have somethin' to tell ya, sweet Girl. When yer momma tole' me I was gonna be a Grammy, the voice a' God spoke as clear as day. He said, 'Grace, this young'un's gonna be courageous, a companion to many."

"Come on, Grammy, God didn't say young'un, did he?" Maddie laughed.

"Now don't ya be interruptin' me, Girl! He said it jes' as the sky is full a them stars. God said, 'Grace r'member the story a Gideon, jes' as he needed encouragement, she too'll need help seein' the strength within.'" Lifting her chin again, she continued, "Maddie Ruth, yer name's ver' special. 'Madelyn' means 'High-Tower,' 'Ruth' means 'Companion' and 'Bennett,' well 'Bennett' means 'Little Blessed One.'"

Holding her breath, Maddie looked up, suddenly interested in her Grammy's prophecy. "God truly spoke to you about ME?"

With a look of disbelief on Grammy's face, she replied, "Well a'course, why wouldn't he?"

Why wouldn't he? She wondered. "I dunno, why would he care about me?"

Grace looked intently into her eyes, "Oh, my beautiful Granddaughter. Ya gotta know how ver' much Almighty God loves you. Those stars in the sky, he promised Abraham he'd have descendants that numbered greater than even them. Ma Jesus said, 'Look at the birds of the air; they don't sow or reap or store away in barns.'" Grammy pointed to the ceiling excitedly. "'Yet yer Heavenly Father feeds 'em. Aren't ya much more valuable than they?'" Grammy looked at her granddaughter and placed her hand on Maddie's arm as she continued, "And my Love, the prophet Jeremiah tole' God's chosen people that the Lord has plans to prosper and not to harm but to give 'em hope and a future. And jes' like them, he loves you, too." Grabbing Maddie's hand, she tapped it lightly on her heart. "Feel that? The beatin' of yer heart is proof. He breathed the breath of life into ya my sweet Girl, do ya feel it?"

Breathing deeply, Maddie said quietly, "Yes, ma'am."

"Now I cain't tell ya what to do, but my God has spoken into me, and now I'm speakin' it ta you." She picked up the book from the nightstand and said, "I give this to you, my beautiful Granddaughter. This book is called The Holy Bible. This is God's Word inspired and written by man through God's Spirit. He gave this book to us so we'd know him, so we'd know who we are in him, and so we'd learn what he wants us to do. I want ya to read it."

Maddie's eyes widened in disbelief, "But it's so big."

Grammy smiled, "Girl, we got a big God. A'course he'd give us somethin' big to get to know him with. Don't worry 'bout the size, Girl. Read a little bit at a time. The Spirit will guide ya." She picked up another book from the bedside table and laid it on Maddie's lap. "I have a ver' special request. Ever' day, when ya read, I want ya ta pray. Pray fer God to reveal himself. Jeremiah 29:13 says, 'You'll seek me and find me when ya seek me with all yer heart.' Maddie Ruth, I want'cha to start seekin' and write your thoughts in this here journal. It's okay if ya don't know him right away. He'll reveal himself."

She picked up the book and responded, "Okay, I'll read it, Grammy. But where do I start?"

"Well, at the beginnin', a'course. Thar' are sixty-six books in the Bible. Ever' book has a meanin' to it. Genesis is all about the beginnin', so start thar'. And don't get discouraged if ya don't understand somethin'. Write it down and pray 'bout it. Ask questions when ya don't understand, got it?"

"Yes, ma'am," she replied, a spark growing deep within.

"Good. Now 'bout your daddy. What 'ya worried 'bout?"

"Mom was crying when Dad told her about this mission. What do you think he's doing?"

"I don't know, my sweet Girl, but I do know this: my God works for the good of those who love him and are called accordin' to his purpose. This means we trust; we praise Almighty God for all he's done, and we ask him to protect yer daddy. Wanna ask him now?"

"Me?"

Grammy answered patiently, "Why not you?"

Looking at a shadow on the wall, she mumbled, "I'm not sure God will hear my prayer."

With a chuckle, Grammy answered, "Beautiful, he hears ya more than you'll ever know. R'member, yer talkin' to God. He loves it when we talk to him. Jes' tell him how ya feel. He'll hear ya. Promise."

"Okay," Maddie responded with hope.

Closing her eyes, she clasped her hands together tightly. With a shaky voice, she said, "God, I don't know if you're here, but Grammy says you are, so I pray you can hear me. My daddy is in danger, and he needs you. God, please protect him, please bring him home safe." Opening one eye, she glanced at Grammy, who was moving her lips silently. "Thank you, God, for making all things for my good. In Jesus' Name, amen."

"That's right, Girl. Keep talkin'; he hears ya," Grammy encouraged as she kissed her forehead and turned off the lamp. "Good night, Maddie Ruth."

ISRAEL

"Commander Bennett, good to see you again. How are Jacque and the kids?"

Shaking the hand of Daniel Reese, Deputy Director of Communications at the US Embassy in Israel, David responded, "Thank you, Dan, they are well. It's been a long time. Are you and Cindy enjoying Jerusalem?"

"Yes, thank you. But, since my promotion, the tension here

has been challenging. Cindy is considering taking the kids home until things calm down."

"Congratulations on your promotion, Dan. Yes, I understand that communications have been interesting. Brief me on the facts to date."

"The team here has uncovered intel that is considerably alarming. We need your help deciphering who is responsible."

Lowering his gaze to the manila envelope on the table, David answered, "Sure, let me take a look."

Dan placed his hand on the envelope and replied, "Dave, before I give you this packet, I have to tell you something."

Looking at the tired features on his old friend, David saw the gray for the first time. With a question on his brow, David waited patiently for the other shoe to drop.

"We believe a new foreign terrorist organization has assembled. David, we have reason to believe that their roots go deep."

CHAPTER 5

A Promising Revelation

As Maddie awoke to Matthew's chatter in the kitchen, she wiped her sleepy eyes and sat up. Annoyed at the sound of a very loud bird outside of her window, she mumbled, "It's too early," to whoever was listening.

Picking up the book on her bedside table, she opened the front cover and squinted to read Grammy's scribble:

Maddie,

My dear Granddaughter, I give this Bible to you as an extension of my heart. Jesus gave you his life as he wrote your name in the palm of his hand. Enjoy every moment as you draw near to your Heavenly Father, the One who wrote these words and the One who loves you most. I look forward to hearing how his Spirit speaks to you through these pages.
Love you dearly, Grammy.

Maddie loved her Grammy, but boy did she have interesting handwriting. Thankfully, she had learned over the years how to transcribe the scribble.

Turning the pages, she finally found the one with Genesis at the top. *Grammy said to start at the beginning, so I guess this is where I will begin.*

"In the beginning God created the heavens and the earth.

Now the earth was formless and empty, darkness was over the surface of the deep, and the Spirit of God was hovering over the waters. And God said, 'Let there be light,' and there was light. God saw that the light was good, and he separated the light from the darkness. ... Then God said, 'Let us make mankind in our image, in our likeness' ... So, God created mankind in his own image, in the image of God he created them; male and female he created them."

Processing a million questions, she picked up the journal Grammy left behind and began to write.

July 28

God, when was the beginning? Do I look like you? Will I ever see you? How old is the earth? Did you give the bird her song? Can you ask her to please not wake me up so early?
Maddie

After an hour of writing, she took her journal into the kitchen to meet Grammy and Matthew. She was so excited to show off her progress.

Maddie shook her head as she crossed the kitchen threshold, not believing her own eyes. Her brother, elbow-deep in flour and dough, was a sight. Laughing, she wondered if Grammy knew about the mess to be cleaned off the floor, the counters, and Matthew's hair. *Mom would have a fit,* she chuckled to herself.

"Grammy, guess what?" She asked.

Taking her eyes off her grandson, Grammy responded, "Good mornin' Love, whatcha got there?"

"I read for a whole hour this morning and wrote a whole bunch of questions, like you asked."

"Really now? Let's see here whatcha wrote?"

"Grammy, how many holes do I cut?" Matthew interrupted.

Looking at her grandson with great patience, Grammy replied, "When I was knee-high to a grasshopper, not much younger'n you, my Memaw tole' me that biscuit makin' was ser'ous business. Fer ever' biscuit ya cut, yer buildin' muscle and storin' up grit."

Scratching his flour-covered nose, Matthew said, "But we aren't making grits, Grammy."

"Young'un, listen to yer ole' Grammy now. See that glass thar'? It's a tool. When ya cover the edges with flour, yer preppin' it to make the cut. Then ya press down hard. Harder'n a one-eyed man doin' push-ups."

"Is that how I store up grit?" Matthew asked as he closed one eye and pushed the glass down as hard as possible.

Grammy laughed.

Maddie loved her Grammy's way of turning a phrase. *One of these days, I need to write a book that includes all her southern sayings.* she mused.

"Is this right?" Matthew asked.

"Well, I'll be, I'd say that thar' is righter'n rain. Now pick up the biscuit, careful like, and set it on the bakin' sheet. That's it, ya got it, Matthew, yer grit is growin' as we speak! Do that five more times, and I'd say we'll have the best biscuits this side of the Mississippi!"

Listening to her brother and Grammy's exchange, Maddie sat at the table and opened her journal. Matthew began whistling an unrecognizable tune. Smiling, she looked up as Grammy grabbed her glasses and sat down.

"Now, let's take a look."

Maddie bit her lip as her Grammy read the questions she wrote.

"Well now, I'd say those are jes' 'bout the most honest questions I ever did see. Whatcha think, Girl?"

"What do you mean?" She asked nervously.

"Did ya learn anythin'?" Grammy asked.

"Yes, ma'am, I did. Did you know that God made mankind in his image? Does that mean that God looks like me?"

Chuckling, Grammy answered, "No, Ma'am, more like you look like him. We may be made in his image, but he is holy, and his glory is greater than anythin' ya can ever imagine. A man in the Bible named Moses wanted to see God's glory. God said he could'na see his face fer nobody could see him and live. He made him stand on the cleft of a rock as he covered Moses with his hand. Moses could only see the Lord's back, but the light from God's glory was so great that the Good Book declared Moses as radiant, so bright that nobody'd come near 'im. He had to put a veil over his face ever'time he saw the Lord."

"Grammy, look, all done!" A baking sheet full of biscuits later, Matthew glowed as he showed off his hard work.

With pride, Grammy said, "Well, I'd say that's finer 'n frog hair. Boy, ya did a fine job, yep a fine job. But I gotta say, ya made a bigger mess'n Max tearin' the stuffin' outta his poor duck."

Maddie shook her head as Grammy helped Matthew put the biscuits in the oven. "Grammy, can we see God?"

"Well, now, I never seen Father God in the flesh, but he is with me."

"How do you know?"

"Well, not shore I can 'splain, but I'll try. When I pray, I get real quiet-like. I close my eyes and breathe in and out slowly. I get a picture of what Jesus might look like. He's invited me into his presence, and I don't take that lightly. I sit and listen 'a'fore I ever speak. When his peace surrounds me, I talk to him. I thank him for his goodness. I thank him for the day. I thank him fer life and our family. I pray fer other people who need a helpin' hand. I ask him to help me in my day, give me wisdom and direction, and go with me ever'where. Sometimes I may even feel a warm light coverin' me."

"Like Moses?" Maddie asked.

Pausing for a moment, Grammy responded, "Well, I guess. Though I doubt I'm as radiant as Moses."

"Grammy, please don't be mad, but I've never seen or felt him before. How can I believe in something I can't see or feel?"

"Oh, my sweet Granddaughter, I ain't gonna say I always felt him. It's only through a relationship built over time that I feel his presence. He's ever'where, even here right this very moment. I know this to be true because he is."

"In this room?" Matthew asked as he looked around.

"Why yes siree, in this ver' room. Ya see my Loves, we are in his presence always. God is ever'where, but it's only when we seek him with all our hearts that we find him. Let's set outside a spell while we wait fer the biscuits to rise."

As they walked outside, Max nudged Maddie's leg with his duck in his mouth. After playing tug-of-war with him, Max surrendered the duck so she would throw it. Max ran after the duck as Grammy licked her finger putting it in the air. "That's a right smart wind we got today. 'Sposed to be a storm comin' in later. D'ya feel it?"

Imitating Grammy, both Maddie and Matthew licked their fingers and put them in the air.

"I feel it," Matthew agreed with a serious look on his face.

"Yes, ma'am, I can feel the wind."

Looking in the distance, Grammy asked, "Can ya see the wind?"

Two heads shook no.

"If yer not lookin' for it, can ya feel it?"

"Sometimes," Matthew answered.

"So, if ya cain't always feel it and ya cain't see it, is it real?"

A smile broke on Maddie's face as she remembered Rachel's response about air being real yet unseen.

"Yes, ma'am, it's real!" She exclaimed. "But what else can we not see that's real?"

"So much more, my Girl. I'll leave one word for ya to chew on: FAITH. But we'll leave that for 'nother day. Fer now, let's go in and eat those yummy biscuits Brother made!"

As the sun was setting on a Tennessee Saturday, Grammy gave a tour of her garden. Maddie was in awe of the gigantic tomatoes and towering sunflowers that reached over her head.

As butterflies' flit through the butterfly bushes, she reminisced childhood memories of playing hide-and-seek in this very garden.

Grammy showed off her squash, cucumber, and peppers. Matthew laughed at the cabbage patches while asking Grammy if a baby was hiding in the leaves.

Running her fingers along the bumpiness of a pea pod, Maddie asked, "Grammy, can I ask a question?"

"A'course, Maddie Girl."

"Do you miss Grandpa George?"

"Ever'day, Love."

"Why did he have to die?"

"It was his time."

Sad, Maddie asked, "But why? Couldn't God let us have him a little longer?"

Grammy placed her arms around her. "Beautiful, ever'thin' on this earth is temporary. We live; we die, it's the circle of life. God needed your Grandpa George, I 'spose. George'd finished his purpose here and was ready to start his purpose in Heaven. I love him, but I cain't change the plan of Almighty God."

"I just . . . "

"What, Love?"

A tear escaped Maddie's eye as she answered, "I wish I told him I loved him before he died."

"Oh, Deary, he knew. You were the apple of his eye. He loved you as big as this sunflower and knew you loved him right back."

"Tell me again how y'all met?" She asked curiously.

"First, let's set a spell. Yer Grammy is plumb wore out this afternoon." Sitting on a bench in the middle of the garden, Grammy fanned her face with a napkin from her pocket. "Ooee, if these Tennessee summers don't get hotter and hotter ever' year! Now, where were we? Oh, yes, now my George was a handsome young man. Full a' life with a boomin' voice to boot. He'd walk into a room, and ever'body would quiet. N'er did George Bennett ever have an enemy. When I was sixteen, I was invited to a Sunday School picnic and was so excited to wear my new pink flower dress and patent leather shoes. After settin' in the church service with my friend, we walked to the lawn fer a picnic. It was blasted hot on that Sunday jes' like today, and ever'body was sportin' a paper fan. Anyway, my friend was talkin' to me 'bout some boy who was irritatin' her, and suddenly, the air left my chest as quickly as I breathed it in. There he was, George Allen Bennett, in all his six-foot glory. Hair as black as coal. Eyes as green as this here bean, penetratin' to the core. Now wouldn't ya know it? He looked at me and all I could think was to hide behind the nearest mason jar. Never you mind that the mason jar was empty 'cept fer a couple a' rocks at the bottom. My George walked over and asked my name, and the rest is history. Wow, that'd be fifty-three years since we met."

"How old were you?" Maddie asked.

"I was sixteen."

"And he was a year older, right?"

"That's right as rain, Love. Time shore does fly."

As Grammy became lost in her memories, Maddie remembered the conversation from the previous night. Was Grammy's revelation the promise Daddy always talked about? What was it she said? Madelyn means high tower. Ruth means companion and Bennett means little-blessed one. *How does this tie into a promise?* She wondered.

The soft, wet palm of her grandmother's hand slid into hers, and she looked up into Grammy's weepy eyes. "Are you okay Grammy?"

"Never you mind, Girl, never you mind. Yer Grammy is jes' fine, reminiscin' a bit is all."

"Can I ask you another question?"

"Always Love, what is it?"

Nervously, Maddie continued, "Last night you mentioned that my name has a special meaning. What does high tower, companion, and little blessed one have to do with me?"

Grammy tightened her grip around her granddaughter's hand and looked her deep in the eyes.

"R'member I tole' ya that Father God tole' me you would

need a little encouragin'?"

"Yes, ma'am."

"Well, that's cause he has a special mission for ya." Grammy squeezed her hand again.

"For me?" Maddie's heart began to flutter.

"Now ya look at me, Girl. Thar' ain't nothin' to be 'fraid of, ya here?"

Maddie looked down.

"No, ya don't. Look at me. Almighty God don't give nobody nothin' he ain't prepared to help 'em with, here?"

"But. . . "

"No ma'am, no buts." Grammy grabbed her other hand and encouraged her to look up.

"Even Moses was nervous. Gideon was hidin' when he was called. Esther needed encouragin'. David ran when his life was in danger. Thar' ain't nobody nowhere that don't feel a little fear when they're called to do God's will, but ya know what?"

Maddie looked at her Grammy warily.

"Fear is a springboard fer courage. Ever' challenge ya face will open that door. I want ya to always r'member that, Girl. God allowed us to see that each a' these men and women had a little fear in 'em, and they all knew where to turn. My God turned their fear into courage." Placing her hands on her granddaughter's shoulders, Grammy held her gaze with reassurance. "Maddie Ruth, he'll be with you, too, and he'll turn yer fear into courage jes' the same. In those moments when you're 'fraid, ask him to take yer hand and walk with ya through that door, an he will.

"Now, 'bout that mission. I had a dream a'fore you were born, where sunflowers were ever'where! They were so tall I could barely see the sky. But the sky I did see was dark and ominous. I was walkin' through the garden enjoyin' the beauty all around me and then there he was."

"Who?"

"Well now, I don't know I can rightly say; but he shore looked important." Raising her hand to her mouth as if to tell a secret, she whispered, "I think he was an angel, truth be told."

Nodding her head, she continued, "Now, he was prunin' these sunflowers here, so they'd grow big and tall. I looked at 'em and gave him my Sunday best greetin,' "Mornin' Sir." And he said, "Mornin' Grace."

"Wait, he knew your name?"

"He shore did, as shore as I know yers. He invited me to set a spell, like we're settin' now, and then he tole' me a story. He said my beautiful granddaughter would be a companion to many who were hidin' from somethin' evil. He tole' me that he would protect them through you, and he would bless the work a yer hand and yer heart. He tole' me to give ya the word a' God and to teach ya that God's Name is a fortified tower; the righteous run to it and are safe."

"Daddy always told me that my name held a promise."

Grammy smiled as she waited for her to process this new information. After a few moments of silence, she asked, "Do ya know what this means?"

Curious, Maddie looked at her.

"When ya take his hand, yer sayin' I trust ya, God. He's yer Tower, yer hidin' place. No matter the shakin', he'll protect ya."

Maddie looked at her Grammy's hand in hers and nodded.

"Okay?" Grammy squeezed her hand.

"Okay."

ISRAEL

"A new foreign terrorist organization? How deep are we talking?"

Shaking his head, Dan looked nervously at his friend and answered, "While monitoring JONAH, our cryptologists found a flurry of obscure communications camouflaged under the guise of world trade."

The tap of David's shoe got louder and louder as Dan took a sip of water and considered what he would say next.

"And Dave, these communications look suspiciously similar to TRU."

CHAPTER 6

Confirmations' Song

Sunday morning shined brightly in Maddie's window, and once again, a bird chirped very loudly outside. *Does that bird have to be so loud?* She wondered. Opening her eyes to peer out the window, she felt a song bubble up inside—a sweet little tune that filled her with joy. *Oh boy, that bird is starting to rub off on me,* she thought grudgingly.

Sitting down for her daily reading, she bowed her head and asked, "God, please show me who you are. Grammy said you made a promise about me; please show me that, too. I don't want to be afraid anymore."

As she finished Genesis nine, she wrote in her journal:

> *July 29*
> *God, you made Noah a promise. You had him build a boat and bring his family and the animals on it for protection. Is that what you want me to do? Do you want me to build a boat? God, please give me Noah's strength and courage.*
> *Maddie*

She couldn't wait to share with Grammy, but first, she had to dress for church. Looking in the mirror at the new blue dress her mom bought before her birthday, she wondered if she looked pretty like her Grammy did when she met Grandpa George. *God, will I meet my future husband at sixteen?*

Taking her Bible and journal to breakfast, she sat down with Grammy. "Grammy, today I read about God's promise to Noah, but can I ask you a question? Why did God destroy everyone but his family in the flood?"

"Well, I'll be, that's a good question, Maddie Ruth. One I'd like to leave for 'nother day if ya please."

"Aw, man. Okay."

"Patience, Love, we'll get there. Today I wanna talk 'bout faith. Do ya know why God made that promise to Noah?"

"Why?"

"Noah was righteous, blameless, and walked faithfully with his God. While ever'body on the earth was wicked, Noah wasn't. Noah loved and trusted God knowin' he would care for him and his family. This is called faith, the confidence in what we hope for and assurance in what we cain't see. Noah had faith and God blessed him."

"Do you think that Noah was afraid?"

"Who wouldn't be? But Noah did it anyway, trustin' God to care fer him no matter what. He had faith in God and his promise, and God blessed 'im for it."

"Do you think I can be like Noah?"

"Are ya askin' if I think ya can love God, trust him, and have faith? Girl, I think ya got gumption more'n ya even know."

Maddie smiled as she helped her Grammy make breakfast.

While it had been a long time since she had gone to church with Grammy, not much had changed. The pews sat straight and tall, with wooden backs and cushioned seats. A book with the name "HYMNAL" was placed in front of every fourth seat. The bright and fragrant flowers that adorned the front of the church reminded Maddie of her childhood years when she would pick a flower and place it in her hair. Grammy said Ms. Lorna picked them from her garden every week.

Grammy's church met for prayer in the sanctuary every Sunday and then afterward they would break into Sunday school groups. Classes were grouped by age and led by one teacher who shared a Bible story. This Sunday, her teacher was Ms. Bonnie.

"Well, I'll be. Is that Maddie Ruth Bennett? Look at ya Girl, yer pretty as a peach. Ya sure have grown up, haven't ya?"

As Ms. Bonnie hugged her, she replied, "Hi, Ms. Bonnie, I just had a birthday."

"Well, now, ya don't say. How old might ya' be now?"

"I'm fifteen!" She declared.

Pretending to be shocked, Ms. Bonnie replied, "I don't believe it! You must be at least sixteen."

"Ms. Bonnie!" Embarrassed, Maddie giggled.

"Come on in, Girl." Ms. Bonnie shut the Sunday School room door behind them.

Maddie was so excited as Ms. Bonnie told the story of Noah. Listening intently to her every word, she was on the edge of her seat through the entire class. Raising her hand, she asked the question which had been nagging her all morning.

Ms. Bonnie called her, "Yes, Maddie?"

"Ms. Bonnie, why did God save Noah and his family and kill everyone else in the flood?"

"Well, that's a great question. The Bible says the earth was corrupt and full of violence in God's sight. It says God wanted to put an end to all people because of their violence."

Amy Jayne Wright, a red-headed girl Maddie vaguely remembered, raised her hand, "But Ms. Bonnie, what about the babies? They weren't corrupt, were they?"

"Were they corrupt? No, no, I don't think they were corrupt," Ms. Bonnie answered.

"Did God destroy them?" Amy asked the teacher.

"His Word says that only Noah and his family were saved." Ms. Bonnie replied.

"Then why did he kill the babies?" Amy asked.

The room was so quiet you could hear a pin drop.

"Truth be told, Ladies, I don't know. I certainly cain't

explain everythin' God does. I can tell ya the facts given to us in God's Word. The world was full of sin, and the Lord saw how wicked humans had become. The Bible also says that the thoughts of the human heart were evil, meanin' people acted from evil thoughts. Mill over this, babies were bein' born in the middle of all that evil. Genesis 6:6 says the Lord regretted that he had made human bein's, and his heart was deeply troubled. What kinda things would have ta happen fer God's heart to be troubled over the creation he loved?"

Amy Jayne thought for a moment, "I guess people hurtin' each other, parents divorcin'?" A sad look passed on her face.

Another girl added, "Cain did kill Abel."

"That's right. Wickedness was great on the earth, and it made God sad. I 'spect the people didn't care about the Lord anymore 'cause Noah was the only one who found favor with him.

"So, he made a way for people to be restored to him. God set a plan of action into place resultin' in Noah and his family bein' one of many who would bring his Son into the world. Was God unfair for allowin' the babies to die with all the others? Perhaps, unfair in our understandin' of what is fair. But he loved his creation enough to save us all through his Son. His Son gave his own life so we could have eternity with him. We may never know in this lifetime why he chose to bring those babies home to him, but I 'spect we can ask him when we get to Heaven."

Maddie's thoughts spiraled out of control. *What must a life full of violence look like for a child? The six o'clock news was full of stories of children being abandoned, kidnapped, left in hot cars, killed even. God needed Grandpa and took him to Heaven; maybe God saved the babies in Noah's time by letting them die and go to Heaven to spare them from evil. Was this a blessing for those saved?*

Lost in her thoughts, she didn't realize everyone had left the room until Ms. Bonnie lightly tapped her shoulder. "Maddie, are ya okay?"

"Yes, Ma'am."

Ms. Bonnie sat in the chair next to her, "Wanna talk?"

"No, Ma'am, I'm okay. Thank you for today's lesson. I was reading about Noah this morning."

She smiled at Maddie, "Ya don't say?"

"I thought it was cool that God saved Noah and his family. Can you imagine what the ark must've looked like?" Furrowing her brow, she continued, "I'm still trying to figure out how he fit all the animals on the boat!"

Laughing at her enthusiasm, Ms. Bonnie asked, "Did ya catch the promise God gave Noah and his family after they found dry land?"

"No, Ma'am, what was that?"

"God gave Noah and his family a rainbow as a promise that he would never again destroy the earth by flood."

"Wait, so every time I see a rainbow, I'm looking at the same promise God gave to Noah?"

"Yes, ma'am. Ever' time we see a rainbow, we receive a confirmation of God's promise to Noah." Ms. Bonnie smiled.

"Wow." Thinking about the promise made to Grammy, Maddie wondered if God would give her a rainbow reminder, too.

"Maddie, this is gonna sound strange, but I feel I need to share somethin' with you. I can tell yer interested in the story of Noah. Have ya ever thought 'bout the gift God gave the world through Noah's family? God called Noah to obey him in buildin' an ark. Then he provided all Noah needed to fulfill the call includin' a right smart number of animals for Noah to care for. Why do ya think he did all that?"

Maddie thought for a moment and replied, "He wanted to save the world?"

Nodding, Ms. Bonnie said, "Yer right, God wanted to save the world, but why did he choose Noah?"

"Because Noah was faithful?"

"That's right, and faithfulness is a choice. Noah chose to trust God and so God entrusted Noah with the people and animals he was gonna use to rebuild the world. God does that. He chooses people he knows'll listen to 'im and step out in obedience. I feel like God is tellin' you to trust him."

"What do you mean?"

"I feel like God is fixin' to do somethin', and he's gonna use you in his plan. I cain't say more'n that 'cept I know the world is gettin' ugly. And God is usin' people willin' to trust him and obey his call. I see somethin' in you, Maddie, and I think yer one of the people. Receive this word or throw it away, but if you choose to receive it, pray, and ask him what he wants ya to do."

Maddie's eyes brightened as she wondered, *is this my rainbow? Is God confirming what Grammy told me?*

With a skip in her step and a song in her heart, she left the room to find Grammy and Matthew.

ISRAEL

As David looked over the intel, his steely gaze did not give away the churning in his stomach. In a few short weeks, the WTO would gather in Geneva for the Ministerial Conference. Leaders from across the globe would gather in one room to discuss new trade agreements. A handful of big corporations would cash in big depending on the outcome of these trade talks. "So, what are these communications exactly?"

With calm authority, Dan answered, "After we found the camouflaged communications, trends revealed themselves through the conversations surrounding the centralization of international global imports and exports of material goods. We saw specific mentions of blockades in key trade ports around the world that appeared to be designed to drive countries into a centralized trade system. These messages were interspersed throughout average run-of-the-mill conversations. It appeared as if the sender knew the communications were monitored."

"Isn't JONAH the telecommunications cable routing internet traffic between Tel Aviv, Israel and Europe?" David asked.

A quick breath revealed Dan's surprise at David's knowledge of JONAH: "Yes. It is also known as the Bezeq International Optical System, owned by Bezeq, respectively."

Reading through the highlighted sections of

communications, David saw Savannah, Georgia, highlighted. "Savannah is listed here. Why would they choose to block the port of Savannah? I can understand California, New York, and Louisiana even, but Georgia?"

"As far as we can tell, the ports listed provide for the world's food supply. Dave, we need you to find out who is responsible for these transmissions and why."

"Who do you suspect?"

"Heck, Dave, anyone, the Russians, Chinese, or even the Palestinians, for all we know. At this point, we aren't sure. But the question of who is responsible has been heavy on the Ambassador's mind."

"If these transmissions are global, why do we suspect a world power is responsible?"

Dan seemed to be irritated over the line of questions, but he continued, "As I mentioned, we suspect a new underground organization that is using dark web tactics. Our intel points toward a potential terrorist group deadlier than even ISIL. Based on the number of communications and the blockade targets listed, it appears big money is behind it. But that isn't the worst of it."

David's stomach began to boil.

"These communications may also be transmitted across other trans-Atlantic cables. We have no idea yet how far this organization's reach extends or how much money is behind it. This is not good, Dave, not good at all." Daniel shook his head.

Counting down the days to the Geneva Conference, David knew the media would have a field day with this one.

"I don't think I need to tell you the importance of finding these operatives quickly. You do realize that the WTO is meeting soon?"

"Yes."

"Dave, you're the best, and we need your experience to find out who this organization is so we can stop these potential attacks. We have a team staying near the embassy awaiting orders. I scheduled a meeting for you with the Ambassador at 0900 tomorrow morning to go over the details of these communications. After this, you will meet with the team to go over logistics."

David sat down with a sigh.

"It's a fallen world we live in, isn't it David?"

"Hmm."

CHAPTER 7

Endless Possibilities

Lost in thought after Sunday school, Maddie bumped into the pungent odor of boy and body spray as she rounded a corner. Embarrassed, she hurried to pick up her Bible that fell to the floor.

"Hey, Blue, you're gorgeous!" A voice said from the group of boys.

Speechless, she wanted to vanish into the wall. "Hi?"

While straightening her dress, she saw the boys elbowing one another.

"Jacob, talk to her."

"Ahem, excuse me." Finding the sass from deep within, she rolled her eyes and prepared for her escape.

"So, what's your name, Blue?" The boy named Jacob asked.

"Maddie." She heard herself respond.

"Maaaaaaadddiiieeee, do you have a mirror? Cause I wanna see how good I look." The raucous laughter filled the hallway.

"What? Uh no. Perhaps you can try the bathroom?" Feeling her anxiety rise, she rushed off before he said anything else.

Hurrying into the sanctuary, relief filled her when she saw Grammy and Matthew. "Whew." She exclaimed as she sat down in a heap next to her brother.

"What's wrong, Maddie Girl?" Grammy asked.

"Nothing."

"Hmmph, nothin' huh?" Grammy looked at Matthew and said, "Looks like a mortified jumble of somethin' to me. Must be a boy involved."

As Jacob walked into the room, Maddie felt her face flush and her hands get sweaty. Worried that he might recognize her, she began fumbling with the paper in Matthew's hand. "What's this?" she asked.

"We got to draw in Sunday school! The teacher told us to draw anything we wanted, so I drew a picture of you."

"Awe, thank you, little Bro." Maddie couldn't stay mad very long when her brother was around. He brought her joy without even knowing he was doing so.

Turning her attention toward the front, she was in awe as a lovely tune arose from the piano. The choir filed into the sanctuary adorned in ruby-red robes. Listening to the music as it danced around her, Maddie pondered, *I must remember to ask Ms. Lorna to teach me that melody.*

After service, Maddie followed Grammy and Matthew to greet Pastor Ron. The line was long as church members waited to shake the pastor's hand.

As she understood it, Pastor Ron had quite a colorful history. He had dropped out of high school and joined a motorcycle gang. With his permission, Grammy would share his testimony.

Pastor Ron had a Road to Damascus conversion, he shore did. He was meaner 'n a wet hen, diggin' his own grave. After a night of drinkin', Pastor Ron woke up to a light overhead, a light unlike anythin' he'd ever seen; a light so bright that he could'na see as a boomin' voice spoke his name, 'Ron.'

Pastor Ron, he was so 'fraid he tried to jump up and run outta the room. But he was paralyzed and could'na move. The voice spoke again, 'Ron, wake up and foller me. I've a church for you to lead.'

After that interestin' meetin', Pastor Ron got up, took a shower, and went to church. Tellin' his story to the local pastor, he never looked back and now leads the congregation of this here church.

"Hello, Grace." Pastor Ron gave Grammy a big bear hug.

"Why hello, Pastor Ron, what do ya know good?"

Smiling at the three of them, he said, "Hm, not a whole lot, 'cept that I'm hungry for some lunch. Who might we have here?"

"My granddaughter Maddie and my grandson Matthew."

"So good to see you both." He gave them both his signature bear hug. "Can we expect you at the church picnic this afternoon?"

"Ya know thar's rain comin' in Pastor," Grammy answered with concern in her voice.

"Yes, ma'am, we'll bring 'er in if it starts to rain."

Grammy relaxed as she answered the Pastor, "Well, we're lookin' forward to it then."

"My Grammy made mac and cheese, Pastor Ron! I can't wait!" Matthew piped in.

"Well now, yer Grammy's got the best mac and cheese this side of the holler," Pastor Ron replied.

"Come along now young'uns. Let Pastor Ron finish with his congregation. Matthew, go get the mac and cheese out of Aunt Lisa's car, and meet us over yonder by the oak tree."

As Maddie and Grammy walked over to the table under the oak tree, Maddie caught a glimpse of Jacob and his friends. *Please don't look at me, please don't look at me.*

"Now what's got yer bee in a bonnet, Girl?" Grammy asked her granddaughter.

"Grammy, what's a holler?" Matthew asked as he ran back with the mac and cheese.

"Well now, a holler is a valley, boy. See those mountains surroundin' us?" Grammy spanned the mountains surrounding them with her hands.

"Yes, ma'am."

"A holler is a valley surrounded by mountains. It's a place where ya can let your young'uns run loose cause ya know ya got plenty a time a'fore it gets dark."

"Why is it called a holler?" Matthew asked.

"Cause you gotta holler over the mountain if you wanna talk to your neighbor over yonder, a'course."

"Ohhhhh." Matthew walked away lost in thought.

Offering Maddie the bench, Grammy gave her some napkins and silverware to unroll. "Now how 'bout this boy ya been gawkin' at?" Grammy asked her curiously.

"I haven't been gawking at any boy, Grammy."

"Guess my glasses ain't as sharp as they used to be." As Grammy seemed to buy her white lie, Jacob walked over.

"Can I talk to you?" Jacob asked nervously.

"Well, now thar's Ms. Lorna. Let me see if she needs any help over yonder. Y'all okay now?"

Fidgeting with her nails, she said, "Yes, ma'am, I'm okay."

"Got my eye on you boy." Grammy pointed at Jacob.

Jacob turned bright red, "Yes, ma'am."

As Jacob sat down next to Maddie, she wiped her sweaty palms on her dress and attempted to quiet her rapidly beating heart. *Breathe.*

Is he nervous too? Maddie wondered as she saw Jacob sitting on his hands and looking around. "Well?" She asked.

"Well?" Jacob parroted.

Maddie began to wonder why he thought she was okay with his sitting so close to her. "Did you have something to say to me?" *Way to blast that sass, Maddie.* she chuckled to herself.

"Oh yeah, I'm sorry for bein' ugly to you earlier."

"You were mean to me? I couldn't tell from your sarcasm."

Looking at her apologetically, he said, "I was wrong."

A bit wary, she muttered, "Apology accepted."

And just like that Jacob got up and walked away.

Shaking her head, she muttered, "Boys" under her breath.

Maddie got up to help her Grammy. As they straightened out the tablecloth, thunder rolled in the distance.

"A storm is blowin' in. Let's take everythin' into the

kitchen." Grammy called out. Picking up dishes, everyone followed her into the church kitchen.

Maddie loved this room. A couple of years ago several of the local lumberjacks had to cut down a bunch of dead trees after a storm. Bringing the trees into town, they carved them into tables and benches. Running her fingers over the glossed wood, Maddie loved tracing initials carved into the wood from lovers' past. Coming across one such carving, she pressed her fingers into the initials MS / EK.

The hair on the back of her neck stood up as she sensed someone's eyes on her. Startled, she jumped up as Jacob commented, "Those are my parent's initials."

"Really?"

"Yup! As high school sweethearts, this was their favorite tree. After this tree was cut down, my Papaw formed this into a table in honor of them."

"That is so sweet!" Her heart began to soften a bit.

"Can we start over? Hi, my name is Jacob Sullivan." Jacob extended his hand for Maddie to shake.

Accepting Jacob's peace offering, she looked up into his gray eyes.

"Maddie 'um Bennett," Maddie said, shaking his hand.

"Maddie 'um, huh? Is that a southern middle name?" Jacob laughed. "My mom said you are Ms. Grace's granddaughter. Are you visitin'?"

"Yes, my brother and I are here for two weeks. Then we'll go home for school." She was quite curious that he asked his mom about her.

"Where's home?"

Distracting herself with a bowl of potato salad, she answered, "Atlanta. We live in a little town north of Atlanta called Marietta."

"Mare 'etta? Like after the Kentucky philly?" Jacob asked.

"Philly? No, it's a city," Maddie giggled.

With a serious look on his face, Jacob replied, "Oh, sorry. Etta was a beautiful mare who won the Kentucky Oaks at Churchill Downs. She has quite the story. Her trainer put her in the race to work her out but she shore showed him by winnin'!" Jacob grinned, "I kinda have a likin' to horses."

A warm feeling came over Maddie as Jacob showed his enthusiasm over the horse. "She sounds like she had a pretty cool life."

"Well, it is said she was a bit temperamental, but I shore do love an underdog story. So how did yer city get called "Mare 'etta, anyway?" Jacob asked.

"Not Mare 'etta, Marietta." She laughed as she shrugged a shoulder. "I don't know."

A shadow of disappointment seemed to cross Jacob's face as he asked, "So, you'll be leaving soon?"

"In a week, yes." The pea salad suddenly looked very interesting.

Jacob handed her a plate as he tilted his head toward the food line. "Oh bummer, I'm going on a mission trip tomorrow."

Bummer, what does he mean by bummer? She wondered. "Where are you going?"

"Our youth group goes ta the Appalatchun Mountains to help our neighbors thar' build and repair homes. It's an older community, but we help 'em as much as we can."

"That sounds cool." *I would love to do something like that.* She thought.

"Thar' ain't no power or water, but I jes' love talkin' to 'em. It's like they live in a different century, ya know? It's so cool to hear the old-world stories and to hear their music. Some of the older men play a mean banjo."

"Wow, the banjo? I love the guitar, but I've never heard anyone play the banjo," Maddie bopped up and down at the idea of playing a new instrument.

Jacob played a pretend banjo on his empty plate. "Yup, they're amazin'. Taught me a couple of licks, they did."

Excited to meet another musician, she asked, "Really? You play?"

"Sure, I can bring mine later if you're still 'round," Jacob promised.

"That would be awesome!" Blushing, she realized their plates were still empty, and people were beginning to line up behind them.

Filling up his plate, Jacob said, "It was nice talkin' to ya Maddie. I'm gonna go sit with my mom. Catch ya later."

"Kay, bye."

After dinner, Maddie and Matthew walked outside to join everyone. Her brother ran off to find his friends, while Maddie's eyes widened at the canopy of green above. *My very own blanket of protection,* she thought as she reminisced over Rachel's picture of God's presence in creation.

Missing her friend, she took a moment to give her friend a call.

"Hello?"

"Hey, Girl! I was thinking about you and wanted to give you a call. I don't have much time. Sorry, I had to leave my phone at home, so I'm calling you on Gram's phone."

"Maddie! It's so good to hear your voice. No worries. How is ole' Grammy doing?" Rachel asked.

In her best Grammy accent, she said, "She's 'righter 'n rain."

Rachel laughed.

Oh, how she missed her friend. It had only been a week, but it felt like a year.

"I met a boy today," Maddie shared nervously.

"Ooooohhhh, a real boy?" Rachel laughed.

"Haha, yeah, he was a bit extra at first. He made fun of me."

"He did NOT!"

"Yes, he did. But then he did something strange."

"Do tell."

Maddie answered softly, "He apologized."

"Really now? Well, it sounds like Maddie has been struck by Cupid's arrow," her friend responded.

"No way, not this girl." She said adamantly.

Rachel laughed at her friend's adamant response. "What does he look like?"

"Brown hair, gray eyes, oh and he's almost seventeen."

Coyly, Rachel replied, "Almost seventeen, you don't say."

"Yes, and he has freckles!"

"Oh, he sounds awful!" Rachel agreed with a smile in her voice.

Maddie laughed as a picture of her friend's amusing, yet horrified response popped into her head.

Changing the subject, she interjected, "I'll be home in a week."

"Yay! We can have a pool date. Want me to invite the girls?" Rachel asked.

"Most def! I can't wait to see you guys." As she pondered the idea of a hangout, she suddenly felt eager to go home.

"Same here. See you soon."

Maddie opened the door to the kitchen. Hearing loud voices coming from the common room, she stopped to listen.

"But what can we do? What if those idiots in Washington are jes' tryin' to scare us ag'in with this threatenin' of food rations?"

"Now you listen to me, Benjamin, yer momma would ne'er stand for you bein' so ugly. Don't be a ninny. The Lord gave us the plan to follow and we're gonna foller it!"

Maddie shook her head as Grammy responded to Benjamin the "Ninny."

Pastor Ron interjected into the conversation, "Benjamin, I understand your fear, but the good Lord will never leave nor forsake us. Jesus gave us specific instructions in Matthew twenty-four. He told us that it would be good for the Master to find us doing what we are called to when he returns."

"Pastor Ron, no offense, but church is over. Can we please

talk about the matter at hand?" A burly man in the corner interrupted.

Pastor Ron encouraged his friend, "Hear me out, Clyde. Jesus was very specific in that he does not want us to be alarmed by the chaos going on around us. And specifically, he says that this is only the beginnin'. So, what can we do? We can pray, we can continue lovin' our neighbor and stand firm as the one who stands firm to the end will be saved."

Maddie's mind was reeling. *I wonder if this is the reason Dad had to leave.* Worried that the thundering of her heart would reveal her presence, she moved into the back corner.

Pastor Ron continued, "We have a real crisis on our hands. Countries experiencin' terrorist attacks are the norm now. Our schools are being targeted through hate. Our families are bein' split right down the middle. And now we are experiencin' food shortages of epic proportions. I understand it seems as if Washington is tryin' to scare us, but somethin' else is at play here. The enemy is movin', and the eleventh hour is at hand. It's my personal belief the four horsemen are ridin' even now. But while the enemy is threatenin' to push us into battle with each other, Jesus has already won the war. So, we must keep our eyes on him, the Perfecter of our faith, and remember that our battle is not against flesh and blood but against the forces of evil in the heavenly realms."

Suddenly, the room went quiet as everyone looked up at Maddie.

Grammy got up and walked toward her. "Maddie Girl, did'na see ya there. Is everythin' all right?" Grammy grabbed her hand.

"Yes, ma'am, I'm good. Can I sit with you?"

"Well, a'course ya can. Meetin's over, right Pastor Ron?"

"Shore 'nough Ms. Grace." Pastor Ron winked at Maddie. "Are y'all stayin' for the pick'n grin'n?"

Grammy looked at her and asked, "Whaddya' think Love? Wanna stay?"

Confused, she whispered to Grammy, "What exactly is a pig 'n grinnin?"

"Silly ole' me, a pickin' n' grinnin' is a bluegrass concert o' strings. The boys'll bring their banjos and their g'itars and the women'll bring their voices. We'll all cut a shine under a blanket of God's stars."

"But do the pigs grin?" Maddie asked with a grin on her face.

"Eh law, you young'uns are keepin' me on my toes now, ain't ya? Grammy tousled her granddaughter's hair as she led her out of the common room.

Clapping her hands, Maddie found herself immersed in a symphony of sound. She loved music, all kinds of music, really, but the strings spoke deep into her soul.

Listening to Ms. Lorna sing to a violin, Maddie turned to her Grammy and asked, "Can I meet with Ms. Lorna this week? I'd like to ask her a couple of questions about a song she played this morning."

"Why, a'course, Love. I'll set that up for ya."

Sparks from the firelight danced to the rhythm of the instruments. Matthew walked up to his sister asking for her hand, "Will you dance with me, Sis?"

Maddie, Matthew, and the other students danced around the fire. Amy Jayne, the redhead from Sunday school, grabbed Maddie's arm with a group of other girls and led her and her brother around the fire. As they danced, her feet deliciously found their rhythm to the pick of each string.

Glancing at the guitar players, she saw Jacob picking a banjo. He gave her a quick nod and smile as he began to play. Oh, the beauty of the banjo—Maddie loved it!

Looking up at the stars, she swung her arms around as all her cares dissipated . . . FREEDOM . . . *Is this what freedom feels like? No worry, no expectations, NO FEAR! The possibilities are endless!*

ISRAEL

"Ambassador Cohen, it's a pleasure to meet you." David shook the hand of the current US Ambassador to Israel.

"Commander Bennett, we've been expecting you. Deputy Reese has briefed you on why you are here?"

"Yes, he has, where are we with the investigation?"

"Unfortunately, we aren't much further along, but I will tell you what we do know. On the fourteenth of May, one of our cryptologists found several overwhelmed internet uplinks. As he monitored the traffic, he noticed IP packets were being delayed while many others were prioritized. While researching the ISP responsible for the throttling, he realized the prioritized messages all had similar digital signatures."

Puzzled, David asked, "Deputy Reese mentioned the communications looked like those used by TRU Mail. What is the indication this is the case?"

"Yes, the XML syntax is slightly different but very close to that of TRU. The cryptologist who recognized the throttling worked with the FBI when they initiated the sting to bring TRU down in 2014. Once he figured out the digital signature, he was able to hack into the packets to see the data being transmitted."

"Packet sniffing, huh?" David laughed. "Foolish mortals- so the data was unencrypted?"

Nodding, the Ambassador answered, "Yes. And as Deputy Reese has explained, each of the internet communications were regular Joe Shmo posts, but with cryptic instructions on how to interrupt and globalize trade. The most concerning posts were the mentions of blockades at major ports around the world. The messages imply an unlimited amount of funds available to inflict global damage to the world's food supply."

"Interesting, and now we are back to global espionage. I still don't understand, I thought TRU was defunct?"

"It appears to have come to life again. Our cryptologists haven't been successful in finding the back-end servers."

David looked at the Ambassador with a smirk, "Have you asked Mordecai Aronoff?"

Irritated, the Ambassador responded, "He's been briefed, yes, but he's currently in the Med on holiday."

"If I know Mordecai, the holiday is well deserved."

"You know Mordecai, Commander?"

"Oh yes, for many years," David answered.

The Ambassador let out a low grunt, "Then you know that he is very good at staying on the down low."

"Yes, I am aware." David turned back to the window and looked to the street below.

"Commander, this situation is of the highest importance. If these messages are real and extend as far as we believe, the WTO Conference may be compromised, which may jeopardize international security."

"I understand, Ambassador. Give me the communications you have copied, and we will go to work."

CHAPTER 8

The Destruction of Peace

Maddie was tapping her foot all the way to Grammy's. Her heart was filled with something new. She couldn't explain it if you asked her, but for the first time, she was aware of everything around her. She could almost feel the blood coursing through her veins. Remembering the visual Rachel gave of God and how he sees us, she could understand her friend's enthusiasm. She couldn't wait to tell her about the night.

As Aunt Lisa pulled into the drive, Maddie gently shook her brother who was quietly snoozing on her shoulder, "Matthew, we're here, time to wake up."

Matthew stretched and yawned. "Grammy?"

"Yes, Love?"

"That was fun, can we do it again?" Matthew yawned.

Grammy snickered, "Now what part might that be?"

Yawning a second time, he murmured, "All of it?"

Grammy chuckled, "Well Matthew, next time ya come and see ole Grammy here we'll set up another pick'n grin'n."

Suddenly, Matthew was wide awake as he asked, "Aww, but do I have to wait?"

"Waitin' makes it all the more fun, Boy." Grammy laughed at his change in demeanor.

Walking up the stairs, Maddie helped her brother into the house. His budding excitement was palpable as he chatted over the night and the pick'n grin'n to come.

Falling into bed, Matthew asked, "Maddie?"

Moving a lock of unruly red hair out of his eyes, she answered, "Yes, Matthew?"

"Can we live here one day?" He asked seriously.

"Live here? Do you mean move here from Atlanta?"

"Yeah, I love it here!"

"But what about Mom and Dad?" Maddie chuckled. There was no way her parents would want to live on Wild Rock Mountain.

Matthew clapped his hands as if the issue was decided, "They can come too!"

Smiling, she asked, "Oh sure, do you see Mom dancing around a campfire?"

Raising to his sister's level, Matthew countered, "Oh Maddie, I'll bet Momma would love it!"

"Hmmm, go to sleep now, little Brother. Love you." She kissed her brother's forehead.

"Love you, Sis. Sleep tight, don't let the bed bug's bite."

"Eek, bed bugs!" Maddie laughed as she teased her brother, turning out his light.

As she walked toward her room, she noticed a glimpse of light spilling into the hallway. Wondering what Grammy might be doing, she tiptoed into the kitchen and observed her sitting deep in thought at the table.

"Grammy?"

"Yes, Maddie dear."

"Are you okay?"

"Why a'course. Come sit with yer ole' Gram a spell."

Maddie shared with her Grammy what her brother had asked. Grammy chuckled over Matthew's innocent question. "Well, ya never know how life'll turn out."

Wondering over her response, she asked, "What do you mean, Grammy?"

Squeezing her hand, she answered, "Well Maddie girl, in all my years I've seen lots of change. I 'spect I'll see lots more a'fore the Father calls me home."

"Can I ask a question? What were y'all talking about in the

kitchen this afternoon?"

Stirring her cup of tea, Grammy pondered a moment. As she looked up into her granddaughter's eyes, she grabbed her hand and squeezed. "Maddie Ruth, some serious things are going on in our nation. Unfortunately, the enemy is dividin' our country into little pieces, and I'm not so shore our leaders 'r strong 'nough to place this chaos into the Almighty's hand. But," squeezing Maddie's hand again, "this I know. God placed our leadership into power for a reason. Jesus said to give to Caesar what is Caesar's, give to God what is God's. He tole' us ta love our neighbor and ta love God. He said ta love our enemy and stand firm till the very end. So, Maddie Ruth, we keep our eyes on him. NO MATTER WHAT happens, we keep the faith that our God will make all things good for those who love him and are called ta his purpose."

Tears threatened to fall as she looked down and asked, "Is my daddy in danger?"

"I don't know Love, I don't know. But this I promise, I'll give yer daddy to the Almighty an' ask for a special batch of supernatural protection over him tonight. Ya hear?"

Maddie squeezed her Gram's hand even more.

Sunlight bathed Maddie's room with glorious light. The bird outside of her window was singing a pretty tune. Remembering Emma's ask about writing a song together, she wondered, *how would this melody sound as a song?*

Humming along to the bird's tune, she made her way into the kitchen. Stomach rumbling from the amazing smells coming from the pot on the stove, she greeted her Grammy. "Good morning, how are you this fine morning?"

Grammy looked at her beautiful granddaughter with a big grin. "Well hello ma Girl, I see ya slept well last evenin'."

"Yes, ma'am, sure did! Can I say that the bird outside of my window is quite the music maker? I didn't like her much at first, but this morning her song was wonderful. My friend Emma and I are going to write a worship song and I wondered if I could use this tune for the melody?" Maddie hummed the tune for Grammy.

"Ah, so you and Ms. Carolina Wren have made friends, did ya? I think she'd be honored. My Memaw always said art imitates life. Is that why ya wanna see Ms. Lorna?"

"Yes, ma'am, has she ever written music?" Maddie asked as she set the bowls and spoons on the table.

"Well, I'd say she's written a song or two. The song we sang yesterday was a Lorna Kyle original."

"Really? I wondered. It sure was beautiful." With stars in her eyes, Maddie wondered, *how cool would it be to have a Maddie Bennett original?*

"Yep, the good Lord shore 'nough gave that woman a gift right up thar' with the birds." Grammy turned back toward the stove to stir the glorious deliciousness coming from the pot. "Well, go on and finish your quiet time while I cook us some breakfast. Then we'll visit my ole friend Ms. Lorna."

"Yay! Thank you, Grammy!" She hugged her sweet gram's neck and then went to spend some time in the Bible.

Finishing her study on Genesis eleven, Maddie had a confused look on her face. Writing in her journal, she wondered:

> *July 30*
> *God, why did you confuse the languages? Were you afraid of what the people would do?*
> *Maddie*

As she walked into the kitchen, Matthew ran past her, "Grammy, Grammy, look what I made!"

"Well, I'll be! You made this?"

Matthew glowed with pride over the boomerang in his hand. Small and sandy, his new toy had quite an interesting elbow on the backside.

"Umm, how exactly did you make this?" Maddie asked.

"Yesterday afternoon, while the little kids were playing, Uncle Tom let me play in his workshop. He's making a whole bunch of boomerangs out of old trees. I asked if he would show me how to make one and he took one of the pieces he had already cut and showed me how to sand it. Next time he said he'd show me how to oil it. Grammy, can I go help, Uncle Tom, this afternoon?" Matthew asked.

"Why a'course Boy, I think that's a grand idea. Come an' help yer ole Grammy put breakfast on the table."

"Amen." Grammy, Maddie, and Matthew released their hands and dug into oatmeal with cinnamon toast.

"Mmmm, this is so good Grammy! Momma never makes toast like this!"

"Ya know the secret, boy?"

Matthew whispered, "What?"

"Butter. Real butter. Ya gotta spread it jes' right and mix up that sugar and cinnamon til it's smooth as yer boomerang right there. Then pour it even-like over the buttered bread. Nothin' like it this side of the holler!"

"Hey, isn't a holler a valley?"

"Well, I'll be, ain't you a good lis'ner?"

"Grammy, can I ask you a question?" Maddie asked.

"Well, a'course Love."

"I read about the tower of Babel this morning. Why did God confuse all the languages and send the people away?"

Grammy looked at her with a keen eye. "Hmm gettin' into some right interestin' readin' now ain't ya? Well, the way I understand it, the people were tryin' to build a tower right into Heaven so God had to stop their buildin' a'fore they could finish."

"But why did it matter? Didn't God want a relationship with them?"

Grammy bit into her toast and thought for a moment. "I think today would be a good day to talk about original sin. But first, let's finish this scrumptious meal the Lord provided."

Walking through the garden after breakfast, Grammy began with the Garden of Eden. "Can you just imagine what it must've been like?" She asked. "Ever' good thing ya'd ever 'magine in that garden, but one thing they could'na eat."

"Why?" Maddie asked.

"Because the Lord said, 'You're free to eat from any tree in the garden, but ya must not eat from the tree of the knowledge of good and evil, for when you eat from it, you'll die.'"

Watching her Grammy run her hands lovingly up a sunflower stalk, she asked, "Why did God plant a tree he didn't want them to have?"

"God created everythin', Maddie Ruth."

"Everything? Did God create evil?"

"Well, I do think yer gettin' a bit ahead of the story, Girl.

"God created everythin', the heavens, the earth. He created all ya see around ya. He also created angels who live with him in Heaven. Now thar' was one nasty bugger of an angel called Lucifer who decided one day he wanted God's throne. So, God kicked ole' Lucifer and his followers right outta Heaven. No Maddie Ruth, God did'na create evil cause thar's no evil in him as the Psalmist tells us. But that Lucifer's prideful heart attempted to twist all that was good in Heaven; and through this sin his heart became evil. Now when Lucifer and his minions were sent out of Heaven, evil found its way to Earth."

"So, the tree of the knowledge of good and evil was there because of these angels?"

"Well, I think the tree was thar' as a reminder that evil was real, kinda like a red light. Red lights warn us to be cautious, or else we'd get run over. God created Adam and Eve as human bein's outta great love, to be companions, not puppets. It was outta this love that he gave 'em free will to choose good or evil."

"What's free will?" Maddie asked.

"Well, have ya ever had to make a choice?"

"Sure, lots."

"Ya see, free will is a choice."

"So, God placed this tree in the garden to give Adam and Eve a choice?"

"Hmm, more so that he wanted 'em to choose correctly. Ya know how your momma gives ya a curfew?"

"Yes, ma'am."

Bending down to check the cucumbers, Grammy stood up and asked, "What happens if ya don't foller it?"

"I'm grounded."

"What would ya call that?"

"Punishment."

"What else would ya call it?"

Confused over Grammy's repeated question, she asked, "Ma'am?"

"Come now Girl, ya know the answer!" Grammy stood up and looked at her granddaughter with those keen eyes again.

Biting her lip, she mulled over the answer.

"A consequence?"

"What if yer parents did'na punish ya? Do ya think thar'd be a consequence?"

Pausing for a moment, she answered, "Yes?"

Grammy tucked a strand of hair behind Maddie's ear as she directed her to a bench. "Ya know I love you, right?"

Looking down, she whispered, "Yes, ma'am."

"Then ya listen to yer ole' Grammy right here. I wish I could tell ya nothin' bad never happens to nobody. But the truth is that evil is all around us. Yer parents give a curfew as a boundary to keep ya safe. If ya come in past curfew, they know somethin' bad could happen. 'Specially in that big city that y'all live in." Pulling her garden scissors out of her pocket, Grammy began picking tomatoes off the vine.

"Now, do ya r'member what Adam and Eve did?"

"Didn't they eat from the bad tree?"

"Well, I'll be, give the girl a 'mater!" Grammy laughed as she bit into the luscious fruit. "Yes, Adam and Eve ate from that thar' tree. They were tricked into disobedience by a serpent in the garden who twisted the words of God. But here's the rub, thar's a consequence to anythin' ya choose—good or bad." Grammy opened her hand so Maddie could see the bite's resulting mess.

"Ohhhh, so Adam and Eve were sent out of the garden because they disobeyed God and realized they had made a mess of things? Did God send the flood because of evil as well?"

"Look 'atcha Girl, yer gettin' it!"

"So, what was the evil at the Tower of Babel? Didn't the people just want to be with God?"

"I don't think they cared nothin' 'bout God. Nope, they wanted to make a name fer themselves. That was prideful, Maddie Ruth. In that thar' pride, they wanted nothin' but to steal God's glory, same as that ole' bugger Lucifer."

Wrinkling her nose in understanding, she said, "Oh, and so God changed the speech at Babel because the people thought they were better than God? Wow, God sure sounds like a parent."

Grammy laughed, "Well a'course Girl, He was yer Creator and that makes him yer Heavenly Father! And as yer Father, he loves ya so much that he wants to protect you and all his chil'ren."

Grammy stood up and hobbled over to a baby sunflower. "See this little seedlin' here?" She asked.

"Yes, ma'am."

"Thar's a nasty little bugger here called a cutworm. Now, if I don't weed my garden, this little worm'll eat ma beautiful plants and kill 'em, destroyin' my peace in the process. So, by cleanin' round ma plants and removin' these stinkers, I'm settin' a boundary to keep my plants safe. Do ya understand?"

"But he looks so cute, kinda like a caterpillar."

"Maddie Ruth, the greatest lie the devil ever told was that he didn't exist. An' the next lie was that he and his temptations were harmless, cute, and cuddly. Once I buy the lie that this here worm is cute and cuddly, I might as well say goodbye to this here garden. The same goes for any good thing I let the devil take from me.

"The temptation was waitin' in the shadows, so God placed a boundary 'round Adam and Eve to protect 'em. Now when they disobeyed and crossed the boundary, they had to face the consequence of leavin' the only home they knew. And guess what else they lost when they had to leave the garden?"

"Their peace?"

"Yes, ma'am, shore did. And ever since, we been tryin' to get that peace back. Ya could say that all peace on earth is threatened by the consequence of sin. Adam and Eve learned that the minute they walked outta that beautiful garden. And this, my beautiful granddaughter, is why we needed a Prince of Peace to return what was stolen from us."

Watching a butterfly land on the flower's petal, Maddie sighed.

"Remember this Maddie Ruth, a bad consequence isna' the only one. Thar' are good ones too. Jesus came to save us from the lies of that ole' bugger Satan, or the devil, mind you, to show us what real peace looks like. He is our Prince of Peace and he taught us boundaries that keep us inside God's protection. We experience a lotta good consequences for follerin' him, like love, joy, peace, hope, and grace. He does'na promise a life free of problems, but he promises he'll always be with us through ever' one. Understand?"

"Yes, ma'am, I think so."

"Good, now let's go round up your brother and see about our date with Ms. Lorna!"

ISRAEL

Sitting in a dimly lit room, David looked at the pages shared by Ambassador Cohen. The crimson-red header reminded him of the blood spilled under the cover of free speech. He would never understand how a group of people were willing to go underground and share information that led to the death of so many innocent public servants.

Mike was a baby when David ran the assignment that almost cost him his life. The fear on Jacque's face when she learned how close the family came to being victims themselves haunted him. Afterward, she begged him to retire permanently, but that was not an option in David's mind. *I will not leave my post.* He mused.

Freedom wasn't free. This truth was ingrained into David by his dad at a young age. George Bennett was a Vietnam Vet. From the moment David took his first step, his dad taught him how to stand tall and salute. As a child, he heard stories of men who stood tall. George and Grace taught their son to be grateful for the freedom found when men gave their lives for the love of family and country. Their bravery inspired him to never give up or give in to fear. In moments like this, his dad's encouraging words were always at the edge of his thoughts, *"No, if anything, Son, do it afraid."*

As a teenager, David found himself entrenched in the football scene. Coach Weaver encouraged the team with a saying borrowed from Vince Lombardi: *"It's not whether you get knocked down; it's whether you get up."*

So, he lived his life getting up and doing it afraid. This was a life motto, something Jacque couldn't grasp. To David, life and death were on the line.

"Coffee, Commander?"

David looked up as Ambassador Cohen offered him a steaming cup of joe.

"Thank you, Ambassador, I'm beginning to think sleep is a pipe dream."

"Please, call me James. You've earned it. Does anything here stand out to you?"

David looked at the messages dated the tenth of June. The sender wanted to make an impression as each message included the same phrase: "IF THERE IS NO ORDER THERE CAN BE NO PEACE" in all capital letters.

"James, what do you think this means?" David asked.

"Hm, if there is no order there can be no peace. The real question here is, by whose order are we talking?"

"Good question."

CHAPTER 9

Searching for Hope in a Fallen World

Aunt Lisa, Eva Mae, Maddie, and Grammy all ventured out to visit Ms. Lorna after leaving Matthew with Uncle Tom.

Lorna Kyle was the nice lady who had the voice of a lark and played piano like Mozart. Maddie was in awe of her musical talent and was so looking forward to meeting and sharing musical ideas with her.

As they drove up the beautifully manicured drive, Grammy shared stories of their younger years. Best friends since they were tikes, they shared everything. In her late teens, Lorna began to sing in the Church choir. One Sunday, a stranger came into town and swept Lorna away into the world of music. Their lives would never be the same.

In the late seventies, Lorna Kyle would be one of the first recipients of the Grammy Award for Best Gospel/Christian Contemporary Music. She would then set the stage for so many who would come after in the creative musician category of Christian Contemporary music.

"Yep, all those Christian artists today can thank good ole' Lorna Kyle for their success." Grammy shared proudly.

Maddie was so excited. *Wow, I knew Ms. Lorna had a beautiful voice, but I had no idea she was so successful!*

As they stepped out of the car, Aunt Lisa called out, "Momma, I'm gonna take Eva Mae to the church and run

79

some errands. I'll be back around threeish. Will that work for y'all?"

"Why a'course Love, see ya in a bit. Enjoy your playtime sweet Girl!" Eva Mae giggled over Grammy's kisses.

As Aunt Lisa drove off, Maddie and Grammy walked up to the door and rang the bell. Suddenly, Maddie was quite nervous. Her palms were sweaty even as her heart beat rapidly. Grammy grabbed her granddaughter's hand and squeezed. Mustering up the courage to meet this icon of music, she squeezed Grammy's hand in return.

The door opened and Ms. Lorna gave Grammy a big hug. Looking at Maddie she said, "Hello there, dahlin'! I've been 'specting you'ns all mornin'! Come in, come in."

Ms. Lorna's home was beautiful. Fresh-cut flowers were everywhere. A beautiful staircase with mahogany railings curved up to the upper floor. Ms. Lorna walked them into the living room where a flat-screen TV was showing the morning news.

"Last night, London experienced another attack. Officials say that an underground group is allegedly staging attacks of war against member countries of the World Trade Organization. But Susan, we have yet to find out who is behind these attacks."

"Let me turn this off so we can chat." Ms. Lorna turned off the TV as she sat in the white wingback chair.

Racing thoughts took over Maddie's mind. *War? Where is Dad? Oh God, please let my daddy be okay.* Previous conversations overheard by Grammy and her parents were overwhelming: war, eleventh hour, martial law. *What is going on here? Is peace on earth even a thing anymore?*

Grammy patted her granddaughter's knee when she saw her face go pale. Attempting to change the direction of her attention, she began chatting about Ms. Lorna's front room. "Whatcha think, Girl? Beautiful, ain't it? Take a sniff of all the flow'rs in here."

"Came right from my garden, they did," Ms. Lorna replied.

"Really, all of them?" Her eyes were wide as saucers at the thought.

"They shore did. I go out ever' mornin' and pick a fresh bunch. There ain't nothin' like fresh-cut flowers."

The fragrance was invigorating. Maddie loved fresh-cut flowers. As she looked at all the beautiful bouquets, her glance fell on the delicate photos of friends and family over the years. *Ms. Lorna is loved.* She thought to herself.

"Maddie Ruth, why don't ya tell Ms. Lorna why ya wanted to visit."

"Oh yeah, Ms. Lorna, at Church on Sunday, you played a beautiful song. What was it?"

"That would be a blessin' from God, child. I call it 'Into Your Hands.' Wanna take a listen? Come on into the music room."

As they walked through the house, Maddie was amazed at all the colors. Walking into the music room, her eyes widened as she stood in awe. In the center of the room stood a beautiful white Baby Grand piano. On top of the piano stood a simple painting on a small gold easel. Stopping to look at the painting, she tilted her head.

"Quite beautiful, isn't it?" Ms. Lorna asked.

"Why yes, but whose hand is that?"

A young girl with long black hair and flawless white skin was sitting on her legs. She was wearing a simple long white dress and had her hands lifted into the air. Her head bowed and eyes closed, she seemed sad, yet at peace. *She looks so peaceful,* Maddie mused; *I wish. . .* Above the hands of the girl, a pair of hands hung in midair, a cloud surrounding them. It was as if someone was reaching down from the sky to touch the young woman.

"That, Ms. Maddie, is the Lord. The girl is givin' herself into his hands, surrenderin' all to him. All her fear and worry, all her struggles, she's givin' it all to him."

Deep in thought, Maddie lifted her hand to touch the hands of the young woman.

"Does he take it all away?" She asked.

Pressure from a hand on her shoulder interrupted her gaze and she glanced toward Ms. Lorna.

"Beautiful, he does something better. He holds her hand as he teaches her to face her fear and give him her worry. He does all this while givin' her strength to face the challenges of life."

Ms. Lorna sat down, patting the piano bench for her to join her. "Let's sing about it."

Long fingers ran over the beautiful keys of the piano, which were like glass. Ms. Lorna's voice was so beautiful, you would never know she was sixty-eight years old. Maddie closed her eyes as she listened to her sing.

Silence filled the air for a long moment after Ms. Lorna finished the simple ballad. Maddie couldn't take her mind off the words; *you see the broken heart I try to hide.* Thoughts of her mom's disappointment and her dad never being home flooded her mind. The comforting strength of Grammy's knobby hand on Maddie's shoulder gave her permission to release the feelings she had been harboring. A wave of emotion overwhelmed her as she began to sob. As her heart rate increased, Maddie suddenly couldn't breathe. She leaned forward as Ms. Lorna and Grammy both began to stroke her arms. Then she heard the quiet prayer.

"Abba Father, please heal this young'un. She's yours God and in this moment, we give her to you. We believe her healin' is in your mighty hand. In the strong Name of Jesus Christ, amen."

Her tears began to ebb as her breathing slowed. *Was prayer really that powerful? Could it truly slow her heart rate down?* Perplexed, she looked up. Overwhelmed by the great love in her Gram's eyes, her fear melted away as she hugged her tightly.

"Mamaw!" Eva Mae toddled down the hallway looking for her Grand. "Hope it was all right Ms. Lorna, we let ourselves in." Aunt Lisa scooped up her baby to give Grammy a kiss.

"Why a'course Beautiful, my home is your home."

"Whatch'all doin'?"

"Ms. Lorna was playing her new song for us," Maddie shared.

"Really now? I jes' love that new song a' yours, Ms. Lorna. I hear there's an awesome story behind it."

"Yes, ma'am, as with any good story, lots of tears."

"Do ya mind sharin' with our Maddie here?"

"Not at all."

Ms. Lorna's soothing voice calmed Maddie's beating heart. Watching her, she was amused by the hands that served to tell a story of pain intermixed with grace. She said that word a lot-grace.

"What is grace, Ms. Lorna?" Maddie asked.

"Why now, it's undeserved favor."

"Favor?"

"Yes, ma'am. Have you ever received a surprise gift?"

"Yes, ma'am."

"Did you deserve the gift?"

Maddie chewed on her lip as she pondered the question.

"The grace of our Lord is a gift none of us deserve, yet he gives to us in abundance. It's the gift that never stops giving. Let me tell ya a story about it."

Maddie listened as she shared her story.

Growing up in a poor Tennessee mountain home, she was rambunctious, a handful to hear her tell it. Her momma died in childbirth. Her daddy was a coal miner who worked long hours and raised her from a tike. At the age of fifteen, Lorna sang at a local fair. An up-and-coming producer heard her performance and encouraged her to audition. Flattered by the attention, Lorna sang Amazing Grace.

The years that followed were a whirlwind for Lorna. Her dad encouraged her to leave their little town in Wild Rock and find her passion. She entered the music industry, leaving everything familiar behind. As her career grew, her old life became a memory. In the beginning, Lorna missed her friends and family, especially Grace; but the excitement of her newfound world pushed the longing for home to the back of her mind.

Over time, she found herself caught up in drugs, greed, and loneliness.

As Ms. Lorna sadly reminisced the years of attention-seeking, Maddie realized that she too felt lost in a sea of others' expectations.

Then one day, she met Jesus.

The look on Ms. Lorna's face was one of great joy. Amazed at the change in her countenance, Maddie leaned in to hear more.

Ms. Lorna referred to herself as a prodigal that Jesus saved from the pit of hell. A near overdose would almost take her life. Waking up in the hospital, the first face she saw was that of her dear friend, Grace, who served to encourage her in the weeks to follow.

After her release from the hospital, she took a hiatus from performing and went home with Grace. She would learn about love, grace, and mercy as her friend encouraged her to recognize the one who created and loved her so much that he died so she could truly live. Lorna found herself covered by the love of her Savior as he peeled back the layers of shame and self-condemnation from her battered heart. Her career would change as she decided to leave rock n roll and pursue a career in Christian music.

Rachel came to mind as Maddie considered the love between Grammy and Ms. Lorna. If she was in trouble, Rachel would never leave her side, just like Grammy.

When Ms. Lorna finished reminiscing, she said, "So ya see

Maddie, I surrendered my all to the one who rescued and made me whole. I've served him ever' day since. The inspiration for this song began on Easter Sunday, 1972. I had the honor to share it for the first time in the church this past Easter."

Aunt Lisa asked the question she was dying to ask. "Ms. Lorna, was the Christian scene different from Rock n' Roll?"

"Oh yes. In the beginnin', rock n' roll was flashy and fun. Every concert was excitin' yet exhaustin'. The audience always wanted more'n I could give. After I left that ole' life behind, God blessed me with a new life in him. I became a Christian on the tail end of the Jesus movement. People like me yearned for a simpler life, very much like the early church in the book of Acts. Worshippin' Jesus was our priority. And there was nothin' like being in a congregation of believers and watching the Holy Spirit move. While the secular audience sucked the life out of me, the Christian audience did just the opposite. It was as if the Holy Spirit filled up ever' person in an overflow to the person standing next to them. Through this exchange, God lifted me up and out of my self-imposed hell and into the reality of heaven on earth. Ya could say the Holy Spirit hovered over us as he did at creation.

"A'course there wasn't much money to be made. But working alongside some amazin' spirit-filled artists allowed God to grow inside of me what was there all along: a deep desire to share the love of Christ through song. It was a very good friend of mine, Camille, who encouraged me to begin writin' lyrics."

Excited to hear Ms. Lorna mention lyric writing, Maddie remembered the whole reason she wanted to talk to her in the first place.

"Ms. Lorna, can I ask you a question?"

"Why a'course, Dear."

"I received a keyboard for my birthday. My friend Emma asked if we could write a worship song together."

"Really now, how excitin'!"

Embarrassed over her lack of experience, she said, "Yes, ma'am, but I'm not sure how to do that."

Ms. Lorna lifted Maddie's chin and placed her hand on her heart as she replied, "It begins here."

"What do you mean?"

"Any good song begins in your heart. Desire buds within, then inspiration fertilizes the bloom into the fullness of beauty. God places the desire in your heart and then provides the muse for inspiration."

"Muse?"

Ms. Lorna lifted the painting from the top of the piano. "Do you remember these hands?"

"Yes, ma'am."

"God is my first Inspiration. I can look to all the things he created: the sky, the water, the flowers, the trees, the birds, a newborn babe, and in these things, I hear his voice and inspiration is born."

Maddie's wheels were turning. She looked up and asked, "Is it possible to write a melody from a bird's call?"

"Why, a'course! Art imitates life, I always say."

Excitement bubbled up inside as she thought about the bird who had been singing to her every morning. *I guess the bird is inspiring me!* She pondered.

"How do we come up with the words?"

Ms. Lorna thought for a moment, "The first thing to figure out is the root of your song. What do ya want to say to God? A worship song is meant to lift worship to God. So, from your root message, play a word game. An example: when I think about God, I consider all his attributes."

Pulling out a piece of paper and a pen, Ms. Lorna asked, "Give me a list of adjectives you would use to describe God."

"I'm not sure I know what you mean," she responded.

"That's okay, let's do this together."

Looking at Grammy, Ms. Lorna asked. "Grace, how would you describe God?"

Grammy smiled ear to ear as she replied, "Well, now, I'd say he's faithful, wise, holy, loving, merciful, good, and gracious."

"That's a good start. Now, let's create a list of actions or verbs we associate with God."

"Oh, can I answer this one?" Aunt Lisa clapped excitedly.

"Why, a'course."

"He loves, gives, redeems, restores, provides, creates, and breathes."

"Okay Maddie, your turn. If you were writin' a letter to God or prayin' for somethin' you needed, what would you ask God for?"

While she loved the exercise, her nervous stomach gave her pause. She wasn't sure she wanted to tell them what she was thinking.

Ms. Lorna waited patiently for a response.

"I think I would ask God to take this anxiety from me."

Lorna looked at Grace with sad eyes for her sweet granddaughter.

After a moment, Lorna said, "That's a brave ask. Would you like to share the things that create anxiety within you?"

Maddie blinked rapidly as she shook her head, "I dunno."

Aunt Lisa piped in, "Ya know, Maddie, I had anxiety at your age, too."

"Really?"

"Yup, shore did. Lookin' back on that season of life, I reckon I was tryin' to be somebody I wasn't. I never quite understood the truth of who I was. I sought affirmation from others and perfection in myself. And the truth is, the two never did meet."

Maddie felt as if her aunt was looking deep into her soul. Nodding her head she responded, "Yeah, something like that."

"And if you're anythin' like me, my heart would beat a hundred miles a minute when I thought I did something wrong or when I couldn't measure up to another person's expectations."

Maddie looked up and asked quietly, "What did you do, Aunt Lisa?"

Tucking a tuft of hair behind her niece's ear, she answered, "Honestly, sweetie, I cain't rightly say I've completely mastered the anxiety monster, but ever' day I sit in the presence of my

Father and allow him to remind me who he says I am."

Confused, Maddie looked at Grammy and asked, "Grandpa George?"

Grammy laughed, "No sweet Girl, not Grandpa George. Yer Aunt Lisa here is talkin' 'bout your Heavenly Father."

"Wait, he talks to you?"

"Why, a'course. Doesn't he talk to you?"

"Well, I've been praying, but I haven't heard a voice yet."

"Oh, I've never heard an audible voice. Nope, God talks to me through his word, his Spirit, or through a friend." Aunt Lisa opened Ms. Lorna's Bible sitting on the side table. "If I open this Bible, I can read verses that define me as God says I am. Such as Ephesians 2:10 which says, 'For we are God's handiwork, created in Christ Jesus to do good works, which God prepared in advance for us to do.' When I read this verse, I can hear the quiet whisper of my Heavenly Father whisperin' into my ear, 'Lisa, yer my daughter whom I love. I have a plan fer you today, a purpose uniquely designed jes' for you.' This gives me hope in a fallen world."

"Wow, it says that?" Maddie leaned over her aunt's shoulder to see.

"Yep, shore does." Lisa smiled from ear to ear.

Looking at the words on the paper, inspiration bubbled up as she sang a bit timidly, "God you are faithful, you give me peace. Father, I ask you to take anxiety from me."

ISRAEL

David walked into a conference room located in the Arnona consular section annex compound of the Jerusalem Consulate General. This new location of the US Embassy hosted Ambassador Cohen and a small staff. As he walked into the room, a group of Navy CWOs stood and saluted.

"At ease." He said to the group.

These Cryptologic Warfare Officers treasured both commitment and confidentiality. David knew this from his own experience. After Officer Candidate School, he spent twelve years working as a CWO. In year twelve, he was promoted to Lieutenant Commander. At year fifteen, he was promoted to Commander where he led a team of ninety cryptologists. This would be his final rank before retirement. He would have made Captain within the year if he remained; but in that season, it had become apparent that his family needed him most.

"It has come to our attention that a new threat is lurking in the shadows." David began. "An influx of data threatening both national and international security has been found, and we must find those responsible quickly."

Laying out the documents before the team, he shared the facts of the mission to date.

CHAPTER 10

An Uncertain Future

As Maddie packed her bags for the long trip home, tears welled up in her eyes.

Echoing her thoughts, Matthew bounded into her room. "Do we have to leave?" He asked. "Uncle Tom and I still have a whole lot of boomerangs to make!" Matthew was so proud of the new toy hanging from his backpack.

Trying to put on a strong front for her brother, she said, "I know, but aren't you excited to go home? School starts in a few weeks."

"Yuck, why should I be excited about school? Making a boomerang is more fun than sitting at a desk!" Matthew chased Max out of the room and left Maddie to her musings.

While sad to leave Grammy's, she was happy to see her friends and her new keyboard. Ms. Lorna gave some great tips for songwriting. Emma would be so happy to begin their worship song project.

Humming the new melody, she rolled the new lyric over in her mind. After she was able to write a couple of lines, Ms. Lorna helped her to align the lyrics to a melody. As they crafted the verse, her inspiration became clear. While she was focused on her anxiety, Ms. Lorna taught her to move her focus to the one who would heal her from anxiety.

God you are faithful.
My source of strength.

Father, I thank you,
For giving me peace.

Ms. Lorna was so proud. "Well Maddie, I think God's Spirit has given you a gift. Continue worshipin' and he'll give you the rest. I encourage you to read the Psalms. David, a man after God's own heart, would turn the burdens of his soul into song. He would cry out to the Lord and declare the truth of God's goodness. This was a form of worship to his King, but also a source of encouragement for his soul. Give it a try and see if this doesn't help you find the peace you need in the moment you're strugglin'. One thing I've learned over the years is that trustin' God covers those times when we're uncertain about the outcome."

Zipping up her suitcase, her thoughts moved to all she had learned over the last two weeks: reading the Bible, journaling her thoughts, and turning her worry into worship. *Can these things truly help me with anxiety?* She wondered.

"All right y'all let's skedaddle. If we wait too much longer, Atlanter'll be hotter 'n blue blazes."

The clackity clack of four paws announced the arrival of sweet Max with his duck in tow. His sad eyes met hers as he dropped the present at her feet. Bending down, she gave him her favorite Bassett hug and rubbed his ears. "I'll be back Maxie; you can count on it."

The drive home from Grammy's always seemed the longest. Maddie would be so excited to arrive at her house, but going home would drag. She loved being with Grammy and had learned so much from the Bible and lyric projects, but she missed hanging out with Rachel and the girls. With Matthew sleeping on her shoulder, she began to think of all the things waiting for her at home. *I wonder what Mom will want me to do. I wonder if Dad has called.* Her mind was in a hundred places all at once.

"Grammy?" A sleepy Matthew murmured.

"Yassir, Matthew."

"Why does Eva Mae call you Mamaw? Isn't your name Grammy?"

Turning the steering wheel around a sharp curve, Aunt Lisa snickered at the out-of-the-blue question.

"To be shore now, my name is Grace, so ya know. But Mamaw is a common name for grammas in these here parts."

"Why do we call you Grammy then?"

"Well now, when y'all were born, yer Momma wanted ya to call me what she was 'customed to. Makes no matter ta me, I love ya all the same. Jes' don't forget to call me, ya here?"

Oh, Grammy, that'll never EVER happen! Thank you for letting me come and play with Max, make boomerangs, and teach me how to cook and everything! You're the best Grammy-Mamaw ever!"

Matthew stretched in his seat belt to hug her.

Grammy laughed big and loud as she patted his arm. "And yer the best ten-year old grandboy ever!"

"Now Grammy, you know I'll be eleven next year!"

"Well now, yer the best almost eleven years ole grandboy ever!"

Matthew beamed at his Grammy's praise.

"Hello, Grace and Lisa. Thank you for bringing the kids home," Jacque declared as she opened the door.

"Mom, look what I made!" Matthew ran up to his mom, dropping his backpack as he pulled out his boomerang.

"That's quite an interesting toy; what is it?" she asked, turning it around in her hand.

"It's a boom-er-ang," Matthew pronounced. "You throw it, like this." Matthew threw it into the yard, narrowly missing a window.

"Well, I think you need to keep that in the backyard, Son."

"Yes, ma'am," he replied nervously.

"Hello Maddie, did you enjoy your trip?" Jacque asked as she turned to her daughter.

"Yes, ma'am, it was so much fun! Grammy introduced me to Ms. Lorna who taught me how to write a song!"

"That's nice. Did you finish your summer reading?"

Looking at the floor nervously, she answered, "No ma'am, I'm not quite finished."

"Well, you know what you need to do then. Up you go. You too Matthew."

Two groans echoed as they turned to the stairs. *So much for calling Emma.*

Opening her bedroom door, Maddie heard murmured voices downstairs. Peeking around the corner, she listened in on their conversation.

"Did they behave, Grace?"

"They were finer 'n frog hair, Jacque. A sight better than you right now."

"What do you mean?"

"Alcohol is quite pungent, my daughter. How much have you taken to drinkin'?"

"I only had a cocktail."

"It's barely lunchtime."

"That's none of your business, Grace."

"I don't mean to be ugly, Daughter, but those young'uns up them stairs are my kin, so your bein' three sheets to the wind is my business."

"I am fine, they are fine, we are all fine!" As Maddie listened, she heard the cabinet door slam shut as her mom started to put away the dishes.

"Don't go gittin' yer gussie up Jacque, we're kin and we're here for ya, 'specially while David's gone. Why don't ya sit down a spell? By the by, where's Michael?"

The sound of sobbing surprised Maddie as she drew near the stairs.

"I don't know," Jacque cried. "We argued Friday night when he came home late after a party. He stormed out and I haven't seen him since."

Hiding behind the railing, she watched as Grammy wiped tears from her momma's face.

Momma rarely cried, but this would be the second time in a month.

"Dear Girl, I'm so sorry. Yer havin' a mess of a time right now, ain't ya? How can we help you?"

Her mom's slumped figure suddenly straightened as she answered, "Thank you, Grace, but we'll be fine. If we need you, we'll call."

An awkward silence filled the kitchen. Confused, Maddie sat down against the wall wondering at the interaction between her mom and Grammy.

"Maddie, Matthew, come say goodbye to your grandmother!" Mom called up the stairs.

Fighting back the emotion of saying goodbye to Grammy, she walked downstairs and into her open arms.

"What's that I see Maddie Ruth, crocodile tears?" Grammy lifted her chin.

"Thank you for letting us stay with you."

"Why a'course, Love. Y'all know yer welcome anytime at ole Grammy's."

"I love you, Grammy."

"And I love you a bushel and a peck and a hug 'round the neck."

Missing her already, Maddie wiped her eyes on her Grammy's dress. Matthew's face reflected her sadness as he wrapped his arms around them both and appeared to do the same.

When the door closed on her favorite person, Maddie felt as if her world was coming down around her. There was something she couldn't shake.

Her mom picked up her backpack and gave it to her. "Time to get to work, Maddie."

Images flit behind closed lids as Maddie thrashed around in her sleep. She saw her father holding what looked to be a spear, as he looked to the danger in the sea. A whale as big as her house was jumping up and around the boat her dad was on. As he threw a spear towards the whale, she screamed, begging him to come to shore, but he could not hear her. Watching the spear meet its target, she breathed a sigh of relief. Relief turned to horror; however, as she watched the tail break the boat in two, her dad thrust into the sea.

"Maddie, Maddie, wake up. Wake up, Maddie!"

Awaking to the small hands of her brother shaking her shoulder, she realized she was in a puddle of sweat. "Matthew, is everything okay?"

"Maddie, you were yelling in your sleep. Are you okay?"

"I don't know," she replied. "I think Dad's in trouble."

"What do you mean?"

"I don't know. I dreamed he was fighting a whale. The whale hit him and pushed him into the sea."

"Isn't Moby Dick a whale?"

Thinking about the reading from the night before, she realized the logic in her brother's question. "Well, yes, but I think Dad is in trouble."

"Maddie?"

Yawning, she answered, "Yeah?"

"Can I sleep with you tonight?"

Sunlight peeked into Maddie's room as a small elbow poked her in the face. Gently moving Matthew aside, she went to the bathroom. Considering the dream from the night before, she couldn't help but wonder, *is Dad in danger?* Recalling her reading, she thought about Ahab and the infamous Moby Dick. *Is he facing a whale of his own?* She wondered. She heard once that her dad was quite relentless in his work. Just as Ahab was relentless in his pursuit of the monstrous whale. A familiar uneasiness filled her stomach as she linked her dream to Ahab's final stand.

Remembering what Aunt Lisa said about God talking to her, she knelt on the cold bathroom floor and looked up as she said a prayer, "God, Grammy says you hear my prayers and while I haven't heard your voice, I pray she is right. God, I'm worried about my dad. Ya see, I can't imagine losing him and while Grammy says I should pray for your will to be done, I'm worried that your will involves taking him away from us. Please God, please don't take my daddy away," Maddie sobbed. "Please protect him from whatever danger he might be in. Please?"

As she walked back into her bedroom, the sweet coo of a bird outside of her window surprised her.

"Matthew, Matthew, come look!" Maddie excitedly called to her brother as she saw a dove staring at her through the window.

Wiping his eyes with his fist, Matthew mumbled, "What is it?"

"It's a dove, come look."

As she turned back to the window, the dove flew away. Enamored with the beauty of the bird's wings, she asked, "Do you think God heard my prayer?"

"Well, a'course he did Sis, God hears all our prayers." Matthew turned over to go back to sleep.

Walking into the kitchen, Maddie saw her mom's quick turn as she placed a glass in the sink.

"Maddiieeee, how are you this fine morning?"

"Mom, are you okay?"

"Okay, I'm more than okay, I'm just peachy!"

Jacque walked over to her daughter. A bit unsteady, she placed her arm over her shoulder. "I can't tell you how glad I am to have you home, Daughter."

"Really?" Skeptical, she raised her eyebrow.

With a smart reply, Jacque answered, "Well, of course. You are in fact, my fav-o-rite daughter."

"I am your only daughter."

"Details, shmetails." Jacque's hand appeared to bat at an invisible fly.

"Mom, have you been drinking?" Maddie walked to the cabinet to find a glass.

Sarcastically, her mom answered, "It's only a cocktail, Maddie-dear."

Giving her mom a glass of water, Maddie added, "But it's only nine o'clock in the morning."

"Why are you bugging me with so many details? Did you finish your reading?"

"Yes, ma'am, I did. I'll have my report completed today."

"Well, good Girl," Jacque patted her daughter on the head. "Where's your brother?"

Turning to call her brother, Maddie said, "He's upstairs, I'll call him down for breakfast."

"That's my Mads, can you pour cereal for the two of you? I think I'm going to lie down; I have a headache."

"Yes, ma'am."

ISRAEL

A week after David arrived in Israel, Dan closed the French doors to the conference room as David and the team settled at the table.

"So, what did you find?" The Deputy Director of Communications asked.

"Joe?" David nodded to the lead cryptologist to share the findings.

"Well sir, we have learned that each message was sent from

a hidden IP. We were able to identify commonalities in the cryptic messages inline and what we found was interesting. The senders regularly used acronyms in their greetings, such as AIP for Agent-in-place, BM for Bagman, BW for Birdwatcher, CO for Case officer."

"Wait so they are using spy abbreviations?" Dan interrupted.

"Yes, sir, straight from the internet."

"It's too simple. Are you sure this isn't a teenager playing a game?" Dan asked.

Joe continued, "I considered the same, Sir, except the amount of detail included in the instructions is not something you can search. Whoever wrote these communications is quite creative. And that isn't all of it."

"There's more?" Dan asked jokingly.

"Yes sir, do you recall the London attack last week?"

"Yes."

"One of those arrested had BAGMAN tattooed on his arm." Joe shared.

Dan shook his head, "So now we have a connection to a physical attack."

"Dan, what are you thinking?" David asked.

Dan looked at him intently, "I think we have an uncertain future ahead of us."

CHAPTER 11

Broken Pieces

Breakfast in the Bennett household was typically low-key. Maddie and Matthew were used to cereal and the TV. With school starting, she thought it was time to switch things up.

"Matthew, you need to set your alarm for six am, okay? School starts next week, and we need to be on a schedule.

"Do I have to? We don't go back for another week. I need my beauty sleep Mads."

"Please don't call me that, Matthew. You know I hate that name."

"How about Ruthie?" Matthew threw a cheerio at his sister.

Maddie reciprocated with a pink marshmallow. War was on!

"Mom will have your heads if she sees you having a food fight in her pristine kitchen." Two surprised heads turned at Michael's entrance.

"Mike!" Matthew ran up to his brother to knock his cap off.

"Where have you been? Mom has been worried sick!"

"NTKB, little Sis," Michael teasingly tugged on her ear lobe while reciprocating Matthew's play.

"NTKB?" Matthew asked.

"That would be need-to-know-basis, little G." Cackling, Michael grabbed a box of cereal and sat down with the milk.

"Seriously, Michael, Mom is really worried about Dad being gone. This is not a good time for you to be disappearing."

"There is a great deal more to be worried about in this world than Dad being gone. By the way, where is the old man?"

99

"I don't know. He told Mom that dangerous things were going on in Washington." Maddie looked irritated as Michael snorted.

"Dad decided to be Superman again, did he?"

"Superman? That's so cool! Does Dad have a cape?" Matthew asked.

"Michael, be serious. I think Dad is in trouble."

"I am serious. Look around you, little sister. You may think you're the main character in the game, sheltered under Superman's cape and all; but in the real world, people are suspect. It's time for a regime change." Michael looked out of the kitchen window.

"What do you mean?"

Locking eyes with his sister, Mike lowered his voice and continued, "Maddie, I want you to listen to me. You need to stay up to date with the news going on in the world and you need to be informed."

"I heard that Washington is trying to scare us about an enemy. Is that true?"

"You could say that. Our President is all about media fear. But hear this, little Sis, we all gotta make sure we're on the right side of history, or else find ourselves canceled."

"Grammy said God is watching over us," Maddie said confidently.

"God schmod, do you see God protecting our schools?"

Remembering Ms. Bonnie's answer about Noah and the flood, she said, "Maybe God has to remove the corruption standing in the way of restoration."

Michael started laughing hysterically. "Restoration, that's hilarious! Watch the news, Ms. Smartie-Pants. There's no corruption being removed in this country, but there sure are a lot of broken pieces."

Sitting in the living room with her laptop and homework, Maddie's thoughts were a jumbled mess. The twelve o'clock news was filled with stories about murder and robbery. *Why am I watching this again?*

> "With the WTO Ministerial Conference only two weeks away, thousands of protestors marched on the capital calling for the impeachment of President Carlton. Susan, the people's demands for food, jobs, and lower taxes were met with deaf ears as the President teed off at Pebble Beach. Pictures of hungry children met with threats of tear gas from officers outfitted in riot gear."

Curious, her ears perked up over this latest story. *Is this why Dad had to leave suddenly? Why do they want the president to be impeached?* She had several friends facing a tough financial time in their life, but she didn't see a lot of hungry children. *Michael was right, perhaps I do need to pay more attention to the news.*

As her attention returned to the plight of Ahab chasing the leg-stealing whale, she wrote the question, "What are you willing to fight for?" Her chest filled with pride as she remembered her dad's response to her mom about fighting for his family. She only hoped that if she were called to stand up for what she believed in, she would be as courageous as her dad and Captain Ahab. "God, I'm not sure that I can be courageous," she prayed quietly.

"Maddie, can you please bring me the ibuprofen from the cabinet?"

Jumping up, she went into the kitchen to grab a glass of water with the bottle of pills, "Coming!"

Making her way to her mom's room, she opened the door. Staring at her pale face as she opened the bottle, she walked slowly to her side. "Mom, are you okay?"

Grabbing the bottle, she snapped, "I'll be fine, I just need to get my wits about me. Did you and Matthew eat breakfast?"

"Yes, ma'am, I'm finishing my paper now."

"Good, good. That's good. Hey, doesn't school start next week?"

"Yes, ma'am, Matthew and I talked about setting our alarms

to prepare for the new schedule."

With a change in tone, her mom smiled and looked at her daughter, "That's nice. How about we go out for brunch on Friday and pick out some school clothes?"

Excited, Maddie exclaimed, "Yes, ma'am, that would be amazing!"

Jacque turned away from her daughter as she yawned, "It's a date. Now can you please turn out the light? I need to sleep off this headache."

Closing the door quietly, Maddie turned and walked back to her homework.

As she finished the last line of her paper, a message popped up on the screen.

Rachel: "Hey, you."

Maddie: "Rachel!"

Maddie typed a myriad of emojis after her friend's name. Her friend replied with a crying face emoji.

Rachel: "Want some company?"

Maddie: "Yes!"

Rachel: "Well, come open the door then!"

Jumping off the couch, Maddie ran to the door and into the arms of her best friend.

"Surprise! You didn't think you would sneak home without my knowing, did you?" Rachel asked.

"I can't keep any secret from you, can I? I'm sorry I haven't texted you. Mom hasn't given me my phone back. I had to finish my project before going anywhere." Maddie closed the door and jumped back on the couch with her friend.

Picking up the book on the side table, Rachel asked, "How is ole Captain Ahab?"

"You didn't have to read the same book?"

"Nope, I read Hidden Figures." Rachel began to write invisible math problems in the air. "And can I just say, goals!"

Plopping down on the couch, Maddie and Rachel were the best of friends all over again. It was as if they had never separated. Watching Rachel's hands move as she shared the stories of the courageous black women who were mathematicians for NASA, she realized how much she had missed her friend's lively gestures.

"Maddie, I can't tell you how much this book moved me." Rachel wiped away a tear.

"Oh, I don't know if I could stand having to work with math problems all day, bleh!"

"It's not about math problems, silly. Well, it is a little, I guess. It's about the pure courage these women had as they faced persecution. Can you imagine being black and being a woman at NASA?"

"I don't understand, women work at NASA now. What's the big deal?"

"Maddie, these women worked at NASA in 1961, during the civil rights movement. One of the women, a "computer" as she was called, had to solve high-key hard math problems which were used to send John Glenn into space. They worked in segregated areas. The computer, Katherine Johnson, was discriminated against because one of the other men accused her of being a communist! Oh, and they had to walk miles to go to the bathroom."

"Wait, they had to walk miles?"

"Well, that's probably exaggerating a little, but let's just say it was a long way!"

"Whoa, that sounds like a good book. Probably not as scary as Moby Dick."

Rachel lightly pulled a strand of Maddie's hair and asked, "Hey, what's going on?"

"Nothing, why?"

"I know that look."

"Oh Rachel, Grammy's house was so fun, I felt free! I met a real song artist who taught me how to write words to a song. Her name was Lorna and . . ."

"Wait, Lorna? You don't mean Lorna Kyle?"

"Yes, that was her name. She's an old friend of Grammy's, and she lives in the town where Grammy lives. She plays the piano at church."

"No way! Do you mean to tell me that you met THE Lorna Kyle? Hold up. She taught YOU how to write a song? Girl, you have no idea what has happened!"

Puzzled, Maddie asked, "What do you mean?"

"Lorna Kyle is only the queen of Christian Gospel music! My mom used to play her songs for me when I was a baby. Goodness, I'm sure I have a onesie somewhere with a Lorna Kyle original lyric on it!" Rachel began to sing a gospel song under her breath.

"Really?"

Rachel's enthusiasm was contagious, "Yes, really! Was she as nice as they say?"

"Oh, she was super nice! And her home was so colorful! Flowers were everywhere! And she had the most beautiful artwork. Seriously Rach, I think I was close to Heaven."

"Heaven, huh? Did y'all talk about Heaven much?" Rachel inquired with a smile.

"Rach, I learned some grounding techniques for my anxiety. Oh, and Grammy had me do a Bible study! I learned about creation, Adam and Eve, Noah, and the tower of Babel. She challenged me to journal my thoughts and prayers. Hey, do you know why God changed the speech of those building the tower of Babel?"

Rachel laughed at her friend's scattered thoughts, "The Babylonians were trying to build a tower to Heaven."

Confused, Maddie asked, "But wouldn't God want them to visit him?"

"No, they wanted to prove they could—and not only a

tower but a whole city. They wanted to make a name for themselves, not for God. It would be like building the king and queen buildings into Heaven and saying, 'Look how great I am because I built these buildings into the sky!'" Rachel beat her chest dramatically.

"So why change their speech? Couldn't God knock the building down?"

"Good question. Let's Google it," Rachel answered.

Rachel was good at researching things. Watching her friend perform a couple of searches, she wondered if she would help her write her paper.

"Ahh, check this out." Rachel shared her phone with her friend. "A man named Josephus said that it was Nimrod who persuaded the people not to ascribe the tower to God as if he made them happy, but instead to see that their courage made them happy."

"Who is Nimrod?"

Scrolling down the page, Rachel answered, "This article says he was the great-grandson of Noah. And not a very nice man. Under him, the government became one of tyranny, so they would depend on his power rather than God's."

"But weren't Noah and his family righteous?" Maddie asked. "Doesn't righteous mean good?"

"Noah was considered righteous because he believed in, trusted, and was obedient to God. His family was blessed because of him. But righteousness does not necessarily pass down to other generations. There is a scandalous story about Noah's son seeing him naked while passed out drunk. Wait a second." Rachel excitedly pulled up another app on her phone. "That's right! The son who saw his dad naked is Ham, Ham is the grandfather of Nimrod. Wowza, how's that for connecting dots!"

"I'm completely confused."

"Don't you see? Noah was righteous, but he made an error in judgment. His son saw him naked and was cursed because of it. The son's grandson led the people to build a tower to Heaven purposely choosing not to attribute it to God because he was resentful." Rachel shook her head in awe over the finding.

"God changed the languages of the people because of their pride. Pride is sin and God is Holy. He changed their speech and scattered them to stop the building of Babel because they were choosing to go their own way. And can you believe, they dedicated it to their god, Marduk? Do you see what resentment does to people?"

"Wait, it's still standing?"

"No, today it's a watering hole in Iraq. Dad told me once that archaeologists have been trying to excavate it but alas, they only see the outline and a big watering hole," Rachel answered dreamingly.

"Whoa, that's crazy."

"Right? I just love history! But hey, don't hold me to this info. We need to research these and confirm they are biblical facts. So, back to that look, what's going on? You didn't think you'd distract me, did you?"

"Oh, Rach, I don't know. Mike has been secretly sneaking around and was missing until just this morning, Dad was called to a Navy mission, and something is wrong with Mom."

"My dad said something about your dad having to leave. What's up?" Rachel asked.

Feeling her chest tighten a little, Maddie breathed in deeply. "After everyone left the party, I overheard Dad talking to Mom about having to leave. Mom was crying and begged him to stay. Dad said that dangerous things were going on in Washington and he was needed." Tears began to well up in her eyes as she said, "And Dad told Mom that if either his family or country were in danger, he must step up and do his duty." She lowered her face into her hands.

Rachel handed her friend a tissue.

Sheepishly, Maddie turned to her friend and asked, "Rach, do you think your dad knows what's going on?"

"I can ask him, but I'm not sure he would tell me, confidentiality and all."

"Thank you."

"Hey, you mentioned something is wrong with your mom?"

"She's been sleeping a lot."

"Well, I can imagine she's struggling with your dad being gone and all.

Looking out of the window, Maddie replied, "Yeah." Worry over her mom and Grammy's conversation gripped her, but she wasn't ready to share that quite yet.

"After a few quiet moments, Rachel piped up. Hey, you mentioned that Grammy challenged you to journal your prayers. Grab your journal and let's lift all of this in prayer right now."

Eyes of gratitude met her friend's as she breathed a sigh of relief. "Great idea, be right back!"

ISRAEL

"Thank you, Joe. Dan, we think the acronyms identify key players. The captured suspect had an interesting tattoo that we need to run through the FTO database. Joe, do you have an image you can show us?"

"Yes, sir." Joe pulled out a photograph and passed it to Dave. He took a Sharpie from his pocket as he pointed to the photograph. "Right here, there are three images in one. The first image in the center is an upside-down cross. The second image overlaying the cross is an obscure bolt of lightning. And the third is the circle." He began to draw the symbol on a blank piece of paper.

"Great artwork," Dan replied appreciatively. "But what does it stand for?"

Joe held up the page to the light and turned it around. "What do you see now?"

"A cross with a backward lightning bolt?" Dan answered.

David took the page from Joe's hand and laid it on the table. Taking the sharpie, he drew a cryptic symbol of his own, "Dan, that looks like a sideways version of the Nazi SS Bolt."

Dan looked up, startled, "Do we suspect a remnant of the Nazi Party?"

"The last war criminal died in 2019. A handful of

functionaries still believe in Hitler and the atrocities he propagated, but I can't imagine anyone still living would be behind these communications. There is one possibility, though."

"What's that?"

With a concerned look toward the Deputy Director, Dave answered, "Perhaps someone wants us to believe the Third Reich has resurrected."

CHAPTER 12

A Cocoon of Fear

Friday morning brought cloudy skies and an equally cloudy mom. Maddie was excited about shopping, but realized her mom didn't feel well.

Concerned over her color, she said, "Mom, we don't have to go if you don't want to."

"I'll be okay, Maddie. I just need a cup of coffee and some ibuprofen, and then I'll be ready. Can you please call Mrs. Williams and ask if Matthew can play with Caleb today?"

Picking up her phone, she called their neighbor and offered to walk Matthew over.

Climbing the stairs to Caleb's house, Maddie and Matthew were surprised when a large Great Dane flew past them and down the street. Curly-haired Caleb ran out the door and past his friend.

"Wait up!" Matthew yelled.

Mrs. Williams opened the screen door, shaking her head as she handed Maddie the leash. "You'll need this." Remember, the secret word is 'heel.'"

"Thor, HEEL!" Three voices called out in unison. Suddenly, Thor stopped and sat down, completely still. Looking at one another, Maddie and the boys walked slowly up to Thor and said, "Good boy." Caleb kneeled to hold the monstrous dog while she placed his leash around his neck.

Thor immediately jumped up and started running once again. "Thor, HEEL!" She yelled. Obediently, Thor stopped.

"Ok Thor, this time we are going to go back home, and you are going to walk like a good dog, right?" Maddie walked slowly up to Thor as he looked at her inquisitively. She grabbed his collar to connect his leash and pulled him back in the direction they came. Thor grudgingly followed.

As Maddie, Matthew, and Caleb walked up the steps, Mrs. Williams came out once again, "Thank you so much. This dog is going to be the death of me!"

"No problem, Mrs. Williams. Mom and I are going shopping. We'll pick Matthew up this afternoon. Is that okay?"

"Of course, y'all have a great time. Matthew can stay for as long as you need."

As she walked back to the house, the phone in her pocket buzzed. Seeing Emma's face brought a smile to her own as she answered. After saying hello, a chorus of voices shouted her name.

"Hi, Girls! What are y'all up to today?"

Jade said, "It's pool time, Baby! We've all voted and decided that you are sun deprived. Grab a suit and join us as we work on our tans."

Disappointed, she answered, "I can't. Mom is taking me shopping."

"Shopping? Like, school shopping? Bleh, look into my eyes, you would much rather go swimming," Jade teased her friend.

"Yes, but Mom said today is the only day we can go. Can I take a rain check and go tomorrow?"

Rachel answered, "I can go at noon."

Emma and Kaitlyn both piped in, "Count us in!"

"It's a date," Maddie replied happily. "Gotta run now; I'll see you, ladies, tomorrow."

"See ya!"

Walking around the mall, Maddie was enamored with all the colors and styles for the new year. She didn't have an eye for fashion, but her mom knew just where to go.

"Maddie, I think you should get your hair layered this year. The ponytail look is a little girlish, don't you think?"

Rolling her eyes, she said, "Mom, I like my ponytail. All the girls are wearing their hair up in some fashion."

"You're coming of age, my dear, and it's time to find your style. I would like to see you wear less jeans and more dresses." Jacque held up a cute off-the-shoulder dress.

"Mom, thank you, but I like my jeans and T-shirts. They're comfy."

"Yes, but you don't know who might be looking. Remember, you never have a second chance to make a first impression."

Anxiety arose in Maddie as she pondered her mom's favorite phrase. *Why should I care about someone's impression of me?* "So, you have told me."

As Maddie and Jacque left the store, Maddie wasn't looking as she ran into a man dressed in black.

"Maddie, what are you doing? I'm so sorry Sir. My daughter is so clumsy."

"I'm sorry." Embarrassed, she began picking up her things.

The man, who appeared flustered himself, began speaking in a weird language. She couldn't understand a word but knew he wasn't happy. A moment later, his friend joined him, and in smooth and perfect English, the man said, "It's okay, Miss. My friend was not paying attention. Please, forgive." The two men straightened up and walked away quickly.

Regaining her composure, Maddie noticed that one of the men had BIRDWATCHER tattooed on his neck. That's strange, Maddie wondered, w*hy would anyone want to tattoo Birdwatcher on their neck?*

Deep in thought, she missed half of what her mom said. Realizing she was talking directly to her, Maddie snapped out of her thoughts and said, "I'm sorry, Mom, what did you say?"

"Really, Maddie, must you be so clumsy? Please look where you are going. I can only imagine the gossip mill buzzing on Monday because of your clumsiness."

"I'm sorry, Mom, but he appeared out of nowhere."

Exasperated, her mom replied, "No Maddie, nobody appears out of nowhere. You need to watch where you are going."

"Yes, ma'am."

"Let's go find a place to eat. I am starved after all that commotion."

The restaurant was bustling on the Friday before the first day of school. Waiting in line, Maddie chewed her lip nervously as she thought back to the encounter outside of the store. The guy seemed to look at her strangely, and she began to wonder if he was following them.

"Mom, can I ask you a question?"

"What's that?" Jacque asked, scrolling through her phone.

"That man back there, did he seem weird to you?"

"No stranger than half of the other people around here."

"Did you see the tattoo on his neck?"

"I will never understand why someone would tattoo their neck. Do they not know how hard it will be for anyone to take them seriously with that kind of display?"

"Mom, lots of people have tattoos. That's not what I mean. Did you see what the tattoo said? It said Birdwatcher. Don't you think that's a bit strange?"

"Maddie, I don't have time to consider a stranger's decisions. Put it out of your mind, and let's sit down to eat."

"Okay."

Jacque led the conversation with small talk amid frequent phone checks. She seemed oblivious to the fact that her daughter wasn't paying attention.

Maddie couldn't stop thinking about the man at the store. He had black hair, all-black clothing, dark olive skin, and that tattoo. There was something not right about him, but she couldn't put her finger on it.

As her mom paid the bill, suddenly the fire alarm sounded. People began scattering everywhere. Jacque quickly paid the bill, grabbed their bags, and said, "Come on." Grabbing her daughter's arm, she pulled her toward the exit.

As she and her mom walked outside, they noticed a group of people congregating in the parking lot. Police cars blocked the exits, and officers were directing everyone to a safe location.

Walking up to two officers, Jacque abruptly interrupted their conversation, "Sir, what is this? Why are these exits blocked?"

"Ma'am, we have a situation and need for you to be patient and stand over there."

"What do you mean 'stand over there?' Do you know who I am?" Jacque was getting quite irate.

Butterflies began to flutter in Maddie's stomach as she encouraged her mom to calm down. "Mom, it's okay. We can wait over there."

"Ma'am, please, we need you and your daughter to stand over there."

Pulling her mom by the arm, Maddie led Jacque over to the crowd of people. She could hear her mom suddenly yelling into her phone. "You will never believe; these idiots are making us wait! I don't know, they won't say anything, only that we need to be patient and wait. Yes, fine, okay. Yes, I will let you know. Bye."

"Who was on the phone?"

"Your Grandpa Jack. Where is your dad when we need him? I don't understand the nerve of some people, making us wait!" Jacque went back to her phone as Maddie pulled out hers.

"It's okay, Mom. Would you like me to call Mrs. Williams?"

"Mrs. Williams? Oh, yes, please do." Jacque answered, distracted. "But stay near, do you hear?"

As she looked around, she realized everyone was quite worried. *I wonder what's going on.* She thought to herself. Dialing Mrs. Williams' number, she took herself away from the conversation to her side to focus on her own. "Mrs. Williams? This is Maddie. There is a situation at the mall. No, no, we are fine, just an alarm, I think. What? A fire? Oh, I see. Yes, do you mind if Matthew eats dinner with Caleb? Thank you."

Turning back to her mom, Maddie shared the information she had been given. "Mom, there was a fire at the mall, but Mrs. Williams said that the news reports say that it's contained."

"Yes, I read here it was outside of the Macy's near a stairwell. That's a weird place for a fire, isn't it?"

Lost in thought, she began to consider what could have happened. What if the fire had spread? What if we couldn't get out of the mall? Her heart pounded with each what-if thought. Suddenly, she wanted to get away. "Too many people," she whispered. Suddenly, she felt dizzy.

"Are you okay?" A stranger next to Maddie touched her shoulder.

"Fine." She could barely think, much less speak.

"Over here, sit down, young lady. Officer, Officer, we need help over here, please!"

An officer hurried over and spoke into his walkie-talkie. "Yes, we need EMS here, stat. Over by the food court entrance."

Her hands were sweaty and clammy. Maddie sat down, clutching her chest. The officer picked up her wrist and looked at his watch.

A paramedic bent down and placed a cloth on her forehead and a cuff on her arm. Taking her blood pressure, he looked her in the eye and asked, "What's your name?"

"M-a-d-d-i-e," she whispered.

"Hi Maddie, no need to speak anymore. My name is Gabe, you are safe here. Now, I want you to look me in the eye. That's good. I see you are having a little trouble breathing. I want you to know that everything is okay. We're going to help you. Look at me, okay? I want you to copy what I am doing."

Listening to the paramedic's friendly voice, she felt as if the crowd around them disappeared.

"That's right, I want you to breathe in real slow like."

As Gabe breathed in, she copied him.

"Okay, now I want you to exhale long and slow, like this. Very good, Maddie."

After a few more breaths, Maddie felt her heart begin to calm. One more tightening of the cuff confirmed to the paramedic what she felt inside her body. Her blood pressure had normalized.

"Maddie, Maddie, where are you?"

Seeing her mom, she immediately burst into tears as she jumped up and hugged her.

"Will someone please tell me what is happening?" Jacque asked.

"It's okay, Mom. I'm okay."

"Are you Maddie's mom?" The officer asked.

"Yes, I am Mrs. Jacque Bennett."

"Your daughter had a panic attack."

Interrupting the officer, her mom said, "My daughter does not have panic attacks."

The EMT technician stood up and looked at Jacque directly. "Ma'am, I assure you that Maddie here experienced a panic attack. This kind of thing happens quite often in an emergency. But she will be okay."

Timidly, her mom responded, "Well, okay, does she need to go to the hospital?"

"No ma'am, she will be fine. Won't you Maddie?"

"Yes, sir."

"I suggest you take her to her primary care physician. Here is my card if you have any questions. Do you mind coming over here to fill out some paperwork?"

Sitting down on the curb, she heard the voice of her friend in her mind. *Breathe in, breathe out slowly*. Rachel would say. *It's okay, Maddie, you are safe here.* The EMT, Gabe, gave her the same instructions Rachel would give.

Jacque walked over to her daughter, "Feeling better? Are you ready to go home?"

Maddie nodded yes.

Grabbing their bags, Jacque looked at her daughter with worry. "It's okay, Maddie, I can carry these. You let me know if you have any issues walking to the car, okay?"

Surprised by her concern, Maddie answered. "I'll be okay, Mom, thank you."

As they entered the car, Jacque began to cry.

"What's wrong?"

"I'm so sorry, Maddie. I thought you were making it all up."

"It's okay, Mom. You know I can't help it. Don't you?"

"Yes, I can see that now." Jacque looked at her daughter. "We will get you some help, okay? I'll call Dr. Richards next week."

Maddie and her mom were both quiet on the ride home. Pulling out her phone, she texted Rachel.

Maddie: "Interesting afternoon."

Rachel: "What's up?"

Maddie: "I ran into a weird guy, the mall caught on fire. Oh, and I had a panic attack."

Immediately, the face of her best friend popped up on her phone as the video chat began to ring.

Accepting the call, she smiled weakly at her friend.

"Come on Maddie, you can't text that kind of thing. You're gonna give me a heart attack!"

"Sorry, I'm okay. Mom's okay."

"Do they know what happened?"

"I don't know."

"Well, I'm coming over. Is that okay Mrs. Bennett?"

Looking into Maddie's phone, her mom answered, "Yes Rachel, that will be fine."

Opening the door to her friend, Maddie found herself in a big bear hug. "Are you okay?"

Laughing, she said, "I'm fine."

Rachel walked her friend to the couch and looked at her seriously. "So, tell me what happened."

Maddie proceeded to share the story again with her friend. She left nothing out and finished with the promise from her mom to see a therapist.

"That's good. You know, my mom had to see a therapist after she left the hospital. Just like Emma's mom, she learned some great tips to help her. I never realized that postpartum depression was a thing."

"Wow, your mom was depressed?"

"Yes, she called it her cocoon. She looked sad and cried a lot. She isolated herself and didn't want to be around us except at dinner time. It was a hard season for all of us. But she came out of it."

"Why did she call it a cocoon?"

"Mom said it was like being in a deep dark place. She couldn't climb out and didn't know how to explain what was happening to her or how to ask for help. Several weeks after she began receiving therapy, she revealed what she was feeling. Her thoughts of dying were overwhelming. She realized how close she came to having to leave everyone she loved behind. It was so very sad."

"I can't imagine." Maddie placed her hand on her friend's. "I'm so sorry Rachel."

Rachel smiled sadly. "She's okay now. Dad thought she was hormonal. I tried to help her, but honestly, I didn't know how to help. We're all learning to ask for help when we need it and to be fully present for each other when needed."

Maddie sat in the heaviness of Rachel's story for a moment. "Rachel, I know what the cocoon feels like. When I can't breathe, I feel like there's a tight cocoon around my chest squeezing the breath out of me."

"That sounds scary," Rachel responded. "Maddie, can I ask you a question?"

"Sure."

"The night before your party, you mentioned being afraid all the time. Do you feel the cocoon when you are afraid?"

Looking down at her tightly clasped hands, she answered, "Yes."

ISRAEL

"Commander Bennett, there is a call for you."

"Thank you, I'll take it in the conference room."

"Commander Bennett speaking."

"I've been trying to reach you all day. Can't you answer your cell?"

David could hear the tension in Jacque's voice. "I've been in meetings all day. Is something wrong? You sound stressed."

"Stressed? I sound stressed. Well, you would be stressed, too, if you found yourself in a mall on fire. Oh, and let's not forget our daughter, who had to be calmed down by paramedics."

"What do you mean? Is Maddie, okay?"

"So, you only care about Maddie, do you?

"Jacque, can we please start at the beginning? What happened?"

Jacque shared the events of the day with David. He sighed as he heard her voice break at the end. "Jacque, are you okay?"

The silence was deafening. After a moment, she answered, "I don't know. David, when are you coming home?"

"Jacque, you know the drill; I can't leave my post until the task is complete."

The long pause on the other end of the line spoke volumes. "Babe, I know this is hard for you. You have had to carry so much in my absence. But you know that I must fulfill my..."

"I know you must fulfill your duty to your country. When, might I ask, will your duty to your family come before your duty to your country?"

CHAPTER 13

Connecting the Dots

A bright beam of sunshine burst through the stained-glass window of Maddie's bedroom. Grabbing her phone to check the time, she was surprised by the thread of text messages from her squad.

Jade: "Who's ready for a girl's day?"

Kaitlyn: "I am so excited!"

Emma: "Wait, aren't we swimming?"

Kaitlyn: "Yes, silly."

Emma: "Eleven am?"

Rachel: "I'll bring the snacks!"

Jade: "Movie After?"

Kaitlyn: "Gotta check with the parental unit."

Rachel: "Not too late, church tomorrow."

"Oh, no!" Jumping up, she realized she had only fifteen minutes. Rummaging through her dresser, she threw her swimsuit on the bed, followed by a pair of shorts and a T-shirt.

As she dressed, she answered the flurry of texts with one of her own:

Maddie: "Woke up late, will be there shortly."

Running downstairs, she grabbed a banana and threw sunscreen into a bag as she scribbled a note:

Mom,
I'm going swimming with the girls. Matthew is still at Caleb's house. I have my phone; call me if you need me. Love, Maddie

The house sure is quiet. Deciding to let her mom sleep in, she quietly locked the door behind her.

Living in the same neighborhood was very convenient for Maddie and her friends. Rachel was the first to move into Brighton Hills. Yesterday wasn't the first time Rachel helped her to process an event. Ever since she moved into the neighborhood, Rachel was always available to help. Maddie still remembered the first day she met Rachel in her first-grade year. Blond curls, blue eyes, and big smile, she always stood out in a crowd. "Hi, Friend, what's your name?" Rachel asked.

"Maddie. What's yours?"

"I'm Rachel, and I'm here to tell you that our bus is the bestest in town. Have you ever ridden a school bus?"

"No, my mom usually drives me to school."

"Did you just move in? Momma and I saw a moving truck last week, and I said, 'Momma, my best friend is on that moving truck.' Wanna be my best friend?" For a second grader to want to be her best friend absolutely made Maddie's day. Rachel never seemed to mind the year difference in their ages, even when she went to high school. Rachel never cared for appearances; she loved Maddie for Maddie. And for this, she was grateful.

Walking past Charlie's tree, she remembered the summer before third grade when Jade moved into the neighborhood. Rachel and Maddie found themselves in a pickle when Charlie the neighborhood cat climbed a tree. Rachel got stuck on a limb when, channeling her inner superhero, she decided to climb after him. Maddie watched in horror as her friend dangled from the tree with one hand and a T-shirt. In a hot second, a girl with long black braids that sparkled with a rainbow of colored beads climbed up the tree like Spiderman. Holding hands, they jumped down from a seated position on the bottom branch and laughed as Charlie jumped off and ran into the woods behind them. Maddie shook her head. Jade and Rachel often found themselves on opposite ends of conversations but were forever marked by the moment Jade saved Rachel's life.

Turning toward the pool, she remembered her friend Emma's entrance into their lives. Maddie faced a particularly difficult seventh-grade year when she had to face the local bully. Walking home from Rachel's one afternoon, a group of girls sitting on the corner called out her name. As she turned around, a wadded-up piece of paper hit her in the face. Laughter drew the girls together as they stood up and made their way over to her.

"What do you want, Ashley?" Maddie and Ashley had known each other for a couple of years but had never really talked until middle school.

"Where's a friend when you need her, Girls?" Grabbing her bag, Ashley taunted her. "What's in here?" Maddie attempted to retrieve her homework as Ashley took it out of her bag.

"That's mine!"

"Yours?" Looking around, Ashley gave her homework to her friend. "Last I looked, you're standing on a public street. That means this homework; well, I would say this homework is public property. Wouldn't you agree, Girls?"

Nodding in agreement, the girls started laughing hilariously.

"Hey, what are you doing?" Suddenly, a girl with short wavy hair and beautiful brown skin ran over and grabbed her bag. Standing nose to nose, she stared Ashley down until she backed away.

"I'll see you again." Ashley nodded toward Maddie, throwing her homework on the sidewalk as she and her friends walked away.

"Thanks." She said, grateful for her rescuer.

"Don't mention it; I don't like bullies." Handing Maddie her bag, she continued, "Hey, my name is Emma. What's yours?" Emma helped her pick up the crumpled pieces of paper.

"Maddie. When did y'all move in?"

"Last Sunday. Have you lived here long?"

"For about six years."

"Hey, come check out our garden. Mom and I are finishing up our prep for planting."

Emma picked up a handful of soil to show her friend. "We just finished tilling. See how soft the soil is?"

To keep from having to touch the dirt, Maddie bent down to look at the freshly tilled soil. "What are you planting?"

"Over here, we'll have tomatoes and, in this corner, peppers. Oh, and on that side, we're planting squash."

Peering at Emma's fingernails, she asked, "Wow, you like getting your hands dirty, don't you?"

"Yes, it's my therapy. Don't you?"

Looking at her own hands, she pondered her mom's response if she came home with dirty fingernails. "My Grammy loves to garden, too. I've always been interested, but my mom would have a field day if I got my hands dirty."

Opening the gate to the pool deck, Maddie laughed at the times she had done just that. Emma loved planting and spent the next two years teaching her friends how to prepare a garden, what to plant, and when to plant. Maddie wasn't as fond of it as her friend, but she loved watching Emma jump into her projects with enthusiasm.

While Kaitlyn didn't live in the neighborhood, she wasn't too far away, and in the last year, they had become close friends. Maddie appreciated Kaitlyn's quick wit and unique way of looking at things. This unique perspective brought them together for a school project, which resulted in many nights of lively debate. Walking toward her friends, she saw Kaitlyn share something from her phone in her unique techie fashion. Grabbing a chair, Maddie had to laugh as she thought of the many times her friend brought them into her world. "The

Butterfly Nebula is in the constellation Scorpius. It's almost four thousand light years from Earth. See? Oh, and check this out!"

"Are those wings?" Emma asked.

"They're cauldrons of gas heated to twenty thousand degrees Celsius. It's said this is one of the hottest stars in our galaxy. Isn't it crazy?" Kaitlyn asked.

"Wow, it's so beautiful! God is an amazing Creator, isn't he?" Rachel peered in awe at Kaitlyn's phone.

Jade looked at her friend, "Not to bust your bubble Rach, but this star is dying. That's why it's called a NE-BUL-A."

"Life or death is all in the hands of the Father," Rachel countered.

"Yeah, but look at the colors, ya gotta admit, that's a lot of gas!" Kaitlyn laughed.

"Kaitlyn, it's always about gas with you, isn't it?" Smiling at her friend, Emma quickly changed the subject. "Hey Maddie, are you okay? Rachel told us what happened yesterday. Were you scared?"

"I'm okay. What're you looking at Kaitlyn?"

Handing her the phone, she renewed her dissertation on the dying star.

"Wild," Maddie answered as she handed the phone back.

"So, tell us what happened," Jade said as she began braiding Maddie's hair.

"It's all a blur now. The mall caught on fire, and I had a panic attack. Oh, and I ran into some guy who had a Birdwatcher tattoo on his neck."

"Birdwatcher? That's weird."

"Yeah, it was weird. I didn't see a bird or anything, just the word. And he looked at me in the strangest way."

Jade stopped braiding and moved to the end of Kaitlyn's chair. Focusing intently on her friend she asked, "What do you mean? How did he look at you?"

"He stared for a long minute like he wanted to say something but couldn't. I don't think he spoke English because his friend came and apologized for Birdwatcher bumping into me."

"Wait, he bumped into you?" Jade was on high alert.

"Yeah, but mom was right behind me. Like I said, the other guy apologized and then they walked away."

"And then the fire alarm went off?" Kaitlyn seemed to know where Jade was going with the questions.

"No, that happened an hour later."

"An hour, huh? Sounds like perfect timing. Hey Girls, check this out. Maddie, is this the tattoo?"

Peering once again at Kaitlyn's phone, she replied excitedly, "Yes, that's it! What is this?"

"Some weird social media page. Check it out; this account has over a million followers."

"Let me see." Jade took Kaitlyn's phone and scrolled through the posts. "Look at all these dudes. They're all pretty sketchy, Maddie. Check it out. Each one seems to have this weird tat, the same but different. It's almost like they're a badge of some kind."

Giving the phone back to Kaitlyn, Jade continued, "Girls, I need you to listen to me. Some high-key weird things are going on right now. Every day, there is a report of another person who has gone missing. Do you remember Casey from last year? Her parents haven't seen her in weeks."

"Wait, what? Casey? What happened?" Rachel asked.

"According to my mom, she was walking to the store and disappeared. She hasn't been heard from since. Her parents called my mom and asked if we had seen her. Then there's Jason Wilson. He went missing after a baseball game."

"Not Jason. He was in my chem class last year," Kaitlyn piped in.

"Girls, NamUS reported almost six hundred thousand people went missing last year. As of now, it's up to five hundred thousand and it's only August."

The girls sat in the quiet of Jade's pronouncement.

"Maddie, I don't want to scare you, but that guy sounds like bad news. This page has a lot of scary dudes on it. Please promise me you'll be careful."

Looking into Jade's eyes, she nodded in agreement.

"Things are a bit too serious over here, what're you girls gabbing about?"

Kaitlyn's face turned bright red when Noah dragged a chair next to her.

Rachel smiled and winked at her friend as she teased the boy she crushed on. "Noah, where have you been all summer? Jade was just telling us how she was so worried you had gone missing."

"Missing? Nah, ain't nobody takin' me. See these? Flexing his biceps, he kissed each one and looked at Kaitlyn with arrogant eyes. "I'm Batman." He laughed as he dove into the pool.

The girls all jumped as water splashed them from his audacious display.

Walking home from the pool, Maddie turned to Rachel and asked, "Do you think that guy was bad news?"

"I don't know, Maddie, but be careful, K? My dad's been talking a lot lately about the end of days. I think he's worried, too."

The butterflies began to rumble in Maddie's tummy as she asked, "What do you mean, the end of days?"

"I'll let my dad explain it to you. But like, the world feels dark, ya know? He keeps saying how Jesus said that in the last days, wickedness would multiply and the love of most would grow cold. Don't you feel it?"

Thinking about Noah and the ark, Maddie looked at her friend and asked, "Rachel, do you think God will destroy the earth like he did back in Noah's day?"

"God promised never to destroy the earth by flood, but the Bible does say it will be destroyed by fire. But Maddie, that same chapter says that God promises a new Heaven and a new earth! Can you imagine?"

"Wow, you really know the Bible, Rach. Grammy encouraged me to read but to be honest I didn't get very far. There's a lot I don't understand."

"I get it. It took me a while, too, and if I'm honest, I needed somebody to help me understand it. My small group leader, Sonya, has been a godsend! I've learned so much since she started challenging me to read. Hey, my church is having a back-to-school bash in a couple of weeks. Why don't you and the girls join me? There'll be lots of great food and fun things to do. And you can meet my leader. Maybe she can help you, too!"

That night, as the girls arrived at the movie theater, Maddie couldn't help but feel a bit of trepidation as she looked around the mall. Honestly, she was surprised that everyone seemed so nonchalant.

Rachel elbowed her as they ascended the escalator to the top of the mall. "Hey, what's up?" She asked.

Looking down at the food court, she said, "Just a few days ago, I was in this very mall. . ."

"We don't have to go to the movie. If you want, I can call my dad and we can go to Top Golf."

"Nah, it's okay. I just wish I didn't feel so anxious." Stepping off the escalator, she followed Jade, who was walking backward toward the ticket taker. Maddie wished she could be as bold and unafraid as her friend.

A big tub of popcorn and Junior Mints later, the girls were settled in their stadium seats. Maddie explored the theater, half expecting a bad guy to start yelling.

"Hey, we're okay, Maddie." Emma laid her hand on her friend's and squeezed.

She didn't realize she was holding her breath until her friend touched her. Inhaling deeply, she told her body to calm down and decided to settle in and enjoy the movie. Thankfully, Kaitlyn chose a comedy. Before she knew it, Maddie was laughing hysterically with everyone else.

At the end of the night, she was glad that she had come to the movies. Looking around at her friends, she was grateful to have a squad that loved her and was attentive to her struggles.

A sigh of frustration popped the bubble of gratitude as she realized how needy she was. *I must get a handle on this anxiety!* She thought. Thinking back to the painting on Ms. Lorna's piano and the song lyrics she wrote, she so wanted that peace for herself. The line, "God, you are faithful, when I am afraid you bring me peace," was curious. *How can I feel God's peace?* She wondered. *Truly, I just want Dad to come home; everything will be okay then, right?* She wasn't so sure.

As they walked out of the mall, she breathed a sigh of relief. Smiling weakly at Rachel, who caught her ruminating, she shuffled the thoughts away and followed her friend to her dad's car. *Oh well,* she thought, *school is right around the corner, hopefully things would settle down then.*

ISRAEL

Opening his laptop to the ring of the secure uplink, David heard the familiar voice of Admiral Osborne, Director of the NSA, "Commander, good to see you again. How is Jerusalem?"

"Hi, Rick. Israel is Israel. How are the girls?"

"The twins are growing like weeds. Did you know Robin is expecting again?"

"Congratulations! Aren't you a little old for having children?"

"Hm, Commander Bennett, what have you learned?"

David and Rick had a friendly rapport, but Rick's tone of voice suggested that he either had company or was short on patience.

"Well, Admiral Osborne, my team reviewed the communications shared by the Deputy Director of Communications in Israel and the traffic is concerning." Sharing the images with the Admiral, he pointed out the messages and symbols of interest. "Have you seen similar reports?"

"I assume you heard about the attack in London?"

"Yes, sir, as I understand, the suspect had an interesting tattoo. When we ran it through the FTO Database, there were no hits."

"Well, we have seen an influx of these images across the country, including a mass shooting in Ohio and a fire at a mall in Georgia. At both scenes of the crime, suspects were reported to have similar names tattooed on their necks. The suspect in Georgia had the same upside down cross tattooed on his arm."

"Where in Georgia?"

"Hang on, let me check." After a few moments, Admiral Osborne continued, "Smyrna, Georgia. Hang on, isn't that near where you live?"

"Yes," David answered tersely as he looked away.

Suddenly, the gravity of the mission hit him. "Rick, in speaking with Jacque, she mentioned a fire at the local mall. I assume this is the same?"

"It appears so, yes."

"How many of these suspects have been captured?"

"I can't say, but I will investigate it. In the meantime, we'll dispatch a team of agents to search for these keywords and do some reverse intelligence to flush out those sending the messages. I'll follow up with the FBI on their findings with these strangely tattooed men."

"That sounds good, Sir. Our team will continue working with the Embassy here to see what else we can glean from the communications on JONAH. I have a call with Mordecai

Aronoff as well to help us decipher the patterns for anomalies. I would also suggest a briefing from the US Trade Rep after the WTO conference in Geneva."

"Already on it."

"Keep me posted on your findings."

"You've got it."

CHAPTER 14

Truth Revealed

The first two weeks of high school were a blur. As Jade would say, they slayed the eighth grade. But High School, well High School brought a whole new dimension of challenge and anxiety for Maddie. New classes, new teachers, new homework, UGGHHHH! Where did summer go? Thankfully, she had her girls to encourage her. But encouragement was the last thing she was thinking about on Wednesday morning as her phone buzzed annoyingly. "It's too early," she groaned.

Adjusting her eyes to the brightness of the screen, she scrolled through the messages from her girls.

Rachel: "I have a great vibe about tonight!"

Kaitlyn: "Really, Rach, it's a bit early, don't ya

think?"

Rachel: "You'll thank me later."

Jade: "Girl, you are high-key extra today!"

Watching the emoji flair, Maddie laughed.

Maddie: "So, what's the fit today?"

Jade: "A crop top and jeans."

*Kaitlyn: "Mom got me a dope velour jacket. I'm
going to pair it with a mini and tank."*

Checking her closet, she pulled out a pair of ripped jeans and a T-shirt. She wanted to look cute but didn't want to overdo it. Looking at herself in the mirror, she considered her mom's suggestion of getting a haircut. Mom's suggestions weren't really suggestions at all. Maddie had decided a long time ago that it wasn't worth arguing over most things, but her style was one of those things she preferred to have control over.

Pulling her hair up into a regular ponytail, she pulled on her tennis shoes, grabbed her book bag, and made her way to the kitchen.

"Matthew, what is that?" Peering over her brother's shoulder, she was aghast at the disgusting mix of foods in Matthew's bowl.

"It's good, here try some." Matthew offered his bowl as milk sloshed out of his full mouth.

"No way." Maddie pretended she was going to puke. "I'll take this banana, thank you. Hey, where's Mom?"

"Dunno. I haven't seen her come out yet."

"Hmm, I'll go check on her." Knocking on her door, she peered in as the door cracked open. "Hey Mom, is everything okay?"

Jacque was passed out, a bottle lying on the floor. She moaned as Maddie picked up the bottle.

"Maddie, where are you?"

"I'm here Mom. Are you okay?"

"Fine, I'm fine. Can you make breakfast for your brother?"

"He's eating now."

"Good, that's good. Think I'll take a nap. Can you please close the door on your way out?"

"Mom, I'm going to church with Rachel tonight."

"Church? That's nice, Dear. Tell Olivia and Tom I said hello."

"What about Matthew, Mom? Do you want me to ask Mrs. Williams if Matthew can hang out with Caleb after school?"

"Oh, that would be nice, thank you. Have a good day."

Worried, she walked out to the garage to throw out the bottle. She didn't want Matthew to see what Mom was up to. *What should I do?* She wondered. Maddie's gut told her something was wrong with her mom, but she didn't know who to talk to, and her mom would have a fit if she shared her business with anyone outside of the family.

"Hey, wait up!" Maddie ran up to meet Rachel as she was getting on the bus.

"Thought you were riding with your mom?"

"She has a headache."

Finding a seat, Rachel said, "She sure has had a lot of those lately. Is everything okay?"

"She'll be fine. I think she's worried about Dad."

"My dad misses him too. Hey, by the way, Dad offered to take us to church tonight. Do you need a ride?"

Maddie sighed in relief, "Yes, that would be great! I need to drop Matthew at Caleb's first then I'll come over."

"Awesome, are you excited?"

"A little nervous, actually."

"Nothing to be nervous about, Maddie. Think of it as going to a family reunion and meeting a whole bunch of family you've never met." Rachel encouraged her friend as the bus rolled up to the front of the school.

"As long as you're there."

"Always!" Rachel fist bumped her friend as she jumped out of her seat.

"Okay, gotta run, I have a quiz to make up before homeroom."

"See ya."

"Maddie, how are you?"

Maddie stepped into the big hug of Rachel's mom as she welcomed her into their home.

"Hi Ms. Olivia, I'm doing okay. How are you?"

"Rachel told us what happened. How are you handling everything?"

"It's a lot, but I'm okay. Mom is going to take me to the doctor."

"I am so thankful you are okay. Rachel will be down in a moment. Hey, it's good to see you." Ms. Olivia always had the warmest smiles for her daughter's friends.

"Hello Beautiful, how is my BFF?" Rachel lit up the kitchen in a flurry of color as she danced into the room.

"Wow, that's an interesting combination." Maddie smiled as she admired the pink tutu and polka-dot hair pieces. *Only Rachel could pull this off.*

"It's the BASH! Gotta make a splash! Oh, Maddie, I can't wait for my squad to meet my church fam!"

Rachel's enthusiasm was contagious. "Is this fit okay?"

"Yes, I love this color on you! I wish I could wear this shade of salmon."

"Am I under-dressed for church? Grammy says we are supposed to wear dresses."

"Oh no, 'come as you are' is our motto. Besides, I'm wearing a tutu." Rachel laughed as she walked an invisible catwalk.

"Hi, Maddie, Rachel, I see your inner ballerina's coming out." Rachel's dad smiled as he kissed his daughter on her forehead.

"Hi Mr. Tom, my mom says hello."

"How is Jacque?" Rachel's mom looked around her husband as she dried a dish.

"She's okay. She misses Dad." Maddie looked down at her shoes.

Rachel grabbed her hand and squeezed.

"This must be a tough season for all of you. Is there anything we can do to help?"

"No ma'am, we're good."

Olivia smiled warmly and placed her hand on her shoulder. "Okay, remember that we are here, and we love you guys."

"Yes, ma'am."

"All right, Ladies, let's go." Tom grabbed his keys and walked through the garage door.

Tom and Olivia Monroe had been friends with Maddie's parents since Rachel and she first met. After David retired from the Navy, Tom helped him procure a job with their vendor, Magnum Lock Security. Magnum Lock was a professional hacking company for the most prominent corporations on the Eastern seaboard. Tom held David in high regard.

"Mr. Tom, thank you for driving me tonight."

"That is no problem, Maddie. You are always welcome to ride with us."

"Us?" She looked at her friend inquisitively.

"Oh yes, Dad goes too. He leads the freshman boys."

"Oh wow, how long have you been a leader, Mr. Tom?"

"I've been serving them since their sixth-grade year. It's been quite the journey."

"Dad is great with them, Maddie! Leaders come and go, but my dad, he is in for the long haul. And the boys love him."

Looking at Rachel, she whispered, "Have you had a chance to ask him yet?"

"Hey, Dad, Maddie is worried about her dad. She, well we, were wondering if you, like, know where he is."

Maddie turned ten shades of red as her friend boldly asked the question that she had been so anxious to ask herself.

Looking in the rearview mirror with concern, Mr. Tom answered, "Even if I did, I wouldn't be able to tell you, girls."

"Well, we thought we would try." Rachel encouraged her friend with a wink.

"Maddie, what are you worried about?" Mr. Tom asked.

"I don't know." Her nerves began to scream red alert.

"It's okay to be afraid, but you don't have to stay that way."

"I guess. I just don't want anything bad to happen to him."

Nodding, Mr. Tom said, "I agree with you, Maddie, and what I know to be true is God's promise that he is with us and for us. I will pray this promise over your dad, including that he will protect him." Looking into the rearview mirror, he said, "And Maddie, we are here if you need to talk."

Rachel looked at her friend solemnly and squeezed her hand. "Me, too."

A sense of relief came over her. Often, when she was afraid, her chest would feel heavy, but this time was different. She didn't have to bear the worry alone; it was like someone else was helping her with the heaviness.

As the car stopped in Jade's driveway, Maddie and Rachel's friends ran out to the van. Opening the side door, Jade led her friends in a symphony of Monster Mash.

"Really, Jade?" Rachel shot a look of disapproval that resulted in a prompt eye roll from her friend.

"I'm here, but only for the food, of course."

"Jade, I predict that you will love it! You may come for the food, but Jesus will tap on your heart, and he'll fill more than just your stomach." Emma winked at her friend.

"Okay, Ms. Optimist, we shall see."

"Hey Maddie, about that worship song?"

"Oh yeah, I've got a couple of lines for you, Emma. I had some help at Grammy's."

"I'll have some free time after service, would you be open to playing a few bars?"

"I don't know. Will there be a lot of people?"

"Oh, I doubt it, everyone will be at the food truck, right Jade?"

Cackling loudly, she answered, "Yup, I'm here for the food."

Jade, attempting to change the subject, looked over Kaitlyn's shoulder and said, "Hey, whatcha doin'?"

"Nothing, just texting someone."

"Someone? He wouldn't be named Batman, would he?"

Kaitlyn snickered as she returned to her phone.

Amused by the banter, Maddie laughed as they turned into the long drive up to the church. The church was huge and so different from Grammy's. Mom had many opinions about the mega-church, as she called it, but Rachel had really connected there. She was intrigued to see the place Rachel talked so much about.

"What are they wearing?" Kaitlyn was suddenly very interested in the organized chaos in the parking lot.

"Oh, that's a Zorb. Two people wear a Zorb and box, see?" Rachel was on the edge of her seat as she pointed to the pair of students engaged in a boxing ring.

"I want to do THAT!" Kaitlyn put her phone away as she watched the ensuing match.

With a bit of sass, Jade asked, "I thought we were going to church?"

"This is church. We have fun while we worship Jesus."

"Grammy says we should always show reverence in the house of the Lord."

"Come on, you don't think Jesus has fun? He did create us which means he created fun!" Rachel laughed as she enjoyed her friend's excitement.

"Whatever, just remember I'm only here …"

"For the food, we know, Jade, but give Jesus a chance, all right?"

Nervous and excited, Maddie walked with her squad through the double doors. Every person she passed smiled warmly. She would never remember all the people Rachel introduced her to.

"Rachel, hey Girl! How was your weekend?"

"Hi Sonya, it was great! I brought the friends I've told you about. This is Jade, Kaitlyn, and Maddie."

"Hi ladies, we've heard so much about you. We're glad you've joined us tonight. We have a great night planned. Did you see the events outside?"

Maddie nodded, "Yes, ma'am."

"In about thirty minutes we'll start our service and then have food trucks after. Rachel, will you help them sign in? Once y'all finish, meet me in the coffee shop and I'll grab you a free coffee."

"Now that's what I'm talking about." Jade elbowed Kaitlyn.

As Rachel signed her friends in, Maddie asked, "Where did Emma go?"

"She's on keys tonight, so she had to practice before service."

"Wow, she performs onstage?"

"She doesn't *perform*. She helps to facilitate worship." Rachel answered.

"What do you mean?"

"When we sing to God, he is our audience. We are lifting our worship to him. Those on the stage only facilitate that worship. They lead us in praise to him."

Maddie read the words on the screen. "I'll follow where Your Spirit leads." Remembering Ms. Lorna's story of David who worshiped his King and found encouragement for his soul, she wondered, *would she too find encouragement?* Never had she seen anything like this in her life. *Who is this spirit?* Confused, she wondered, *were they talking about God?* As she stood in the dark room, the electricity was palpable. She looked around and saw people talking and, on their phones, but then there were these people with their hands up and eyes closed. *This is so different from the amens of Grammy's worship.*

Rachel grabbed her hand as she stood perfectly still. Maddie didn't know what to do. As they sang the song *"Available,"* she squeezed her friend's hand while pondering the words.

Looking around the room, a boy dropped to his knees and began weeping. *What is going on?* As strange as she found the things going on around her, she wasn't anxious. Her voice wanted to sing the words on the screen, even if she was a little self-conscious.

Jade stood perfectly still. Following her gaze, Maddie saw her staring at Emma. Playing the keyboard, Emma had her eyes closed. She had never seen her friend so at peace. Something remarkable was happening.

The lights dimmed as the audience quietly listened to the words of the pastor. The air was thick as he told the story of God's love and Jesus' sacrifice. Grammy told the story of Jesus a dozen times, but something about the way the pastor interlaced it with his own made it seem real to her. Rachel and Emma hung on to his every word, writing everything in their journals. Jade and Kaitlyn, on the other hand, laughed quietly at something on Kaitlyn's phone. *How can they be so absent?* Maddie wondered as she listened to his words.

Pastor Derrik broke into her annoyed thoughts. "The song *"Available"* in our worship set tonight had the lyric, 'Yes, Lord, I am available.' Some of you came tonight feeling broken, anxious, and afraid. Others of you are worried about an uncertain future. I am here to tell you that God's promise of peace in the middle of chaos is real. In John's gospel, he shares Jesus' promise with us, 'For God so loved the world that he gave his one and only Son that whoever believes in him shall not perish but have eternal life.' This is extravagant grace. And no matter what we face in this world, the truth is that Jesus, our Prince of Peace, made it possible for you to not only have his peace but to know his peace."

As Emma softly played the keyboard, Maddie felt the pastor speak directly to her. Everyone else fell away as she listened to his message.

"God so loved you that he poured out his grace through the gift of his Son, Jesus. Jesus is calling you and asking, 'Are you available?' Will you say yes to him tonight?"

Time seemed to stand still as the pastor prayed. With her eyes closed, a yearning grew within her heart. Months of worry, fear, and anxiety from all the things weighed on her heavily. She wanted to be able to count on this extravagant grace that was promised but didn't know if she was good enough. *Can I truly break free from all of this?* She began weeping as a picture of the painting on Ms. Lorna's piano popped into her mind. Remembering her deepest desire at that moment, she whispered, "I want to feel peace like that."

She heard a whisper in return, ***"You can."***

Opening her eyes, she looked around to see who spoke to her. *Wait, did I say that?*

"His invitation is for you. You are not too broken for the Father to mend. And you don't have to be good enough to accept his invitation." She was astonished as her thoughts were reflected in the pastor's words. "Jesus is here waiting for you to say yes to him. If you would like to give him your yes, we have leaders around the room who would love to pray with you. Here is how that's going to happen. As the worship band comes up to play, find your leader. I know this may be difficult for some of you, but we want you to know that you are not alone."

Maddie's stomach was in knots, but there was also a tug on her heart that would not go away. Looking at her friend, she asked, "Will you go with me?" Rachel smiled and led the way to Sonya.

ISRAEL

The hotel in Jerusalem where David stayed was covered in beautiful stone and architectural windows. Admiring the timeless architecture, he awaited his long-time friend, Mordecai Aronoff.

"Mordy, how are you? How was your holiday?"

"Shalom, my friend. It's been too long."

Mordecai and David went way back. While on active duty in Naval Intelligence, he worked with Mordy's team in Israel on several high-profile cases. The most complex case is that of the planned kidnapping of the Israeli Prime Minister. David remembered the intel they found leading them to the Prime Minister's deputy PM. *Some people will do anything for money.* He thought to himself.

"So where did you and the family go?"

"We took the boat to the Mediterranean. The Research Institute needed my boat for an expedition, so we took advantage of the opportunity to show our boys the real world."

While working for the Israeli Intelligence Service, Mordy had purchased a survey ship that he used to hire out for underwater oceanic exploration. It had been a dream of his for years to sail around exploring the "real world," as he called it. The R/V Whitestone was outfitted with the finest sonar equipment and ready to sail at a moment's notice. No expense had been spared in the outfitting of the vessel. While David had his suspicions of possible reconnaissance missions, he kept them to himself and chose to enjoy the conversation with his old friend.

"So, enough about me, what can I do for you?"

"Mordecai, we have a critical issue at hand. Are you aware of the uncovered communications from the JONAH?"

"Yes, yes, the Ambassador briefed me. What have you uncovered so far?"

"The intelligence is garbled, but tactical messages that appear to be directives are interspersed throughout. The signatures of the communications are very similar to those we uncovered from TRU. We aren't certain, but we do suspect a lucrative and well-funded terrorist organization is responsible. We've uncovered covert names throughout the communications that have corroborated with national and international attacks."

David laid out the photographs sent to him by the FBI.

Looking at the photographs, Mordecai asked, "How many attacks are we talking about?"

"We've counted eighteen to date: five in the United States, one in Brazil, four in the UK, two in Australia, three in Germany, one in Singapore, one in Shanghai, and one in South Korea."

"Interesting, is it a coincidence that each country is a member state of the World Trade Organization? And they are meeting soon, yes?"

"Yes. We feel certain a coup of global proportions is in the works. We need you to analyze the patterns of these communications for any anomalies that would lead us to the group responsible. And quickly.

"Oh, and Mordy, please keep this under wraps. One of the attacks was in the city where I live. My wife and daughter were present when it occurred."

Mordecai looked at his friend with concern, "Were they harmed?"

"No, they are fine. The local authorities believe it was a fire set by teenagers, but you can understand my concern."

"Yes, David, I understand. I will run some tests immediately, and I will pray to Yeshua on your behalf. Shalom to you and your family."

"Thank you, Mordy."

CHAPTER 15

Light Shines in the Darkness

"Hi Maddie, how can I pray for you?"

"The pastor said that God's promise of peace in the middle of chaos is real. Is it?"

"Yes, ma'am." She smiled sincerely. "Tell me, what's going on."

"Nothing, no, everything. I don't know. My dad is somewhere, probably putting his life in danger. My mom is worried about him and has started . . ." Maddie took a deep breath. "My brother left, and we don't know where he . . ." She couldn't say another word as the sobs racked her body.

"Oh Girl, come here." Sonya simply let her cry. After a few moments, she led her and Rachel over to a chair. Giving her a tissue, she asked, "Better?"

Maddie nodded. "I just don't know what to do anymore. If God is here, we sure do need him."

"Tell me what you're feeling right now."

"Sad, no afraid, I guess.

"Yeah, I get it. I would feel overwhelmed, perhaps worried?"

"Yeah."

"You know it's okay to feel these feelings, right?"

Maddie wasn't sure how to answer that question.

"Oh, sweet Girl, God gave you feelings and not only did he promise peace, but he promised his presence and his comfort in the middle of your pain. Did you know that God is right here, right now?"

"I guess. How do you know?"

"His word says he is with us and for us. God is always true to his word, Maddie, and so we can trust that what he says is true."

"But how do I feel him?"

"Well, the truth is that we don't always feel him in the way we think of feelings. His presence is found in our worship, in other people like your beautiful friend here, in his creation, and in his Spirit."

"That song tonight talked about a spirit; is that God?"

"Yes, ma'am. Jesus sent his Spirit, God's Spirit, to be our Helper. He is the one who leads us to all truth. He speaks to us and guides us."

"Wait, he speaks to us?"

"Yes, ma'am."

"I heard a voice tonight that said, 'you can' when I said I wanted to feel peace."

"Well, there you go."

"But it was weird. It wasn't like a real voice, but almost like something that I thought. Oh, I don't know, it all sounds so weird."

"It's not weird at all. God's Spirit speaks softly; it almost sounds like our own thoughts, but we know that it's his because it is encouraging and convicting and always leads us to God and his word. And it typically comes out of nowhere." Sonya laughed softly at that last revelation.

"Oh."

"So, do you want God's peace?"

"Yes, ma'am."

"Well, if you would like, we can ask the Prince of Peace right now to give us his peace."

"Really?"

"Yes, we can. And Maddie, he not only wants to give you his peace, but he wants a relationship with you, too. Jesus loved you so much that he came to die for you. But his gift didn't end there, he resurrected on the third day and ascended into Heaven to become your High Priest."

"What is that?"

"Our High Priest is the one who fights for us, kind of like a defense attorney. When the enemy attempts to condemn a believer before the Father, Jesus stands at his right hand and says, 'That Sonya, she is mine. Her sins are forgiven.'"

"Sins?"

"Yes, the Bible says that all have sinned and fallen short of God's glory. Sin is anything that separates from God. God has condemned sin, but we stand condemned through our sin. The good news is that we are justified freely by his grace through the redemption Jesus gave at the Cross."

"Justified?"

"Yes, ma'am, justified means saved. The word says that it is by grace we have been saved, through faith- not from ourselves, but it is the gift of God. Think of it like you falling into a deep dark pit and a hand reaches down to pull you out."

Remembering the painting, she had an epiphany, "That's why she had so much peace."

"What's that?" Sonya asked.

"There was this painting with a girl on her knees, praying, I think. Anyway, a hand was reaching down. She had so much peace on her face. That is what I was talking about when I said I wanted to feel peace like that."

"Wow, it sounds like a powerful painting."

"Yeah."

Sonya placed her hand on Maddie's shoulder, "Do you know where that peace comes from?"

Looking up, she shook her head.

"According to God's word, when we lift our requests to God the peace that transcends all understanding will guard our heart and mind in Christ Jesus. God's peace is what surrounded that girl in your painting."

"So, I can lift my requests and feel his peace?"

"Yes, ma'am. And if you choose to follow him, he will walk with you and lead you all your days, even into eternity."

"Is that why we tell him we're available?"

"You've got it! Would you like to pray?"

"Yes, ma'am. But I don't know what to say."

"It's okay. I'll tell you what. I will pray first; I will ask him to hear our requests. Then, I will pray a prayer of invitation. You will receive his invitation by repeating after me. Do you understand?"

"I think so."

"What would you like to ask the Father?"

"Well, I guess for peace and to help my momma and protect my daddy. Oh, and my brother too."

"What are their names?"

"Jacque is my mom; my dad is David, and my brother is Mike. Oh, and can we pray for Matthew too?"

"Of course, let's pray. Rachel, would you like to join us?"

"Of course." The three grabbed hands and bowed their heads to pray.

Calm washed over her as Sonya prayed for her family. Listening to her words gave her hope that she wasn't alone in the world. Perhaps letting go wouldn't be so hard after all.

"Okay Maddie, this is the part that I want you to repeat after me."

> *"Father,*
>
> *Thank you for the sacrifice that Jesus paid on my behalf. Tonight, I choose to follow your Son, Jesus, and to receive him as my Lord and Savior. I know that I am a sinner, and Jesus chose to save me through his sacrifice, and I choose to say yes, I am available. I choose to follow Jesus all my days. Thank you, Jesus, for grace. Help me to grow my faith. In Jesus' Name, Amen."*

After praying, she was suddenly overwhelmed by a huge group hug. She had no idea who was around her, but she felt greatly loved in that moment. Suddenly, she noticed the lights were up and the room was empty except for those who prayed over her. *I wonder where everyone went.*

Rachel was talking a million miles a minute. Maddie could tell her friend was excited, but she didn't know what to say. She only knew that a rock had been removed and she hoped it stayed that way.

Walking to the parking lot, everyone was waiting in line for the food truck. Suddenly, she remembered Emma and their worship song. She ran back into the sanctuary as Emma was packing up.

"Hey, you!" Emma ran up to her friend to hug her. "Congrats! I am so happy for you!"

"I don't even know what happened."

"I'll tell you what happened, Jesus met you where you were and brought you close to him. Trust me, you'll never be the same!"

"How so?"

"Hmm, how to explain. Wait, do you know what it feels like to take a pop quiz and have all the answers?"

"Yeah."

"Having a relationship with Jesus is even better because I know the One who has all the answers. No matter what I face, I can go to him, lay it all at his feet, and receive his peace. But what makes it even greater is that I can walk in his light every day and experience his joy. The Light shines in the darkness and the darkness has not overcome it. This is who Jesus is, Maddie. This is what he has given us!"

"It sounds too good to be true."

"Oh, don't get me wrong, it's not easy. But I don't have to worry because God's got me! And Beautiful, he's got you too!"

"Now, how about that worship song?"

Maddie was walking on a cloud. She played the lyric for her friend and Emma lit up like a Christmas tree. Before they left, two verses were added to the chorus she and Ms. Lorna wrote.

On the ride home, Maddie, Rachel, and Emma were singing the new song in harmony. Kaitlyn was on her phone and Jade was quiet. The night was surreal, one she would never forget.

As Rachel's dad pulled into her driveway, the sight of an ambulance popped the bubble Maddie had been floating on. The car barely stopped before she jumped out and ran into the house.

"What happened?" She asked.

A paramedic was picking up her gear as Maddie ran in. "Sweetie, it's okay. We're going to take your mom to the hospital."

"Where is she?"

"She's in the ambulance and in good hands."

"Where is my brother?"

"Maddie, Maddie." Matthew ran into her arms with Mrs. Williams not far behind.

"Mrs. Williams, what happened?"

"Thank you, Leslie, we appreciate all your help. You go on and I will bring Maddie and Matthew to the hospital shortly."

"Wait, what do you mean? Mom? Where are you taking her?" Anxiety threatened her composure as she looked into Mrs. Williams's sympathetic eyes. "It's okay, Maddie. We will take you and your brother to the hospital."

Rachel and the girls rushed in to hug their friend as she sobbed. It was all too much. *What happened to the peace?*

As she cried, Mr. Tom began praying, followed by Rachel and Emma. Maddie's heart rate began to normalize as a concert of prayer arose above her and her brother. As they prayed, she lifted a prayer of her own: "God, please, please help my momma."

The car was quiet all the way to the hospital. Maddie had Rachel on one side and Matthew on the other, both holding her hands. Mrs. Williams was driving them as Rachel's dad took the other girls home. She was thankful to be surrounded by her friends, but if truth be told, she felt so broken.

What happened to her mom? Was she okay? A litany of questions rushed through her mind. Rachel squeezed her hand.

"Rach?"

"Yeah?"

"What was that prayer you prayed for your mom when she was in the hospital?"

"Oh…. God, please don't take my momma away, please heal her."

"God, please, please don't take my mom away, please heal her."

"Yes, Lord, amen."

The doors to the hospital opened as Maddie and Matthew walked up to the glass. Suddenly, Grandpa Jack grabbed them both and hugged them tight.

"Grandpa!" They cried out in unison.

"Hello to you. Fancy meeting you both here."

"Is Mom okay?"

"Your momma will be fine. We have the best care that money can buy for your momma so don't you worry, ya hear?"

"But what happened?"

"Let's come over here and sit."

Walking over to the couch in the ER, Maddie sat next to her grandpa while Matthew jumped in his lap. Grandpa Jack looked to Mr. Tom and Mrs. Williams and asked, "Can you give us a minute?"

"Of course, we'll be right over here."

"Maddie, Matthew, your momma is very sick right now."

"What do you mean, sick?" Feeling sick herself, Maddie remembered the bottle she had thrown away from her mom's room just that morning.

"Your momma misses your dad, and this has made her very sad. To make herself feel better, she took some pills and got sick. The doctor is working now to help her feel better."

"Wait, did she OD?" Maddie asked.

"What is OD?" Matthew asked innocently.

Grandpa Jack looked at her as he said quietly, "Your momma thought she would feel better, Maddie Girl, but she wasn't thinking in her right mind. But she is going to get better. I'll see to it, I promise."

Reeling, her thoughts began to run away with her. *My mom tried to kill herself.* She didn't understand. *Oh goodness, this was all my fault! If I had said something to someone if I hadn't gone to church. If I had BEEN THERE for Mom, this never would have happened!* Maddie covered her face with her hands as she cried softly. Grandpa Jack clinched her in his arms with quiet sobs of his own.

As the two quieted, Rachel came over and sat next to her friend. Grandpa Jack gestured, "OK?" as he picked up his cell phone and walked away.

She nodded but then cried anxiously into the shoulder of her friend.

"Oh, Rachel, it's all my fault,"

"What do you mean?"

As anxiety began to burn within her belly, Maddie wrung her hands like a dishcloth.

Rachel took her hand and said, "Hey, look at me. Now breathe. It's okay, it's going to be okay."

Covered in shame, she couldn't look at her friend. "Mom has been drinking for a while. She has been so worried about my dad. Grandpa Jack said that she took pills to feel better."

"Maddie, I am so sorry." Rachel hugged her friend tightly.

"I don't understand. Rach, do you think she tried to kill herself?"

Rachel's dad walked over and asked, "Is everything okay?"

Rachel shared what Maddie told her.

Bending down before them, Mr. Tom said, "Maddie, you did nothing wrong, do you hear me? Your mom is sad, but this is not your fault."

"But I should have said something to somebody."

"Maddie, people get sad. We cannot control the feelings or the actions of others. And often we do not see what is happening until it is too late, but that never makes it your fault.

What we need to do now is concentrate on helping your momma get better, right?"

Maddie nodded as she said, "Yes, Sir."

"Hey, a little birdie told me that you invited Jesus into your life tonight."

"Yeah."

"Well, why don't you pray for him to meet you here and bring his peace?"

"I prayed for him to help my mom tonight."

"Well, dear Girl, I would say he answered that prayer. What do you think?"

ISRAEL

"This is a day that will stand in the history books. The nations represented in this chamber have chosen to place world peace above personal gain. Bob, the world can thank one man for this feat- Lucien Baldur. Listen in as he gives his speech before the World Trade Organization."

> "Ladies and Gentlemen, today we have the honor to stand before the world to declare an end to world hunger. I have, in my hand, the plan to eliminate world hunger forever. As world changers, we have a responsibility to bring this to pass in our lifetime. If we do not, then people will die, children will die. And we cannot eliminate world hunger until we bring about world peace. But can we bring about peace without order? No, we cannot. Where there is no order, there can be no peace. We must first stand together to bring about order to all nations so that peace is realized. And in bringing peace, we will eliminate world hunger once and for all. Thank you."

"Well, Bob, it sounds like an impossible feat. Time will tell whether Lucien Baldur is the real deal."

A red alert went up for David as he heard the words, "Where there is no order, there can be no peace." Looking through the documents on the table, his eyes focused on one phrase: IF THERE IS NO ORDER THERE CAN BE NO PEACE. *Surely, this is a coincidence.*

Distracted by the buzz of his phone, he was relieved by the break from his frustrating thoughts.

CHAPTER 16

A New Normal

The waiting room was filled with people. In the corner, a woman was wringing her hands with worry. A child ran around a chair. An old woman was holding hands with her husband, who was snoring softly on her shoulder.

Maddie thought she had put her fear of the unknown behind her, but here it was once again staring her in the face. She remembered the first time she experienced anxiety. She was twelve. Seeing her Grandpa George in the hospital was gut-wrenching. He was always big and strong, but pneumonia came and took him quickly. While Grammy had her faith to keep her strong, Maddie felt lost in a world of uncertainty. Who would be next? Would God take her Grammy? The what-ifs filled her with fear and dread. When Matthew got sick, she thought she would lose it. Seeing the wires connected to her little brother like Grandpa was overwhelming, and she swore she would never step foot in a hospital ever again, yet here she was.

"I wonder what their story is." Rachel must have been reading Maddie's thoughts.

"Which one?"

"The woman over there looks especially worried. Do you think she has a child here or perhaps a husband?"

"I don't know. I guess it could be anything."

"Come on, let's go talk to her."

"Wait, Rach."

"It's okay, Maddie; God has given us one another for this very reason. Let's see if we can help her."

Her stomach was in knots. She didn't know if she could handle another sad story. But she trusted her friend and followed her anyway.

"Hi, ma'am. My name is Rachel, and this is Maddie. What's your name?"

"Hi, my name is Jessica."

"It's busy tonight, isn't it? We couldn't help but see you here by yourself. Is everything okay?"

"No, it's not okay."

"Is there anything we can pray for? I know sitting in a hospital can be hard. My mom was in the hospital and almost died. We found great comfort in others who prayed for us."

"That would be nice, thank you. My son is here for a drug overdose. We aren't sure he'll make it through the night." Looking through the glass, she continued, "My husband couldn't stay. Please pray for them both."

Suddenly, Maddie was overwhelmed with compassion for Jessica. She was here for the same reason! It suddenly seemed very important to sit with her. Following Rachel's lead, she sat down next to her and listened to her friend. As Rachel prayed, the anxiety melted away, and all she could think about was this son and his mom's prayer to see him healed and free from drug addiction.

"Amen." After praying, she and Rachel sat with their new friend and learned more about their family and what God was doing. Hearing how God was moving amid a stranger's addiction meant a lot to her. *Perhaps Mom will be okay,* she pondered.

"How were you able to do that?" Maddie asked her friend later.

"I follow God's prompting. I ask God to show me who he wants me to serve, and I obey. We're all called to serve."

"Grammy prays for waiters and waitresses at restaurants. I never considered that she was serving them."

"I love your Grammy. Yep, every prayer is an opportunity. Sonya says we're carriers of hope and to always be prepared to sprinkle hope to those in our path. Hey, remember your panic attack at the mall?"

"Yeah."

"You said that someone took you to an EMT who helped you, right?"

"Mm-hmm."

"Well, when we pray for someone, we're taking them to the Father. We're asking God to help them."

Pondering her friend's encouragement, Maddie asked, "Hey, your dad said that God answered my prayer about my mom. What do you think he meant by that?"

"Come on, let's go ask him." Rachel grabbed her hand to walk over to her dad.

"Hey, Dad, Maddie has a question for you." Rachel plopped down in the seat next to her dad as Maddie sat beside her.

Putting down his phone, Tom looked at Maddie and asked, "What can I do for you, young lady?"

"Mr. Tom, you said something earlier that I have a question about. You said God was answering my prayer for my mom. What did you mean by that?"

"Great question, Maddie. If I might ask, what did you pray?"

"For God to help her."

"And what were you hoping God would do to help her?"

Shrugging her shoulders, she said, "I hoped everything would go back to normal, like when Dad was home."

"When we pray for someone, we are asking God to meet them in their need. Do you think her need just started?"

Remembering the bottles, she answered, "No."

"I don't know the whole story, Maddie, but I expect your mom has been in pain for a long time. Her response to this pain was like a simmering pot boiling over. Normal lives often mask the feelings of pain and trauma that we harbor. But God wants to heal her, and so he used you to pray for healing, and now she is in a hospital- a place where she can get help, right?"

"I guess."

"Maddie, God often reveals before he heals. This is a moment of revelation for your mom that will help her find healing if she chooses to receive it. Keep praying for her; she is going to need a lot of God's strength in the days to come."

"I never thought about it like that."

Rachel grabbed her friend's hands, "Just like the EMT, Maddie. You brought your mom to the Father and now he will go to work to help her find healing. Perhaps he's creating a new normal for your family."

Grandpa Jack walked over as Maddie, Rachel, and Matthew slept, slumped over on each other's shoulders. Kneeling, he gently tapped them on the shoulders, "Time to go home."

"How's Momma?" Maddie asked sleepily.

"She's facing a long road of healing, but she will be okay. They're keeping her for a couple of days and then they'll move her to a place where she can get the help she needs. I'm going to stay with you both tonight and your Grammy will be here in the morning."

"Grammy is coming. YAY!" Matthew was suddenly wide awake. "Grammy is coming, Grammy is coming!"

"Jack, let us know if there is anything we can do." Tom clapped her grandpa on the back.

"Thank you, Tom. We need to get in touch with David to let him know what is going on. I understand you have his number?"

"Yes, I'll call him directly."

"Please tell him to call me. Here is my number. He can call me day or night."

Maddie was stuck in her thoughts on the ride home. Ruminating over every conversation of the last few days, she tried to pinpoint a time when she could have intervened. Mr. Tom's voice interrupted her thoughts, *This is not your fault*, but she sure did feel responsible. And if she were honest, she felt responsible for a lot of things—her mom, her brothers, the expectations of others. *I wish Dad were home*, she sighed.

Driving up to the dark house, she felt a heaviness in her chest. Turning to her brother, she noticed he had gone pale. "What's wrong, Matthew?" She asked.

Tears began to fall as he said softly, "I don't know if I can go in there."

Looking him in the eye, she agreed, "I know, little Brother; this is hard for me too. Hold my hand, and let's do this together, okay?"

"Okay."

Maddie had trouble going to sleep. Deciding to journal for a while, she turned on her light and grabbed her journal and pen.

September 7
Jesus,

I said yes to you tonight. I felt so happy when everyone prayed over me. But if I'm honest, I don't feel so happy right now. I don't understand why my dad left, and my mom doesn't want to live. Mr. Tom said that you reveal before you heal. Can you heal my momma? Can you heal our family? Truly? I want to believe just like the girl in the painting, but I need your help. Please help us. Oh, and if you could, please help Jessica and her son, too.
Maddie

ISRAEL

"David, this is Tom."

"Hi Tom, it's late there, isn't it? Is everything okay with Olivia and the girls?"

"My family is fine, Dave, but there has been a situation. Jacque is in the hospital. Jack asked me to call you. He needs to speak with you."

After speaking with Tom and Jack, David hung up and closed his eyes. First, the mall, and now this. He and his team were on the precipice of answers, but his family needed him now. For the second time in his career, he felt the need to lay everything down. Holding his head in his hands, he felt so conflicted. He made a promise to his wife that he would protect her, their family, and their country, but he didn't know how to protect her from herself. He felt powerless.

Dialing the familiar number in Wild Rock, Tennessee, he heard his mom's sleepy voice, "Hello?"

"Momma." His voice broke.

"Oh, David." After a moment of quiet, "I'm so sorry, Son."

"What do I do? For the first time in my life, I feel helpless."

"The only thing ya can do, my boy. Give 'er to the Almighty."

"I don't know how soon I can leave here."

"Now David Bennett, never you mind, we're family. Lisa and I are leavin' in the mornin'. We'll take care of everythin'."

"Thank you, Momma."

"I love you, Son. And David?"

"Yes, ma'am."

"God loves you too."

As he laid the phone on the table, he broke down. It had been a long time since he had prayed. But if there was ever a time for divine intervention, it was now. Years ago, his mom had taught him to lay his hands out and his burdens down. Getting on his knees, he prayed.

Connecting to the secure uplink, he heard the voice of Admiral Rick Osborne, "David, the FBI was very interested in your team's findings. They have uncovered an underground organization that has kept a very low profile until recently."

"Who are they?"

"An organization called PeaceKeepers. They have factions around the world with a large media following. They recruit young men and women who are disconnected from their families- runaways, children from broken homes, and foster children. They appear to be grooming these young adults with nonconformist ideologies, leading them into committing local terroristic crimes."

"Local?"

"Yes, the intent seems to lean toward imploding the local government from within. Crimes of chaos that create division inside of communities."

"Can you pinpoint a ringleader?"

"Not yet, the organization is very well formed, but as I mentioned, in factions. We are still working on figuring out who is providing the financial backing."

"Rick, who is Lucien Baldur?"

"Lucien Baldur, why do you ask?"

"One of the things he said in his speech to the WTO was similar to this message we found in the JONAH communications: IF THERE IS NO ORDER THERE CAN BE NO PEACE."

"As far as I know, Lucien Baldur is a well-respected Israeli businessman who has made many financial contributions to the medical community worldwide. But I hear the concern in your voice. Would you like me to check him out?"

"I think it would be a good idea, yes. But please keep it confidential. I don't know how connected he is here. On another note, Rick, remember the mall fire in Georgia?"

"Yes."

"I mentioned my family was there."

"Yes, I remember."

"My wife is in the hospital."

"What happened?"

"After the fire, she fell into depression and is being sent to a mental health facility. Rick, as soon as this mission wraps up, I am going home."

"Of course, David. Would you like me to re-assign you?"

"No, we are close to resolution. After I receive Mordecai Aronoff's report, I will follow up with Deputy Reese and Ambassador Cohen and then go from there."

"Of course. We are here for you, Son."

"Thank you."

CHAPTER 17

Releasing the Burden

Maddie awoke to the sound of her brother shouting in excitement. Running downstairs to investigate, her heart swelled with joy at the sight of her brother embraced in Grammy's arms. Tears came out of nowhere when she joined in the hug.

"Well now, you'd a thought you'ns ain't seen me in a coon's age." Grammy sat down to catch her breath.

"Grammy, I didn't think you'd ever get here!" Matthew was jumping up and down.

"Yer seein' me, ain't ya?" She laughed at her grandson's excitement.

Catching Maddie's eye, Grammy asked, "How're ya doin', Girl?"

Not sure how to answer the question, she placed her head on Grammy's shoulder.

"Good morning, Grace. Thank you for coming so quickly." Grandpa Jack buttoned the sleeve around his wrist as he walked into the kitchen. "Would you like a cup of coffee?"

"Why mornin', Jack. I'd do anythin' for these two young'uns. And no, thank ya fer the offer, though. How's our girl doin' this mornin'?"

Looking at Maddie and Matthew, Jack replied, "Do you mind if we take this in the den?"

"A'course." Lifting Maddie's chin, Grammy walked out of the kitchen.

"Maddie, why do adults do that?"

"I don't know. I guess they think we can't handle the truth."

Matthew plopped down on the stool with a grimace on his face.

Opening the refrigerator door, Maddie asked, "Hey, want some breakfast? We still have school today."

"Ugh. Do we have to? I'm feelin' puny, Mads," in his best Grammy imitation.

"It'll be good for us both, Brother. And don't call me that! So, what'll it be? Fruity Pebbles or Pop-Tarts?"

"Strawberry with frosting?"

"You bet."

"Pop-Tarts, Pop-Tarts!"

"You've got it."

Returning to the kitchen with Grammy in tow, Grandpa Jack said, "Eat your breakfast, then grab your bookbags, kids. I'll take you to school." Grandpa Jack's command left a somber feel in the air.

With a half-hearted smile, Maddie tousled her brother's hair and mouthed, "It'll be okay."

"Hey, I didn't expect you to be here today." Surprised by Rachel's light tug on her shoulder, Maddie turned to look at her friend. "How are you doing? How's your mom?"

If she were honest, she would tell her friend that she was numb, but she wasn't in the mood to be vulnerable now. "I'm all right. Grandpa said she's stable, whatever that means."

"Sounds like she's doing better?"

"Yeah, but he wouldn't give us any details. He and Grammy kept the convo to themselves."

"Oh, Grammy is here? Yay! I can't wait to see her."

"Madddddddddie!" Overwhelmed by the love, her spirit began to lift as her friends ran up to greet them.

Emma grabbed her hand as she exclaimed, "Maddie, you

accepted Jesus last night! I'm so excited for you!"

"Wow, I did, didn't I?" She had almost forgotten the excitement of the night before her world came crashing down.

Her friend's excitement calmed into her regular quiet demeanor as she said, "He is with you right now. Do you know this?"

"Yeah, I'm just a little confused right now."

"If you need to talk, I'm here." Wiping away a tear on her friend's face, she repeated, "She'll be okay; Jesus has her in his hand. Right, Girls?"

"Right!"

As she and Rachel walked into math class, Maddie suddenly became self-conscious when it seemed that everyone's eyes were on her. Rachel grabbed her hand and squeezed. "It's okay," she mouthed.

"Good morning, Maddie, and Rachel, how are you ladies this morning?"

"Oh, we're finer 'n frog hair," Rachel replied, winking at her friend.

Maddie turned red when giggles echoed from the back of the classroom.

"And what exactly is a frog hair, Ms. Monroe?"

"Oh, come on, Ms. Davis, don't you golf?"

"That would be no."

"Really? You've never picked up a golf club?" Rachel pretended to swing a golf club as their teacher, Ms. Davis, gave an exasperated look.

She had to giggle as her friend sat in her chair with a big smile. Rachel always knew how to break the tension.

"All right, settle down, everyone. Let's get to it, shall we?"

As the teacher wrote out the word problem on the board, Maddie found herself looking out the window.

"Maddie, tell us how far you can travel?"

"Hm, what? Travel? Travel where?"

"Back to earth, Ms. Bennett. Read the problem on the board and tell the class how far you can travel with twelve dollars?"

Wiping her sweaty palms on her pants leg, her stomach responded to the teacher's ask as she pondered the jumbled words: *A cab ride costs $3.25 for the first half-mile and $0.70 for each mile after the first half-mile. How far can someone travel for $12?*

"Um." Maddie felt like she was going to throw up as everyone turned to her.

"Thirteen miles," Rachel whispered from behind.

"Thirteen miles?" She answered nervously.

"That's right, thank you, Ms. Monroe."

Maddie turned red as she looked down at her math book. *I guess it's time to pay attention.*

As class ended, Maddie and Rachel stood up and walked toward the front.

"Maddie, can I speak to you for a moment?" Ms. Davis asked.

"You've got this, Champ. I'll be waiting for you outside." Rachel pumped the air with her arm as she walked away.

With sweaty palms, she awaited Ms. Davis' rebuke.

"Ms. Bennett, you were a bit distracted today. Is everything okay?"

"Yes, ma'am, just stuff going on at home."

"Anything I can help with?"

"No, ma'am. It's all under control now." She mimicked her Grandpa Jack while wondering if his words were true.

"Well, if you need anything, let me know, okay? You don't have to bear heavy burdens alone."

Pausing for a moment, she almost spilled everything but caught herself as Ms. Davis turned her attention to her desk.

"Thank you, I will remember."

"Have a good day, Maddie."

"Yes, ma'am, you, too." Walking out of the classroom, she breathed a sigh of relief as she met her friend.

"Good?" Rachel asked.

Smiling, she said, "Yup, righter n' rain."

Laughing, they hooked arms to walk down the hallway.

Determined to hurry home after stepping off the bus, Maddie felt a tap on her shoulder.

"Hey, Maddie?"

Turning around, she was surprised to be face to face with Ashley, the neighborhood bully. Frozen, she didn't know what to do. She wanted to run but was stuck in place for some reason.

"Hi, I uh, I'm so sorry about your mom, and I'm praying for you and your family."

Looking at her cautiously, she was overcome with emotion, unsure how to respond. "Thank you, Ashley."

"If there is anything we can do, let me know, K?"

"Okay, I will."

Confused, she made her way to her house. Ashley had not talked to her in the two years since she terrorized her. *What changed?* She thought to herself.

Maddie found herself smiling as she looked up the sidewalk and saw her Gram. Suddenly, urgency carried her up the steps as she ran up and slung her bookbag onto the porch and sat down.

"Well, hello, sweet Girl. And how was your day?"

"Long. Oh, but I got a B on my Language Arts test!"

"Well, I'll be. I'm plumb tickled to hear that! And ya know what? I'm prouda your hard work. Ya know it's not about the grade but about the effort, right?"

"Well, if I want to go to college..."

Grammy interrupted, "College schmollege, I ain't here to disrespect yer parents, none, but get outta yer head that ya gotta have college to succeed, ya hear me? Find what God has called ya to and go after that. If'n he calls ya to college, then he'll give ya the money, strength, and the grades to go. Got it?"

"Yes, ma'am."

Getting up from her chair, Grammy said, "Well I ain't had no sweetenin' today. I'd shore like some pie and some sweet milk."

"I'm sorry, Grammy, but I don't think we have any."

"Well now, don't ya worry none. I made an apple pie just

this mornin'. Do ya got some ice cream?"

"I think so, yay! But are you sure? Mom never lets us have dessert before dinner."

"Dahlin', Grammy's here now. Supper can always wait."

Matthew chose a healthy helping of chicken strips, green beans, and macaroni and cheese for supper.

"So, Matthew, how was your day?"

With a mouth full of mac and cheese, he answered, "Pretty rotten."

"Really now, do tell- after ya swaller."

"This boy won't leave me alone. How do you say it? He's as crooked as a dog's ugly leg."

Grammy laughed, "A dog's hind leg, do ya say?"

"Oh yeah. What does that mean again?"

"When somebody's crooked as a dog's hind leg, it means he's crooked as a jay bird- a thief."

"Yeah, that. He loves to take my ice cream money."

"Well now, that's a might unfortunate. And what do ya do when he takes yer money?"

"I get mad."

"I reckon I'd be mad too. And what do ya do after that?"

He shrugged, "Walk away, I guess."

"Have ya tried talking to the teacher?"

"Yeah, she doesn't care."

With a mouth full of green beans, Matthew asked, "Grammy?"

"Now I love to hear my name come from your mouth, Boy, but I'm a bit grieved to see your food. Swaller it down and continue. You have permission to wait until you've finished chewin' a'fore callin' my name, hear?"

Matthew chewed like he was eating a steak. After swallowing, he asked, "What would Jesus do?"

"Well, his word says if someone slaps ya on the right cheek, turn to them the other. And if someone wants to sue ya and take yer shirt, hand over yer coat as well."

"Whoa, whoa, whoa, why would he say that? I'd be naked!"

Grammy chuckled, "The idea is that God will provide fer all yer needs, and by givin' what ya have away you have a chance to show 'em the love of Christ."

Putting his fork down in protest and crossing his arms, he said, "That sounds pretty weird to me, Grammy."

"So, have ya forgiven the boy?"

"Forgive? Naw, don't know how to do that."

"Hmm, Jesus said we forgive seventy times seven. It's a command to do so."

"But if we forgive, won't he just do it again?"

"I reckon he might, but God says that vengeance is his, so we let him mete out justice as he sees fit. We forgive so resentment don't build up in our hearts. Resentment is a cancer, jes' so ya know-a cancer that destroys. Our Father doesn't want our heart to be destroyed, instead, he wants us to release our burdens to him, so our heart is free to love. Ya see?"

"I guess."

"Hey, Grammy." Maddie piped in.

"Yes, ma'am."

"I had a weird encounter today. There's a girl who bullied me all of seventh grade. She stopped me today and said she was praying for me. Now that was weird."

"Why now, sounds ta me like the Holy Spirit's been workin' on her heart."

"I guess."

"Have ya forgiven her?"

"No, ma'am. I can't forget what she did to me."

"Oh, sweet Girl, forgivin' ain't forgettin'. Forgivin' is givin' her and what she did to the Lord and sayin' I'm not gonna be bitter about it. Ya both seem to need some forgiveness tonight. Would you'ns like to pray for it?"

Matthew nodded while his sister agreed silently.

"All right then, give me your hands."

As they clasped hands, Maddie and Matthew bowed their

heads.

"Now Father, we come to ya as our provider, our comforter, and our redeemer. We thank ya, Lord, fer the forgiveness Jesus gave us at the Cross. Yer word says that we must forgive as we are forgiven, and so we ask ya, Lord, to give us the strength to forgive.

"Now, Maddie, put yer hands out and lay the girl in yer hand. Give 'er to the Lord and ask him to give ya his forgiveness."

As Maddie prayed for Ashley a weight lifted from her shoulders. Almost as if all she could remember were the words spoken over her at the bus stop.

"Alrighty, then, Matthew, it's your turn. Put your hands out and lay the boy in your hand. Give 'em to the Lord and ask him to give ya his forgiveness to pass on."

"But I can't see him; how can I put him in my hand?"

"Boy, do ya recollect the ladybug ya had in your hand this summer?"

"Yes, ma'am."

"Pretend he's in your hand and see it as your friend."

"Oh, he's not my friend."

"Now Boy, it ain't never too late ta mend. Jes' ask yer Lord to help ya."

"All right." Matthew clasped his hands and his eyes tightly and prayed, "Father, help me to forgive Justin. Maybe he can be my friend? Amen."

"Why now, that's a right, obedient prayer. Amen."

"Amen, well, if it isn't the wise and beautiful Grammy?" All heads turned as Mike walked into the room with a friend.

ISRAEL

"Mordy, it's good to see you again, Friend." David lifted his seltzer water as his friend took a seat in the booth next to him. The atmosphere in the Israeli bar on Hillel Street was noisy and Americanized, yet culturally rich at the same time. The bartenders did a fantastic job of maintaining the attention of the tourists. This would be a good place to disappear for a few hours of intense conversation.

"Shalom, David. How is your family?"

"Not good, I'm afraid. Jacque is in the hospital."

"Hashem Yerachem! May God have mercy on your family, my friend. Is she okay?"

"She had a breakdown of sorts and is suffering from alcohol poisoning and a pill overdose. The doctor thinks she is suicidal, so they are keeping her for evaluation."

"I am so very sorry, my friend. Is there anything I can do?"

"Well, as my mom would say, I guess you can pray."

"Of course, of course. Yeshua is with you, my friend; you and your wife are not alone."

"Thank you. I know I can count on you. Mordy, I chose this place because of its isolation. Are you comfortable here?"

"I was going to ask if we might take a walk?"

"Certainly, let me pay the bill for our drinks and we can go."

A sense of foreboding stole over David as he walked through the throngs of people, checking his surroundings suspiciously. As he paid the bill, he glanced to the end of the bar and saw someone sitting alone. The man seemed very interested in the table where he and Mordecai were sitting. Nodding to the bartender, he pointed to the cash on the bar and proceeded to meet up with his friend.

As he walked back to the table, the man at the end of the bar stood up. David bent down, pretending to tie his shoe. Noticing the tattoo on the man's ankle, he knew it was time to leave.

"Mordy, don't look behind me, but we are being followed. Keep the conversation casual."

David and Mordecai walked out of the bar and down Hillel Street. Their gait increased as they turned onto King David Street. The man seemed intent on keeping pace with them as they walked swiftly into Rubin Square. Disappearing into the crowd celebrating the yearly Arts festival in the artists' colony of Hutzot Hayotzer, the two hid behind a booth selling pottery.

"I think we lost him. Come with me." Mordecai hailed a taxi. Quietly sharing an address with the driver, he motioned for David to be quiet for the ride.

Peering at the crowds of people, he missed his family. Experience had long since numbed him to danger, but the possibility of his family being in danger only increased his urgency to finish the mission.

"Shalom."

"Shalom to you, my good man. Here you go." Mordecai paid the driver and led David up the walk.

"Did you actually pay him seven hundred shekels?"

"It's a drop in the bucket, my good man. More to keep him from telling anyone about his American fare. Nothing to worry over; you are worth two hundred US dollars."

Stepping out of the taxi, David marveled at his friend's home. The traditional stone cladding combined with large Kurkar stone-adorned walls and arches looked straight out of an Italian magazine. "Welcome to my humble home. David, this is my safe place, the place where I release my burdens to my Lord and enjoy the comfort of friends and family. You are welcome here."

He followed Mordecai to the door and watched as his friend touched the doorpost and kissed his fingers before opening the door. He had never been to his friend's home and was interested to meet his family and perhaps release a few burdens of his own.

CHAPTER 18

All in a Day's Work

Mike looked terrible. Weeks had passed since Maddie last saw him. Although, judging by his dark circles and dirty hair, it might as well have been months.

"Hey guys, this is my friend, Mac. Mac, this is my family." Immediately distracted by the food on the counter, he picked up a piece of chicken and said, "Wow, that chicken looks great, do you have any more?"

"Well now, you'ns look like ya been chewed up and spit out. Mike you, and your friend here can go get warshed up first, then I'll fetch ya both a plate."

Mike grudgingly ran up the stairs with his friend not far behind.

Maddie and Matthew looked at each other and giggled as they listened to Grammy, "That boy ain't learned nothin', eh law. Ya can lead a horse to water, but ya can't make him drink."

"Can I help you, Grammy?" Maddie asked.

"Naw Girl, jes' finish yer supper. I got this."

"Mike, guess what?" Matthew asked as his brother returned to the table.

"What's that, Champ?"

"Caleb and I built a fort! Wanna check it out?"

Tousling his brother's hair, Mike said, "I'm not going to be here very long. How about next time?"

Disappointed, Matthew groaned, "I guess."

"Where have you been, Mike? We haven't seen you in weeks." Maddie was angry that Mike only seemed to come around when he needed something.

"Not your business, little Sis. We've talked about this before."

"Boy, don't ya be talkin' to yer sister like that! I reckon you've been busy, else ya wouldn't be here lookin' as if ya hadn't eaten in a coon's age, but that ain't no reason to be ugly to yer kin."

"Yes, ma'am."

"This is good, Mrs. Bennett." Mac knew when to change the conversation.

"Mike, Mom is in the hospital," Maddie spoke quietly.

Mike's face turned white as he laid his fork down. "What happened?"

She had no idea where the courage came from, but she felt compelled to tell her brother the whole truth. "Mom has been drinking. I didn't know how much, but apparently so much that she tried to kill her..." She may have been filled with courage, but for that moment, she didn't know how to make the tears stop.

"Oh, Maddie Ruth." Grammy got up and put her arms around her granddaughter.

The quiet sobs cut through the room like a knife. Matthew put his chin on his arms as Mike and Mac sat quietly. Nobody knew what to say.

After a few moments of silence, Mike whispered, "It's not your fault." He then jumped up and ran up the stairs, slamming the door behind him.

After what seemed an eternity, Matthew broke the silence with, "Hey Mac, do ya know how to play Dominoes?"

Matthew was the resident king of Dominoes in the Bennett household and had no problem telling everyone. With a shrug, Mac said, "Nope." So, Matthew took it upon himself to teach him.

"Now, Mac, you gotta have a stragety. This is very important." Maddie laughed as her brother mispronounced 'strategy' with a serious look on his face. "You must play your doubles early. This way, you'll have more moves available later. Do you understand?"

As Matthew tutored Mac, Maddie kept an eye on the doorway for her older brother's return. She had to admit, Matthew's comical way of leading the table helped her anxiety to lessen; and watching Grammy, who had no idea what she was doing, led her to laugh more than she had in a hot minute.

Matthew was the master at keeping everyone on task, which helped his sister keep her mind from worry.

After a while, Mike walked down the stairs. It was obvious that he had been crying. For the first time, Maddie was sad for him. What was it that kept him away from the family? Her fifteen-year-old mind couldn't work it out. She wished her dad was here to make everything right again.

"Can I play?" Mike humbly asked.

"Of course," Matthew answered excitedly. "Here, sit next to me and Mac." Matthew scooched over to give his brother room and proceeded to pass out a new set of dominoes to everyone at the table.

A short two hours later, Maddie was jarred by a raucous roar of laughter at the end of the table. With a yawn, she stretched and shook her head as her brothers argued over who won. She couldn't help but smile. Perhaps everything would be alright.

Early Saturday morning, Maddie walked downstairs and grabbed a banana and a jacket. She needed to clear her head.

While she'd hoped to catch up with her Fam, they were all busy. Rachel had her PSAT test, Jade and her mom were at some homeless place, Emma was helping her mom and Kaitlyn was visiting family. So, Maddie was left to her thoughts.

It was a little cloudy, but otherwise, it seemed to be a great day for a bike ride, so she went into the garage to grab her bike. "Oh no," she cried. Bending down, she looked disappointedly at the flat tire on her bike. She attempted to add air to her tire but to no avail.

"WHY?!?" The tears she fought so hard to keep at bay threatened to spill over. Nothing seemed to be going her way lately, and she was so frustrated!

As she sat on the floor discouraged, she noticed her dad's bike sitting against the wall. After wiping her face, she stood up and walked over to inspect the tires.

The news mentioned the possibility of rain, so she put on her jacket and jumped on the bike. Dad was taller than she, so it took a moment for her to adjust to the height and the crossbar.

Looking both ways at the end of the driveway, she pulled out and rode toward the back of the neighborhood. She knew the perfect spot to find the quiet she needed.

After the girls met Kaitlyn last year, Jade took them to a secret place. It was a place of escape where they could find happiness when they were sad. Maddie desperately needed that today.

As she neared the curb behind Charlie's Tree, she jumped off and walked the bike to a clearing in the trees. Thankfully, she found what she was looking for as she climbed back on the bike. She quickly realized her mistake when her backside experienced the discomfort of a banana seat ill-suited to absorb the jolts of rocks and pits in the ground. UGH! She grunted as she decided to walk the bike instead.

Her demeanor changed as soon as the invigorating fresh air caressed her face. The shade inside the shelter of trees created the perfect environment for the explosion of red, brown, and gold colors interspersed among the green. Maddie enjoyed the change in color this time of year. As her eyes beheld the beauty, her ears delighted in the sounds of birds singing, and leaves crunching. The whole palette brought peace to her wavering heart as it found its rhythm in the magical shelter. Breathing in deeply, she smiled as the dark and threatening thoughts she had pondered dissipated with the clouds.

Suddenly, the sun burst into her oasis like a candle as she made her way around a bend. Stopping for a moment, she bent down to pick up a few leaves to take home with her. Pulling the warm banana from her pocket, she peeled it and took a bite. After a few moments, she pulled her journal from the other pocket and began to draw the tree before her. Relief filled her as she realized that peace could be found in quiet places.

"Father, I thank you for giving me peace." The song she and Emma wrote bubbled up and out as she wrote a prayer of thanks in her journal. This was exactly what she needed.

An hour later, she noticed the leaves making quite a racket as the wind picked up. A sound from behind startled her as she rose. Looking toward the opening, she craned her neck to find the source but couldn't make anything out. Her heart began to race as she suddenly realized she was all alone and without her phone.

As she stood and turned to leave, she couldn't believe her eyes! The bird from Wild Rock was right next to her, perched on a tree. Fear dissipated as she decided that was the sound that she heard. Cocking her head to the side, she was surprised as the bird did the same. Cocking her head to the other side, the bird mimicked her, singing its song as it flew away. In awe over the wonder of the moment, she jumped back on her bike and made her way out of the forest.

She didn't like the look of the sky. Menacing clouds replaced the bright sunlight that had teased her in the oasis. Little drops soon turned into big plops as she placed the hood of her jacket on her head. To make it home before the skies opened, she picked up the pace. She had wanted to ride around the neighborhood a bit more but decided maybe it wasn't the best idea. In the nick of time, she rode up the driveway as the skies opened and poured out the promised rain. Thankful for her raincoat, she hunched inside the safety of her hood, jumped off the bike, and opened the garage door.

"How's my Maddie Ruth?" Grammy asked as she brushed her wet hair.

"I'm okay. It was nice to have Mike back. And you, of course. Thank you for coming to stay with us."

"Why a'course, Love. I would'na do anything different. Whatcha feelin'?"

"I'm sad. I wish I could tell Mom how sorry I am."

"Now whatcha got to feel sorry 'bout?"

"I wish I would've asked her how she was doing. She was hurting, right?"

"Sweet Girl, I 'spect she's been hurtin' a long while. But ya know, this was not and is not your fault, right?"

"I guess."

"Not, I guess, it was not your fault. Now I wanna hear you say it."

"It was not my fault," Maddie replied with uncertainty.

"It's okay to feel sad, Love. When ya talk to yer momma you can tell her so. But ya cain't take responsibility fer her actions. We all make our own choices, and this was hers. We, as her family, well, we love her through it. When she comes home, she'll need yer love, listenin' ear, and yer support. Do ya hear me?"

"Yes, ma'am."

"So, whatcha wanna tell the Lord tonight?"

"Grammy, if I'm honest, I think I've prayed too much."

"What? Too much? Never! Almighty God is with us and fer us all day, ever' day, Maddie Ruth. Ya can never pray too much."

"I've just asked for so much, and there are so many people who need way more than I do."

In a stern yet quiet voice, Grammy answered, "Now, ya listen to me, Girl. Our God tells us to seek him first, and then he tells us ta ask. Ya gotta know this is all in a day's work fer the Lord. He ain't never too busy for you'ns, and he can handle ever'body's prayers all over the world. It's who he is. Now, what do ya gotta say to the Almighty?"

"Well, I guess that he'll heal Mom and that he'll give us strength."

"That's a mighty strong prayer, Maddie Ruth. Let's lift it up."

ISRAEL

"Papa, Papa!" A set of identical twins ran to meet Mordecai and David at the entrance to Mordecai's home.

"Benjamin, Elijah, meet my friend David. David, these are my boys."

He bent down and looked into the bluest eyes he had ever seen. "Well, hello, and how old are you?"

"Seven," the boys replied in unison. "Do you work with Papa?" one of them asked.

David stood up to ask his friend how he should respond.

Mordecai chuckled as he placed his hand on David's shoulder, "I understand your struggle, my friend. I also find it difficult to tell them apart."

"Benjamin, your dad and I do work together sometimes."

Elijah piped in, "Do you drive the boat?"

David laughed and looked at Mordy, "Boat? They have no idea, do they?"

"And they should not.

"Boys, go find your Imma. Mr. David and I have important business to discuss. I will come to find you and tuck you in shortly."

"Yes, Papa. Bye, Mr. David!"

"They are not much younger than my Matthew. We will have to introduce them one day."

"I would like this, yes."

Closing the door to his study, Mordecai motioned for him to sit. "Would you like a drink?"

"Water would be great, thank you."

Mordy reached into a personal cooler to grab two bottles and gave one to his friend. Sitting in the chair opposite David, he sighed.

"Well, this can't be good," David responded with a concerned laugh.

"I do not know how to say this, but have you ever heard the prophecies of the End of the Age?"

"Hmm, you aren't about to tell me the world is falling, are you, Mordy?"

"In 1948, emerging from the horrors of the holocaust, Israel declared independence, claiming the legitimacy of the promised land given to her by Adonai. In 1967, a six-day war once again forced Israel to fight for her survival, and against all odds, she prevailed over the armies of her neighbors- Egypt, Syria, Jordan, and Iraq. Do you recall the casus belli that justified war?"

"I am certain you will tell me," David ribbed his friend.

Not taking the bait, Mordy replied, "Egypt closed the Straits of Tiran to Israeli shipping, cutting off her only route to Asia and Iran, which was her main supplier of oil."

"Hmm, interesting tactic."

"Indeed. We won our independence once and for all. This led to the beginning of an awakening of my people. What you may not know is that a moment in time called the 'fullness of the Gentiles' has been prophesied. According to prophecy, this moment ushers in a national awakening of my people where blindness will cease, and Yeshua will be recognized as our Messiah. The Deliverer, Yeshua, will then come out of Zion and turn away ungodliness from Jacob. But before Yeshua returns, we are told of a global tribulation that will take place in which an antichrist will rise into power."

He smirked, "And how does this have anything to do with our current situation?"

"David, do you not see the culmination of chaos in the world? Perhaps the prophecies are being fulfilled in our hearing. We cannot overlook or ignore what is happening all around us."

"What about these prophecies brings you to this conclusion?"

"I am not saying the prophecies are being fulfilled. Perhaps they are, or perhaps not." Mordecai leaned forward. "Yeshua said that not even he knew the day. What is certain, based on scripture, is Satan will assert his wrath over Adonai's people by raising up an antichrist who will substitute himself in Christ's place. Then, Adonai will assert his wrath over Satan, sin, and death. Perhaps Adonai allowed moments in time when mankind has experienced a dress rehearsal of sorts to see how Adonai's people would respond. Nero Caesar, Adolph Hitler, and Napoleon, among others.

"If this is so, how many more reprieves can we expect? A sign of the times is that the love of most will grow cold. Are we not witnessing this in our generation? I am only saying that all signs point to prophecy. Israel was restored and is surrounded by conflict. Global antisemitism is rampant. The Jewish people are returning to the land of Israel. If the Gospel hasn't been proclaimed to the whole world, it soon will be. And as I mentioned before, the Jewish people are recovering from their blindness. Thousands of people are awakening to Yeshua. All just as Adonai promised. The signs are right in front of us, David, and Adonai desires that we be wise as the men of Issachar, who understood the times."

"Okay, let's say I buy your theory. Whom might this antichrist be?"

"Well, curious, is it not that Lucien Baldur enters the world's stage at the WTO Conference?"

"I wanted to ask. What do you know about him?"

"He is a very tactical man. He came by his money, honestly, David. He is suave and very well respected, a gentleman to the core."

"Not exactly your world domination kind of guy."

Mordy looked his friend in the eye and gestured toward his own, "It's his eyes. There is no love in them. When he smiles, it's almost sinister, yes?

"David, these messages you have shared with me are evil. It's no coincidence that Lucien Baldur speaks to the world as these messages are being transmitted. Much tactical planning has gone into what appears on paper to be an attack of global proportions. And Lucien Baldur's no order, no peace- well, this certainly sounds like a call an antichrist would make, no?"

"So, is it your theory that Lucien Baldur, a well-respected entrepreneur and philanthropist, is somehow involved with these messages and perhaps some sort of antichrist?" He shook his head, not quite believing what he was hearing.

"I am saying, my friend, to read between the lines. These messages are tactical—very well planned. And didn't you say they weren't encrypted? Do you not find it curious that these were released before Baldur's speech? It is almost as if he wanted them to be found."

"Do you think this is all a ruse?"

"Perhaps."

"What exactly did you find in these messages? Is there a pattern I can give to the FBI?"

"Actually, yes, there is." Mordecai laid out the pages before them.

Looking at the lines with circles covering each page, David looked at his friend. "What am I looking at?"

"Maps."

"Maps?"

"Yes, maps of prime locations with GPS coordinates and instructions to build what looks to be what you would call a commune. The ports appear to be a diversion. Within each set of coordinates, instructions on building what appear to be communities. Do you see? Every sentence includes an instruction."

> *Bagman esahcrup ytreporp detacol create ta a blockade at mraf the port of uoy Savannah close to lliw dnif ship ta 32.091566 x -83.674090. yap renwo I will be waiting hsac.*

"If you don't have a keen eye, you would see, 'Bagman create a blockade at the port of Savannah close to 32.0915566 x -83.674090. I will be waiting.' But look between the lines, and you will see 'Bagman, purchase property located at farm you will find at 32.091566 x -83.74090. Pay owner cash.'"

"Have you identified these GPS coordinates?"

"This one is in a town called Baldersville?"

"Baldersville, Georgia? Hmm, that looks right. Baldersville is approximately three hours from Savannah. What is the indication this is for a commune?"

"Further down, you will find instructions on building structures, planting farms, setting up leadership, and even inviting community members."

"Rick shared with me an underground organization called the PeaceKeepers. They recruit young men and women and groom them into committing local crimes. Do you recall seeing this name within the messages?"

"Not this name, no. However," Mordy pulled out the drawing from Joe on David's team, "do you know what this is?"

"Yes, it is the Nazi SS Bolt."

"That is correct. We have before us maps with instructions on building camps. We have images like the Nazi SS Bolt, which stood for double victory by the German SS. And now we have a philanthropist calling for global peace and order. Does any of this sound familiar?"

"Adolph Hitler comes to mind."

"Yes, perhaps Hitler served as a dress rehearsal for the real thing? If Lucien Baldur is the antichrist, prophecy tells us that he will set himself up in Adonai's temple, proclaiming himself to be Adonai. If these PeaceKeepers are connected, they might be his followers."

"I have no proof that Lucien Baldur is setting up communes all over the world. And even if I did, it's not against the law to build communities."

"If Mr. Baldur is the antichrist, he will trick the whole world, my friend. He won't hide; his evil will be in front of all. And if I had to guess, all under the guise of law and order. The question is, what will he do to force the world into law and order?"

"The question is, will anyone even believe us? I will work with the FBI to see if I can find a connection between Lucien Baldur and the PeaceKeepers. Then I will go undercover to figure out what Mr. Baldur is truly up to. Well, as you say, it's all in a day's work, right?"

"May the Lord bless you and keep you, my friend."

Chapter 19

Homecoming

Twinkling lights distracted Maddie from her brooding. Taking a break from her journal to enjoy the lights on the Christmas tree, she pondered the last three months.

After her mom went into the hospital, she followed Mike's advice to stay in tune with what was going on in the world. The news wasn't good. Every night, a new shooting, fire, or earthquake. Whole cities were burning. Whales were washing up on Atlantic shores. Bees were swarming major cities. A friend's family had been broken apart when her dad was called up to the National Guard- twice. Since school had started in August, two of her classmates were missing. Remembering the overheard conversation over the summer, she couldn't forget Pastor Ron's words, *"The enemy is moving, and the eleventh hour is at hand."* Stenciling these words in her journal, her anxious thoughts found themselves on the page: *What is the eleventh hour?!?!*

In other news, a man by the name of Lucien Baldur had become a celebrity on the world stage as the new Czar of food insecurity for the WTO- whatever that was. Maddie couldn't understand the media frenzy going on about this man. You would've thought he was the savior of the world.

On a lighter note, a letter from Jacob detailing his exciting mission trip to the Appalachian Mountains lifted her spirits.

Oh, and Mom was finally showing signs of healing. She was coming home on Saturday.

Maddie wasn't quite ready for her mom's homecoming, and she wondered if Grammy felt the same, as she seemed to be lost in thought quite often. Dad called and said he would be home soon, but in his daughter's book, soon was an eternity. Matthew seemed to be the only one holding it together. His silliness and constant encouragement that everything would be all right was a breath of fresh air.

The harmony of blinking lights distracted her brooding once more, reminding her of Sonya's teaching on Christmas lights. "They remind us that Jesus Christ is the Light of the World." *I guess that's why they make me happy.* She reasoned. *Maybe Jesus will shine some light on our family this Christmas.*

Reading her journal entry from three months ago, Maddie recalled the day after their Dominoes game when Mike and his friend Mac left in a huff.

August 15
It didn't even take twenty-four hours for Grammy to kick their cans to the curb, as she delicately put it. Grammy's words to Mike, "Mikey, I love ya, but Boy, when ya choose to lie down with dogs, you'll get up with fleas." Mike slammed the door behind him. God, what did Grammy mean? Is Mike homeless? He and his friend were dirty and hungry. But if he's so hungry, why does he only come home every couple of months? Who is feeding him now? Please help him, Lord.
Maddie

Picking up her pen, Maddie turned the page to today's entry:

December 10
God,
where did we go wrong? Our family is torn to pieces, and I don't know what to do . . .

As a tear blurred her writing, she realized she was grateful for this routine her Grammy had encouraged. The journal was a mess, but she didn't feel as much of one.

*Thank you for Grammy, Rachel, Matthew, and Sonya. I
honestly don't know where I would be without them.
Maddie*

According to Sonya, they were her tribe, those who would
stand in the gap for her. No matter what battle she faced, she
had someone to turn to.

"Hey, Maddie." Matthew must've heard her praying for
him.

"Yeah?"

"Are you okay?"

"Sure, Bud. Why do you ask?"

"You've been quiet lately. Are you sad? Remember, you can
share how you feel. This is a safe place."

Tousling his hair, she said, "I am a little sad, yes. But I'll be
okay."

Looking down at his hands, Matthew asked, "Is Momma
okay?"

Pulling her brother in close, she answered, "I hope so."

"We'll all be okay, right Maddie?"

"Are you asking me or yourself?"

Matthew put his hands in his pockets, "I guess both of us.
Ya know, like Mr. C tells us to encourage each other to share.
I guess I'm sharing."

Maddie hugged him. Matthew was taking Mr. Coleman's
advice to heart.

After their mom went into the hospital, she and Matthew
began seeing a counselor. He taught them to name their
feelings like a person. Matthew was getting quite good at it:
"Sad, I see you, and I'll talk about you nicely, but you can't stay
here forever." He would then share with Grammy and Maddie
what he was sad about and go about his day.

While Maddie appreciated Matthew's ability to let the
sadness go, she didn't find it quite as easy. She would talk about
her feelings but still feel them. Grammy encouraged her to use

her journal to tell Jesus about them. She would then place them in her hands and lay them at his feet. It helped. Even if she did pick them right back up again.

"Jesus, why am I sad?" A voice in her head answered, *what did Sonya say?* Sonya explained to Maddie that the voice of God often sounded like the one in our heads. "God's Spirit is encouraging and convicting, never condemning. And it always aligns with God's Word," she would say. "Sonya said that you gave us feelings, but why do I have to feel so much?"

"Why don't you ask Grammy?"

Amazed, Maddie laughed as Grammy happened to walk into the room.

"Grammy, are you busy?"

"Never too busy for my Maddie Ruth. What can I do fer ya, Girl?"

"My small group leader told me that God gave us feelings. Is that true?"

"Well, now, I shore do love Ms. Sonya. She's a right fine leader to ya, Girl. Yes, she is. And yes, ma'am, God shore did give us feelins'. Ya know that yer made in his image, right?"

"Yes, ma'am."

"And how many times have you read that God was riled up or sad."

"Well, he was mad at the people in Babel. I don't remember him weeping, though."

Pulling out her Bible, Grammy pointed to a verse. "What does this say?"

"Jesus wept." Looking up at her Grammy, she asked, "But why?"

"Well, now, one of his best friends had died. I 'spect he cried cause ever'body around him was sad. I woulda thought he'd let it roll off 'em like water off a duck's back, but not my Lord. Nope. He was feelin' their pain and sharin' in it."

"Sonya said that when we are sad, God promises his presence and comfort. After Grandpa George died, did you feel God?"

Grammy sighed after a moment of quiet. Grabbing her hand, she said, "Maddie Ruth, I loved yer Grandpa George more'n I could ever 'splain. But I have ta say those years follerin' his homecomin' with the Lord were some of the sweetest years of my life."

"Why?"

"Ya see those lights right thar'? Constant, they are. When I plug 'em in, they light up the room ever' time. The Lord, why he's even more so. We're in his presence all the time and any time we need 'im we can trust 'im to be constant. Those days were sweet cause no matter how sad I felt, my Lord was thar. Lookie here, he gave us a promise. Here, read it."

"Those who sow in tears will reap with songs of joy. What does that mean?"

After a pause, she said, "My garden don't plant itself, now does it? No ma'am. When I harvest my 'maters, I praise the Lord fer his bounty. But fer 'em to grow; thar's hard work ta sow 'em. When I cried over my George, Jesus shared in my sorrow. And when you cry, my Girl, yer sowin' with tears jes' as if ya planted a seed."

"Grammy, can I ask you a question? When we stayed with you over the summer, I overheard a conversation between you and some of the church people. . ." Suddenly, she was nervous that she might get into trouble.

"Hear what, Girl?"

"Well, I, uh, overheard Pastor Ron mention something about four horsemen and something called the eleventh hour? What was he talking about? Does it have anything to do with Dad or what's happening on the news?" That old familiar feeling in the pit of her stomach was starting to rise again.

"I recollect that conversation. Thar' was heap o' fear in that room, Maddie Ruth. My God did'na give us a spirit of fear; no, he did not. So, are you 'fraid?"

"No, oh, I don't know. I just wonder if all this with Mom is related. With all the bad things going on in the world, is something bad going to happen?"

"Now ya listen to me, Maddie Ruth. Don't you be lettin' fear grab hold. Do ya hear?"

"I just…"

"Granddaughter, do ya know what I learned in my season of plantin'?"

She shook her head.

"When ya sow with tears, Jesus shares in yer sorrow, and his word says he takes yer burdens. Joy comes from him, my Girl. When my George went to Heaven, my God exchanged my sadness for his joy. He took my fears, my worries, ever' burden jes' as the Good Book promised. Ya know what that means for you?"

"I have to give him my sadness, then he'll give me his joy?"

"Why now, my granddaughter through and through, Maddie Ruth. You're gettin' it!"

Later that night as she prepared for bed, she picked up a note that dropped from her journal.

Hi Maddie,

How are you? Jacob here. If ya don't remember, I'm the one you ran into at your Grammy's church. Anyway, I wanted to tell ya how our mission trip went in the mountains. A group of us went to a town called Picker's Hill in Kentucky. The hills were amazin'. It ain't like Wild Rock, where we have a Piggly Wiggly, Nelly's Market, and Wild Rock General Store all in the same place. No, ma'am, Picker's Hill has one general store.

Ya might ask, but how do they feed their families? Well, most of 'em have farms. There was one lady who couldn't tend a farm anymore, so the neighbors'd bring their best garden picks, and she'd cook us up a mess for supper that was so good. (That's a heap o' vegetables, if ya didn't know.) We had chicken and dumplin's, biscuits and gravy, rabbit stew. Oh, and Maddie, she made the best Apple Cobbler that just melted in your mouth!

Oh, and Ms. Abby (that's her name, by the way) had a pig named Holler. He'd get all our leftovers in the slop bucket. Ms. Abby tole' us there ain't nothin' wasted in Picker's Hill!

While we were there, we got to rebuild a porch for Mr. and Mrs. Cline. (No, not Patsy Cline.) It was fallin' down when we got there. But we lifted 'er right up. Mrs. Cline was plumb tickled; she and Mr. Cline had a pick'n' grin'n for us that night. She a'course wanted to test the porch with a little jig, so Mr. Cline pulled out his banjo, and we went to pickin'.

Oh, Maddie, it was great fun. The thing I liked the most was seeing God in them. They don't need much to be happy. I think that is how God wants all of us to be.

I wish you'd been there! So, how is Matthew? He was really interested when we played around the campfire. Tell 'em I'll teach 'em next time y'all come 'round.

Well, gotta go now. I'll give this to Grammy for ya. Write me back. I liked talking to you. You're awesome.
Jacob

She must've read Jacob's letter fifty times. Her heart pounded as she read the last sentence. *He* thinks *I'm awesome!* Unfortunately, every time she would sit down to write to him, she didn't know what to say. *I had a panic attack at the mall. My mom is in a mental hospital. My world is falling around my ears.* Maddie didn't have any cool stories to share and didn't think Jacob would be too interested in what she had to say right now.

As she prayed, she asked the Lord for a story worth telling and perhaps some insight into Pastor Ron's warning. "God, Grammy talks about the prophecy surrounding my name. There must be a story in there somewhere. Will you show me?"

Saturday morning, Maddie awoke to the sound of Ms. Carolina Wren outside her window. When she realized the bird had followed her from Wild Rock Mountain, she was so excited that she had to share with Emma. Using the bird's call in their song, "Peace," Emma shared that God sent them a bird to remind them that he was their peace.

"I'm going to need peace today, Lord." She prayed.

Seeing her Grammy at the stove making breakfast, Maddie snuck behind her to give her a hug.

"Well, look at you, Maddie Ruth, what's got you grinnin' like a possum?"

"Oh Grammy, you know. I am happy to see you, of course!"

"Well, now, how about me?" A familiar voice from behind her spoke softly.

Maddie turned around and squealed, "Daddy!" as if it was her birthday all over again.

"Good morning, Ruthie. It's nice to see you too."

"When did you arrive?"

"Late last night."

"He 'bout skeered me outta my house shoes, that's fer sure!" Grammy grinned at her son.

Matthew ran into the kitchen when he heard his dad's name. Jumping on his back, he whooped and hollered as his dad carried him around the kitchen.

Noticing the silent tear on her gram's cheek, she asked, "Can I help you, Grammy?"

"Why a'course, Girl. Set the table for us? I'm fixin' to put the biscuits in the oven."

"Yes, ma'am."

"How's my Ruthie doing?" Sitting down at the table, David looked at his daughter.

Shrugging her shoulders, she answered, "I'm okay. It's been rough, Dad, I'm not gonna lie."

"I know, my Girl. I wish I would have been here to make things easier."

If you had been here, none of this would have happened. Maddie couldn't stop the errant thought, but she did keep it to herself. She could just hear Mr. C, *"Laying blame isn't helpful, Maddie, but do you know what is? Being vulnerable and honest about your feelings, and choosing to listen to understand, while seeking to forgive."* She tried to do just that.

"It's okay, Dad. I just want Mom to feel better."

"And she will. She comes home today." He said with a smile on his face.

"Yay! I can't wait to see Momma!" Matthew clapped his hands.

With a concerned look on her face, she asked, "Dad, is she ready?"

"Her therapist says she has made great progress and believes she is ready to come home. Maddie, as she is still healing, we, as her family, will need to support and help her in the days to come."

"Yes, sir. Mr. C told Matthew and me that we are to calmly share our feelings and allow her to share as well."

"Mr. C said that we need to listen really hard!" Matthew said as he made the C gesture with his right hand on his ear.

"Can you do that?" David asked.

"Yes, sir!" Matthew responded with a perfect salute.

"That's Good. Let's eat breakfast then, and your mom will be home before you know it."

ATLANTA GEORGIA

Walking through the double doors, David and Jack walked up to the front desk to ask for Jacque. As they waited, Jack updated him on his daughter's progress.

You could cut the tension in the room with a knife. David didn't expect his father-in-law to greet him as his children did, but he did hope for something more than a cold nod. They had never been close, and David always knew he wasn't his first choice for a son-in-law. Jack, never one to mince words, made it clear from the beginning that his daughter was worth more than David could give her. Unfortunately, for a man who gave his daughter everything, he was incensed that her first choice for a husband had to be his last.

Anxious over the silence, David did not doubt that he was at fault in Jack's eyes. However, he couldn't miss the sadness permeating his eyes. It was time to have a hard conversation.

"Sir, I want to thank you for being here when I couldn't. Jacque loves you so much, and I know she appreciated you being here."

"Well, that's what family does, Son."

Jack's words cut into the guilt that he couldn't shake. *Can't he see that this is hard for me too?*

"Mr. Bennett?"

"Yes, ma'am." David stood up.

"Good morning, Mr. Ruby, good to see you again."

"Hello, Dr. Smith. I've briefed my son-in-law on Jacque's recovery. How is she doing? Can we take her home today?"

"Yes, she is free to go home today. All her paperwork is in order. "Mr. Bennett, I must tell you that your wife is in a fragile state. She must continue her therapy; otherwise, she will be back. I also suggest she continue in a twelve-step program. Tell me, will you be with her?"

Taken aback by the doctor's question, David answered, "I will be with her, yes. But I cannot guarantee that I won't be called up."

"I understand. If I may, I am not certain Mrs. Bennett is in a state to manage your home alone. Do you have assistance?"

"I do. My mom has offered to stay if I need to leave again.

"Good, good. Please understand that we agree that the best care for Mrs. Bennett is one of complete support. We only want to be sure she is going home to a healthy environment."

Catching the steely gaze of his father-in-law in the corner of his eye, David bristled at the doctor's insinuation that he couldn't care for his wife. "I assure you, Doctor, Jacque will be well cared for."

"Good, then we understand each other."

"Yes."

CHAPTER 20

Letting Go

Jingle bells on repeat magnified Maddie's already agitated state. Typically, the season brought joy and expectation, but right now, joy seemed as far away as the truck that she and her mom were trudging toward. Covered in bags, you would have thought they were supplying gifts for a small village, but the bags they were carrying were all for the house.

Since her mom's homecoming, she was in power-shopper mode. Each day introduced a new need. A drape here, pillowcases there. "Oh, look, Maddie, wouldn't this nook be so cute with a violet vase?" For some reason, her mom wanted to drag her daughter everywhere. "We don't have too many years left, Maddie; I want to make the most of what we have."

Blah, blah, blah. If she were honest, she was tired of her mom's pandering. She was tired of the ruse; it was obvious that her mom was trying to buy her silence.

In the beginning, Jacque was excited to be home. She checked all the required boxes but was eager to "get back to normal," as she put it. Only grudgingly did she go to therapy. It wasn't two weeks before Maddie noticed her missing a session or two. "I'll reschedule," she would say. Maddie didn't have much faith that she would.

Jumping in the front seat, she pulled out her phone to chat with Rachel.

Maddie: "Hey, you."

Rachel: "Hello, Beautiful! What are you up to?"

Maddie: "Another shopping trip."

Maddie couldn't help but add a thousand vomit emojis.

Rachel: "This is all part of the healing process. Your mom is trying to get her life back together."

Maddie: "I'd be okay with that; except she isn't thinking of anyone but herself."

Rachel: "Sounds like we need a coffee date. Meet me at The Coffee Bar?"

Maddie: "Sure, I'll ask Mom to drop me off."

Rachel: "Great, see you in a bit!"

"Hey, Mom, can you drop me at The Coffee Bar? Rachel needs to talk."

"Oh, Mads, I wanted to watch a movie. Are you sure?"

Maddie cringed when her mom used the hated nickname. "I'm sorry, Mom, but she needs me."

"Okay, sure. Maybe we can watch the movie later?"

Twitching one eyebrow slightly, Maddie managed a forced smile as she looked at her mom. "Yeah, that sounds good."

The rich aroma of coffee beans and freshly baked cookies hit Maddie right in her happy place. She had a great love for coffee shops. Colorful wreaths interspersed with white lights reminded her of their visit to Helen last Christmas. *If only I could go back.* She mused. The atmosphere helped her to de-stress no matter the mood she was in. *Oh, how cute.* Admiring the Christmas tree in the corner, she was considering who might enjoy a coffee bean ornament.

"Hi, Maddie, can I help you?" Her calculations were interrupted by Jackson Reese from church and her mind suddenly went blank.

"Oh, hey, Jackson. I didn't know you worked here."

"Yeah, I'm working through the holidays so I can save up for college."

Smiling, she said, "Oh, well, I'm just looking while I wait for my friend."

"Hey, are you friends with Rachel Monroe?"

"Yeah, she's my best friend. Why?"

Jackson looked around Maddie when the bell sounded over the door. "Hey, Rachel."

"Hi, Jackson! Fancy meeting you here!" Rachel blushed as she grabbed her friend's hand and squeezed.

Maddie laughed quietly. "Jackson and I were just talking about whether we knew each other."

"Well, I uh." It was Jackson's turn to blush. "I asked if she knew you. I mean, we do go to the same church."

"Yes, of course." Rachel wiggled her eyebrows at her friend. Maddie, what lovely concoction would we like to imbibe today?"

Giggling at her friend's dramatic display, Maddie asked Jackson, "What would you suggest?"

"Well, all the girls seem to be buying the Peppermint mocha, but my favorite is Caramel Brulée Latte."

"Two Caramel Brulées it is then." Rachel paused for dramatic effect, then winked. "My treat."

After paying, the two walked over to a sofa. Rachel plopped down and crossed her legs. "Oh, Maddie, isn't Jackson the cutest? When I grow up, I so want to ask for his number."

"When you grow up, huh?"

"Well, he is driving. Mom would never let me go out with someone who is driving."

"Will she let you go out with anyone?"

Rachel laughed as she looked dreamily toward the object of their conversation, "Hm, you have a good point there."

"Here you go, two Caramel Brulées. Enjoy!"

The girls laughed as they noticed the foam heart on top.

"Okay, Jackson, here goes. There's no pressure, but if this isn't as good as promised, I will write a strongly worded letter to management."

"Big yikes, Rachel." Maddie's eyes widened as she waited for her friend's verdict.

With a big foamy smile, Rachel winked, "Yum! This is the best Jackson! You've got this girl's A+ review!"

As Jackson walked away, Rachel swooned. Mouthing the words, HE IS SO CUTE to her friend, she went back to drinking her coffee. "Okay, Friend, tell me what's up."

Maddie frowned as she remembered the reason for their impromptu coffee date.

"Rach, I am beyond frustrated. Mom is so fake right now. She is trying so hard to be friends with me while she is making everyone think everything is fine. She's not fine. She's missing appointments and going shopping every day. She thinks her shopping is therapy but really, it's just another addiction."

Rachel grabbed her hand as she listened to her friend.

"What are you afraid of?" Rachel always struck at the root of the problem.

"What if she starts drinking again? She was hiding it before. It was too late before we knew what was happening. I guess I'm afraid I won't be able to save her."

Rachel squeezed her hand again. "Maddie, remember what my dad said; this is not your fault. Do you know what that means?"

Shaking her head, she looked at her friend with weary eyes.

"It means that you are not responsible for your mom. You cannot control her decisions. You cannot save her. You can only love her and be there for her when she needs you."

She appreciated her friend's patient quiet as she processed her thoughts. Focusing on the white lights, she remembered Grammy saying that God was constant.

"Rach?"

"Yeah?"

"When your mom almost died delivering Hannah, what did you feel?"

"Lost, afraid, like I couldn't control what was happening."

"Yeah. Didn't you say you got mad at God?"

"I was afraid and yes, I did yell at God. Was I mad at him? Yeah, I guess I was. But I knew that he was faithful. God has answered every prayer I have prayed. The only thing is, I didn't know how he would answer. So, in the moment of my yelling, I guess I was mad that I didn't know how he would answer.

"Maddie, can I ask you a question? Are you mad at God?"

Focusing on the wall painting in front of their table, Maddie released a deep breath and said, "I guess a little bit. I'm so frustrated that I can't fix this!"

"No, you can't. But God can."

Looking at the lights again, Maddie said, "Grammy says he is constant."

Following her gaze, Rachel agreed, "Yes, God is faithful. He will never let you down, Maddie. Never. But, if you are holding on to anger at your mom, you've got to give it to him."

She wrinkled her nose at the thought.

Rachel reached out and said, "I want to show you something that Sonya taught me. Give me your hands."

As she placed her palms on her friend's, Rachel continued, "Now close your eyes."

Maddie closed her eyes.

"I want you to open the eyes of your heart."

Confused, she peeked one eye open.

"No, not your real eyes, LOL! Open the eyes of your heart and see all the pain, the hurt, the fear, and the anger. See each one as a rock inside of your heart. Some are little, some are large. Do you see them?"

"I guess."

"Now, I want you to take your right hand and see yourself picking one rock out of your heart and placing it in your left hand. That's good, now name it."

"Name it?"

"Yeah, name the rock you put in your hand."

"Fred," she smirked.

"Very funny. Okay, now name the hurt."

She saw where her friend was going with this. "Abandonment."

"That's good. Now grab another."

"I can't fix this."

"Keep going."

"Left alone."

Over the next ten minutes, Maddie continued to list every hurt and pain she had: guilt over her mom's failed suicide, fear that it might happen again, worry that she couldn't care for Matthew, anger at her mom for wanting to leave her behind.

"Okay, now I want you to see all the rocks in your hands. Are they heavy?"

Maddie nodded her head in agreement.

"Yeah, they look heavy. Jesus said in the Bible, 'Come to me, all you who are weary and burdened, and I will give you rest. Take my yoke upon you and learn from me, for I am gentle and humble in heart, and you will find rest for your souls. For my yoke is easy, and my burden is light.' So, we are going to stand on his promise, and we are going to give him those heavy rocks. Are you ready?"

"I'm ready."

"Okay, I am going to pray and when I squeeze your hand, I want you to turn your palms over, so that the rocks fall to the floor. I want you to see them fall at the feet of Jesus."

After Rachel prayed, Maddie rotated her hands. In her mind's eye, she could see rocks falling from her hands. Somehow, her heart felt lighter. After her friend said amen, she opened her eyes.

"What do you feel?"

"It's weird, but like, I feel lighter."

"Hey, did anyone order a glass of rocks?" Jackson broke the tension as he brought over a vase full of rocks.

Rachel laughed as she mouthed, "I see you."

"Bye, Rach!" Placing her key in the door, she waved bye to her friend.

"There you are, Mads. How was your visit with Rachel?"

"Oh, hi, Mom. It was good."

"That's good. Can you help me put these drapes up?"

"Oh sure. Give me a minute." Maddie ran upstairs to put her phone on the charger.

A glimpse of her mom staring out the front window caught her off guard. She looked lost like she was waiting for something or someone. Maddie wondered at her thoughts.

"Okay Mom, how can I help?" Remembering her friend's encouragement to be there when her mom needed, she smiled at her mom.

Maddie had no idea how to hang drapes. Her mom had always hired someone to do difficult tasks. But she seemed intent on doing this herself, so she was determined to help her figure it out.

"I don't know which way to hang them; what do you think, Maddie?"

"Well, the darker color should be on the outside, right?" Rummaging through the box, she found the directions and pointed to the picture where they had to thread the rod through the holes. "And then it looks like we install the rod like this."

Standing on the step stool, she penciled in the rod location, helped her mom drill the holes, and then balanced as she hung them.

After they were finished, her mom was beaming. "Wow, they really make the room pop, don't they?"

Maddie felt a wave of gratitude as she watched her mom smile over their success.

"They really do."

"Thank you, Maddie, for your help. I didn't realize your talent with projects."

Blushing at the affirmation, she realized it had been a long time since she had heard her mom's appreciation. "How about that movie?"

"Sure, I'll make the popcorn. Where are Grammy and Matthew?"

"Aunt Lisa is in town. She picked up Grammy and Matthew and took them to the aquarium."

"Oh, that's fun. Anything good on Netflix?"

Getting ready for bed, Maddie debriefed the day. She awoke so full of anger, but after praying with Rachel and hanging out with her mom, she was at peace. Just like Rachel felt after she prayed for her mom. Journaling the events of the day, she wrote:

> *December 15*
> *God,*
> *I guess it's time for me to start letting go of some things.*
> - *bitterness*
> - *anger*
> - *unmet expectations*
> - *fear*
> *I am tired of holding on to these heavy rocks.*
> *I place them in my hand, God, and give them to you.*
> *Maddie*

CHAPTER 21

Love's Gift

The sun was shining brightly through the kitchen's stained-glass window. It was Christmas Eve, and Maddie felt joy for the first time in what seemed like ages. *Perhaps Christmas could be saved.*

"Good morning, Grammy."

"Well, good morning to ya, Sunshine! How's ma Maddie Ruth this mornin'?"

"I'm feeling pretty good today. It's Christmas Eve!"

"Yes, ma'am. I've been thinkin' about Christmas breakfast. How would ya feel about waffles and bacon?"

"Sounds yummy! Can I help you make the waffles?"

"Why a'course! Christmas breakfast wouldn't be the same without a little help."

"Mom said that Aunt Lisa came into town?"

Grammy smiled, "She shore did. She took sweet Eva Mae (Maddie's cousin, Aunt Lisa's daughter) and Matthew to the store so yer parents could sleep in."

"Is she staying through Christmas?"

"No, ma'am. Jes' through breakfast."

"Grammy, can I ask you a question?"

"Yes, ma'am."

"I've been reading the Christmas story, and I was wondering, well, Luke talks about Mary pondering things in her heart. What exactly was she pondering?"

"Why d'ya ask?"

"Well, Grammy, like, you know she was only fourteen?"

"Yes, ma'am."

"That's a year younger than me." She whispered.

Grammy chuckled, stirring the waffle batter, "Well, yes, that's 'bout right, ain't it?"

"I'm just wondering if Mary was a little angry that she had to give up her whole life to bring a baby into the world. I mean, she was only fourteen!" Maddie was aghast at the thought.

"Now, Maddie Ruth, ya hear me now. Mary was fourteen, but life back then was much differ'nt than today. It was a gift she was chosen as Jesus' momma. When the angel came to visit her, he told 'er she found favor with God. It was an honor to be given such a gift."

"I guess. It's just so weird, ya know? Mary's sitting there, and an angel comes to her and says, 'You're gonna have a baby.' I mean, what are you supposed to say to that?"

Looking at her granddaughter, Grammy smiled. "You're my baby Girl, Maddie Ruth. Do ya recollect that story I tole' ya 'bout your name?"

"Yes, ma'am, that I would be a companion to many who would need God's strong tower?"

"That's a right fine memory you got, Girl. Well, did ya know that Mary had a prophecy 'bout her too?"

"Really?"

"Yes, ma'am, it'd be the prophet Isaiah, I think. Yeah, that's right. Isaiah said, 'Behold, the virgin'll be with child and'll give birth to a son, and'll call him Immanuel."

"But Grammy, how does that even work?"

"What, Child?"

"She was a virgin," Maddie whispered.

Laughing again, Grammy said, "Yes, ma'am, she was. The word says that God's Spirit blessed her with a child."

"But how does a Spirit . . ."

"Girl, let's sit down a spell while the oven heats up. Now, are ya goin' ta listen to me or take us down a rabbit trail?"

Placing her hands in her lap, she closed her lips tight to signal she was ready to listen.

"So that Isaiah foretole her deliverin' the Savior into the world. Now, jes' like I tole' you what was shared to me in my dream, she too was told stories all her life 'bout the virgin who'd be with child. So, the angel, while a surprise to her personally, wasn't a surprise at all."

"I guess, it's just weird."

Tousling her granddaughter's hair, Grammy asked, "So what is it you're really gettin' at, Girl?"

"I guess I'm wondering about God's will for my life. When I was reading about Mary and thinking about how her life was turned upside down, I could feel her pain a little, ya know? I mean, I'm not going to have a baby, but I feel like everything has been turned upside down. Reading how she pondered everything in her heart, I couldn't help but wonder how a fourteen-year-old girl who had her life flipped upside down could feel good about any of it."

"Well, I'll be, that's a whole feelin' ya got thar'. And, my Girl, it's okay to feel like things have gone a bit haywire, but thar' ain't nothin' written nowhere that says life's gonna go like we planned. Now, Mary, she wasn't thinkin' 'bout herself an her own life. Well, the Good Book doesn't say so anyway. But what it does say is that she loved her son so much. Even up to the moment, she had to watch him die on a cross. Now, I 'spect the gift she was given to ponder his birth filled those empty moments of pain afterward. But she knew that his life was a gift from the very first moment. Love's gift, in fact."

"Love's gift?"

"Yes, ma'am, the word says that God is love, so God, in fact, gave her the gift of a son, his Son, whom he entrusted her with. This was an honor, Love. God trusted her with his Son. Life ain't 'bout you or me, we're jes' a breath in the wind. Life is 'bout our Creator weavin' us all in his great story of redemption. And one day, we'll all get to be together in the land of milk and honey, rejoicin' in his love fer all of us. That, my Dear, is Love's gift."

"Grammy, do you think things will ever be normal again?"

"Well, who promised you normal, Girl? Ain't nobody said

life was gonna be normal. In fact, James said jes' the opposite."

"Is it too much to want to know what's coming?" Maddie asked, frustrated.

Grammy laughed, "Now, where would the fun be in that?" Grabbing her granddaughter's hand, Grammy squeezed and said, "Maddie Ruth, I know yer hurtin'. The world must seem a little scary for ya right now. But sweet Girl, that's why we trust the One who is faithful. Yer gonna have heartache and pain yer whole life, and you gotta choose what yer gonna put your faith in. If ya put your faith in people or things, yer gonna get let down. Now look at me."

She tried to hold back the tears, but looking into Grammy's loving gaze, Maddie lost it.

"It's okay Love; let it go. R'member, he captures ever' tear in his bottle."

After a few moments, she looked up again. "Grammy, I'm just so angry. Mom tried to kill herself! She didn't care enough about me and Matthew to stick around. Why would she do that? This world is falling apart around our ears, and she wants to abandon us. Does she even love us?"

"Oh, sweet Girl, yer momma loves you, but she's hurtin' too. Her feelin's jes' got the better of her."

Laying her head on Grammy's shoulder, sobs softened into a hiccup as she sought to gain control over her emotions. Breathing deeply, she could feel the battle that anxiety was stirring inside, but she was determined not to let it control her this time.

"Let me tell ya' a story. Yer Grandpa George was the most handsome boy in Wild Rock. With eyes greener 'n Sycamore Lake in deep summer and hair black and shiny as a Sunday shoeshine. He was quite the looker." Grammy wiggled her eyebrows and smiled. "Do you recollect how I tole' ya we met at a picnic?"

Maddie nodded.

"Well, it weren't a year later a'fore we were hitched. Now I know what yer thinkin', that weren't much of a courtship. And ya know what they say, weddin' without courtin' is like vittles without salt. But we was chasin' the clock cause ma George went to the Navy. His pa was a Frogman and expected his son ta foller in his footsteps and so foller 'im he did. Not too long afterward, we got word he was shipped to Vietnam. Maddie Ruth, I was so skeered. I cried enough tears to fill the M'ssippi on the day we said goodbye. I was so worried I'd never see ma George again. But he left somethin' behind on that fall day. In November, I found out I was expectin'."

"Was that Daddy?"

"Yes, ma'am, it was. Anyway, I was plumb tickled to be carryin' ma David, but I had no idea where yer grandpa was. The first time he came home, he was a different man. He left with stars in his eyes but came home a little lost. He did'na know how to be a dad, and I had a hard time lettin' 'im. We fought a lot in those early years. If I'm honest, I couldna let 'im be all God called 'im to be. I wanted things ma way. I could'na see the hardships he was experiencin'. I only wanted 'im to see mine. Learning to give love, grace, and mercy took me a long time. And the truth, Maddie Ruth- the only one I was wrestlin' with was me."

After a few moments of contemplating that last statement, she asked, "Grammy, do you think Jesus can help me forgive Momma?"

Squeezing her hand once more, Grammy said, "I know he can. His grace and mercy were the very gifts that Love made real for each of us. Now, how about them waffles?"

It was good to be surrounded by family. Mom was smiling at Dad again. Little Eva Mae was babbling to the salt and pepper shakers. Matthew had Grammy's attention as he shared about his new bow and arrow escapade. The only one missing was Michael. Maddie couldn't help but wonder where he was living, if he was eating, did he ever think about them. She bought him a present when she went to the mall with her mom.

Afraid to tell anyone, she wrapped and placed it on the backside of the tree. Anxiety began to bubble up as she began to worry. *No, he will be okay.* "*God, please take care of my brother. Protect him, wherever he is, and bring him home for Christmas so I can give him my gift.*"

A knock on the door surprised her as she prayed. Matthew excitedly yelled Michael's name as he opened the door for him. *God, was this coincidence, or did you just answer my prayer?*

You could see the hunger on Michael's face as he walked into the dining room.

Mom grabbed him a plate as her dad added a chair. Maddie had never seen her parents cater to her brother like this. While there was worry in their eyes, the love they showed as they served their son filled the room like a warm blanket.

Grammy grabbed Maddie's hand and smiled at her. She must've been thinking the same as her granddaughter. This was that love Grammy spoke of, wasn't it? Love made real, indeed.

MARIETTA, GEORGIA

"Michael, do you have a moment?" David asked his son to join him in the den as the rest of the family sang Christmas carols.

A glimpse of fear quickly faded as Michael squared his shoulders and stepped into his dad's office.

"Shut the door behind you."

Intelligence had given David the skills needed to read people. Michael had all the features of someone hiding something. *Don't show your cards yet. Allow Michael to come to you.*

The quiet was too much for Michael to bear. Fidgeting in his chair, he began to mumble. David thought better of interrogating his son now. It was Christmas, after all.

"How are you doing?"

"Fine."

"The way you scarfed down breakfast would speak otherwise."

"So now you're going to lecture me about how I eat?"

David sat back in his chair. *Easy...*

"No, Michael. Your mom and I are worried about you. You've been gone for months. Is everything okay?"

"Worried? Hmph. And where have you been over the last six months?"

"Now Michael, you know…"

"I know NOTHING!" Michael shouted. "You don't tell anybody anything, yet you, MR. HIGH AND MIGHTY, want to tell me how to live?!?"

Guilt overwhelmed David in a flurry of emotion as he walked over to his son and touched his arm, "Michael…"

"NO! You preach duty and responsibility, yet you can't even take care of your own family. This world needs peace and order, and it starts here- in this house. One day, you're going to have to protect this family. What are they going to do if you aren't here, huh? I mean, you couldn't even be here for Mom! I am tired of your empty promises and your endless preaching. I've found a new family who accepts me for who I am. So, leave me alone!" Michael left the room, slamming the door behind him.

Perplexed over his son's tirade, emotion turned to shock when he recognized the Bagman tattoo on his son's arm. Sinking into the chair, he released a long exhale as he recalled the culmination of six months of work. The memory of his final conversation with Ambassador Cohen echoed in his mind.

Israel is grateful for your thorough investigation, Commander Bennett. David could see the relief on the Ambassador's face as he extended his right hand.

Acting on the reports of his team, the FBI thwarted a global coup planned by a group called The PeaceKeepers. The group's intention was to disrupt the world's food supply through a blockade of all major ports. When David handed over his team's intel, the agents were giddy to connect the dots to the riots taking place across the nation and swiftly made arrests.

Obviously, not everyone was arrested. David speculated.

Presenting his left in return, he curiously replied, *Thank you for the opportunity to serve, Ambassador Cohen. I do have a question; however. In our investigation, we uncovered quite a bit of intel on Lucien Baldur. We find it interesting that he just happens to deliver a speech that landed him the role of Czar at the same time these communications are released. Even more interesting, we found parallels of his message, 'If there is no order, there can be no peace,' interspersed within the messages that your office asked us to decipher. What are your thoughts?*

Ambassador Cohen dropped David's hand like a hot poker. *Why are you investigating a man who is working to end world hunger and usher in world peace? Come on. These PeaceKeepers are obviously just trouble-making miscreants looking to be on the six o'clock news. They have nothing to do with this more than generous benefactor.*

I didn't say we were investigating him. Should we? Mr. Baldur has very deep pockets. The PeaceKeepers were very well funded, weren't they?

Yes, well . . .

David sat quietly, considering his next move.

Aggravated, the Ambassador continued, *Lucien Baldur is a fine and upstanding citizen of this community. Certainly, you make no implications to his involvement in this coup.*

Hmm, no implications whatsoever, Ambassador. Thank you for your time.

Anger arose as he considered the possibility that Michael was connected to the PeaceKeepers. And if Lucien Baldur was involved as well. . . *Oh, Michael, what have you gotten yourself into?*

Closing his eyes, David mused, *this case is certainly NOT closed.*

CHAPTER 22

Tending to the Roots

When Dad was home, Christmas Eve in the Bennett household was lively. The house was decorated floor to ceiling in red, white, and gold. Twinkling lights framed the drapes in the living room. Even Mom embodied the Christmas spirit in her pretty red dress. Maddie willingly went along with the cheerfulness filling the room, but deep down, she was feeling a bit anxious. Whatever happened between her dad and brother seemed to have fizzled, but the expectation of a brewing argument tempered her cheerfulness.

Grammy decided today was a good day to make cookies. "Gotta feed them neighbors and share the love of Jesus," Grammy said. "Thar' ain't no better way than to whip up a batch of sweetness!"

"Grammy, how does this look?" Matthew was so proud of the Santa cookie he had made.

"Whoo, doggie, that's the most perfect Santa I ever did see. I do declare, thar's more flour on you than in the cookie, Boy. I'm startin' to see a pattern 'ere."

Giggles came from the table as Mom and Dad whispered over their batch. "What are y'all doing over there?" Maddie asked.

"Never mind. Pay attention to your cookies, and we'll pay attention to ours." Mom giggled as her dad chose that moment to tickle her.

Michael walked into the kitchen and sat down at the bar

next to Maddie. "Can I help?"

Wrinkling her nose at the strong odor wafting from her brother, she said, "Sure." She rolled a ball of dough and placed it in front of him.

"Are you okay?" She whispered.

While everyone created their masterpieces, Grammy was responsible for cooking them. It seemed a good trade, considering her hovering presence. Maddie loved it when Grammy hovered. She brought joy everywhere she went—even when she was *chewin' on somethin',* as she put it.

Engaging in small talk with Michael was challenging. She could tell he didn't really want to be there. Looking over his shoulder, she complimented his rendition of Frosty the Snowman. "Is his head upside down?" she teased him.

"Ho! Ho! Ho! Merry Christmas!" A chorus of voices entered the kitchen as Maddie put the finishing touches on her last cookie.

"Oh look, the gaggle has arrived," Michael whispered to his sister.

"Hush!" Maddie's eyes reflected the joy of seeing her girls even as she rolled them her brother's way.

"We heard there was a free concert going on over here," Jade piped in.

"Free, nah, we don't perform for less than a nickel," Maddie laughed.

"Come on, Maddie, let's play Peace for everyone." Emma grabbed her friend.

Maddie and Emma sat together at the keyboard in the living room and began to play as everyone walked in from the kitchen. Creating this song was so much fun. Emma taught her how to add chords to the melody they gleaned from the bird's call. They then transcribed the melody and played it over and over until it was tuned to their liking. Then they added the lyrics with Ms. Lorna's help and beamed as she clapped and congratulated their "fine work" over video chat.

They had played the song twice at church, but Maddie realized that playing in front of her family was terrifying. This song reflected some of her most anxious thoughts. She wasn't sure she was ready to share with her parents.

Sensing her friend's apprehension, Emma began playing the low notes in succession. Whispering, she encouraged, "It's okay, Friend, God has us."

Taking a deep breath and exhaling slowly, Maddie began playing the high notes as she sang the lead vocal. Emma focused on the chords and complimented her lead with harmony. The two worked well together as a duet.

As she ventured into the first verse, it didn't take her long to get lost in the emotion. The cries of her heart were so deeply rooted that when she chose to sing them, the crescendo moved the audience. Emma would say that this was a result of God blessing the audience with the opportunity to hear his response to her heart's cry. The final note left an eerie echo in the room as everyone sat quietly.

Rachel attempted to hide a silent tear as Jade and Kaitlyn broke the quiet with their loud applause.

"Ruthie, that was simply beautiful." David was in awe over his daughter's performance.

Maddie nervously looked at her parents. Her mom's face lost all color as she stared behind her daughter, speechless.

"Isn't that right, Jacque?" David encouraged his wife to answer.

"Yes, yes, great job Maddie, Emma." Maddie's mom clapped quietly.

"Maddie did most of the work, with a little help from Ms. Carolina Wren, of course." Elbowing her friend in the ribs, she smiled.

"Carolina Wren? Who is that?" David asked.

Flushing, Maddie looked at her friend as if to say, *I can't believe you said that!*

"It's okay, tell them."

"There's this bird. . . "Maddie began anxiously.

Sensing her granddaughter's anxiousness, Grammy placed her hands on her shoulders. "Art imitatin' life, my boy. God sent a bird to give Maddie an idea."

"A bird? Do tell."

"Well, there's this wren that hangs outside my window every morning and sings."

With a look of contempt, Michael looked down his nose at his sister and laughed, "Now, I have heard everything."

"Michael, that will be enough," David interjected.

"I see. Now, I can't even have an opinion in this family. I don't even know why I listened to you, Mom," he said with disdain.

"Michael."

"See, I'm not welcome here." Michael left the room, slamming the front door behind him.

Emma grabbed her friend's hand as Maddie sat shaking. She didn't know what to say.

"Maddie Ruth, I want'cha to hear me now. My God loves you'ns song. Why, I 'spect He's smilin' in Heaven right now at the both of ya. Emma, thank ya for helpin' our girl."

"Yes, ma'am, it was my pleasure, truly. Maddie has a gift."

Attempting to break the tension, Rachel smiled at her friend. "Speaking of gifts. Maddie, we thought we would bring your gift early."

"Hey, give me a minute?" Maddie jumped off the bench to grab Michael's present from under the tree and ran out the front door. *Oh good, he hasn't left.* Happy to see him sitting behind the wheel of his car, she softly closed the door behind her.

"Hey, Mike." Maddie knocked on the window.

"What do you want?" Mike refused to look at his sister.

Maddie was sad. She didn't know what to say to make this easier. "I just wanted to say Merry Christmas." Maddie left his gift on the hood of the car and walked back into the house.

Everyone quieted as Maddie walked into the living room. Nobody was willing to address the elephant in the room, so Maddie took a deep breath and said, "Rach, did you say something about a gift?"

"Yep!" Rachel walked over and gave her an envelope. "Go ahead, open it."

Opening the envelope, she looked at the folded paper inside. Confused, she looked up from the church's logo at the top. "What is it?"

"You're, well, we're," Rachel gestured to all the girls, "going to Winter Retreat!"

"What? Yay!!!!!"

"Wait, we're all going?" Jade and Kaitlyn were just as surprised as Maddie, while Rachel and Emma grinned like Cheshire cats.

Nervous, she looked at her parents. "It's the second weekend of February. Is that okay?"

Dad smiled, "We've already discussed this with Tom and Olivia. You can go."

"Really? Thank you, thank you!" Elated, Maddie ran over to both parents and hugged them tight.

"Can I go?" Matthew stuck out his lower lip, dejected.

"Not this time, Son, but don't worry, we'll do something together that weekend."

"Really? Can we shoot arrows?"

"We'll see."

"Yay!!"

"Come on, Slugger, show me that bow again."

Maddie's family left the room so she and her girls could exchange gifts. Grabbing presents from under the tree, she hoped her friends would like them.

Passing them out one by one, she asked that they wait to open until they were all passed out. "Okay, open them."

As Emma and Maddie were writing Peace, Emma shared a revelation with her friend. "Maddie, you know that your love language is words of affirmation."

"What is that?"

"It means that you are good at telling others how you feel about them, and you love to hear how others love you. Words are your gift from the Lord."

This revelation gave her an idea for the perfect gifts.

"Oh, goodie, a journal!" Rachel excitedly announced. Jade looked confused. Kaitlyn was trying to find the book's title.

Emma looked up at her friend and smiled.

Maddie wished she could video this moment; the expression on each of her friends' faces was priceless. She gave each one a different-colored hardback book—a simple book with nothing on the front or the back.

"Kind of, but not really," she answered. "Open it."

As each girl opened her personalized book, they sat quietly for a moment as they read and then began sharing what they were reading. Maddie smiled. She had worked on these books for the last three months. Each one had personalized notes to her friends. She wrote notes of encouragement, memories that brought her joy, and, of course, letters detailing how much each one meant to her. They were the most difficult yet most rewarding gifts she had ever given. The girls were pleased.

"Do you like them?"

"Like it? I love it!" Jade exclaimed as they all surrounded Maddie in a big group hug. "But really, Spiderman?"

"Well, you did climb that tree like Spiderman when you saved Rachel's life."

"Oh yeah, Charlie's tree!" Rachel got everyone howling as she animatedly shared the story of Jade's (aka Spiderman) lifesaving escapade.

The night ended tenderly at church. Grammy encouraged David to pack up the family and take them to a candlelight service. "There ain't no better way to celebrate our Savior's birth than to be with family in his house."

As they traveled to the church, Grammy turned to her granddaughter and said, "Maddie Ruth, I shore did like that song you'ns wrote."

"Thank you, Grammy."

"Do ya know what God did in that?"

She looked at her Gram expectantly.

"He planted a seed."

"What do you mean?"

"There's a verse in Isaiah that says, 'Rain and snow come down from Heaven and do not return without waterin' the earth, makin' it bud and flourish so it yields seed for the sower and bread for the eater, so is my word that goes out from my mouth: it will not return to me empty, but will accomplish what I desire and achieve the purpose for which I sent it.' The peace you're singin' 'bout: he is the provider of that thar' peace."

She had heard her Gram recite this verse before. Maddie used to be so afraid of storms, especially hard rains on her Gram's metal roof. But Grammy would always console her with this promise.

"Grammy, isn't that the story you tell when it rains?" Matthew asked.

"Well, I'll be, that's one good memory you got, Boy. Yassir, one of my favorites. But Maddie Ruth, he ain't jes' givin' ya peace in this moment, he's plantin' a seed to remind ya in ever' moment that he is the Prince a' peace. Everythin' he plants has a purpose and never returns void. And my beautiful Girl, them be roots he'll always tend to, never you forget."

Maddie had never been to a midnight service; the atmosphere was beautiful. There were no fancy lights or smoke machines, only white candles with soft light. With a candle in hand, she found herself singing to the lyrics on the screen. Remembering her conversation with Grammy, she considered the night of Jesus' birth and the memories Mary pondered. Looking around the room, there were many who quietly sang of the gift of a Savior. Closing her eyes, she silently prayed, *Father, thank you for the Prince of peace. I pray for your peace to fill my heart.* As the clock overhead struck midnight, she had a revelation: just as Mary pondered the promises given to her by God, she too was learning to ponder the promises given by her Heavenly Father.

"Merry Christmas, Brother."

"Merry Christmas, Maddie. Did we miss Santa?"

"No, Matthew. But I'm sure he'll be here soon. Go to sleep; I wouldn't want you to miss him."

"Do you think he'll like the cookie I made him?"

"I think he will love it."

"Good. Hey Maddie?"

"Yeah?"

"I love you a bushel and a peck and a hug around the neck."

She grinned at her brother's attempt to copy Grammy. "I love you, too."

Turning out his light and closing the door, she ran into Grammy in the hallway. "Merry Christmas, my beautiful Granddaughter."

"Merry Christmas, Grammy. Thank you for being here."

"Why a'course, Love, I wouldn't have it any other way."

"Grammy, about that seed?"

"Yes, ma'am."

"Do you truly think God will use it?"

"I have no doubt, Maddie Ruth. In fact, right now, he's tendin' to that seed and the roots sproutin' from it in the garden of yer heart." Placing her hand on her granddaughter's shoulder she said, "R'member his promise to ya, Love. Ya only need faith as big as a mustard seed."

CHAPTER 23

Winter Retreat

Maddie awoke on the second Friday in February, elated for winter retreat. Even Ms. Carolina Wren was sharing in her joy. Once the bird realized she had a daily meal of mealworms, she would return every morning to sing her benefactors a song. Once upon a time, Maddie would have been irritated at the wake-up call, but she had come to enjoy the reminder of God's gift to her.

Life had gone back to normal in the Bennett household. So much so that Grammy finally felt the confidence to return home. Maddie and Matthew were sad to say goodbye, but Grammy promised, "It's never goodbye chil'ens, only see ya later!" Grammy always knew what to say to "turn their frowns upside down," as she put it.

Maddie's mom seemed to be more of her old self. She was happy to have Dad home every night for dinner, but her daughter still couldn't do anything right for whatever reason.

She was done with her mom's insistence on hovering over her every decision. They spent an hour arguing over what she packed for the retreat. She finally gave in and packed the heavy coat, even if it meant her suitcase was a million pounds.

The retreat! Choosing to pack her bitter thoughts away, she checked her suitcase for a third time and left it by the door. Preparing a text for her friends as she ran down the stairs, her mom interrupted her typing.

"Maddie…"

"Sorry, Mom, I've gotta run. I'm late."

Placing her hand on her daughter's shoulder, Jacque replied, "You need your jacket, young lady. Here. Oh, and here's a banana. Have a good day."

Thanking her mom, she ran out the door with her arms full.

Out of breath she caught up with Rachel just in time. "Hey, you."

"Hey, Girl, you made it!"

"Sorry, I started a text but never got to finish. Moms, you know."

"No worries, you're here; that's what matters. Now breathe."

As they took their seat on the bus, Maddie began complaining about her mom. "She wants me to bring my heavy coat. Really? Who even wears a heavy coat anymore?"

Looking out of the window, Rachel responded, "Oh, Maddie, I'm sure several people will have their heavy coats. It is February, and we will be in the North Georgia mountains. This isn't a trip to the beach."

"It's just so heavy. My suitcase is a million pounds."

"Really, a million?"

She could hear her friend's raised eyebrow. "Well, at least a hundred."

"You're funny. Let's talk about the weekend. What did you sign up for?"

"Against my better judgment, I signed up for zip-lining. Thankfully, Dad was around to persuade Mom."

"Oh, Maddie, I'm so happy! Imagine a canopy of trees below you and flying alongside your Ms. Carolina Wren. You'll love it, I promise."

"How high are you off the ground?"

"I think it's about a hundred-fifty to two hundred feet. But that's nothing. When my dad and I skydived, we were about ten – thirteen thousand feet off the ground."

Maddie's heart fell into her stomach. "I'll leave skydiving to the experts."

Rachel laughed.

"How did you get your parents to agree to that anyway? I

practically had to beg my parents to let me zipline."

"Oh, you know, my dad was a Leap Frog."

"A leap what?"

"A Leap Frog. He was part of the parachute team when he was a Seal in the Navy."

"I didn't know that. So, he jumped out of a perfectly good airplane on purpose?"

"Yup!"

Shaking her head, Maddie laughed nervously. "Frogs and seals, wow. What else do I not know about you and your family?"

"When I was little, Dad didn't want me to be afraid of hard things. This was one of those things he wanted to teach me. 'Place your life in the hands of God every time you do hard things, Rachel, and you will learn to command fear rather than allow fear to command you.' Every time I face something scary, I remember those words."

"You aren't afraid?"

"I didn't say that. Sure, I'm afraid, but I do it anyway. And I pray every time."

"I'm still trying to figure all that out. Do you ask God to take away the fear?"

"More like I ask him to give me the courage to face the fear. Dad taught me to see fear like a person. Sometimes, fear alerts us to danger, in which case we move forward cautiously. At other times, fear tries to keep us from doing hard things. This person is like a bully on the playground. You've gotta stand up to him and do it anyway, with God's help, of course."

"How do you know the difference? I mean, jumping out of airplanes is dangerous. You could die."

"I could, yes. But I have a hundred percent chance of dying at some point in my life. Should I keep from doing hard things because I may die? Or should I trust God to protect me and place people in my life who will teach me to do hard things well?"

Thinking of her mom's breakdown and her dad's constant absence, she began to wonder if God had placed anyone in her life whom she could trust to teach her.

"Hey, what's wrong?"

"Nothing, I just wish I had someone to teach me to do hard things."

Rachel placed her arm around her friend, "Hey, you've got me."

Maddie smiled, "Yeah. So, you'll be there for this zip-lining thing?"

"Of course! Right behind you."

"Promise?"

"Pinky promise." Sealed with their familiar pinkie shake, she felt better already.

A symphony of worship filled the bus as Maddie and her squad traveled to Woodlands with their church family. Never had she experienced anything so loud and beautiful. Emma played her ukulele with ease as the boys toward the front of the bus joined in with their guitars. Rachel clapped her hands and pretended to conduct as the entire bus followed her lead. Even Jade joined in on the excitement. *If this is what Heaven is like, sign me up!*

Kaitlyn was the only one not participating in the fun.

Curious about her friend's activity, Maddie threw a piece of bubble gum over her friend's shoulder. "Hey you, whatcha doin'?"

Locking her phone, Kaitlyn looked at her friend with a smile. "Nothing, just finishing my homework."

"It's the weekend."

Looking out of the window, Kaitlyn replied, "Ms. Turner is on me to finish my paper."

"Hey, if you would've started it earlier in the week, you wouldn't have to do it now," Jade piped in.

Kaitlyn stuck her tongue out at her friend as she went back to her phone.

Everyone on the bus began singing "Good, Good Father." As Maddie listened to the lyrics, she closed her eyes and worshipped quietly.

"Where did you go?" Rachel asked her friend as the song ended.

"I was thinking about the day I said yes to Jesus."

"Oh, that was a great day, wasn't it?"

"Yes, before the world blew apart."

"What if that moment in time was perfectly chosen to prepare you for what was to come?"

"What do you mean?"

"Well, before you knew the peace of God, where do you think your thoughts would have gone?"

She turned to look out of the window, "I would have had a panic attack."

"Yeah, but you didn't."

"You're right, I didn't."

"In some of my darkest moments, I sing "Good Good Father." This song reminds me of who God is when my thoughts venture into darkness." Rachel began to write some of the lyrics in her journal.

"What does it really feel like?"

"What?"

"Being loved by the Father. What do you feel?"

"Hmm, it depends on the situation. If I am worshiping, I may get excited knowing that I'm singing with the angels, or I may be overwhelmed by his presence, in awe. If I am praying, I sometimes feel like God is covering me with a blanket. Sometimes, I get chills, but I always feel his peace. You felt his peace that night, didn't you? Even with everything going on with your mom?"

"Yeah, I did. Of course, you were there."

"That's part of it, Maddie. God doesn't leave us alone in our grief. He is always with us and in moments when we need a human touch, he provides."

"Just like he provided you for that woman whose son OD'd?"

"Oh yeah, I forgot about that." Rachel smiled as she remembered. "Just like that. But Maddie, I do have to say that I don't always feel Him physically. It is knowing that He is with me that gives me the greatest peace."

"Yay, here we are!" Jade had everyone looking out the window as the bus rounded the last bend to Woodlands Camp.

Maddie was excited all over again. *This place is amazing!* Surrounded by huge log cabins and a lake, she couldn't believe the size of the campground.

"Are we in the country?" Jade looked in awe at the nature around them.

Rachel laughed, "Naw, Girl, we're in the mountains. Wait until after worship tonight. Be prepared to be awed once again. Come on, let's grab our bags and meet up for dinner."

Maddie could not believe her eyes and ears. Once again, she felt like she was taking a trip to Heaven. Most everyone seemed so happy as they worshipped—everyone except Kaitlyn, that is. She couldn't stay off her phone for more than five minutes. Maddie wondered if something was wrong with her friend.

After worship, the girls left the worship center pumped up. Even Jade was excited. Suddenly, she grabbed Kaitlyn's phone and ran away.

"Hey, give that back!" Kaitlyn ran off after her.

Maddie, Rachel, and Emma looked at each other in surprise and ran after them both.

At the bottom of the stairs, the girls stopped as Jade was looking intently at Kaitlyn. "So, who's Todd?"

"None of your business. Give me my phone back."

"Kaitlyn, you're not supposed to have your phone. You need to put it away before we get in trouble," Rachel interrupted.

Holding her hand out, she turned to Rachel and then back at Jade and said, "I will but give it back."

"Not until you tell us who Todd is," Jade insisted.

Shrugging her shoulders, Kaitlyn answered quietly, "He's a guy I met online."

"Wait, what?"

"I met him online, okay?"

"Kate, you know the rule. No talking to strangers online." The worry in Emma's voice was palpable.

"He's fine. He goes to a school on the east side of Atlanta."

"Which one?" Jade asked.

"What? Oh, I don't remember. It starts with a C, I think?"

"Let me get this straight." Jade was getting snarky. "You are talking to a guy you met online, and you don't even know what school he goes to? We talked about this, Kaitlyn. There are hundreds of students missing EVERY WEEK! How do you think this happens?"

"Hi Girls, how is everyone?" Sonya interrupted the tension as Kaitlyn quickly put her phone away.

Rachel broke the silence, "We are awesome, Sonya! Worship was fire tonight!"

"Yes, ma'am. There is nothing like leaving everything at the Cross so you can receive a fresh anointing from the Father." Sonya referred to their prayer time. The Pastor encouraged everyone to take everything they were carrying and lay it at the Cross. This reminded Maddie of the time when Rachel encouraged her to see her pain as rocks in her hands. There seemed to be a pattern of letting go here.

"Well, I think Kaitlyn forgot to lay her phone at that Cross." You could see darts in Jade's eyes.

"Jade!"

"Okay, Ladies. Kaitlyn, you know this is a no-phone zone, right?"

"Yes, ma'am."

"You ladies are adults and I'm not going to keep after you, but you only get out of this weekend what you put into it. Do you understand?"

Kaitlyn shrugged her shoulders.

"I trust you will do the right thing." Sonya smiled at Kaitlyn.

"Now, ladies, enjoy the bonfire. I will see you at eleven; I have a treat for you!"

Looking at her friends, Kaitlyn turned off her phone and placed it in her pocket. "I'll put it away, okay?"

Jade grabbed the crook of her arm and said, "Thank you BFF. Now, let's go get some marshmallows!"

Maddie and her squad walked to the cabin with such joy. Even Emma, who was typically one to be in bed early, was filled with energy after the night. "Hey, Rach, I saw Jackson looking at you tonight."

"No, you did not!" Rachel exclaimed.

"I sure did. How much do you wanna bet, ladies, that he'll say hello tomorrow before lunch?"

"I'll take that bet!" Jade laughed. "I'll wager that he'll wait until tomorrow evening at the earliest."

"You guys, just stop. No more boy talk!" Rachel wasn't typically one to get embarrassed, but when it came to boys, you could hear it in her nervous laugh.

"Hey, look!" Everyone stopped to look up at Rachel's announcement.

"What are we looking at?" Jade whispered.

"There's a shooting star! Let's make a wish!" Kaitlyn exclaimed, pointing to the sky.

"Hey, I have an idea. Can we say a prayer and thank God for this moment?" The girls circled up as Rachel said a prayer of gratitude for the night.

Rachel never failed to amaze Maddie. She always knew what to pray and when, and her words expressed exactly what she was feeling. "Hey, Rach, can you teach us?"

"Teach you what?"

"Teach us to pray."

"Sure. But you know we're just talking to God."

"I know, but I never know what to say."

"Okay. If he was standing here right now, what would you say to him?"

"That I'm thankful to be here with you guys."

"Okay, now tell him."

"Just like that?"

"Yep, just like that."

Maddie closed her eyes and said the words, "Father, thank you for this night. Thank you for the stars in the sky and for my friends. Amen."

"Perfect! See, was that so hard?"

"But is that all there is?"

"No, Beautiful, it's only the beginning."

The girls settled in for the night with their small group and Sonya, who surprised everyone with a journal for the weekend. Inside the journal were scriptures for every day. Sonya even went so far as to write personal notes throughout each journal.

After Maddie's mom went into the hospital, Sonya invited her on a coffee date, which would be the first of several. Maddie learned that her leader was a nurse with four children, including one who was in their youth group. Sonya was very smart and was teaching Maddie how to read the Bible. They would spend hours talking about bible stories. It was like having a second Grammy.

"Tell me what you ladies learned tonight?" Sonya asked.

One of the other girls in the group responded with, "That boys have no idea how to eat s'mores. So messy, YUCK!"

Sonya laughed. "All right, what else?"

"I learned not to get too close to Jeremy because he needs a shower!" All the girls laughed at Jade's comment.

"Come on, Ladies, I love your honesty, but let's be nice and go a little deeper, shall we? Rachel, what was the topic of the teaching?"

"Taking our thoughts captive."

"Very good. What were some of the thought examples given by Pastor Derrik?"

"Thoughts like I am ugly or I'm stupid," the room was suddenly quiet as Emma answered Sonya's question.

"That's right. Have any of you had thoughts like this?"

Several hands, including Sonya's, went up in response.

Puzzled, Rachel asked, "Wait, you've had thoughts like that, Sonya?"

"Yes, ma'am, I have. I grew up listening to many well-intentioned but hurtful voices. In my day, it was believed that to toughen the skin, you said things that would, well, toughen the skin. Unfortunately, I internalized these thoughts, and the result was a lot of insecurity.

"And that is the point. When we meet tomorrow, be prepared with your Bible and journal. As you spend quiet time with the Lord tomorrow morning, ask him to reveal to you any thoughts that you may be harboring. We'll talk about them tomorrow. Do you have any questions?"

Kaitlyn raised her hand, "What if we don't have any thoughts worth sharing?"

"Well, that's a great question, Kaitlyn. We all have thoughts that are worth sharing. But I'm not going to force anyone to share anything they don't want to share. I would ask that you come with an open mind, an open heart, and a willingness to be respectful to those who do share. And, if God calls you to share, feel confident that everyone here will do the same for you. Okay, ladies?

"All right, now let's get some sleep; eight am comes early!"

Maddie listened to the soft snores of the other girls in the room. Emma was talking to someone in her sleep. *Must be a good dream.* Maddie; however, could not go to sleep. She had so many thoughts rolling around in her head that she had no idea what, if anything, she wanted to share. Rachel made her promise to be real this weekend, and she wanted to, truly. But to be 'real' meant that she had to be vulnerable. She wasn't sure she could do that.

MARIETTA, GEORGIA

"Shalom David, it's good to hear your voice. How are you?"

"Good evening, Mordecai. Is it too late?"

"Not at all, my friend. Any time before midnight is still early. What can I do for you?"

"I need to talk to you about the PeaceKeepers."

"Sure, what's on your mind?"

"Well, I thought our case was wrapped up. The FBI seems to think they have all the PeaceKeepers in hand, but I'm not so sure."

"What makes you suspicious?"

David closed his eyes and paused for a moment. He knew that there was no going back once the words were out of his mouth. "I think my son, Michael, is a PeaceKeeper."

CHAPTER 24

Captive Thoughts

"**W**ake up, sleepyhead, it's time for breakfast."

"Just another five minutes, Mom, I promise." Stirred from a dream about Jacob in Wild Rock, she was not quite ready to open her eyes.

Rachel was insistent on waking her friend. "Come on, Maddie, let's hurry, or we'll miss out on the waffles."

"Waffles, I'm up!"

Jade walked into the room with a yawn, "Is there coffee? I'm not going anywhere without coffee."

"Of course, come on, ladies. I, for one, am not missing out on the waffles."

At the top of the stairs, Jade stopped, "Woah." Each girl stared in awe at the sunrise over the lake.

"Isn't it beautiful? I could sit here forever," Emma was sitting in a rocking chair with her journal.

"Come on, Girls, waffles are calling."

"Yes, ma'am," Kaitlyn saluted Rachel as she ran down the stairs.

Emma jumped up and joined the girls as they made their way to the dining hall.

"Whatcha writing about?" Maddie asked Emma.

Emma pulled her journal to her chest in a hug, "My thoughts about my mom's panic attacks."

"Oh, that's heavy."

"Yeah."

"What are you writing about?"

Maddie shrugged, "I don't think anyone wants to hear what I'm thinking."

"Why would you think that? Our thoughts are powerful. My mom's therapist always told her that holding her thoughts and feelings in was like filling her heart with rocks. But sharing them was like watching them skip across a pond. This is one of the ways she learned to ground herself."

"Sounds like something Mr. C would say."

"Isn't he your counselor?" Rachel asked.

"Yeah."

"Have you shared your thoughts with him?"

Kicking a rock into the grass, Maddie felt a little guilty for not having processed more. "Not Really. I've only been able to name my anger."

"Well, that's a start," Emma grabbed her hand. "I know this is hard, but you're not alone. Hey, let's just start with one thought. You can share one thought, can't you?"

Inspired by her friend's encouragement, she smiled, "I think so."

The dining hall was filled with people, and there was a flurry of activity. You had to yell over to your neighbor to be heard.

"Oh man, I hope the waffles aren't gone." Kaitlyn was worried when she saw the line was at least a mile long.

Rachel, ever positive, encouraged her friend. "They have plenty. I haven't come to a retreat yet where we didn't have enough food for everyone."

"There's always a first time. You know there's a food shortage going on right now."

"Jade, does it look like we have a food shortage?" Kaitlyn asked, looking over the kitchen tables.

"I'm just saying. We should all be conserving now."

Maddie's stomach rumbled. She wasn't sure she wanted to ask what she was thinking but figured now was as good a time as any, considering they would be in line for a while. "Mom and I saw the food lines on the news the other night. Wasn't that in New York?"

"New York, California, and Washington State have been reporting lines miles long. My mom and I were thinking about going up to New York for spring break to see how we can help."

"You don't think we'll have a shortage at home, do you?"

"It's hard to tell. Right now, the big cities are suffering because they don't have many local food producers. My mom says the US has always been self-sufficient when it comes to food production, but with gangs attacking major farms and food processing plants, it's become difficult to recover the supply for the demand. It's a mess. There needs to be better protection around these facilities."

Maddie never thought about being helpless to criminals. *Aren't the police supposed to protect us?* Shivering, she thought about someone breaking into their home. *Please, God, don't let that happen.*

"Waffle?"

"Oh yes, please." In a daze, she looked at her plate.

"Bacon or sausage?"

"Their bacon is the best!" Rachel nudged her friend out of her thoughts.

"Bacon, please."

As they ventured over to their table, she couldn't shake the foreboding of Jade's last statement.

"Hi, Rachel."

Maddie's thoughts were interrupted by a male voice behind her. Giggles from the table caused her to turn to see who was behind them.

"Hi, Jackson. Are you enjoying the retreat?"

"Oh yeah. Wasn't last night's worship amazing? God's presence was palpable."

"Yes, it was. Especially that new song. What was it called?"

"Faithful? Yeah, the band has been working on it for a while."

"Well, I thought y'all did a great job. I was impressed with your guitar solo."

Jackson Reese had been in the worship band for a while. Ever since Rachel saw him at the coffee shop, she swooned over his dark red hair and blue eyes. Jade loved to tease her blonde-haired friend that their babies would be so cute.

"Thanks." Embarrassed, he looked ready for a quick exit. "Well, I guess I should go. Gotta get back for rehearsal. What are you doing this afternoon?"

Rachel gave Emma a sharp look as her friend giggled behind her hand.

"We're zip-lining."

"Awesome. See you there."

"Can't wait!"

"Can't wait! Oh, Jackson, you're so cute, Jackson," Jade was smooching her hand as he walked away.

"You guys are so wrong!" Rachel laughed as she blushed.

"Well, I don't know, somebody owes me for the bet we made, so I would say we're so right." Emma held out her hand for Jade to collect on their bet over Jackson's timing.

After breakfast, Maddie and Rachel found a pair of rocking chairs to sit in for their quiet time. The lake was so peaceful, like glass. Watching a pair of geese fly in, Maddie sighed as she tried to make sense of her jumbled thoughts. Opening her journal, she sat looking at the page.

February 11

. . . .

The morning service included more worship with a message. The message was all about taking thoughts captive. Pastor Derrik explained the three places where our thoughts originated: ourselves, God, and Satan. He shared how the enemy aggressively whispers lies that we would begin to believe. These lies disguised as negative words, hate, condemnation, persecution, and rejection would eventually be repeated in our minds if we didn't guard our hearts. "But", he said, "when we have a thought that is negative, condemning, or untrue, we can speak truth to it, and it no longer has a hold on us. God's truth counters the lies of the enemy."

Maddie remembered how Mr. C would encourage them to hold their feelings in their hands. *Is that what it means to take a thought captive?* She wondered.

On her way back to their cabin, she wished she'd taken the time to write in her journal. Maddie promised Emma she would come up with at least one thought. *God, what should I share?* she asked the Lord quietly.

"How about sharing your fear of rejection?"

Do I have to? What if they reject me, too?

"Maddie, I am with you."

Pastor Derrik said God's thoughts were encouraging, even when convicting. She was learning to discern God's voice.

Courage began to fill her as she walked up the stairs. She could do this; the Lord was with her.

Grabbing their bibles and journals, the girls circled up with Sonya, who began with a prayer.

"Okay, Ladies. Last night, I challenged you to share some thoughts you are having. Who wants to go first?"

Emma raised her hand and said, "I'll go."

"Great. Now, before you go, Emma, a reminder to all of you Ladies: this is a safe place. We will respect one another inside and outside of this room. Be kind and listen to those who are sharing, and remember, what is shared in this room, you are not to repeat. Does everyone understand?"

"Yes, ma'am."

"Awesome. Okay, Emma, share away."

"If it's okay, I'd like to read from my journal."

Sonya smiled and nodded.

"My mom is a graphic designer. She loves to design things and taught me how to design and build gardens. I haven't known a time when I didn't love her. After I was born, she had postpartum depression, which led to anxiety and panic attacks. My first memory was at about six years old. My mom was cooking dinner, and she dropped a dish that broke into a million pieces. She said she couldn't breathe and asked me to dial 911. I remember that call like it was yesterday." Summoning the courage to continue, Emma said, "Dad was at work when the ambulance came and so I got to ride up front with the driver. They wouldn't let me see what they were doing to her. I was so afraid for her. After this happened, she went into a mental health facility for a little while. She has had issues off and on ever since."

"Oh, Emma, I'm so sorry this happened. Tell me, how did this make you feel when it happened?"

"I was afraid for my mom, that I wouldn't ever see her again."

Jade grabbed Emma's hand.

Sonya asked, "I can see this still affects you greatly. Did you write down what thoughts you are having now?"

Emma closed her eyes. Maddie placed her arm around her friend as she saw her fighting tears.

"I have nightmares. Terrible nightmares that I'm the one who caused my mom's anxiety. I mean, the anxiety didn't start until she had me, so it must be my fault, right?"

"Oh, beautiful Girl, you are carrying a heavy weight. I would be afraid too, but I can assure you that what happened is not your fault. Some illnesses, whether mental or physical, can be in the body for years. They can be triggered by an event, but you- Emma- your entry into the world wasn't the event that triggered the attacks. Tell me something, you said that you didn't know a time when you didn't love her. I'll bet that she loves you very much, doesn't she?"

"Yes, ma'am."

"And I'll bet she would say that *your* life was one of her greatest gifts. Would I be right?"

Emma smiled and nodded.

"I think she would want to know about these nightmares you are having. And I think she would agree with me when I say that she loves you very much and wants to see these thoughts become thoughts of hope instead of fear. So, let's talk about that. Open your bible and read Romans 5:3-5 to us."

"We rejoice in our sufferings, knowing that suffering produces endurance, and endurance produces character, and character produces hope, and hope does not put us to shame, because God's love has been poured into our hearts through the Holy Spirit who has been given to us."

"Tell us what you think that means."

"That we should rejoice in our suffering because it gives us hope? But how can suffering give us hope?" Emma asked.

"That's a good question. Why don't you read that last part for us again."

"God's love has been poured into our hearts through the Holy Spirit who has been given to us."

"Remember when Pastor Derrik taught us today about the voices we hear? Well, when God speaks to us, he speaks through his Spirit. When you accept Jesus, you are given the Holy Spirit, who is your helper and your comforter. So, when you suffer, the Holy Spirit comforts you. What does suffering produce?"

"Endurance," Emma responded.

"That's right. Endurance comes from his strength. What does endurance produce?"

Rachel grabbed Emma's hand and enthusiastically responded with her, "Character!"

"That's right. Endurance produces character because you don't quit. Jade, you're a runner, right?"

"Yes, ma'am."

"How hard is it to keep going when your tank is empty?"

"Impossible! But I've got wind beneath my wings!" Jade flipped her braids back as everyone laughed.

"That wind, my beautiful friend, is the Holy Spirit. He gives us the strength to keep on when we have none left. Okay now, what does character produce?"

"Hope!" All the girls chimed in.

"Look at you ladies. That's right! So, Emma, when you are thinking that your mom's anxiety is your fault, what are you going to do?"

"Speak the truth to those thoughts!" One of the girls in the group responded.

"That's right, Nicole." Sonya lifted her Bible. This book is true, Ladies. I challenge you to memorize the scripture you just read, Emma. Allow God's word to be written on your heart for those moments when you feel like your mom's anxiety is your fault. And know that there are many more where that came from. Got it?"

Emma beamed, "Yes, ma'am."

"All right, who's next?"

Maddie was speechless. She had no idea her friend was suffering from these thoughts. The girls were all crowding around Emma's Bible, reading the verse together.

"SECH! Suffering, endurance, character, hope, suffering, endurance, character, hope." They continued to repeat it until Jade started to rap.

Maddie shook her head and laughed.

"Okay, ladies, quiet down now. Who wants to go next?"

Feeling the butterflies rolling around in her stomach, Maddie nervously raised her hand.

"Awesome. Tell us some of your thoughts," Sonya smiled at her.

"Well, um." She looked at Emma, who grabbed her hand and squeezed. "Y'all know that my mom tried to commit suicide." She began shaking.

After a few moments, Ms. Sonya encouraged, "This is a safe place; you've got this."

"Well, my brother and I have been going to a therapist who is teaching us to hold our feelings in our hands. My feeling is anger." Maddie held out her hands and practiced turning them up and over. "I'm over being angry at her for drinking too much. But I'm angry now because it's obvious that she didn't want me." Her voice escalated as she clenched her fists. "My dad is never home, and my brother is always disappearing. WHAT IS WRONG WITH ME?!? WHY DOES EVERYONE WANT TO LEAVE ME?!?"

The echoes of her sobs haunted the quiet room.

"Oh, sweet Girl, do you feel rejected by your mom, your dad, and your brother?"

"Yes," Maddie said as she hiccupped.

"Hmm, will somebody with a bible open up and read Genesis 16:13 to us?"

"I will," Rachel answered.

"She gave this name to the Lord who spoke to her: 'You are the God who sees me,' for she said, 'I have now seen the One who sees me.'"

Sonya closed her eyes for a moment and continued, "There was a woman named Hagar. She was a handmaiden to Sarah who was the wife to Abraham. Sarah couldn't bear children. But ya see, God made a promise to Abraham that he and Sarah would have descendants as numerous as the stars. So, guess what Sarah did? She got tired of waiting and asked her husband to have a child with her handmaiden and they conceived a child."

"Wait, so you're telling me people are cheatin' in the Bible? I thought it was holy?" Kaitlyn piped in.

"Yes, ma'am. Oh, the Bible is holy but also quite scandalous.

"Once Sarah did conceive a child, the Bible says that she began to despise and mistreat Hagar, so Hagar left."

"Well, that's not fair. Sarah told her husband to cheat!" Jade exclaimed.

"Well, she wasn't thinking about it in those terms. But yes, it was Sarah's idea."

Picking up her Bible, Sonya read, "The angel of the Lord found Hagar near a spring. So, not only did the Lord see her, but he looked for her and in verses eleven and twelve, the angel of the Lord told her that she would have a child and would name him Ishmael. After this, she spoke that she had seen the Lord, and he had, in fact, seen her. The name she gave him was "El Roi- the God who sees me." Sonya quietly waited for Maddie to understand.

"So, Hagar was rejected, and God saw her?"

"Yes, ma'am, that's right. Girls, I'm going to cook your noodle with this one, but believe it or not, there is story after story in God's word of people being rejected by others. We hear that the Bible is a book of rules, but truly, it is a love story of God's great love for us all, including those who are rejected by man. Jesus himself was rejected by the very people he came to save. But he gave of himself anyway. Do you know why?"

"Cook your noodle." Everyone giggled as Jade mimicked Sonya.

"Why?" Maddie asked seriously.

Sonya smiled, laser-focused on her, "Because God so loved YOU. God sees you, even if your family doesn't. And do you know what? God sees your mom, too. If I had to guess, she probably experiences some of these same thoughts and feelings we've been talking about."

The room was heavy. Everyone felt it. After a few moments, Sonya looked at Maddie and asked, "You asked the question, 'What is wrong with me?' What about your family's behavior leads you to believe that something is wrong with you?"

Maddie wasn't sure how to answer this question. "I mean, if I did everything right, they wouldn't want to leave, right?"

"Hmm," Sonya sighed. "If only that were true. Maddie, we're all a complicated bunch. I mean, look at Hagar's story. What did Hagar do wrong? She was obedient to Sarah, right?"

Maddie nodded.

"Sometimes, others make decisions that have nothing to do with us and just don't make any sense. We can't control the actions of others.

"Girls, what do we have control over?"

Emma raised her hand and answered softly, "Our thoughts."

"Yep. Anyone else?"

"I can control my emotions," Rachel said.

"That's right. Now, pretend you have a remote control. What can you control in others?"

Everyone got quiet. Suddenly, Jade took out an invisible remote and pretended to click it toward Kaitlyn. "Hey, this thing isn't working."

Kaitlyn rolled her eyes at her friend's attempt at comic relief. "Really, Jade, as if."

"Just helping Sonya," Jade laughed.

"No, but thank you, Jade, that's exactly right. We can't control anyone else's actions, but we can control our response to them." Turning to look at Maddie, she continued, "God sees you, Beautiful, and he knows your heart. Let's pray that he will help you navigate this season."

After everyone finished praying, Sonya decided to lighten the mood as she stood up, "Okay, ladies, this has been awesome! I want to give everyone else time to share, but right now, I need a snack break; who's with me?"

Grabbing two packs of cookies, Sonya walked over to Maddie and gave her one with a hug. "You've got this, and God's got you."

"Thank you." Her heart suddenly felt lighter under the encouragement of her leader.

As the session continued, Rachel shared her fear of losing her sister and several of the other girls shared their experiences with anxiety, depression, and loneliness. Maddie was in awe. For the first time, she had a safe place to share the fear that was consuming her. What a relief to know that she wasn't alone in these thoughts! She was so thankful Rachel invited her. This truly was the greatest Christmas present ever.

"Hey, wait up!" Maddie and the girls turned around to see Sonya running to meet them after their small group.

"Hi, Sonya! That was a great group, thank you." Emma said.

"And I would like to thank you ladies."

"For what?" Rachel asked.

"It took a lot of courage to share. Vulnerability is hard. I am very proud of you, all of you."

Jade, embarrassed over the affirmation, said, "Well, I'm excited to finish this rap."

Maddie, Rachel, Emma, and Sonya all laughed as Jade and Kaitlyn rapped all the way to the dining hall.

MARIETTA, GEORGIA

"What is the indication that your son is a PeaceKeeper?" Mordecai asked David.

"He came home for Christmas and had one of those tattoos."

"Which one was it?"

"BAGMAN. What do you think it means?"

"Well, the intel we uncovered seems to indicate that Bagman is a collector or a distributor. Whatever the PeaceKeepers are involved in, the bagman is the one who receives or delivers whatever is needed to do the job."

"So, a runner."

"In the beginning, yes. But they are groomed to pay spies and to bribe local authorities."

"That doesn't sound like Michael. What were the other designations?"

"The Agent-In-Place is someone in leadership who defected from an outside authority. A Babysitter is a bodyguard, or someone charged with watching someone. The Case Officer appears to be the guy who manages everyone, and the Birdwatcher is the spy."

"As I recall, that was the tattoo on the guy who was rounded up by my house."

"I wonder what, or who, he was spying on?"

"That information was never shared with me," David said. "What are the others?"

"Cobbler is the guy who creates fake identification cards. These guys are good at becoming invisible."

"Hmm."

"Oh, this one is good. The Ghoul is the guy who, get this, vets obituaries and graveyards to obtain names for the Cobbler to use. Then, there is the Raven, who is used as their internal intelligence."

"So, Agent-In-Place, Babysitter, Case Officer, Birdwatcher, Cobbler, Ghoul, Raven, and Bagman. Are there others?"

"I think that is all of them. I expect there are more, but this was all my informant had for me. The FBI thought they had rounded them all up, but David, this is an international organization. Is your FBI working with the international authorities to round them up in other countries?"

"That information has not been made available to me. Once you helped us figure out the code behind the messages we found, I was told that our mission was complete, and my team was released for a new mission."

"If your son is part of this group, and they are still running loose, then that means…"

Bracing himself for the repercussions of saying what he was thinking aloud, he interrupted his friend, "That whoever is in control has bigger plans."

CHAPTER 25

A Mountain of Doubt

Maddie was relieved to see so many students waiting to zipline. *Perhaps the girls won't want to wait?* She hoped. "Oh no, look at the line. Do y'all want to go to the coffee shop instead?"

"No ma'am. Not on my watch will you run from this challenge, Maddie Ruth! This is a character builder." Rachel said.

Rolling her eyes over her friend's insistence, she crossed her arms in objection.

"Are you worried?" Jade asked.

Holding her thumb and index finger to her eye, she said, "Just a little."

"Look at the guide as he gears up. See, you'll wear a helmet, gloves, and a harness with ropes. The key is to listen to the guy who straps you up and make sure there is no damage to your gear."

"What if I fall?"

"You won't fall, Girl. There have been lots of people on this ride, and nobody has died."

Maddie quietly pondered Jade's last comment and began mouthing a prayer to God. Seeing her fear as rocks in her hand, she laid it at the Cross and asked for courage to move forward.

"Hi, Rachel!" A group of guys walked up with Jackson in the center.

"Hi, Jackson. Have you ridden yet?"

"Oh yeah, going for round two! Have y'all gone yet?"

"No, we just got here."

"Hi, Noah! I didn't know you were going to be here." Rachel elbowed Kaitlyn.

Suddenly, Kaitlyn's ears perked up. "Oh, hey, Noah."

"Are you two a thing?" Jade gestured toward Jackson and Noah. "I didn't know y'all were bros."

Noah hugged Jackson and said, "I never leave the cave without him."

"Look at this line, Bro. We gotta get back if we're going to ride again," Jackson said impatiently. Before he walked away, he winked at Rachel.

"Girl, did you see what Jackson did?" Jade began jumping up and down.

Rachel blushed.

"I think somebody's got a crush!"

Kaitlyn whispered to Emma, "Did you know that Noah was coming?"

"Nah, I didn't. But now we can see if he truly flies like Batman."

Everyone laughed at Emma's sass.

Noah Whitney was a free spirit. Kaitlyn and he had met last year, and she crushed on him all summer. After the Batman incident at the pool, he and Kaitlyn hung out until Halloween, when something happened. Kaitlyn wouldn't talk about it, but Maddie knew it must've been something big. Kaitlyn was introverted, but she had no problem with bluntness. She did; however, overthink everything due to her analytical mindset, and that tended to push people away, especially free spirits like Noah.

"Hey, Kaitlyn, what happened to you and Noah? Y'all were joined at the hip last summer." Jade asked.

"Nothing, I don't want to talk about it."

"Okay, okay. I got 'chu. One more question: Did Todd have anything to do with it?"

Kaitlyn looked at Jade with fire in her eyes and walked away.

"Hey, what did I say?" Jade asked.

"Jade, can't you keep your *thoughts* to yourself?" Emma chased after Kaitlyn.

"I didn't mean anything by it."

"I know," Rachel said, "but this is a big deal. Give her a few minutes to chill and we'll go and check on her."

Before they knew it, Maddie, Rachel, and Jade were at the front of the line. Maddie didn't have a lot of time to ruminate on her anxiousness. She was a little excited to try something new. Climbing the stairs to the platform, she began to look at the scenery. It was wintertime, but there were a lot of evergreens that made the ground look not so far away.

As she reached the top, the guide asked her, "Hi, what's your name?"

"Maddie."

"Hi Maddie, have you zip lined before?"

She blushed as she answered, "No, Sir."

"It's okay; we have a lot of first-timers here. Let me tell you how it's done." He gave her a helmet, harness, and what looked to be ropes with wheels, just as Jade said.

Examining the ropes, she confirmed they were new and pliable. The helmet looked solid with a cushioned inner core. "How do the wheels work?"

"This is a pulley. This is a cable. The pulley has what's called a sheave. Have you seen those movies where the hero puts his jacket over the wire and slides down?"

"Yeah."

"Yeah, don't do that. This pulley allows for less friction, and less friction means more speed. And speed is the name of the game as you're going down a slope."

Unnerved by the guide's promise of more speed, she gulped for air.

"Now, once you get about three-quarters of the way through, you'll notice the cable slopes up. This is okay. This will help you to stop at the end. We do have a manual brake here that you can use to stop. But be careful because your friend here, what's your name?"

"Rachel."

"Yeah, Rachel will be right behind you."

"Yes, ma'am, I'm right behind you. You can do this, and I

promise you will love it!"

"Okay, let's do this." Gearing up, she stood on the edge of the platform, looking down. Things looked a good bit higher from the platform than they did from the ladder. But she took a deep breath, gripped the handles, and LEAPED!

Seconds passed before Maddie was zipping fast. She didn't have time to be scared because the scenery took her breath away, and before she knew it, she was at the end. Just as the guide said, she began going upward, and the ride slowed. She began to depress the brake, and then she came to a full stop at the end platform.

"How was it?" The guide at the end asked her.

"Amazing." Suddenly, Maddie wanted to cry. How many things had she missed out on because of fear? Perhaps ignorance is the parent of fear. "Can we do it again?"

"Of course, go back to the end of the line, and they'll get you geared up again."

She waited at the bottom for Rachel and Jade. As Rachel descended the ladder, her face glowed and her eyes filled with joy. "Wasn't that amazing? Want to do it again?"

"Yes, I think so," Maddie answered with a smile.

"All right, let's go!"

As the girls crested the hill, Maddie saw Emma and Kaitlyn sitting in a pavilion by the lake. Emma was waving them over.

"Hey, Emma is calling for us," Maddie told the girls.

Walking over to the pavilion, Jade asked, "Can we interrupt?"

"Grab a rocking chair," Emma said.

"Check out that lake. I think I could live here," Rachel began to rock as she gazed at the lake.

Jade drew her chair close to Kaitlyn, "Hey, Girl, I'm sorry. I didn't mean to hurt you. What's going on?"

"Noah ghosted Kaitlyn," Emma whispered.

"I thought he liked me, but only when it was convenient. Every time we made plans, he bailed. I finally told him to stop texting. I don't want something that isn't real." Kaitlyn stared off into the distance.

Jade grabbed her friend's hand, "Hey, Kate, look at me."

Kaitlyn jerked her hand away.

"Hey, I am so sorry. I didn't know."

"Well, you would if you LISTENED! I don't know what to say anymore without you making it into a joke." Kaitlyn narrowed her eyes as she expressed her anger.

"I didn't mean to," Jade said.

"I know," Kaitlyn sighed. "I just need you to listen to me instead of thinking the worst or making fun of me."

"I can do that, Kate. I'm sorry Noah ghosted you."

The corner of Kaitlyn's mouth lifted as she looked at her friend. "Thank you."

"Forgive me?"

"Of course." Kaitlyn hugged her friend.

"Whew, I thought we were going to have to drag you ladies up to the zipline. Are we all good now?" Rachel asked as she made her way up the hill.

"Yes, we're good, let's go," Kaitlyn said.

As the sun set, the girls sat in the room, waiting for worship to begin. Maddie's heart felt full. They all had such a great time zip-lining and even had a chance to play Maddie and Emma's new song for the worship team. The worship pastor asked Maddie if she would be interested in joining the group, but she wasn't sure she was ready for that big of a leap of faith.

She loved this part. There was something about being in a room of people happy to worship. She couldn't explain it, but it felt like electricity was all over the place.

After worship, Pastor Derrik taught about the power of prayer, which serves to help us overcome dark thoughts. He told a story of a missionary to Mexico by the name of Lane Myers who taught, "Don't tell God how big your mountain is, tell the mountain how big your God is." As he read from Mark 11:22-24, Maddie highlighted the scripture in her bible. "If we focus on the problem," Pastor Derrik said, "the problem gets bigger and bigger, but when we focus on God, we realize that he is always bigger than the problems we face. When we focus on God, we learn that his grace truly is sufficient as his Word promises, and we no longer are bound to the dark thoughts that lead us into fear, anxiety, depression, and ultimately sin."

Wow, how often do I focus on my problems? She never considered that she could be making her problems worse by allowing her thoughts to consume her. Drawing a mountain around the question she had written, she remembered when Grammy gave her journal to her. "Girl, we got a big God," Grammy told her as she encouraged her to journal. Maddie had not been reading her bible and journaling as she'd promised.

As guilt began to cover her, she heard Pastor Derrik say, "Today is a new day. And tonight, I want to talk to two groups of people. It's possible that right now, you are overwhelmed by the mountains in your life that lead you to thoughts of hopelessness. Perhaps you even feel guilt and shame over those thoughts. May I encourage you with this? Galatians 5:1 says, 'It is for freedom that Christ has set us free. Stand firm, then, and do not let yourselves be burdened again by a yoke of slavery.' Today, my friends, Jesus wants to set you free. And to the second group, perhaps you question whether God truly is bigger than your mountain. It's okay to have doubts. Remember that even Thomas, Jesus' disciple, had doubts. And Jesus lovingly allowed Thomas to process his doubts by touching his wounds. Like Thomas, you don't have to stay stuck in your doubts. Today, you can ask Abba, our Big God, to reveal himself to you. Jeremiah 29:13 in the Message Bible says, 'When you come looking for me, you'll find me. Yes, when you get serious about finding me and want it more than anything else, I'll make sure you won't be disappointed.' This is who our Big God is, and he is ready to meet you right where you sit. So tonight, I'd like to lead both groups in a prayer. We encourage those who are struggling with doubt to be vulnerable tonight in your groups. You are blessed with amazing leaders who want to introduce you to Jesus, the One who will walk you through your doubts."

As Maddie prayed, she felt Jade beside her shaking. Placing her arm around her friend, she felt Emma do the same from the other side. Suddenly, Jade began sobbing. Rachel left her seat, crouched down before them, and began to pray. Emma joined her and they quietly prayed over Jade. Maddie followed suit and added a prayer of her own. Their combined prayers, like their worship, seemed to swirl around them and into Heaven. As Jade's sobs quieted, Maddie placed her head on her shoulder.

After service, Jade looked at her friends and whispered, "Thank you." There was nothing left but to wrap their arms around one another in a big group hug.

As the girls walked up to the cabin, Rachel asked, "Wanna talk about it, Jade?"

"Not yet, I will share in our group. I'm getting my thoughts together."

Maddie sighed. *I don't want to go home.* Everything at Woodlands was perfect. She felt like she was in a safe bubble and wanted to stay there forever. Walking over to Kaitlyn she asked, "Hey you, how are you doing? You've been quiet."

"I'm good. I'm thinking about what I'm going to say tonight."

"You're going to share?"

"I think so," Kaitlyn said with a faraway look in her eyes.

Maddie hugged her friend. "You're not alone."

"I know. Thank you."

The excitement of last night seemed to have disappeared. Nervousness hung in the air like static, even as everyone seemed to want to cling to one another.

Sonya pulled out snacks and said, "It feels a bit heavy in here. Let's play a game, shall we?"

Before everyone knew it, they were laughing and throwing

"Squirrel" at one another. (Oh, if you didn't know, "Squirrel" is a stuffed squirrel that Sonya uses to reel everyone in when they go off on rabbit trails.)

"Okay, okay, let's start by praying for the group. Who would like to open us up?"

"I will."

"Awesome, Emma, thank you."

After Emma prayed, Sonya reminded everyone of the group's rule of respect. "Remember, what is said here stays here, right?"

"Right!"

"Who wants to go first?"

Jade raised her hand. "I never knew my dad," she began. "My mom is a doctor and works a lot. If it weren't for these girls, I would go nuts." She looked at her squad and smiled. "Mom didn't ever talk about my dad. I mean, she worked so much, ya know? But I heard from my auntie that he wasn't a good guy. She said he was manipulative and verbally abusive. One day, I told her I wanted to meet him, and she said, 'You don't wanna meet that man. He was evil. Besides, he's dead anyway.' That was the first time I had heard that my dad wasn't alive. I asked her what happened, and she said, 'Who knows? He probably deserved it anyway.' I've never dared to ask my mom about it. Auntie made me promise I wouldn't say anything, but I want more than anything to know. I feel so alone sometimes. Like you said last night, Maddie." Tears fell as she gulped for air.

"Oh, Jade, I'm so sorry. That's some heavy stuff. Would you like to share what you are feeling?"

"Powerless. I mean I want to know what happened and to help my mom, but I don't even know where to start. Pastor Derrik talked about moving mountains tonight, but I don't think God can move this mountain."

"That's fair. I, too, would feel helpless. But, Jade, helpless, is not hopeless. Hey, look up this verse for me and tell us what it says, Psalm 46:1."

"God is our refuge and strength, an ever-present help in

trouble."

"What do you think that means?"

"He will always be there?"

"Bingo! What do you think it means when it says that he is our refuge and strength?"

Jade began to twirl one of her braids around her finger as she said, "That I am strong through him?"

"That's right! Refuge means escape, retreat, and shelter. There is a Hebrew word called 'machaseh' pronounced 'ma-ha-se', which refers to a shelter from storms and danger. Not knowing the whole story, it sounds to me as if God was sheltering you and your mom from danger. So even if you didn't know your earthly father, your Heavenly Father had you in the palm of his hand the whole time."

"Machaseh, that's nice," Jade said.

"Now, Ladies, we have all learned how to take our thoughts captive this weekend. But the truth is, Machaseh shelters us as we go to God's word for all truth. Everyone here has a mountain they are facing; would you agree? Just as Pastor Derrik told us tonight, God wants us to go to him with all our storms. He wants us to stand in the authority that Christ gave us and tell the mountain to move. This doesn't mean we won't have problems in this world. It means that our Refuge and Strength will help us to navigate every mountain we face."

Kaitlyn raised her hand and said, "Sonya, I think I'm ready to share now."

"Get it, Girl!" Sonya smiled as she tossed a candy bar at her.

"I met this guy online named Todd. He's seventeen and logical like me. We have a lot in common, including our love for all things nerdy. He's nice." She looked at her friends. "Anyway, he wants to meet me in person and I'm a little scared. I had a bad experience with a relationship last year and I'm kinda afraid to jump out again. I want to be courageous, but I'm thinking logically about all the what-ifs that could happen. I know, I'm overthinking it as I always do. But what should I do?"

"Kaitlyn, thank you for sharing. It took great courage for

you to share as you did. I am proud of you. I am curious, though, how did you meet?"

"I liked a social media post on an account he follows, and he DM'd me," Kaitlyn answered.

"Can I ask you a question?" Sonya asked. "I know you seek courage, but fear can be a red flag, too. Do you think you may be nervous because you don't know this guy?"

"Yeah, Kate, he sounds a little sketch to me," Jade said.

"No, no, you don't understand. He is so nice! He is respectful and tells me I'm pretty. And we have so much in common! He isn't a bad guy." Kaitlyn defended.

Jade opened her mouth and immediately closed it when Sonya gave her a look.

"I believe you, Beautiful. Would you be willing to share the what-ifs that bother you about him?"

"Well, he wanted to come over to my house one day when my mom was gone. I like scary movies and so does he, so he thought we could watch a movie together." Kaitlyn looked around the group for someone to agree with her.

"What did you think about that?" Sonya asked.

"That my mom would kill me!"

"It sounds to me like you received a word of wisdom in that moment. I assume you agreed and didn't invite him?"

"Yeah, but I do want to meet him. Would it be okay to invite my friends?" She looked expectantly at Jade, Rachel, Emma, and Maddie.

"How about this? Girls, I would like you to help Kaitlyn here. Don't tell her what to do, but pull your bibles out, and let's help her find what God says to do when we aren't sure about a situation. Give me some words that we want to search for."

"Wisdom."

"Discernment."

"That's good, Rachel. Does anyone else want to share?"

Maddie thought about the things they had talked about this weekend and said, "Trust?"

"Ooh, look at you girls go! Okay, look up those words in

your index in the back of your bible and come up with some scriptures. Remember, you are looking for scripture that you can apply to your life. Go."

Everyone circled up. Each girl looked in her index and began writing scriptures in her journal. Then, they shared them with the group. They landed on Proverbs 3:5: "Trust in the Lord with all your heart and lean not on your own understanding; in all your ways submit to him, and he will make your paths straight."

"That's good, Ladies! Who knows what this verse means?" Sonya gestured to Rachel, who was excited to share.

"Trust God with everything in you. Do not merely lean on what you know that is outside of who God is and what his word says but trust him completely to lead you into truth. Sonya, what does making our paths straight mean?"

Sonya drew two paths on a piece of paper and said, "God gives us a choice through free will, right?" Drawing arrows toward a house with light, she continued. "We can choose to follow him on the straight path, or we can choose to go our own way and get lost. How many times do we lean only on what we think or what someone else says and end up in a dark place, not understanding how we got there?"

Kaitlyn fiddled with her journal as she pondered the dark place of Sonya's drawing, which was a spider's web.

"What do you think, Kaitlyn?"

"It sounds good, but if I'm honest, I don't know if I believe in God. How can I trust him if I don't believe?" Kaitlyn asked.

"That's a great question. And again, I'm proud of you for your honesty. We," Sonya looked around the room, "can't make that decision for you. God gave you free will to choose him or not to choose him. And as Pastor Derrik taught tonight, it's okay to doubt. But remember, you can take your doubts to God, and he will reveal himself to you. He will guide and direct you when you learn to trust him."

Jade grabbed Kaitlyn's hand, "What was that verse Pastor Derrik shared? 'When you come looking for me, and you want it more than anything else, I'll make sure you won't be disappointed.' If I can do it, then you can too, Kate."

CHAPTER 26

Protective Covering

Maddie and her friends arose Sunday morning with happy hearts. Compared to Saturday night, Sunday was a breath of fresh air. Listening to everyone's stories was hard but powerful, and it seemed to lift the heaviness that everyone carried into the weekend. Rachel always said, 'God is in the midst of everything and everyone,' and she was right. It seemed that every story had God in it, even for those who didn't believe.

At the end of the group, Jade told Sonya that she wanted to believe. She was tired of doubting and living in the shadow of her past. Sonya asked if she wanted to receive the gift of grace that Jesus had for her. Jade said yes, after which time she knelt on the floor and prayed to receive him. Everyone surrounded Jade and quietly prayed over her.

Maddie was so happy. It was as if an invisible bond connected her with her friends, even outside of their friendship. *Now, if only Kaitlyn would say yes.*

After group, everyone met at the bonfire pit and sang until midnight. It reminded her of the pick'n' grin'n at Grammy's. The ukulele and guitars came out and they were soon singing worship songs. Jackson and his small group were leading, and Rachel was mesmerized. Her eyes were like saucers as she watched Jackson play. It wasn't long before everyone without an instrument had their arms around one another and were swaying to the song.

Rachel nudged her. "Banana for your thoughts," she said.

253

"Oh, I'm full, but thank you."

"You looked like you were a million miles away."

"Just thinking about last night. Ya know, that's kinda what the pick'n' grin'n was like at Grammy's. But they were dancing."

"Sounds like a dream," Rachel said. "Do you miss Grammy's?"

"Yeah, kinda. But I loved it this weekend. Thank you, by the way."

"For what? I only passed on an invite."

"For everything. Rachel, you have no idea how thankful I am for you. This year has been hard, but you have helped me to see things differently."

"Well, thanks, but that wasn't me. That was Jesus. He has a plan for you, Maddie, and he wants you to be free from fear. Remind me to read to you about God's armor. My dad taught me all about how to put God's armor on to help me when I face challenges."

"Armor? Like what police wear?"

"Kinda like that, but different. I'll tell you about it on the bus."

Everyone cleaned their rooms and packed up their things to leave. Maddie was a bit sad as she thought about leaving, but then Rachel would encourage her with, "We'll be back."

As they jumped on the bus, she was surprised to see Ashley wave at her as she jumped on the bus in front of them. Sitting down beside Rachel, she asked, "Hey, what's up with Ashley Gordon? She used to hate me, but when Mom was in the hospital, she said she would pray for me."

"Oh yeah, she came to retreat last year and had a radical change of heart. It was so cool to watch God transform her. As I understand, she has a rough home story, but God healed her from the trauma she experienced and now she is a different person."

"Jesus does change hearts, doesn't he?"

"Yes, he does." Rachel's determined gaze reflected how much she believed this to be true.

Whispering a quiet goodbye to Woodlands, Maddie said aloud, "I'll be back."

As the bus started rolling, Rachel opened her bible. Sonya was sitting on the bench across from them and Rachel took that moment to ask her a question. "Hey, Sonya, I was gonna read Ephesians Six to Maddie. Do you know anything about the armor of God?"

Sonya put her book away and turned to the girls. "What would you like to know?"

"Well, it says here that our battle isn't against flesh and blood but against the powers of this dark world and against the spiritual forces of evil in the heavenly realms. My dad explained it to me, but it was kind of confusing, and I was wondering if you could explain it to us."

"Well, what would you define as flesh and blood?" Sonya asked.

"I guess anything or anyone that has flesh and blood?"

"That's logical. You, me, and everyone on this bus, right?"

"Yes, ma'am. But when it says that our battle is against the powers of this dark world and against the spiritual forces of evil in the heavenly realms, who is it talking about?"

"That's a good question. The word here that leads us to the answer is evil. If God is our machaseh or our refuge, then it stands to reason that we need shelter, right? The ones referred to in this passage are those who are in direct opposition to God, and in direct opposition to those whom God loves."

"So, Satan and his demons?" Rachel asked.

"That's right. But these fallen angels don't come to us as we see in movies. They are invisible and speak into our thoughts. They study, tempt, and attempt to oppress us. They also speak through oppressed people. So, it's important to remember that our battle isn't against other people because they are only speaking what they hear from God's enemy."

"So, these people have demons in them?" Jade asked in horror.

"Well, they could. But in most cases, it's more of an impression they make on them. True evil behavior could signify a demonic presence within a person. But responding to another in anger, lying to another, and losing control of self typically comes from our unguarded flesh that is susceptible to the temptation of the enemy. There is a game that we played when I was a kid. It's called 'Telephone.' The game goes like this: I whisper a secret (typically a rumor) into Rachel's ear. Rachel then whispers in Maddie's ear. It continues down the line until the last person at the end of the line has a completely different story from the one that I gave Rachel. Gossip like this destroys nations because of pride that leads to lies, offense, confusion, and, ultimately, division. Today, we call this disinformation and misinformation; you guys call it spilling the tea." Everyone giggled at her analogy. "But they are all the same. This is only one example, but you understand the concept, right? That is why it's so important to keep our eyes on Jesus, guard our hearts, take our thoughts captive, and yes, put on our armor."

"So, then, it's a demon's fault that someone gossips?" Kaitlyn asked.

"No, ma'am, not at all. It is your responsibility to guard your heart, which means you must know that there is a thief intent to steal, kill, and destroy you. He'll do it subtly. When we sin, we open a door to the enemy, who will then do anything in his power to take us down a path that leads to death. And Girls, he doesn't care about you. He wants to destroy the relationship you have, or could have, with God. So, we must be alert and guard our hearts so we can hear and be led by God's Spirit."

Agitated, Kaitlyn asked, "But what if I don't know?"

"Well, truly, God has placed within each of us a moral compass. When you are two years old and your parents tell you no, you want to rebel out of immaturity. Throughout your whole life, the enemy will continue to dangle temptations before you that encourage you to rebel in the hope that you would believe that someone, and ultimately God, is holding out on you. This is exactly what happened in the Garden of Eden. And for some, the rebellion grows until they have hearts that are cold toward God and others. When this happens, battles are fierce. Lives are destroyed, families are destroyed, and yes, even nations are destroyed."

"But, these demons, we can't see them, so how do we even know they exist?" Kaitlyn said loudly.

"Kaitlyn, I love your heart. You have a wonderful and beautifully logical mind that questions everything. God gave you that mind so that you would question everything. And he isn't afraid of your questions. If you allow him to guide you, he will lead you into all wisdom and discernment. So, I have a challenge for you. I want you to go into your Bible app and search for demons. Read the chapters that speak about demons, specifically those in Matthew, Mark, Luke, and John, for that is when Jesus contended with them. After you have done this, let's chat some more."

Maddie was quiet during the exchange. She thought demons were the bad things in movies and cartoons. She didn't know they were real, and that people could be controlled by them. "Sonya, does this mean that when I sin, that I am controlled by a demon?"

"I wouldn't call it control, Maddie. Perhaps in the case of those who are most evil, but if you follow Jesus, then his Spirit dwells in you. He isn't going to share you with the enemy. But you can be influenced or oppressed. When you give in to temptation, you open the door to the enemy through sin. This gives him the right to influence you and tell you lies. Ephesians 4:27 calls it giving the devil a foothold. But Jesus gave you his blood to renounce the sin and his authority to rebuke the enemy. That goes back to our lesson this weekend: when you take your thoughts captive, you are saying, 'I'm not going to allow the darkness to influence me. Instead, I am going to turn to the light and speak truth to the lie.' That leads us to the rest of Ephesians six. Rachel read through the end of the section for us."

Maddie pulled out her Bible to read along as Rachel read about a belt, a breastplate, shoes that carry the gospel of peace, a helmet, a shield, and a sword. "Okay, but do I have to wear all of these? My heavy coat was heavy enough; I don't think I can wear all this."

Sonya laughed, "The armor isn't physical, Maddie. It's spiritual. When you asked Jesus to come into your heart, did you feel somebody physically enter your body?"

"Well, no."

"So, it was spiritual, right? Just as Jesus' Spirit dwells within you, he gives you his armor that allows you to spiritually put it on through prayer. And ladies, I pray on the armor DAILY. This protects us from the enemy's schemes. Truly, this is God's protective covering over you in the battle."

"Oh, so prayer applies it. That's the part I never understood," Rachel said.

"Yes, but you must understand, God is your Shelter, but when we pray on his armor, we are acknowledging its presence and use. So, we must actively use the armor. Consider each piece a tool that you use in your everyday life." By this time, everyone had turned to listen to Sonya. "Well, I didn't expect to have to teach a lesson today, but are there any other questions?" She asked.

Kaitlyn looked up from her phone and said, "Sonya, this verse says that Jesus cast a demon out of a little boy. How can a child have a demon?"

"The word doesn't tell us how the boy was demonized. But what we know is that the enemy can influence our free will. He can also influence the free will of another toward us. If I had to guess, that boy experienced some form of trauma resulting in a demonic presence in the child."

"I don't know, Sonya. This all sounds too weird."

"I get it, Kaitlyn; this is heavy and hard. Unfortunately, sin and death are heavy and hard. That is why God sent his Son to set us free. Jesus came for that boy, and he came for you. As we learned last night, it was for freedom that we are set free *through* Jesus. I wish we could all live in a world filled with joy and peace, but the enemy is real, and we can't ignore him. On the other hand, we can't focus on him, either. Jesus didn't give us a spirit of fear but one of power, love, and self-discipline. He also gave us his authority to rebuke the enemy in his name. It is up to us to keep our eyes on Jesus and to operate in the gifts he has given. And Girls, this world isn't all there is. Jesus will return one day and usher in joy and peace for eternity. He has made us this promise."

"That's in Revelation, right?" Rachel asked.

"Yes, ma'am, twenty-one, I believe. But that is a conversation for another day. If you would excuse me, Ladies, but right now, I have a book to finish."

Everyone on the bus went back to singing while Maddie opened her bible to Revelation twenty-one. She had never read Revelation, but she remembered Grammy telling her dad that we all needed to read it these days. *I wonder why she said, these days?* Perhaps it was time to read it for herself.

> *"And I heard a loud voice from the throne saying, Look! God's dwelling place is now among the people, and he will dwell with them. They will be his people, and God himself will be with them and be their God. He will wipe every tear from their eyes. There will be no more death or mourning or crying or pain, for the old order of things has passed away. He who was seated on the throne said, I am making everything new! Then he said, write this down, for these words are trustworthy and true."*

As Maddie read the words, she considered the challenges she had faced. *How nice it would be to have Jesus physically here,* she thought. No mourning, no crying, no pain—*wow, that will be a beautiful day!* No more tears. Feeling a jolt of confidence, she quietly spoke to the window, "God, I want that!"

MARIETTA, GEORGIA

Mordecai paused, "Yes. David, I did some research on Lucien Baldur. But first, may I ask you a question?"

"Sure."

"Is this a secure line?"

"Yes. What is it?"

"Do you remember when we talked about the antichrist? My informant shared information with me that references the purchase of properties all over the world from the company BALDR Industries."

"That is Lucien's company, correct?"

"Yes, publicly traded, I might add. They have many investors." Mordecai's voice began to sound strained.

"These properties are in the United States as well?"

"Yes, including your Baldersville, Georgia."

"Well, that is interesting news indeed. Why do you think he needs these properties?"

"His speech referred to NO ORDER, NO PEACE, no?"

"It did, yes."

"He also promised that he had a plan to usher in peace and end world hunger, correct?"

"That is correct." David wondered where Mordecai was headed.

"I do not believe it to be a coincidence that Lucien Baldur spoke to the WTO conference at the same time a threat to international trade was encountered. The antichrist is prophesied to be a form of "christ" who promises a solution to the world. The Bible refers to him as "the man of lawlessness." When he comes on the scene, he will oppose everything that is God and will set himself up in God's temple and proclaim himself to be god. The Word says that along with the beast and the false prophet, he will use power through signs and wonders to deceive the world into following this counterfeit world order.

"At this time, people will be required to have a mark on their right hand or on their forehead that will be used to buy and sell. Some believe this could be a microchip or a tattoo. I'm not so sure. Just as the Lord seals his people through his Spirit, who deposits fruit within them, I believe perhaps that the antichrist will seal those who follow him through their fruit.

A counterfeit seal, of course, as the enemy cannot create anything on his own. There is a story in the Book of Daniel where the people were told by their government that they must bow to King Darius. If anyone prayed to a god other than the king, they would be thrown into the lions' den. The prayers of the people to the king were their fruit. When Daniel opposed the edict and chose instead to bow to Adonai, his God, he was placed in the lion's den. It is my belief that the people of God will be directly persecuted during the rule of the antichrist due to their refusal to bow down to him and/or whatever system that he proposes."

David trusted his friend implicitly but couldn't place a great deal of weight on the story he was telling. He had heard it all before from his mom, of course. But logic and experience informed his beliefs and logic told him that the Bible was nothing more than a history book, perhaps a moral barometer. History repeats itself, and the revelation of one person who could have so much power as to deceive the world in the manner that Mordy spoke was inconceivable. In respect, however, he decided to stay quiet.

"David, if your son is truly in the PeaceKeepers, and if they are somehow connected to Lucien Baldur and these properties he is purchasing, then he potentially is in grave danger and will need protection."

"Yes, I hear you, my friend. Thank you for the information. I will be in touch."

CHAPTER 27

Revenge of a Bird Watcher

Maddie was excited to see her dad when the bus drove into the parking lot.

After exiting the bus and grabbing her stuff, she waved bye to her friends and rushed to meet her dad, who was leaning against their SUV. "Hi, Dad!" She exclaimed.

"Well, hello, Ruthie, how was the weekend?"

"It was awesome. I zip-lined and everything! It was the best!"

"You zip-lined? That's my Girl." David jumped in the truck after placing her bags in the back.

"What did you do?"

"Matthew and I went to the park. He's getting pretty good with that boomerang."

"Yeah, he loved making it. Did he tell you that he wants to make a series of them?"

"He did. I expect they'll be all over the house before we know it."

"Hey, Dad, guess what? We stayed in a real bunkhouse and had a campfire late at night. Matthew would have loved the campfire. It was so cool, Dad. Thank you for letting me go."

"Well, of course. I'm glad you had the opportunity. Were all your friends there?"

"Oh yeah!"

"How did your big heavy coat fare?" Knowing the answer, he smiled and winked at his daughter.

262

Maddie laughed, "It was safe and sound in my big heavy suitcase."

Their combined laughter set her at ease.

As they sat at an intersection awaiting the light's change, she began bobbing her head to the tune on the radio as David considered his next question.

"Hey, Maddie, can I ask you a question?"

"Yes, Sir?"

"Do you remember the fire at the mall last fall?"

Butterflies began to stir in her stomach at the reminder.

"I just wanted to ask. Do you remember anyone saying anything about a bird watcher?"

Nausea overwhelmed her in a flash. That name stirred up feelings she did not want to face. She hadn't had a panic attack in months and didn't want to bring on one. She began taking deep breaths as Rachel taught her and tried to recall something good from the weekend. After a moment, she asked, "Do we have to talk about it?"

"No, we don't. I was only wondering. Your mom said you had a panic attack. Have you had any since then?"

"No, I haven't. Rachel and Mr. C have really helped me with coping skills."

"Good, that's good. You know I'm here if you need to talk, right?"

Maddie looked out of the window, "Yeah, Dad, thanks."

Monday morning was excruciatingly punctual. *Why can't I still be at Woodlands?* Getting up, Maddie texted her squad,

Maddie: *"What's the fit today?"*

Jade: *"Jeans and a sweater."*

Rachel: *"I'm wearing a dress."*

Kaitlyn: *"Pink hair!"*

Emma: "Wait what? Selfie, please."

Kaitlyn: "I dyed it. Check it out!"

Kaitlyn sent a picture of her pixie hair an extreme color of pink.

Jade: "Well, that's bright."

Kaitlyn: "Don't you love it?"

Emma: "Pink is your color, Kate."

Maddie added a heart to the picture and decided to wear jeans and a sweater. The morning was chilly, and she expected Mom would want her to wear a jacket, so she paired her white sweater with a lime green jacket and walked downstairs.

Grabbing a banana, she walked over to her mom and gave her a kiss on the cheek.

"Well, that was unexpected. Good morning, Maddie."

"Good morning, Mom. How are you feeling today?"

"Much better, thank you."

"Dad said you went shopping this weekend?"

"I did. The lamps in the front room were looking so drab, so I replaced them. Did you see them?"

"No, Ma'am." Going to the front door, she looked at the new lamps her mom had purchased. "I like the tan color. Where did you get them?"

"Macy's, they were on sale. Can you believe it? I bought something on sale!"

"They look great, Mom. Thank you for keeping such a great home for us. I don't say it enough, thank you, that is."

Jacque beamed, "Oh, my daughter, it is my honor. You know I love to keep a beautiful home, but I do it so you can come home to something you are proud of."

"Thank you, Mom. I've gotta run. I love you." After kissing her on the cheek, she left to catch the bus.

On the way to the bus, she thought about what Grammy told her about forgiveness. She had been forgiven and so she should forgive. She wasn't as angry at her mom and dad, but she couldn't say that she had forgiven them. "Jesus, Grammy told me that you would help me to forgive. Can you help me?" As she walked around the corner, she saw Rachel and smiled.

"Hey, you."

Before Maddie could say hello, a flurry of pink approached.

"Kaitlyn, look at you, pretty in pink! I didn't know you were going to ride today." Rachel was in awe of her friend's new hair.

"Mom couldn't take me all the way to school, so I asked her to drop me off so I would bless you two with my pink presence."

"So, why the change? We were just together twenty-four hours ago." Maddie asked as she followed the two to their seats on the bus.

"I feel alive, ya know? Ready to take on the world! Oh, and I'm planning to meet Todd this weekend. Do you think he will like it?"

Maddie looked at Rachel, who had a concerned look on her face. "You're meeting Todd? He's the guy from online, right?"

"Yeah, but Mads, he is cool, promise. He is so nice and respectful."

"What does Mom say?" Rachel asked.

Kaitlyn stared blankly at something in front of them as she said, "She's cool with it."

"Where are y'all gonna meet?" Maddie asked.

"The new Boba place downtown. It's nice and public. I'm getting my license on Wednesday, so I'm gonna drive."

"Wait, when did this happen?" Rachel asked.

"Mom made me an appointment last week."

Maddie was so excited her friend was finding her freedom. "Oh, Kaitlyn, that's awesome! Maybe we can go to the movies on Saturday night?"

"Well, not yet. I am supposed to wait six months before I can drive others around."

Maddie sighed. "Oh yeah, that's right."

Rachel's eyes looked worried as she placed her hand on her friend's shoulder. "Kate, promise me you will be safe.

Kaitlyn looked at her friend and said, "I'll be fine Rach, promise."

"Wait, Kaitlyn's meeting with Todd? We told her that was dangerous, didn't we?" Jade's jaw was tense as she paced back and forth while listening to Rachel and Maddie explain Kaitlyn's weekend date.

"She said she'd be okay. Besides, they're meeting in a public place." Rachel didn't sound too convinced in her response.

"Where?"

Maddie pulled out her phone, "The new Boba Tea shop on First Avenue. Here's the link."

Jade stopped and held her breath, "Do you know what time?"

"No, but I can find out."

"Good, find out and let me know. I've got a class. Let's meet up after school." Jade made the peace sign as she ran down the hallway.

"Sorry, I'm late. Mrs. Turner kept me after class to retake a quiz. Where's Jade?" Rachel was out of breath as she sat down next to Maddie.

"How's my girls?" Jade sat down on the edge of the bench and wrapped her braids on top of her head. "What's the scoop?"

Maddie pulled a piece of paper from her pocket, "Seven PM on Friday night."

"Okay, this is the plan. I have a hankering for some Boba Tea. Wanna join me?"

"Let me guess, Friday at seven?" Rachel asked.

"You've got it."

Maddie fidgeted with her nails as she waited for Rachel. Her mom had encouraged her to stop biting her nails a while ago and they looked healthy and strong. But her nerves threatened to destroy her efforts. Rachel's dad drove up just as she was ready to bite the nail on her index finger.

As she opened the car door, her mom called out, "Bye, Maddie, home by eleven, okay?"

"Yes, ma'am."

Rachel turned to her friend as she slid into the back seat. "Hey, Girl." Rachel's brow furrowed as she smiled at her friend, but the smile didn't quite reach her eyes.

"Thank you, Mr. Tom, for picking me up."

"Of course. So, you two are checking out the new Boba Tea shop?"

"Yes, Sir."

"I never liked sweet tea much." Tom turned the wheel toward First Avenue.

Rachel laughed, "Oh, but Dad, boba is the best! It's like a bubble in a glass. By the way, it closes at nine and we're going to check out Girlfriend's Place after. Can you pick us up at ten?"

Rachel's dad stopped the car and placed it in park. "I don't know Rachel. Walking downtown after dark is not a smart idea."

"We'll be fine, Dad. We've got each other. Right, Maddie?"

"Yeah, we'll be fine, Mr. Tom. We're in God's hand, right, Rach?"

"Right."

Rachel and Maddie waited on the corner for Jade. The sun was just going down at the six o'clock hour. They decided to come early so they could grab a seat in the back of the shop before Kaitlyn showed up.

Maddie watched as the wind blew the flag across the street. Swaying from side to side with the wind, she realized how nervous she was. She was determined to keep it cool as she struggled with all the feels. "Rach, I don't know about this."

"I know, I'm a little nervous too. But I'm more worried about Kaitlyn."

"Yeah, me too."

"Hey, Girls, are you ready?" Jade came up from behind and surprised the two.

"Okay, so I've been thinking how this will go down." Walking into the shop, Jade pointed to the back left corner, "Grab that table. I'll grab our drinks. Two Matchas?"

"Sounds great, thank you." Rachel led Maddie to the back of the shop.

Jade brought the game of Balderdash for them to play as they waited. As they neared the seven o'clock hour, they found themselves laughing over the answers rounding the table as the bell over the door rang. Jade quieted Rachel and Maddie as they watched Kaitlyn walk in with a man behind her.

The man was tall with black hair and dark brown eyes that darted from side to side. He placed his hand on the small of Kaitlyn's back as he walked her to their table.

Jade rolled her eyes and said, "He's not seventeen."

Maddie's nerves screamed as she watched the exchange. Memories of her experience at the mall flooded her mind, leaving a sense of apprehension in their wake. Jade was right; the man Kaitlyn was with was not a teenager. Maddie could see a tattoo on his arm but couldn't make out the words. "Hey, he's got a tattoo, can you make it out?"

Jade squinted toward the front of the shop, "I think it says babysitter? What does that mean?"

"I don't know."

"Okay, this is really sketch; I don't trust this dude." Jade took a picture and sent it to her Google Photos account with the tag BABYSITTER.

The girls sat nervously as Kaitlyn and Todd chatted. Kaitlyn looked down and tucked a tuft of hair behind her ear as Todd touched her hand.

Looking at Jade, Maddie asked, "Should we go talk to them?"

"No, she would be so mad. We'll just wait and see what happens.

As Jade finished talking, Kaitlyn and Todd got up and walked to the front of the shop. Todd once again had his hand on her back. "Okay, let's go."

"Wait, where are we going?" Maddie asked.

"Don't worry, I just want to go out front and see where they go. Do you know where she parked?"

"There's a parking lot in the back," Rachel answered.

"Maybe we should grab somebody to come with us," Maddie said worriedly.

"Do you know anybody here? Let's go to the parking lot and watch. There are streetlights everywhere. We'll be fine. I'll record the walk if it makes you feel better." Jade turned her phone to record.

As they walked around the corner, Maddie watched in horror as she saw her friend pushed into a dark car. "Kaitlyn! Kaitlyn!!" Jade dropped the game she was holding and ran toward the car as it sped off. Maddie's heart was pounding so hard, and her body was paralyzed with fear.

"Get them!" A man's voice shouted out from the darkness somewhere, but before Maddie and Rachel could turn around, someone grabbed them from behind.

MARIETTA, GEORGIA

"David, it's Tom."

"Hi Tom, how's my Girl? Is everything okay?"

"I came to pick the girls up and they weren't anywhere to be found. I walked into the Boba Tea Shop and then Girlfriend's Place, where they said they would be, and there was no sign of them. I've tried to call Rachel, and it goes straight to voicemail. That isn't like her."

David went into investigation mode as he balled his fist. "Are you still there?"

"Yes, and I've called the police." The concern in Tom's voice was palpable.

The nightmare of his family being in danger had come home, but he didn't have time to ponder it. "I'll be there in fifteen minutes."

CHAPTER 28

An Unexpected Drop

SOMEWHERE IN GEORGIA

Maddie awoke to road sounds. A low, rumbling voice was singing along to the radio, but she couldn't make out the words. She felt groggy and couldn't see anything. "Rachel?" she whispered.

"I'm here. Jade's here too." Her friend moved closer to her.

"Oh, good. I can't see you." Maddie felt disoriented.

"I know, we're blindfolded. Shhh, before they hear us."

With her heart pounding, she attempted to pull her sweaty hands out of the glove contraption that locked them together.

"It's okay, Maddie. Breathe deep, remember God is with us."

MARIETTA, GEORGIA

"What do you mean, they vanished? How could they vanish?"

The manager looked nervous as he answered David's question, "I'm sorry, sir. The three girls were in here, and then they walked outside. We never saw them walk back inside."

"The black girl told the blond to follow the girl with the pink hair," the barista added.

"Girl with pink hair?"

"Yes, sir. She was with a tall guy with black hair, about six feet, I think. I've never seen him before."

"Did you catch a name?" David knew this wasn't his jurisdiction, but the more facts he gathered before the police arrived, the faster they would find his daughter.

"Wait a minute, I think I've got their receipt here." The barista went through the receipts on the spindle and said, "Here, I think this is it."

"Baby S. Are you sure this is the receipt?"

"Yes, sir, I am sure. They had two lavender teas."

Tom said, "That's a weird name for a guy."

David did not like where this was going. "I need to make some calls. Let me know when the police arrive." Pulling his phone out of his pocket, he dialed his father-in-law.

"Jack, this is David. Can you do me a favor, please? I need you to go to the house and sit with Jacque and Matthew, there's been a situation. What? Yes, Maddie and some of her friends are missing. I know, yes, we're on it. The police have been called. I will keep you updated. Jack? Do you mind telling Jacque gently? I would prefer not to do it over the phone. No, I don't think I will be home tonight, but I will let you know once we find her. Yes, I promise I will. Thank you. Oh, and Jack, I appreciate you."

He paced the parking lot, considering his next call. He had a suspicion that Michael had something to do with his daughter's disappearance, but he didn't want to divulge what he knew to those responsible. Instead, he decided to call Israel. It was eleven thirty pm Eastern Standard Time, which would be six thirty am their time, not too early to call his friend.

"Mordy? It's David. Yes, I know it's early. I need a favor. No, everything is not okay. Maddie is missing. Can you check something for me? I want to know all the properties that have been purchased by BALDR Industries. Can you get them to me? A couple of days? I don't think we have a couple of days. Okay, thank you, yes. Upload them to Box. Yes, encrypt the upload, and text me the code. Thank you, Friend. Yes, thank you, we need all the prayers we can get."

"David, the police are here." David and Tom walked over to the policemen standing on the corner.

Hi John, Jerry." Shaking the hands of two of Marietta's finest, David was grateful to know that the officers working on his daughter's disappearance were two that he knew. David had earned the respect of many here through his willingness to collaborate on local crimes.

"Hi David, what's going on?"

"My daughter and several of her friends are missing. They were dropped off here around 1800 and were to be picked up at 2200. The barista here said they were following a girl with pink hair and a six-foot man with black hair out of the shop. Here is the receipt of the two they followed."

Officer John asked, "Can you give a description of the girls?"

Pulling his friend aside, Tom whispered, "David, I've got this. Can you please do me a favor and call Jade's mom? I called her and asked that she wait at home until we hear something."

David walked over to the side of the building to make the call. As he was dialing Jade's mom, he noticed a black and white wristband on the ground. Picking it up, he noticed the writing on the side said Woodlands. "Hey, I've got something."

Officer Jerry came over to see what he found. "David, you know the drill: Don't touch anything. I know it's your daughter, but this is an active scene, and we must keep the evidence clean."

Evidence. He couldn't believe they were talking about evidence of his own daughter's disappearance.

"I know. Jerry, I have a theory. Do you think they went back here?" He pointed to the parking lot behind the building and started walking.

"David, why don't you let us investigate, and you go and make your call?"

"I will, but, hey, do you hear something?"

David and Officer Jerry walked behind the building. A ring from behind surprised them both and led them to turn around to see where the sound was coming from. David saw a light flashing under the bush as they walked toward the building. "Jerry, over here. Is that a phone?"

"It looks like it. David, don't touch it." Officer Jerry spoke into his radio, "John, we need you back here."

The phone on the ground stopped ringing. While he waited, he decided to call Jade's mom to give her an update. "Hi Alisha, this is David. No, we haven't found anything yet. You've tried to call her?" Placing his phone on mute, he said to the officers, "Jade's mom says that her phone just rings and rings. Both Rachel and Maddie's phones went straight to voicemail. Do you think that is Jade's phone on the ground?" Taking his phone off mute, he asked, "Hey, Alisha, can you do me a favor? Do you know Jade's passcode for her phone? In case we find it, we want to be able to identify it. Yes, we will stay in contact as soon as we know something. Yes, ma'am, they will be okay; I'll make sure of it."

Officer John picked up the phone and entered the passcode David gave to him. "Bingo."

"Do you think there are any pictures that might show us what they were doing?"

Navigating to the photos on the phone, Officer John said, "Well, there are quite a few here."

David and the officer swiped through Jade's photos, "Hang on, what's that one? Can you expand it?" David looked closely at the picture of a girl with pink hair sitting with a guy with black hair in the tea shop. "I need to see his arm." The officer zoomed in as much as he could. The picture was pixelated, but David knew exactly what was tattooed on the man's arm.

"BABYSITTER, Is this Baby S? Does the name mean something to you?" Officer John asked.

"Are you familiar with the FBI's roundup of the PeaceKeepers?"

"Yes, we were briefed. We arrested several of those troublemakers here, in fact."

"Well, it is my belief that this is another one."

"Why do you think that?"

"I can't say yet, but it's a trail I'm following for a federal case." He felt bad lying to the officer but thought the urgency of finding Maddie and her friends demanded it. "In the meantime, can we get the tapes from this parking lot?"

Officer Jerry responded, "On it."

Officer John said, "Hey David, there's a video on this phone."

"A video? Can you play it?"

They listened to the video and heard the girls talking about their friend Kaitlyn. They were walking around the building where David now stood with the officers and Tom. The video was blurry and disjointed, but he could make out two people several yards in front of them, one of them with pink hair. Suddenly, the girl with the pink hair was pushed into a car and the video ended.

David's heart fell as he saw Kaitlyn pushed into the dark car. "It appears that we now have four missing girls."

"Okay, David, let us do our job." Officer John pointed him to the front of the building and gestured to Officer Jerry, "Call in the troops. We need to tape up this parking lot. This is officially an active crime scene."

David fought his growing anger as he walked away and dialed Michael's number. *What to say to my son?*

"Michael, thank you for answering my call. How are you? No, we're okay, well, mostly. No, Michael, please let me speak." David sighed when the phone went dead.

SOMEWHERE IN GEORGIA

Maddie, Rachel, and Jade had drawn near to one another in the moving vehicle. Maddie felt a shag carpet beneath her instead of a seat. When the vehicle hit a bump, she was jostled around. *We must be in a van.* She thought to herself. Hearing the breathing of her friends was comforting. She knew if they were together, everything would be okay. Stretching out her legs, she attempted to find something that would help her to sit up straight. Suddenly, the van stopped.

"Ladies, I see you are awake. Time to play musical cars." The foreign voice that spoke smooth and perfect English sounded very familiar to Maddie.

"Who are you? What do you want with us? Where is our

friend?" Jade was never one to back down from a fight.

"Tsk, tsk, so many questions. Your friend is fine. In fact, you will meet her very soon. As to who I am, I am nothing but a birdwatcher who will be passing you off soon."

"Birdwatcher, hey, that was the guy I saw at the mall. I thought I recognized his voice," Maddie whispered to Rachel. She took a few deep breaths and counted to ten as she felt her nerves respond to the reminder.

"And that little lady is why you are here. Americans are so nosy."

"What do you mean?"

Maddie could hear Jade's sass coming out. *If she isn't scared, then I can be strong too.* She thought to herself.

"You took a picture. We do not allow pictures. Where is your phone?"

"My phone? What phone?" Jade asked innocently.

"You had a phone in the coffee shop. Where is it?" The girls began to feel their kidnapper's angst.

"I don't have a phone. Take these gloves off and I'll show you."

Maddie heard rustling as Birdwatcher took the gloves off Jade's hands. "Don't try anything, little Lady; you are well surrounded here."

Jade's sigh signaled the girls of her relief, "See, I don't have a phone."

"We found nothing on the other two phones. What did you do with the picture?"

"Honestly, I do not know what you are talking about. Take us back to the tea shop, and I will look around for you?"

"Don't sass me, little Girl."

"Well, I guess we are at an impasse then. Sorry, I couldn't help you." Jade began humming as the gloves were put back on.

A female voice said, "Come on, ladies. It's time to go. Thank you, Birdwatcher. We will be in touch."

"Bagman said I would be paid when the drop was made. May I remind you that I am NOT a babysitter. This unexpected drop was not on my radar."

"Yes, Birdwatcher. Has the CO ever stiffed you? Your money is coming."

Maddie felt someone yanking her arm out of the vehicle as she listened to the exchange. She wanted to remember every detail.

"Do you need to go to the bathroom?"

Relieved the voice was female, she said, "Yes."

"Okay, let's go, and no funny business. You are surrounded."

"We need our hands," Jade said.

"Do not worry; I will remove your gloves in due time."

Maddie was breathing hard, trying to ease the panic rising from her stomach. The woman must've known something was wrong as she began to rub her arm. "We mean you no harm; you are safe."

The girls went to the bathroom and then were hurried into another vehicle. With blindfolds on, Maddie had no idea where they were.

"Can you remove the blindfolds?" Rachel asked.

"Not yet, but soon."

"Where is our friend? Birdwatcher said we would see her." Jade pleaded.

"You will, soon."

CHAPTER 29

A Shield of Faith

SOMEWHERE IN GEORGIA

The new van had what felt like the same shag carpet, but this time the girls were allowed to sit against the wall. Maddie attempted to get comfortable, stretching the weariness out of her arms and legs. She was exhausted. *Just think, twenty-four hours ago, I was warm and comfy in my own bed. Will I ever see my bed again?* She contemplated that thought again. *Maddie, take your thoughts captive. I WILL SEE MY BED AGAIN!*

After what seemed hours, the van stopped. as the back doors opened, the woman's voice from earlier spoke quietly. Maddie strained to listen to what she was saying.

"Bagman, we have a new drop. This one isn't on the books. We have three packages that will need a home."

Maddie couldn't hear the other voice very well, but it sounded as if Bagman didn't like the command.

"I understand, but this comes from the top. Make it happen."

The girls were all pulled out of the van. Rachel touched Maddie's arm and said, "Stay calm; we'll be okay." She was anything but okay, but she kept repeating in her head, *God is with me,* over and over.

The woman from the van gave an instruction to someone and then said, "Okay, Ladies, freedom is yours."

Relief flooded Maddie as the blindfolds and gloves were

278

removed. It took a moment for her eyes to adjust to the grim fluorescent lighting overhead, but the flickering didn't help the headache she was fighting.

As she regained her focus, she noticed a tall woman with red hair wearing a pencil-straight suit. She was standing next to two men who did not appear happy to be there.

"Welcome to the PKO ladies. I am Carissa, your host. This is Billy and Mac. And this is Todd... Suddenly a door opened, and the six-foot man from the Boba Tea Shop walked into the room with Kaitlyn not far behind.

"Kaitlyn!"

"Jade!"

The girls forgot their captors and nearly knocked one another over as they rallied together in a big group hug. Overwhelmed with emotion, each of them began crying and talking all at once.

"Okay, ladies, that is enough. Please sit down. Mac, can you get them some breakfast? I expect they are starving."

The girls obediently quieted and sat down at the nearest lunch table. Maddie could have sworn she had met Mac from somewhere but couldn't put her finger on it. Looking around the room, she saw white walls and a big black symbol that looked like an upside-down cross with a lightning bolt down the middle enclosed in a circle. She shivered. *I wonder what it means,* she wondered. If it weren't for the fact that the walls were mostly bare and they were the only people in the room, she might have thought she was at school. Sighing, she thought to herself; *I wish I was at school.*

"Please excuse the chaos surrounding your entry, Ladies. We pride ourselves on order, and the experience you three had last night was not how we operate. Before I share the house rules, why don't you each share your names?"

The girls looked at one another, not quite sure how to respond.

Jade went first. "My name is Jessie."

"I'm Reagan."

"My name is M-elissa." Maddie quickly understood what

the other girls were doing but wasn't good at lying and tripped over her fake name.

"My name is Kaitlyn."

The room was so quiet you could hear a pin drop. Looking at the woman with red hair and an equally red face, the girls waited for her to continue.

"Okay, Ladies, that was a test, and three of you failed. Let's try again, shall we? We already know your names, but we wanted to know if you were trustworthy enough to be part of our community. Obviously, we have some work to do in that area."

Jade responded a little too bluntly, "Jade."

"Rachel."

"Maddie."

"That's better. Now, was that so hard?" If you follow the rules around here, things will go very easily for you."

Jade raised her hand.

"Yes, Jade?"

"May I ask a question?"

"Well, of course. We have an open-door policy here."

"What exactly is PKO?"

"That is a great question! I am so glad you asked. We are an all-inclusive community that serves the world by providing food and supplies to those in need."

"So, you *kidnap* people to provide for those in need?" Jade's sass was showing again.

"The word kidnap is so last decade, Jade. We are providing a service for the community, and so we invite people into our organization and teach them to love and serve their community. If they don't want to stay, then we, of course, let them go."

Maddie was so confused. Was Carissa unaware of what Birdwatcher did?

"Carissa," Jade responded loudly, "I don't think you understand. There was no INVITATION. Your BIRDWATCHER snatched us off the street like we were garbage! Then he threw us into a van and brought us here. Tell me where the invitation is in that?"

"Jade, shhh," Rachel tried to calm down her friend.

"Don't tell me to shhh; that's what happened!" It had been a long time since Jade's anger was unleashed. Her yells could rattle windows.

Carissa walked over to Jade and stood directly in front of her. "May I see your hands?" She asked calmly.

Maddie, Rachel, and Kaitlyn all looked at one other in fear. Jade, on the other hand, looked at Carissa like a cat placed in water as her captor waited patiently. Jade finally complied.

"Oh, these are lovely. Did you just have them done?" Carissa stroked Jade's hands like silk blankets.

Jade turned to look at the girls as if to say: THIS GIRL IS CRAZY! Turning back to Carissa, she said, "I had them done last Thursday."

"That's good; then you've had time to enjoy them, and you won't mind if I remove them." Carissa ripped the nail off Jade's right index finger like it was a band-aid.

"Hey, that hurts! Why did you do that?" Jade squealed.

"Jade, my dear. This is a community. We believe in order here, and we expect everyone to act respectfully and, of course, orderly. Those who are orderly are rewarded with peace. For those who are disrespectful or disorderly, well, let's just say they learn very quickly the consequences of being disorderly." Carissa folded her hands together and smiled.

Her words were sweet, layered with honey. However, her eyes carried a look of disdain. Just as the black symbol on the wall gave Maddie a shiver, the look on Carissa's face was one of calculation. Like a spider preparing to pounce on a fly.

Jade held her hand tightly as she fought back tears. Maddie wanted to cry on her behalf. *God, can we please wake up from this nightmare?* She prayed quietly.

"Now, I recommend you remove those beautiful nails because otherwise, they will quickly be damaged in the days to come.

"Oh good, Mac, thank you. Ladies, Mac is the best at putting a spread together. He knows exactly what we need to be healthy and strong. Don't you, Mac?"

Mac didn't seem to want to look at the girls, so he turned slightly and said, "Yes, ma'am. Thank you, Carissa, ma'am."

"Okay, ladies, eat up. Afterward, we will show you where you will be sleeping and working."

Working? What did she mean by working? Maddie didn't like that statement but didn't spend too much time mulling over it as she looked down at the eggs, bacon, and fruit cup. She was starved and would eat anything they placed in front of her.

Over breakfast, the girls devoured their food. As they ate, they studied the room. Guards stood post at each exit. They didn't appear to be armed, but they did look quite formidable. Rachel gestured toward the symbol on the wall and whispered, "What is that?"

Maddie looked confused as she shrugged, "I don't know."

"Kaitlyn, what happened last night?" Maddie whispered.

"Todd offered to walk me to my car. Next thing you know, I was dragged into a dark car with dark windows. I don't remember anything."

"You weren't dragged, Todd pushed you," Jade interrupted.

"No, he didn't. I remember an arm reaching out and grabbing me."

"We saw you, Kate. You were pushed," Rachel chimed in.

"Well, anyway. Next thing you know, I woke up here. They held me in a room until you guys got here."

"I wonder why they waited on us. How could they have known we were coming?"

"I don't know. They didn't say anything to me. In fact, Todd was completely quiet all morning. He hasn't even looked at me. Almost as if he isn't quite there if you know what I mean."

"Why did you agree to go out with him, Kate?" Jade asked.

"He was so nice. I've never had a guy talk to me like that. I really thought he was okay. Oh guys, I'm so sorry," Kaitlyn began crying quietly.

Jade looked around the room and briefly touched her friend's hand. "Kate, it's done. Now we need to figure out how to get out of here."

"My dad will save us," Maddie whispered confidently.

Kaitlyn wrapped her arms around herself and began rocking slowly, "Your dad doesn't even know where we are, Maddie."

She didn't know where it came from, but she felt a jolt of courage. "This is his job. If there is any time that I can expect him to show up, it's now."

Jade looked upward as she said cynically, "We'll see about that."

Rachel had been quiet all morning. It was time to be encouraged, and Rachel was the one to bring it. "Ladies, we've been prepared for this trial. It's time to put our shield of faith on."

Kaitlyn rolled her eyes, "Come on, Rachel. This is not a good time to bring out your God theories."

"Kaitlyn, we need God now, more than ever. He is with us. Nobody can take him away from us. It's time to stand on that truth."

"Well, I'm with Jade; we'll see about that."

"Okay, tell us how we put on our shield of faith?"

"Prayer."

"Hurry, let's do this, give me your hands.

"Quickly," Rachel said a prayer, asking God to protect them and cover them with the blood of Jesus and his shield of faithfulness. Quoting from a Psalm, she thanked God for allowing them to dwell in his shelter. Maddie was amazed at how well Rachel remembered the scripture.

"Amen." They each said in unison.

Looking around the room, Maddie noticed that the guards were still standing at the doors, looking forward as if into space. She wondered if they would even respond if the girls got up. Jade must've been thinking the same as she began to rise.

"No, Jade. Wait until they tell us to go," Kaitlyn whispered.

Jade was ready to run. "I only want to see what they'll do."

Rachel pleaded with her friend, "Please, Jade. Don't make trouble. We will be rescued, I promise."

Sitting down obediently, Jade nodded her head. Jade and Rachel debated on many subjects, but Jade always listened to Rachel when push came to shove.

MARIETTA, GEORGIA

"I don't care what it takes! Get me that clearance!" David slammed the phone down.

Taking a deep breath, he attempted to calm his frayed nerves. The past forty-eight days had been harrowing. Within forty-eight hours, the police had found the perpetrator responsible for taking Maddie and her friends. David was not surprised to learn that he was the same person who started the fire at the mall last summer. The police spent hours interrogating the man called Birdwatcher and got nothing, but the evidence against him was overwhelming.

They had yet to find Babysitter or Baby S. The video footage from Jade's phone was released to the media in the hopes that someone could help identify him. But no luck yet.

If there was any silver lining, it was the community response. Even after a month and a half, the story was still alive and parents were bonding together to help find the girls, but also to encourage one another and David. He was thankful for this but found it ironic that every week, hundreds of children went missing around the country, and you rarely heard more than one alert. The media had no problem asking the question, "Who is next?" but offered no solution, no peace, and as a result, fear and chaos gripped the nation, leading to more and more kids being pulled out of school by their parents.

David had a pretty good idea of where the girls were based on the information given to him by Mordy. But each compound was locked up tight. When he got a copy of the properties purchased by BALDR Industries, he immediately called Admiral Osborne who shut him down quickly. "Son, I know you love your daughter, but please let the police do their job. If they find any credible evidence that she is being held against her will in one of these communities, then I will be the first to send in the cavalry." David could not believe his ears. They didn't believe him! He began to wonder if loyalty to his country even mattered when it was his family who was victimized.

The world seemed to be falling apart. Communities were on fire, major cities were running out of food supplies, thieves were openly breaking into houses at all times of the day, and children were being abducted. Chaos was in charge and the media was serving fear up to the public on a platter. What was happening?

Sitting down, his gaze drifted to their family picture from Maddie's birthday last Summer. Everyone looked so happy, including Jacque. Shortly after the abduction, Jacque had a relapse. Jack took her back to the mental health facility to help keep her stable. Matthew went to stay with his mom, while Michael was nowhere to be found. David placed his head in his hands as he lamented over his family falling apart. He needed some of his mom's faith about now. He could hear her voice as if she was sitting right next to him. *Son, get on your knees. Yer Heavenly Father be waitin' for ya.*

He looked at the picture of his family again. If there was ever a time faith was needed, it was now, even if he had to borrow it from his mom. Slipping out of his chair, he fell to his knees.

"God, it's David here. It's been a while since I prayed. And if truth be told, I haven't thought about you since Jacque went into the hospital. Forgive me. Father, my mom believes in you. She says you are faithful and hold true to your promises. I need you now, God. My family needs you now. Our world needs you now. We need a miracle! Please, help us find my Maddie and cover us with your shield of protection. Please God? In Jesus' Name, amen."

David released silent tears that made their way to the floor.

Rubbing his eyes with his hands, he was jolted out of his thoughts by the buzzing of his phone.

"Dad?"

"Michael?"

"Dad, I need your help."

CHAPTER 30

A Counterfeit Peace

BALDERSVILLE, GEORGIA

It had been two months since the girls arrived at the PKO. Maddie was keeping count by making small marks on the wall next to her bed. Of course, she would cover them up.

Every day was the same. She and those in her bunkhouse would get up at six am, go to breakfast, and then work out in the garden. They called it a community garden. Truly, it was a large farm on hundreds and hundreds of acres. Jade had determined there to be about a thousand teens and children working with young adults supervising. Some would work in the garden; others would care for the animals. Those who had been indoctrinated (Jade's words) were allowed to go into public. Everyone else had to stay in the community and work until they earned the right to go into town.

Carissa and her posse (as Jade called them) were a force to be reckoned with. Nobody messed with Carissa or else. Maddie didn't know what "or else" meant, but she wasn't looking to find out.

One day, as she worked, she ventured into the flower beds. Elated that the guard responsible for the area was missing from his post, she was able to freely walk the beds without feeling as if she was being watched. Rows and rows of sunflowers bunched together like a deep forest. This was her safe place. As she wandered, the pads of her fingers brushed over the buds beginning to bloom. Reminiscing over her Grammy's sunflowers, she began to feel sad. *Will I ever see Grammy again?* Maddie was dutifully taking these thoughts to the Cross, but it was so hard. She wanted nothing else but to have Grammy hug her and hear her dad call her Ruthie. *God, please give me a sign. Please tell me that I will see my family again.* Suddenly, she heard a familiar bird call. *Certainly, that isn't Ms. Carolina Wren way down here,* she wondered. Turning around to find the source of the song, she saw her. All in her beautiful brown and white wonder, looking straight at her. Maddie was in awe. She stood perfectly still so as not to scare the bird away. But, as quickly as she came, there she went. *Thank you, God. I, too, will be free again, just like her.* Maddie realized that these moments helped to build her faith. Little signs of God's wonder were everywhere around her if she only looked. Recognizing the guard had returned to his post, she decided it was time to go. Thankful for the moment of peace, she slipped out quietly, humming the song she and Emma wrote.

In their free time, they were allowed to congregate, but their conversations were recorded. If anything was said out of order, they would be reprimanded. They were allowed to pray and to hold church, but open worship was restricted so that order would be maintained at all times.

Maddie was confused over all the order talk. Every day, they heard the same thing: "If there is no order, there can be no peace." They said it at every meal and over the loudspeakers. Rachel reasoned that this was how they kept chaos at bay.

Jade countered, "No, this is how they indoctrinate us."

So, everyone mostly kept to themselves. If a fight were to break out, the offenders would be taken away and placed in what they called the Dark Room. Someone who had spent time in the room stared at Jade in glassy-eyed terror when she asked what it was like.

The girls decided to make friends to see if they could figure out how people were *invited* into the community. Many around them were runaways or wards of the state. Not many were outright kidnapped from loving homes as the girls were, but there were some. Oh, there was the time that Kaitlyn swore she saw Jason Wilson. (He was the one who went missing after a baseball game last year.) But as soon as she saw him, he was gone. She spent every day afterward looking for him.

"I guess I understand why they are taking in runaways and fosters, but why do they need people like us? I don't get it." Maddie didn't know what Jade was more frustrated about, the system or their part in it. Jade became very suspicious of the process, especially after hearing about Kaitlyn's sighting of Jason.

While everything appeared "peaceful," it was a weird kind of peace. Rachel would say, "It's kind of like when you give your dog Benadryl and he's just there." She called it a counterfeit peace. There was no love, no joy, only law and order.

While Maddie was thankful to have her girls with her (truly, they were helping to keep her sane), she missed her family dearly, especially her Grammy. If there was a bright side to this experience, she learned to plant and was even looking forward to harvesting. Something about partnering with God to bring life into the world gave her a new sense of purpose.

Strangely enough, her anxiety was almost gone, and she began to realize that everything she had learned over the last year had prepared her for this moment in time. Rachel, Jade, and she spent every day praying and worshiping in secret as much as they could. This new routine was helping her to stay grounded.

The girls invited Kaitlyn to worship with them, but she was too busy with Todd. He ignored Kaitlyn for the first week, but once she got over being angry with him, suddenly, he wanted a relationship. It was a weird relationship, but Kaitlyn was smitten. Todd DID NOT like Kaitlyn's friends and worked to keep them separated as much as possible. Maddie prayed for her friend's heart. She could see so many red flags.

At the end of one evening, she and Rachel stopped their work and watched the sunset. "Isn't it beautiful?" Rachel asked.

"Yes, it is." Maddie was once again reminded of summer nights at Grammy's in Wild Rock.

"Maddie, what are you asking God for?"

"To see my family again."

Rachel put her shovel down and sat down on the soft earth. "Yeah, me too, but what about for yourself?"

Joining her friend, she grabbed her hand and sat as well, "If I'm honest, I haven't thought much about it."

"What about that prophecy Grammy spoke over you? What was it again?"

"Oh, I had forgotten all about that. Let me think, Madelyn means 'High-Tower', Ruth means 'Companion' and Bennett means 'Little Blessed One.'"

"What do you think God meant by that?"

Fighting back tears, Maddie said, "I don't know. I'm not feeling too blessed right now."

"Didn't you tell me once that when she told you the story of your name, she would tell you the story of Gideon?"

"Yeah."

Picking up a clump of dirt, Rachel said, "You know that Gideon was afraid and anxious. It was in a moment of anxiety that the angel came to him and called him, 'Mighty Warrior.'"

Removing the rocks from the clump Rachel picked up, Maddie said, "Grammy told me he actually said the Lord had abandoned them."

That's right, and the Lord told him to go in his strength and that he was sending him."

"Sending him?"

"Yes, to save Israel. Maddie, your name means High-Tower, Companion, and Little Blessed One. What if God is sending you to save his people?"

Shaking her head, she answered, "Oh, I don't know about that. Who am I?"

Rachel laughed, "Ironically, that's exactly what Gideon said."

As she watched the sunset, Maddie felt a restored sense of peace as she was reminded of a much bigger picture.

"Seriously, Rachel, I know that God promised to save his people, but how can I save anyone?"

"It's not you who would do the saving. Jesus is our Savior. But Maddie, God chooses humble people to do mighty things for his kingdom. He chose Gideon, and he chose you. Think about it."

Rachel stared at the horizon. "The more I think about it, the more I believe there is a reason we are here. Look around you. These people are walking zombies. There's no happiness here. Everyone here is just existing. But we have God in us! It's time we start praying for God to change things, just like he did in the valley of dry bones."

"Isn't there a story about that in the Bible?"

"Yeah, I think it's somewhere in Ezekiel. Goodness, I miss my Bible! But God knows." Rachel grabbed her tired hands, "Maddie, I think we're being prepared for something bigger. What if we are living in the end times? The Bible says that the love of most will grow cold. Haven't we seen that? Perhaps God is preparing these hands to serve those who are walking dead in these last days."

"Oh, Rach, I don't want to think about the end times. Haven't we suffered enough?"

"Remember what Sonya said: It is an honor to suffer for our King. But we can't think about that. God has a purpose for you, for me, and for all the people in the world who are walking around lifeless."

Rachel grabbed her hand as she looked seriously into her eyes, "Perhaps Grammy's prophecy means that YOU are the little blessed one who will be a companion to many. Perhaps your first name is YOUR reminder that God is your strong tower. This could be the purpose he has for you, and now you get to choose if you will join with him in this calling." Rachel was quiet as she pondered her friend's thoughts. "Promise me you'll pray about it?"

"I promise."

MARIETTA, GEORGIA

"Dad, I saw Maddie."

"What? Where? Where are you?"

"Please don't be mad, but I'm in a town called Baldersville, south of Macon. I'm not supposed to be talking to you, Dad, but when I saw Maddie, I just . . ." Sobs kept Michael from finishing.

"Michael, I think I know where you are. Can you get to a safe place and wait for me?"

"There aren't any safe places here, Dad. Everybody knows everybody."

Okay, give me twenty-four hours. Can I reach you on this line?"

"Yes, Sir."

"Good. And promise you'll stay clean?"

"Yes, I will. I can never go back."

Twenty-four hours later, David dialed the number Michael called from. There was no answer. Tapping his foot impatiently, his phone buzzed.

"Michael?"

"Yes, it's me, Dad."

The heaviness in his son's voice was heartbreaking. But he couldn't ponder that right now. "Good. Can you get to a church called New Covenant in Westboro?"

"Yes, I think I know where that is."

"Meet me there Friday night at 2200 hours. We will go over the plan."

"Dad, who are you bringing with you?"

"Just me and Tom."

"Dad, you'll need more than that."

"We'll be fine. This is what we do, Michael." David did not feel the confidence he was projecting, but he didn't have a choice but to keep moving. *Do it, afraid Son.* Remembering his dad's words had pushed him so many times before, he leaned on them now.

"I hope so."

"See you on Friday."

"See ya."

"Mom, it's David."

"Hello, my Davie boy. How's the Lord keepin' ya?"

"I'm tired, Mom."

"I know, Son. How can I pray for ya?"

He hadn't asked for prayer from his mom in years, and he wasn't sure it even worked, but he needed a miracle now and he knew that his mom believed in miracles. "We know where Maddie is. We're going to try and get her and her friends out this weekend. Will you pray over me?"

"Of course, Son, you know I will.

> "Father, God, yer sovereign, and yer good. Thar' ain't nothin' that surprises ya fer you are the Alpha and the Omega, the beginnin' and the end. Lord God, we are trustin' ya to go before my son. Jes' as ya did fer the Israelites; we are believin' that you will part the Red Sea and give him victory. We thank ya, Lord fer protectin' our Maddie Ruth, and we pray Jesus that ya would protect all our loved ones as they are rescued. You, God, are our Rescue, our Dwellin' Place, and we trust that You'll provide for all their needs accordin' to the riches of yer glory. Thank ya' Lord, we love ya. In Jesus' Name, amen."

"Thank you, Mom."

"May the Lord bless and keep ya, my boy."

WESTBORO, GEORGIA

On Friday afternoon, David and Tom drove the three hours from Marietta to the New Covenant Church in Westboro, Georgia. He chose New Covenant because his mom knew the Pastor from way back, and the Pastor knew all about the PKO, as he called the PeaceKeepers unit in Baldersville. And to quote the pastor, "I didn't like them rabble-rousers one bit."

David knocked on the door of the locked church and was greeted by a man a good foot shorter than he, but what he lacked in height, he made up for in girth. Surprised as the man met him with a warm hug and a firm handshake, he said, "You must be Pastor Joe."

"That'd be me," the pastor said. Come in, come in. How was your drive?"

"It was good. This is Tom. He is the father of one of the girls."

Pastor Joe shook Tom's hand briskly. "Good to meet ya, Son."

"We thank you for allowing us to meet Michael here. Would you mind if we laid out our things so we could devise a game plan to get into the compound?"

"Why shore thing, but you're gonna need some help."

"It's okay. We've done this a time or two."

"Trust me, Son, you're gonna need help. And I've got just the men you need."

Surprised, David turned around and saw a group of eleven burly men standing with rifles and shovels.

"Meet the warriors of The Way."

"The Way?"

"Yes, sirree. The first church in the Book of Acts was called The Way. We figured we'd walk in the footsteps of those courageous twelve and start an undercover church right here in Westboro."

"Why do you need an undercover church?" He asked.

"Well, that'd be cause the people here are dead. They're just walkin' around existin'. God's sendin' us out cause he wants to breathe on dead spirits and bring 'em back to life. We're goin' undercover in the most sinister places of South Georgia to be used by the Lord to do just that."

"What kind of things does The Way do?"

"Well, that'd be the Lord's will to reveal, but I'll share one story with ya. See this girl right here?" Pastor Joe pointed to a picture of a girl on a horse waving at the camera. "She was fourteen years old when her parents kicked her out of her house. On the streets, she had to live until an evil man wooed her and began to sell her off to equally evil men."

David shuddered at the thought. *Oh God, please don't let that be what Maddie is going through!*

"Well, we caught wind of this evil scheme straight from the pit of Hell and we prayed, and the Lord was with us as we rescued that young'un and found her a good home. We found her and she found Jesus. That guy ain't selling young girls off anymore." A couple of the men laughed at the Pastor's declaration.

"Can I ask you a question?" David asked.

"Why a'course."

"Did you rescue her from the compound?"

"Oh no. As far as we know, they don't sell off young women … yet. But, with the things comin' out of that place, it's only a matter of time. There ain't no life there. Satan himself could live there and be happy as a lark. In fact, I 'spect he is."

Pastor Joe stopped at the sound of another knock on the door. "Well, I'll be, I think that's you're young'un."

Michael walked into the church. He looked gaunt and underfed. David grabbed his son and hugged him tight. He could feel his ribs through the thin shirt he was wearing. "How are you?"

"I've been better. Dad, I'm so sorry; this is all my fault."

"No, Son. If anything, I am at fault."

"If I had stayed home and gone to school like you told me, I could've helped you protect Maddie." His voice cracked on his sister's name.

"Michael, this could've happened no matter how many people protected her. How did she look when you saw her?"

"She looks good. Your daughter Rachel, as well, Mr. Tom." Michael smiled weakly. The kids are well fed because they're the ones doing all the work." Michael looked around the room and saw the twelve men standing behind them. "Who are they?"

David released a sigh of relief. "You said we needed help. It appears someone else thought we needed help, too. Now, let's get down to business. Show us where the girls are and how to get in."

CHAPTER 31

Rescue!

BALDERSVILLE, GEORGIA

Friday nights were the only time the people in the PKO let their hair down. Monday through Saturday, they worked hard for ten hours with a few hours of school in between. Sundays were spent listening to the person called CO, or Case Officer, teach law and order. On Friday nights, they were allowed pizza, soda, and a movie. The movie was, of course, orderly. They were all pretty good, actually. Maddie didn't realize how many movies she had missed growing up.

On the first Friday in May, they watched Life of Pi. Afterward, Carissa spoke about the importance of finding order in nature and learning how to survive and work together, even amid conflict. Maddie was surprised to see Jade and Kaitlyn listening. Typically, they were working on plans to escape. But, for some reason, they were compliant.

"What's up with you guys?" Maddie asked.

Kaitlyn looked at her nails in an obvious attempt to ignore her friend's gaze. "What do you mean?"

"You're just awfully … good."

Rachel laughed at Maddie's pause.

"If ya can't beat 'em, join 'em, right?" Jade asked as she stuffed pizza in her mouth.

Rachel pointed at Maddie and herself, "We know you better than that. What are you two up to?"

297

Maddie felt nauseous as she watched Jade smile like a Cheshire cat.

Lights out always took place at eleven o'clock sharp. Everyone worked so hard throughout the day that there was never an argument. The cots they were given were not the most comfortable, but they were clean. In fact, everything was spotless. While some worked in the garden and on the farm, there were others who kept the communal spaces clean. *I'm glad that isn't my job.* Maddie mused.

The bunks were arranged in order: Rachel, Maddie, Kaitlyn, and Jade. Thankfully, they were close to the bathrooms which were at the front of the dorm. For some reason, the CO thought it a grand idea to keep the four of them together. *If Grammy were here, she would tell him that he wasn't thinking with all his marbles.* Maddie laughed at the thought.

While she missed her family, she strangely felt safe. The routine worked best for her. Change and spontaneity were more Rachel and Jade's thing, but she loved schedules and clear instructions. So, the time they had spent at PKO, while weird and unsettling, was quite pleasant.

Maddie closed her eyes as she settled into her covers. She could hear slight rustling and whispers from the vicinity of Jade and Kaitlyn's beds. She was so tired that she didn't want to open her eyes. It seemed minutes had passed when she was suddenly awakened by a light in her face. Before she could scream, a warm hand covered her mouth as a man placed his index finger on his lips. As her eyes adjusted beyond the light, she recognized the warm brown eyes of her dad. *DADDY!* David picked up his daughter as she placed her arms tightly around him. "Never let me go," she whispered as tears began to stream down her face.

The next few moments passed quickly. Having to maneuver through the manicured landscaping, David ran until he reached the unmanned exit.

The warriors of The Way had quietly and expertly removed the man who was stationed at the exit so they could get in and out without being seen.

David set Maddie down on the grass next to a man she had never met. Touching her face, he quietly said, "Maddie, this is Joe; he is safe and will stand here with you. Are you okay?"

Maddie had no words. She nodded, overwhelmed with feelings she couldn't communicate.

Soon, she watched as Rachel was set down by her dad. The two girls hugged and cried tears of joy.

"Maddie, where are Jade and Kaitlyn? When we checked the beds, there wasn't anyone there." Mr. Tom asked.

"I don't know. They were in the two beds beside us. Wait, I overheard Jade whisper sunflower. I know where they are!"

Rachel grabbed her hand and began praying when she saw her friend begin to panic.

"Sir, we have Michael on the radio."

"Michael, two of the girls are missing." Maddie could hear the static on the other end and then the voice of her brother.

"Dad, I know where they are; I can take you there," Maddie cried out.

"Tell me where they are, and I will send Michael for them."

"No, Dad, there's no time. I'll take you there."

Maddie was in agony as she waited for Joe, Mr. Tom, and her dad to decide their next action. Finally, she ran out of patience and grabbed his hand, leading him toward the fence.

Over the last two months, Maddie spent many hours in the PKO gardens. After seeing Ms. Carolina Wren, she noticed her almost every day. She seemed to lead her to the same place, the sunflower garden. One day, as she followed the bird, she found a small opening in the fence at the back of the garden. Maddie told the girls about it but didn't know how to get through it or where it would lead. Maddie knew that was where Jade and Kaitlyn were going.

Her dad and Joe finally seemed to listen to her and followed her as she ran through the fields. Maddie felt empowered, like when she zip-lined at Woodlands. She knew she should be afraid, but all she could think about was the safety of her friends.

Once she reached the sunflower fields, she turned around and motioned for her dad not to say a word. Not far from them was a gate with an armed guard. They had to be very quiet, or else they would capture attention.

Standing on her tiptoes, she tried to catch a glimpse of her friends. *Oh God, please, please, help us find them!* She screamed in her thoughts.

Before she knew it, she saw rustling in a group of flowers to her left. Her dad must have seen it, too, as he jumped out in front of her. Suddenly, Jade and Kaitlyn made their way into the clearing and were surprised when they saw Maddie. She was never so happy as to see her friends than at that moment. Relief, mixed with joy, as the girls embraced each other tightly that they never wanted to let go.

"We don't have time, Girls." David whispered. "We need to get you out of here. Joe, do you see Michael?"

Joe looked around the property with his binoculars and whispered, "Yes, I do. He's being questioned by someone."

"Give me those." David grabbed the binoculars from Joe.

"Oh no," he pointed at the girls. Get them out of here. We will meet you at the church." Joe grabbed the three girls and led them through the fence's hidden opening to a hidden SUV up the road, where Tom and Rachel were waiting.

After letting go of her friends, Maddie yelled, "Wait, we can't leave them!" Fear grabbed hold of her once again. *She had just reunited with her dad; she couldn't lose him again!*

"It's okay, ma Girl. God's got 'em."

Hearing Joe's drawl reminded her of Grammy. It was as if she was encouraging her through him. Maddie felt at ease as she grabbed her friend's hands and began praying.

◆◆◆

An hour passed as the girls waited for Maddie's dad and Michael to return. Rachel decided this was a grand time to lecture Jade and Kaitlyn on their stupid decision to leave the dorm. "You could've been killed!"

"But we weren't."

"I never told you where the opening was; it could've taken you hours to find it. Why did you go without us?" Maddie asked.

Kaitlyn looked mischievous as she said, "I'll spill the tea. So, Jade and I decided it was time to break free. We went out to the sunflower bed just as you said and found the back gate unmanned again. Guess whose time it was to guard it?"

"Let me guess, Todd's." Rachel shook her head.

"You've got it! Anywho, once we realized that Todd was nowhere to be found, we started to walk the back fence but there was too much brush. We decided to return to the dorm, and don't you know how happy we were to run into you before having to run all the way back!"

Annoyed over her answer, Maddie said, "I don't understand why you decided to go without us." The adrenaline was winding down and anxiety was starting to set in.

Jade placed her hand on Maddie's shoulder. "We wanted to find the opening and have a solid plan before bringing you two out. Four would easily draw a great deal more attention than two. Maddie, I'm sorry, we knew you and Rachel wouldn't like our plan. But we just had to get out of this place!"

The girls hugged once more. Two months of pent-up fears released in an outpouring of tears from all four of them.

Wiping her tears, Maddie was thankful they were out of danger, but she couldn't stop thinking about her dad. Her body was shaking at the thoughts running through her head. *God, you'll get him through this, right?*

Joe introduced the girls to his wife, Peggy, who sat in the front cab of the SUV. She must've seen Maddie shaking as she grabbed her hand and began to sing quietly. Just as with Joe, the Tennessee twang in Peggy's soft voice reminded her of being with Grammy. When they arrived at the church, she brought them each a blanket and a bottle of water and proceeded to tell them stories about her grandchildren to pass the time. Maddie placed her head on her shoulder and closed her eyes. She wished that for one moment she could be back in Wild Rock; then everything would be okay.

All at once, an army of men barreled through the doors. They were all laughing at something one of them said. Four pairs of eyes opened wide as they peered up at the men who looked like giants. Maddie looked around them to find her dad. Jumping up, she saw him hobbling up the steps.

"It's only a flesh wound; I'll be okay," David tried to console his daughter as she helped him to a chair.

"What happened?"

"When we entered the compound, we went to the general vicinity where Joe saw Michael, but we didn't see him at first. As we rounded the bend, one of the guys saw him tied up against a tree with a swarm of armed guards standing over him. One of the guards saw me and took a shot, but he didn't get much." David looked at his leg as Peggy cleaned the wound.

Maddie looked toward the door. "Where is he?"

"I don't know, Maddie. It was too chaotic."

Her eyes filled with tears as she asked, "We aren't going to leave him, are we?"

Tucking a tuft of hair behind her ear, David said, "Maddie, no, we aren't going to leave him behind. But right now, we need to get you and the girls home safely."

"Wait, so you're staying?"

"Yes. Tom will take you girls home and we'll go back in to get your brother." He melted over the worry in her eyes. David wanted to comfort his daughter but knew how precious minutes were. "Ruthie, we will bring your brother home. I promise."

Joe parroted David's promise, "Yes, ma'am, we'll get him out. The warriors of The Way ain't never left a man behind."

Maddie sat still for a moment, "Dad, I trust you. God protected us, and I believe he will protect you, too."

Epilogue

June 23
Wild Rock, Tennessee

Maddie awoke from her dream safe and sound in Wild Rock, Tennessee. Wiping the sleep from her eyes, she wondered, *how long will I have to relive the past year?* The nightmares plaguing her were lessening but when she had one, she felt as if she was right in the middle of the chaos again. She just couldn't shake the symbol in the mess hall. While she wanted to believe the danger was over, intuition told her otherwise.

Pulling out her journal, she read the entry from the day she came home:

> *May 13*
> *Father,*
> *Thank you for bringing me home and thank you for my daddy. I am so grateful that you led him to us. I've never understood why he worked so hard, but now I see that he works to keep all people safe. Please protect him and the warriors of The Way as they look for Michael. Thank you, Lord, for Rachel, Jade, and Kaitlyn for keeping us safe and helping us through the last two months. Lord, there are still a lot of people in PKO who are lost. I pray, God, that you will rescue them like you rescued us. And in the meantime, please protect them and reveal yourself to them. And Lord,*

please protect Mike. I pray that he will not be punished for saving us! I place him in your capable hand, God. Oh, and thank you for Ms. Carolina Wren. I truly believe you sent her to me to remind me of your presence.

Grammy says I should always ask myself what I have learned when I face a challenge. I have learned that you are faithful. You reveal the truth to us through your word, through those around us, and through the challenges we face so we will know you more and recognize that we can trust you. Well, that's what you did for me, anyway. Thank you for teaching me to speak truth to the enemy's lies. And I have learned not to allow fear to keep me from moving forward but that you will walk with me. Help me, Lord, to take these lessons with me on my journey. I give you my fear, Lord; and I put on the shield of faith you have given me. Whatever you have for me, I am your daughter and am ready to walk in your light. I trust you, God.
Maddie

Thinking about that day was hard, there was so much that happened, but Maddie made it a point to write what she remembered down. Mr. C challenged her to jot down her experience at the PKO as it came to her. He said that she NEEDED to remember so she could heal from the trauma she incurred. He said that this was a big rock that God would help her to excavate. It was going to be hard, but she promised she would do it. She knew that God would help her every step of the way.

Mr. Tom brought the girls home the Saturday after their rescue. Maddie was never happier to be home and in her own bed. An overwhelming welcome was given from those she loved, including her mom, who was at the mental health facility getting a "health lift," as she called it. Mom was okay, but she still had moments when she looked sad and lost.

Going back to school was weird. Everyone at school was happy to see Maddie, but she felt disconnected. Her friends at school had moved on with their lives, but she was in a different place and didn't know how to get back on track. Maddie knew comparing herself to others wasn't healthy, but she had to acknowledge the feelings she was having along with the fact that re-integrating was hard, as Mr. C said. The good news was that they weren't too far behind in their studies. She had one online class to make up over the summer; otherwise, the school administration gave each of the girls a pass for the semester.

Shortly after the girls came home, Mom told her that her dad went undercover again so he could bring Michael home and their family would be complete. Maddie prayed for them both every day. She HAD TO BELIEVE they would be okay. Her new routine included watching the news in the hopes that she would hear that they were safe. Grammy said this wasn't healthy, but she felt she had no choice. Strangely enough, it seemed the newscasters found a new angle every day to report on.

The night she watched Carissa, Todd, and Birdwatcher led away in handcuffs was the night she could finally breathe. Oh, and she couldn't forget Mac. She finally remembered him. He was the one she and Matthew played dominoes with when her brother visited last fall. He, too, was led away for hopefully a very long time. Maddie didn't understand why the CO wasn't arrested, but she expected the investigation was still pending.

Emma was so happy to have her girls home. On the Saturday of their homecoming, she came over to her house and hugged her tight. *I prayed every day!* She cried out. Once again, gratefulness washed over Maddie like waves in the ocean. Before school let out, both Emma and Maddie worked on perfecting their song.

Jade and Kaitlyn both re-integrated as if nothing ever happened. Maddie knew they thought about it, but whenever one of the girls brought it up, they would raise their hand as if to say, nope, not today. Kaitlyn placed her nose in a book and pursued her study of the solar system. Jade chose instead to focus on her faith, reading everything she could about Jesus and the warrior he called her to be (her words.) She and Rachel would have lively debates that always intrigued Maddie; she learned so much from them both. And now that Jade had chosen to follow Jesus, she was working on Kaitlyn to see God in everything. Maddie believed she would be successful.

Maddie's birthday was in a month. After the school year let out, Grammy picked her and Matthew up for the summer. Her mom and Grandpa Jack felt they would be safer there until things calmed down. She couldn't think of a better place to be! Grammy said her friends could visit her for the week, and she even encouraged her to invite Jacob Sullivan!! She was a little nervous about that, but this new Maddie was going to face fear with faith.

Hearing the lively voices of Rachel, Grammy, and Matthew, she decided it was time to join the party and walked into the kitchen. Bending down to pet Max as he chewed on his favorite duck, she laughed at his concentration. Nothing was taking him away from his new friend.

Matthew grabbed her hand and dragged her to the table. "Maddie! Did you enjoy your dream? Rachel said to let you sleep because you were having important con-vo-sa-tions."

Smiling at her little brother, her eyes got all watery as she thought about where she was and where she had been. "Matthew, I had the best sleep ever; thank you for letting me sleep in." Tousling his hair, she walked over to the counter where Grammy was standing.

"Well, Maddie Ruth, what'll it be for breakfast? We got waffles, eggs, bacon, and freshly squeezed OJ."

Grammy looked so beautiful in the morning sun. Maddie never realized how beautiful she was. She truly radiated God's love in everything she did.

"I would love a waffle and some coffee, but can I help?"

"Why a'course ya can Love! Come on over here and help yer ole' Grammy."

As she watched Grammy's old knobby hands, she thought of all Grammy had done for her. From the moment she was born, Grammy had lovingly guided her to this moment. She prayed for her, taught her how to trust in God, and loved her more than Maddie could ask.

"Grammy, can I ask you a question?"

"Why, you know it."

"You have always been so strong; what do you do when you're afraid?"

Grammy stopped her stirring and turned to her granddaughter. "I pray a'course."

Maddie opened Grammy's Bible on the counter, "Sonya taught us that we needed to put on God's armor."

"I always loved Ms. Sonya!" Grammy smiled. "Yep, I put on my armor ever' mornin', my Girl."

"I was wondering about the shield of faith. It says here that it extinguishes all the flaming arrows of the evil one."

"Ever' single one."

"So, is faith the opposite of fear?"

"No ma'am. Love is the opposite of fear."

Looking at her Gram, she said, "But faith extinguishes the arrows."

"That's right, Girl, but it's love that applies the shield. If ya think ya can put on a fancy shield by yerself to fight the devil, yer gonna lose real quick. Our faith comes from hearin' God's message of love. In First John, it says, perfect love drives out fear, 'cause fear has to do with punishment. We're 'fraid cause we don't believe or trust God to do what he says, so we think the worst'll happen. But, when we hear God's message of love and receive it through prayer, our faith grows. Ever' time we trust in God to do what he says, our faith grows. And through God's love, Jesus applies the armor that we're prayin' on, includin' the shield of faith. Our faith is built from his love, so truly, love is the opposite of fear. If you dwell in God's love, then ya don't have to be 'fraid. But Maddie, ya gotta know, there's a reason God said, 'Do not be 'fraid.' It's because he knows that fear is real and not from him. So, he reminds us that we have a choice to walk through the fear with him by our side."

"Can I ask another question?"

"Why a'course, Love, ask as many as ya need."

"Being afraid is a feeling, right? Is faith a feeling, too?"

"No, ma'am, faith is not a feelin'. It's a choice. Ya choose whether to walk in fear or faith. And when you choose to walk in faith, God walks with ya."

Maddie pondered her Grammy's wisdom. It was time to begin praying Psalm ninety-one and Ephesians Six.

Maddie looked at her friend enjoying her time with Jesus on the back deck. Rachel seemed to have recovered the most from their experience at the PKO. She kept reminding her friends what the Bible said, "We will face trials, but they will serve to make us mature and complete." She considered it an honor to have gone through the experience they had at the PKO and felt it would only grow them for the next season of their life. Maddie couldn't say that she was quite there yet, but she felt her faith growing day by day.

She was grateful for her baby faith. The moment she ran through the fence at the PKO, she knew God was with her. Sonya spoke of the power, love, and self-discipline that Jesus gives. Maddie felt that very power jolting through her when she ran after her friends.

Rachel was right; these challenges would mature each of them, but even more so, Maddie realized that God would walk with them through every challenge to come. *Where would I be without you, God?* A wave of thankfulness washed over her. He had taught her so much in the past year and had blessed her with an amazing squad to walk alongside her on her journey. Maddie felt especially blessed to have Grammy and Rachel in her life. They challenged her to be all God created her to be.

The past year was super hard. The scars on her hands were proof. Rachel called them her PKO battle scars. They would never allow Maddie to forget all God had brought her through. Somehow, she knew that this was only the beginning. But as Emma said, "We don't have to worry because God's got us!"

Maddie gave a silent prayer as she looked up, "Father, please grow my faith."

And don't you know that he will?

APPENDIX

Appalachian Dictionary

Grammy was born in Appalachia, where the vocabulary is very colorful. While this isn't a comprehensive list, you may find several of these sayings sprinkled throughout the book.

'bout = about	
'Cause = because	
'Cept = except	
'em = Them	
'er = her	
'ere = here	
'fraid = afraid	
'im = him	
'Magine = imagine	
'Mater = tomato	
'maters = tomatoes	
'Nother = another	
'Nough = enough	
'Spect = expect	
'Splain = explain	
'Sposed = supposed	
'Tater = potato	
A' = of	
A'course = of course	
Acrost = across	
Acrost the waters = from overseas	
Afeared = afraid	
A'fore = before	
Aggin = against	
A'growin' = growing	
Aimin' = have been going to	
Ain't = is not	
Ain't got a dog in that fight = It's none of my business	

Ain't no hill fer a climber = Not a big deal for someone with experience
Anxi'ty = anxiety also Jim Jams = Anxiety (Appalachian)
Any word with "g" on the end is abbreviated with an apostrophe at the end
App-a-LATCH-un = Appalachian
Appa-latch-uh = Appalachia
As the twig is bent so shall the tree grow = The direction you point something/someone in is the direction it/they will go
Back in the day = years ago
Bad off = very sick
Bad turn = someone ill-tempered
Barking up the wrong tree = you're wrong
Bat = quick blink of the eye
Be a-waitin' on 'em at the house = I'll be waiting for them at the house
Beauty never made the kettle sing
Bein' ugly = being hateful, rude, cross, cruel
Beside Oneself = confused or worried
Better git on = need to leave
A bird in the hand is worth two in the bush = It's better to have the certainty of what you do have that the possibility of what you might have
Bite yer tongue = be quiet, don't say it
Black dark = night time
Blackberry winter = time when there is cool weather at the same time as the blooming of wild blackberry shrubs in May
Bless yer pea-pickin' lil heart = you poor, unfortunate soul
Blind house = windowless cabin
Blinked milk = sour milk
Bobble = mistake
Britches = pants

Brung up = raised, as in from childhood
Bugger = frightful (wooly bugger = anyone who is frightful looking)
Buggy = shopping cart
Bumfuzzle = confused or puzzled
C'mon = come on
Cain't = Can't
Cain't tell nobody nothin' that ain't ever been nowhere! = They think they know more than they do
Cain't think of nothin' right off = Can't think of anything at the moment
Cake a' soap = bar of soap
Call on = to visit someone
Care = will do something, don't mind to do something
Carry on = to misbehave
Catawampus = askew, awry
Cause = because
Cheer = chair
Chewed up and spit out = feeling poorly
Chil'ens = children
Chock Full = full to running over
Clean fergot = I forgot
Commode = toilet
Conniption = a mad fit
Could'na = could not
Courtin' = dating
Crayun = crayon
Crick = creek
Crooked as a dog's hind leg = a person who is crooked or deceitful
Cut on the light = turn on the light
Cuttin' up = acting a fool
D'ya = Do you
Dab = cooking measurement – small amount
Dahlin' = darling

Dawg = dog
Did'na = did not
Differ'nt = different
Diggin' his own grave = messing up
Do what? = What did you just say?
Dodge = to avoid
Don't go gittin' yer gussie up = don't get upset
Done = finished
Don't you blare yer eyes at me = don't give me a dirty look
Dope = soda water - coca-cola
Dorter = daughter
Drawers = underwear
Dreckly = directly
Druthers = things one would rather do over anything else
Duns = bills
Ears are burnin' = someone is saying bad things behind your back.
Eat up = consumed. "I'm eat up with love."
Eh law = Oh well
Ever'body = everyone
Ever'time = every time
Ever'where = everywhere
Ever'thin'll be fine, good Lord willin' and the creek don't rise = something should happen unless
Fair to midlin' = I'm okay
Fair up = when rainy weather clears up
Far = fire
Farboard = fire place mantle
Faster than a hot knife through butter – fast and easy
Fatback = fatty meat from the back of a hog that is salt cured
Favor = to resemble
Feisty = spunky, lively

Fer = for
Ferget = Forget
Fetch = to get or bring
Finer 'n frog hair = Things are going well.
Fisticuff = a fist fight
Fit = suitable, ready to use
Fit as a fiddle = fine
Fit ta be tied = angry
Fitified = frozen with fear
Fixin' = fixing to or a side dish
Flatter'n a flitter = something is pretty flat
Fler = flour
Flares = flowers (I chose to substitute flow'rs instead)
Foller = follow
Foller = follow
Follerin' = follow
Foretole = foretold
Fotch = fetch
Frail = old, feeble, sickly
Fret = to worry
Friz = frozen
Fuss at = to scold
Gall = nerve
Galoot = an older man who acts like a fool
Gander = look, stare
Garden sass = greens-turnip, mustard, lettuce
Garntee = guarantee
Father up = to assemble; to collect
Gimme some sugar = Give me a kiss
Gittin' = leaving
Gob = a large amount of something
Gom = make a mess or stop up something
Gonna = going to
Go on = talk at length
Good turn = someone with a pleasant personality

Got that straight = You are correct
Gotta = Have to
Gotta = must or got to
Grinnin' like a possum eatin' a sweet tater = someone who is a mite too pleased with themselves.
Hand = worker or hired hand
Hanker = want or crave
Hard feeling = animosity between people
Harder'n a one-eyed man doin' push-ups = Doing something really hard- with all your strength.
Haul off = to take action
He 'bout skeered me outta my house shoes = he scared me.
He ain't got no sense a-tall = He doesn't make any sense
He ain't no count a-tall = of any account
He gets my goose = irritated
He's as crooked as a dog's hind leg = he's a thief
He's as happy as if he had good sense = Happy and that's a good thing
He's crooked as a jay bird = a thief
He's lower 'n a snake's belly in a wagon rut = bad character
He's mad as a mule chewin' on bumblebees! = He's really angry
He's probably just laying off drunk somewheres = drunk and passed out
Heap o' = a lot of
Hear tell = to be informed or learn of
Heared = heard
Hep = help
Hesh up = be quiet
Hissy fit = tantrum
Hold yer horses = wait
Holler = valley

A holler is a place where ya can let yer young'uns run loose cause ya know ya got plenty a time a'fore it gets dark.
Holp = help
Hootenanny = a part with fold music and dancing
Hotter 'n blue blazes = really hot
Hunker = to work in a determined manner
I better git on = I have to leave
I don't chew my cabbage twice = I'm not going to repeat myself
I feel like I've been chewed up and spit out = Yelled at and criticized
I knowed = I knew
I reckon = I guess
I'm just loaferin' today = I'm just hanging out
Ideal = idea
Iffen = if and
Ill = hateful, angry, combative, always ill-tempered.
If I had my druthers = If I had my way
Infare = wedding
In a great while = a long period of time
In under = beneath, underneath or below
Is all = that's all
It's blowin' up a storm = really windy
It's rainin' cats and dogs = it's raining hard
It's never to late to mend = It's never too late to forgive
It's ver' airish = a little bit chilly outside
I've a mind to = of a particular inclination
It doesn't amount to a hill of beans = something that has little of no value
Jack = bust, tear, steal
Jasper = a bad person, a dishonest person
Jaw = talk
Jerk = pulled

Jim jams = to be restless or feel anxiety; nervous
Jes' = Just
Jist =Just
Job = poke
Jump the broom = get married
Jumped out of the fryin' pan an' into the fire = someone went from one bad situation right into another
Keer = care
Kilt = past tense of killed
Kin = family
Kinda = kind of
Kindly = kind of, somewhat, rather
Knee-high to a grasshopper = someone or something is short
Knee-deep = a bull frog
Knock a tater in the head = Let's go eat
Knows'll = knows will
Knowed = past tense of know
Laid up = sick, hurt, bedridden
Latch = lock, close
Lay down = to give up or surrender
Leastways = at least, at any rate
Leave things in the floor = leave things on the floor
Lemme' = let me
Lessen = unless
Let on = pretend
Lie down with dogs and you'll get up with fleas = bad pals will rub off on you
Like it or lump it = deal with it
Lil' = little
Lipping full = filled to capacity
A little birdie tole me = Juicy gossip that you don't want to share who told
Lookie = look

Lookie here = Look here
Lookin' like the hind wheels o' destruction = You look terrible
Looks to me like = I agree
Lotta = lot of
Ma = my
Makin' a mountain outta molehill = exaggerating
Mayhap = perhaps and maybe
Meaner 'n a wet hen = making someone really mean or meaner.
On the Mend = to improve in health
Mess = enough food for your family
Might could = it's a possibility
Mighty = very, especially, exceedingly
Mill over = to study or ponder
Mind = to watch or attend
Mite = little
Mizzle = fine misty rain
Mock = imitate
More'n = more than
Mushmelon = cantaloupe
N'er = never
Nary = none, not one
Naw = no
Near about = nearly
Never get yer horse in a place where ya cain't turn 'round = don't do something you'll regret later
Never mind = makes no difference
No bigger 'n a minnow in a fishin' pond = not very important.
No count = of little value
No how = in any case
Not shore = not sure or Shore = sure
Notion = inclination
Now that's the pot callin' the kettle black = don't

criticize someone for something you do
Now y'all don't be bad-mouthin' her = Don't talk about her in a mean way.
Of a mind to = to decide to do something
Offer = To try
Offish = quiet, unfriendly, hard to get to know
Ole = familiar with somethin', an attachment.
Oh, my country alive = an expression of unbelief
Old as methusaleh's housecat = pretty old
Oodlins = a large amount
Ornery = hard to deal with or get along with
Outlander = a stranger; outsider
Paper Poke = a bag to carry groceries
Pick = to play a stringed instrument
Pick'n' grin'n = A party with stringed instruments
Piddlin' = dawdling, wasting time doing something
Pig in a poke = not having all the information about what's about to happen
Pinch = small amount in cooking
Pitch a fit = to become uncontrollably upset
Plumb foolish = stupid (Plumb added to a word = completely)
Plumb give out = exhausted
Plumb tickled = pleased to hear
Plumb wore out = tired
Point blank = exact; precise
Pot callin' the kettle black = accusing someone of something you're guilt of
Pole cat = skunk
Pray'r = prayer
Prouda = proud
Puny = sick or sickly feeling
Quit piddlin' around and get ta work
R'call = recall
R'member = remember (In a command, you always

say r'member)
Racket = a noisy fight, a sudden loud occurrence
Ragler = regular
Rare up = to raise up
Reach me a = hand me a
Recollect = remember to do something
Reckon = suppose
Rern = ruin. Past tense: rernt
Resternt = restaurant
Right quick = quickly
Right smart = pretty good amount
Righter'n rain = You did that correctly
Rightly = correctly
Riled up = angry
Ruckus = a commotion
Ruination = total destruction
Run together = spend time together
Salat = salad
Ser'ous = serious
Settin's cheaper'n standin' = sit down and rest yourself
She's as pretty as a peach = she's pretty and sweet
Shine = to like
Shiny britches = dress pants
Shivaree = a loud noisy celebration occurring after a wedding
Sight = a large amount
Sigogglin = not built correctly, skewed or out of balance
Silly ole' me = I should have known better
Sit with me a spell = sit with another typically for conversation
Skedaddle = leave immediately
Skeered = scared
Skift = A dusting of snow

Sleep tight, don't let the bed bug's bite = can lids filled with oil were placed under each bed post to discourage "bed bugs" — this was a hint that it was time to leave.
Slew = a large amount
Slip off = ran away and got married
Slower than a Sunday afternoon = slow
Smack = to chew loudly on food
Smidgen = small amount in cooking
Sorry = worthless
Stout = physical strong
Stove up = hurt, arthritis
Sweet milk = regular milk (as opposed to buttermilk)
Sweet on = you like someone
Swipe off = to wipe off
T'know = to know
Ta = to
Take after = to inherit qualities from someone
Talkingest = talkative
Tell a man what fer = tell him off
Thar' = there
Thar's a fox in the hen house = someone is somewhere they don't need to be
That dog don't hunt = the story doesn't add up
That possum's on the stump = that's as good as it gets
Thataway = that way
Them polecats are from my neck of the woods =
Thick = dense, numerous, plentiful
Thick as fleas on a dog's back = Where there is a lot of something- such as a crowd
Til the cows come home
Toboggan = snug wool cap- like a beanie
Tole' = told
Too big fer his britches = conceited, self-important

Tore up about it = upset
Torn up = something is broken
Tote it in the house = carry it in the house
Upscuddle = A quarrel
Ustocould = past tense of could
Varmint = a wild animal
Ver' = very
Wanna = Want to
Want'cha = want you
Warsh = wash
Warshed = washed
Was you born in a barn? = shut the door or you don't have manners.
Ways = a distance
Worter = water
We just live right 'round the bend = we live around the corner
Weddin' without courtin' is like vittles without salt = salt seasons food just as courting prepares for and seasons a marriage.
Well, I'll be = surprise or astonishment
Well, it's six of one, half dozen of the other = no difference between two choices
Whaddya' = What do you.
What can't be cured must be endured = Be patient and endure
Give someone what fer = Going to tell them just what you think
What's got yer bee in a bonnet = someone who is agitated about something
Whatch'all = what are y'all
Whatcha' = What are you
Where thar's bees thar's honey = something attractive to a person or group
Whoo-wee = astonished

Whoo-wee doggee = astonished	
Whoop and a holler = a short distance	
Winder = window	
Windshaken = a crack or twisted grain in timber, produced by high wind	
Woulda = would have	
Ya = You	
Y'all = You all	
Y'all come back now, ya hear? = Come back soon	
Yassir = yes sir	
Yer = Your	
Yer not from 'round these parts are ya? = You're not from around here, are you?	
Yer slower than molasses = slow	
Yonder = Over there	
You favor yer Momma = You look like your mom	
You'ns = You all	
You'ns ain't seen me in a coon's age = You haven't seen me in a long while	
Young'un(s) = One or Multiple young people	
Younger'n = younger than	

Many thanks to:

Backroads Living
Blind Pig & the Acorn
Directory of Smoky Mountain English
Dancing on Mountaintops
These Storied Mountains – John Parris
Three Ladies and their Babies
And many more who lovingly share the beautiful Appalachian culture.

Acknowledgments

Thank you to my Heavenly Father for pouring Your Word into me and giving me a deep desire to serve you. May this work glorify you.

To my amazing husband, Tony. When the Lord laid this daunting task on my heart, I had no idea where to begin. You encouraged me through your excitement. You led me to people and places that would help me on my journey. I am so grateful for your support my Love!

Mom, thank you for always loving us. I am eternally grateful for the life you gave and the love you taught. Thank you for sharing your love of reading with us.

To my Grandmomma and Granny, thank you both for being my Grammy! Your love and consistent faith have helped me on my journey. I am forever grateful for your prayers over my life.

To my sisters, Jennifer, Patricia, Amanda, and Beth, thank you for helping me to become a better sister.

Thank you, Lauren, for helping me sort out my jumbled thoughts and make them legible. Thank you for being a prayer warrior and an encouragement master. You never let me quit, and for that, I am eternally grateful. Now, go write that story!

Thank you, Natalie, for dotting my I's and crossing my T's. You make me better.

Derik, you unlocked the zeal for God's Word within me that I never knew I had. You had no idea that as you taught my girls, you were teaching me. God has changed my life through His word. I thank you for allowing Him to work through you.

Acknowledgments

Dave, thank you for leading students so well. Your intentionality makes others feel seen. We are eternally blessed through your shepherding heart.

To my Flourish girls, thank you for saying yes. You have forever marked me with your love for the Lord. Thank you for allowing me to be part of your journey.

Thank you to every young woman who has allowed me the honor of walking alongside you. You have blessed me in your journey. Keep the faith, Beautiful, and run your race knowing God is always with you.

Nelum, thank you for your yes to Jesus! I am so thankful for your servant's heart and for all that God does through you. It is an honor to serve alongside you, my sister!

Olha, thank you for sharing your beautiful creative eye with the world! I am so grateful for this photograph that you have allowed me to use for this book. You can follow her at @life.by.olia on YouTube and Instagram.

Rachel, you are a world changer, my friend! Thank you for shining the light of Jesus everywhere you go.

Thank you to my launch team! You have inspired me more than you know.

Thank you to The Chosen for your beautiful portrayal of Mary Magdalene. I am forever marked by the understanding that Jesus saw me in my mess, and He sees me even now. Thank you for allowing me to use an excerpt from season one, episode one. You can download the app here: https://new.thechosen.tv.

Thank you to the many who publicly share the lives and speech of our Appalachian neighbors. And a special thank you to @CelebratingAppalachia for sharing the love of your culture so well. Your heritage is rich and beautiful, my friends!

Acknowledgments

Thank you to the Spy Museum for your intriguing language of espionage.

Thank you to every reader who joined me on this journey. I hope you loved it as much as I did. If so, please take a moment to post a review and tell a friend.

Thank you to Creative Fabrica and designer genesislabstudio for the beautiful Malibu Script Font used under license for the book and chapter titles.

I love feedback! You can submit feedback and suggestions directly to me on my website at https://adaughtersjourney.net.

<u>**Additional works from Eve M. Harrell**</u>

Confessions:
A Mom's Journey from Hovering to Hope

Hello Beautiful:
See Yourself Through the Father's Eyes

Hello Beautiful:
Companion Journal

Running with Zebras:
A Daughter's Journey Through the Fire

Revealed Book Series™
Book 1 – Revealed Truth: A Journey from Fear to Faith
Book 2 – Revealed Mercy: A Journey to the Tower of Trust
Book 3 – Revealed Courage: A Journey Forged Through Fire
Book 4 – Revealed Hope: A Journey For Such a Time as This

Revealed: A Journey Through Prayer Journal
Revealed Pocket Journal
Living Revealed: A Discipleship Journey

#revealedtruthbook

About The Author

Eve Harrell and her husband, Tony, serve their local church as Small Group Leaders to some amazing future leaders. In addition to serving students and their leaders, Eve encourages women of all ages to rest in the love of their Heavenly Father.

Singing, blogging, speaking, writing, spending time in nature, and watching others find freedom in Christ are some of Eve's favorite things.

Eve's passion includes encouraging the next generation to recognize the great value, purpose, and strength they have been given while finding the Father's little gifts along the way.

You can connect with her at https://evemharrell.com.